W9-BUV-689

Who's Loving You

Who's Loving You

MARY B. MORRISON

Dafina
BOOKS

Kensington Publishing Corp
http://www.kensingtonbooks.com

DAFINA BOOKS are published by

Kensington Publishing Corp.
850 Third Avenue
New York, NY 10022

All Kensington Titles, Imprints, and Distributed Lines are available at special
quantity discounts for bulk purchases for sales promotions, premiums, fund-
raising, and educational or institutional use. Special book excerpts or customized printings can also be created to fit specific needs. For details, write
or phone the office of the Kensington special sales manager: Kensington
Publishing Corp., 850 Third Avenue, New York, NY 10022, attn: Special Sales
Department, Phone: 1-800-221-2647.

Dafina and the Dafina logo Reg. U.S. Pat. & TM Off.

Library of Congress Card Catalog Number: 2008928211

ISBN-13: 978-0-7582-1514-7
ISBN-10: 0-7582-1514-2

First hardcover printing: August 2008
10 9 8 7 6 5 4 3 2 1

Printed in the United States of America

With much love, respect, and admiration for my wonderful son,
Jesse Bernard, Jr., to all the single mothers like myself . . . love yourself first,
and to King MaxB Byrd, our loving baby Yorkshire terrier.

Why I Love You

Date:

Given To:

Given By:

Personal Message:

A Special Message to Women Everywhere

Please take time to learn who you are. Know that you are worthy of greatness. You do not need validation from anyone, for those who judge you know not the content of your heart. They do not know the unpaved roads you've traveled. In the still of the night and sometimes in broad daylight, while no one was listening to your cries, you found the strength within and the faith to sustain the challenges you, yes, you, have overcome.

No matter what your journey, you have so many reasons to be proud of yourself. Go on and smile. You know it's true. Respect yourself. Love yourself. Your true value derives not from your bank account, your house, your car, or the clothes you wear. Your self-worth is predicated on how well you know yourself, how well you treat yourself, how much you love and value yourself.

Hear me when I say, "No one will ever treat you worse than you treat yourself," and no one should treat you better. When times get hard—we all experience hard times—and there seems to be no way out . . . keep breathing. Live another second, hold on another minute, hang in there another hour, and with each passing moment, know that your internal beauty is the pure essence of the greatest love, because without you; without your womanly nurturing, your motherly instincts, your ability to breathe life into every living human being; without women, men would cease to exist.

Don't let men brainwash you into believing they hold the power in a relationship. They don't. Giving birth is the highest power of procreation. Men can't do that. So, ladies, don't have babies for men who aren't worthy of your power.

I hope you enjoy reading *Who's Loving You* as much as I enjoyed writing it.

CHAPTER 1

Honey

Love sucks! I swore on my sister's grave, I wished I'd never met him. His voice had lingered in my mind with crisp clarity every damn day, like he was standing behind me, leaning over my shoulder, whispering in my ear. But he wasn't. Not anymore.

"Baby," he used to say to me, and I would answer, barely above a whisper, "Yes?" Seductively, he'd say it again, "Baby," in a tone that quieted me. "Yes?" I'd say softly. We'd go back and forth: then his long fingers and strong hands would gently caress the side of my face and massage my ears.

I'd quiver whenever he'd moan, "Ummmm, you're fucking incredible. You know that? And I'm not talking about your bedroom skills. Baby, you are an amazing woman."

His eargasms would make cool waterfall secretions flow from my pussy, wetting my lips, before he'd ease his hand between my thighs, pressing his middle finger against my clit. He was left-handed. I'd heard Dr. Oz say on *Oprah* that left-handed people were smarter, more balanced, and better capable of processing information than those of us who were right-handed. His index and ring fingers would straddle my shaft, nestling in the crevices of my lips, as he strummed my black pearl with his middle finger. That was my favorite finger.

Gasping at the sound of his voice in my head, I knew . . . I was incredible. But no other man had told me that. No other man had said to me, "I love you." Grant was my first. I let the tears fall, then closed my eyes, visualizing our moments together, lifting my lids to see only me, surrounded by olive painted walls, bright lime cabinets, dark forest granite countertops, and a kitchen floor covered with new hundred-dollar bills that had been permanently laminated into clear ceramic tiles.

Green was my favorite color. I loved walking on men and money. I'd admit I was a little extravagant. A grand total of one million dollars—in hundred-dollar bills—was embedded in every floor of my home, including the bathrooms. Some preferred to walk on sunshine. Money was my visual reminder of where I'd come from. I wasn't proud of how I'd stepped on and over a countless number of people to get where I was. *Live and Let Die* was my favorite James Bond movie and my motto. Standing in front of the kitchen counter, I slid an already sharp knife along the steel sharpener.

Grant had been my joy. We'd loved sharing Cherry Garcia ice cream while watching *The Boondocks* DVD series, and making love. In between orgasms, we'd laugh at Huey, Riley, and their granddad. One time we stayed in bed all day, eating, sleeping, and fucking until we wobbled like ducks when we made our way to the bathroom for a much-needed piss.

"Quack, quack," I'd teased him.

"Quack, quack, quack," he'd tease me back.

Then, suddenly, our relationship had faded to dark. He was out of my life, as if I had frantically awakened from the best dream of my life. Shutting my eyes, I fought to go back to him, to go back to sleep and pick up where we had left off, before he left me. I tossed and wrestled with my empty bed. I opened my legs, easing the memory foam pillow between my thighs, then pulled my red satin sheet around my erect nipples, trying to forget he was no longer mine. Opening my eyes, I found myself standing in the kitchen, staring at a blue crystal bowl filled with red potatoes.

How could my past ruin my future? I had tried my damnedest to give that man my best, and he had slammed the door to his heart in my face, as though I was a Jehovah's Witness trying to save his spiritual behind so he would become the one-hundred forty-four thousandth person to make it . . . Where? To Heaven? Wherever that was. Who'd been there? What did they do to get in? Mistreat others?

From hot to cold, within seconds he had swatted me away like I was a fly landing on his food, regurgitating shit. I'd meant nothing to him. It was as though he'd truly awakened to a stranger.

Words were powerful beyond measure, but his silence hurt me more. He'd made me make myself go crazy. Wow. Love or the lack thereof could do that. Make one go crazy.

"Answer your damn phone. You wrong for this shit, Grant! Dead wrong!" I yelled. I grunted loud enough to release my frustrations, but not so loud that someone in the house would come running to my aid with a straight jacket. My house had thirteen bedrooms. Twelve upstairs. Mine was the only one downstairs.

"I should kill him. Goddammit, son of a bitch!" I screamed. Sucking the stream of blood oozing from my finger, I threw the knife, the potatoes, and the crystal bowl in the damn trash can. "Fuck this shit!"

Love hadn't hurt me. I was clear that I'd hurt the one I loved. Now I was the one suffering. Every time I got angry, so angry that I could harm Grant, something bad happened to my ass. Unzipping the first-aid kit, I pulled out a bandage.

"He probably has some other bitch in his bed, sucking his dick right now, while I'm over here trippin' on unresolved issues that I can't control." *Not by myself.*

As I wrapped the Band-Aid tightly around my middle finger, thoughts of the way we had constantly been together replayed in my mind, reminding me of the irreplaceable love I'd lost. Where was I going to find another six-foot-five, 235-pound, twenty-eight-year-old, successful black man with a body sexier than any Chippendales dancer I'd ever seen? Grant was my man, and I'd be damned if I was gonna let him leave me. I just knew some ex-chick or someone hoping to be the next chick had been waiting for me to fuck up so she could move in on him, with him.

"Not on my watch, bitch! Get your own man!" I grunted.

Each morning I reached out my hand to touch him; rolled over, expecting to kiss him; opened my eyes, longing to see him. I called out his name, but he wasn't there to answer, "Yes, Honey?" as he had so affectionately done. Had he been sincere when he'd said, "You're the best thing that ever happened to me"? I wanted another chance. Hell, I deserved the opportunity to explain why I'd lied. Not everything I'd told him was a lie. Actually, most of what I'd shared about my past was the truth.

"Grant, listen to me," I said. "Are you seriously going to take someone else's word over mine? So what if Benito is your brother! Hell, your own mama don't like his ass. I can't believe you're upset with me about something that happened before we met. You're not making any sense. Okay. Answer this one question. 'Do you still love me? Yes or no?' "

I wasn't getting the answer I wanted; he wasn't here to respond. All of this vacillating in the kitchen, talking to myself, had to stop. One minute I loved him; the same minute I hated his ass to death. I stood topless and barefoot in the middle of the kitchen, text messaging him: *Baby, it's not what you think. Please call me.* I was trying to give him the impression I was being patient with him, but my patience had run out a long fucking time ago.

CHAPTER 2

Grant

You thought you knew a woman; then you found out shit you wished you hadn't. The saying "What you don't know won't hurt you" could actually kill you. In retrospect, I wished our relationship would've remained platonic. That way even if our friendship hadn't flourished, I could have continued respecting her.

We consummated our acquaintance the first day we met. From the airport to dinner, to dicking her down really good, Honey was one sweet lady. Nah, she wasn't a lady; she was a woman. But was she that easy with every guy? Honey was hot and sexy, and my dick was hard and horny, and we clicked. My dick fit her pussy perfectly. I never wanted to wait to have sex with a woman I liked. What were we waiting for? The one thing I could've avoided this time, if I had waited, was having my heart broken. Broken heart and all, life went on. That was for sure.

Parking in my parents' driveway, I contemplated whether to go in. I didn't feel like pretending I was happy again today. Stopping by to check on my mom and dad was routine. As usual, my old man peeked out the front window; then he opened the door, motioning for me to get out of the car. I read Honey's text message, slipped my iPhone in the holder, then smiled at my father.

We walked up the seven steps to the house, with my arm over his broad shoulders. Five inches taller, I towered over him. My dad retired five years ago; Mom hadn't worked a day since they'd married. Her stay-at-home-wife job entailed taking care of my dad, my brother, and me, and although we could take care of ourselves, Mom still enjoyed taking care of us.

Inside the house, I greeted my old man, hugging him tight. "You got a class this morning, old man?" I asked my dad.

He lectured to high-school students during the day and taught entrepreneurial courses in the evening. I took over managing his rental properties when I opened my business, GH Property Management and Development, seven years ago. With Dad's guidance, I'd done well for a twenty-eight-year-old.

"Still trying to outdress me, huh, son? You gotta figure out where my new tailor is first. Close the door before one of those nasty flies creeps in."

I had the best mom and dad. I loved my parents. Would do anything for them. "Hi, my angel," I said to my mother, kissing her cheek. She hugged my waist, holding on a few seconds longer than usual. Mom's hugs reassured me that everything was good. The prolonged hug made me wonder if everything was okay.

Mom whispered, "It's already all right, son. Let go and let God. I know you want us to accept her, but she's not the one for you." Patting me on the back, she said, "You see your brother sitting over there? Speak."

Like I said, I would do anything for my parents.

Benito got up off the sofa and hugged me. Mom hadn't said anything about hugging that fool.

"Hey, bro," he said. "You dump Lace yet? I told Mom all about Lace's past. Take it from me, I keep telling you I dated her for three years. She's bad news."

Pushing him away, I said, "Her name is Honey, and I'm positive she'd plead temporary insanity for the entire three years." Distancing myself from my brother, I followed my dad into the dining room.

Benito was right behind us. "Whatever you wanna call her is cool, but I'm tellin' you—"

Dad interrupted him. "Benito, that's enough. Why don't you stop all the madness about that woman and tell us the truth about what's going on with you? We haven't seen you for twelve years, since you went off to college. And your mother just mailed Tyra a check for ten thousand dollars to pay your son's tuition. You haven't been home in a long time, but I raised you better. Even if your relationship with her is over, you need to go see your son. Now, why'd you come back here?"

Thank God. I wanted to keep the focus on Benito, so I asked him, "Yeah. Why?" I smiled, waiting for my brother to answer. Benito was two years older than me, but he looked forty. His years of partying and drinking were etched on his face. I wasn't having any kids until after I got married. I wanted two, maybe three. All boys.

"I told y'all I kinda made a few bad investments, lost all my money. Then Lace kicked me out. I just need to stay until things settle. A few months. No longer than a year or two," that fool said. Problem was he was serious.

My mother walked into the room, sat a plate in front of my dad, then me, and went back into the kitchen.

"What about me?" Benito yelled. "Why does Grant always have to be first?"

" 'Cause I check on my parents every day I'm in town," I said. "Your behind didn't call after you left, not until you needed us." I really wanted to say, "Nigga, your sorry black ass need to get up outta here and stop leeching," but my parents wouldn't have approved of that.

"Thank you, dear God, for this wonderful bounty, my mother, and my father. Amen," I said. I blessed my stack of pancakes, strips of peppered bacon, and scrambled eggs and started eating. I had a business to run. Benito didn't have shit else to do all day but lay up on my parents. I couldn't believe my mother had paid his cell phone bill. He knew better than to ask me to do anything for him.

Staring at my brother, my dad didn't blink once. Dad said, "You have one more time to disrespect my wife and you're outta here."

Benito was stupid, but not that stupid. He knew when to shut up. Mom walked back into the room and sat Benito's plate in front of him. No thank you, no grace, no comment. Benito started chewing with his mouth open.

"Man," I yelled at him, shoving his plate to the floor. "If you don't stop disrespecting my mother, I'ma beat your ass! Show some fucking appreciation for her. She ain't your damn maid!"

I stood over him, wishing he would push his chair back. My fists were tight. I wanted to punch him in his face. My dad scurried out of his chair and held my arms behind my back.

"Son, calm down. Sit. Finish your breakfast," said Dad.

Benito slid my plate in front of him and started eating my food. Through a mouthful of my pancakes, he said, "You not mad at me, bro. You pissed because you didn't know your sweet Honey baby was a hooker. Pass me the syrup, would ya?"

CHAPTER 3

Honey

The morning was three hours away from noon. The sun was too bright to go back to sleep. The red potatoes were in the trash, my finger was aching, and I was still in the kitchen.

I texted Grant again. *I give. You win.* I stared at my phone until the time and date confirmed exactly when my message was sent. I waited five minutes, then an additional ten minutes, for his reply.

"Ughhh. Motherfucker! What or who are you doing that's more important than me?" I yelled. Again, he had refused to answer. He was lucky I lived in Atlanta and not in D.C., or else . . . or else . . . What was his fucking problem? "Forget you, too, Grant. You're too old for this childish bullshit. A real man would have the decency to give closure to his relationship." Who was I fooling? I was angry because Grant was a real man. A real man with parents who loved him.

Lionel Richie's voice resonating through the kitchen's intercom created a much-welcomed distraction. One of the girls upstairs had decided to play songs, and since I insisted on the best, we had speakers in every room of the house, including the bathrooms. Softly, Lionel sang, "I do love you . . . still."

As Lionel's voice faded, I heard Luther singing, "Time rushes on. And it's not fair. When someone you used to love, is no longer there . . . now you're running back to me, to forgive you your mistake. Kinda makes me sad to say . . . it's a little too late."

Rushing into the spacious white-marbled foyer, I yelled up the U-shaped stairways. "Turn that shit off!"

Grant had helped me find this eight-thousand-square-foot home in Buckhead, which I'd paid cash for, so my escorts could quit fucking men for a living and for once be comfortable and focus on what they really wanted to do with their lives, and this was how they thanked me?

Whosoever had decided to play Luther Vandross at nine o'clock in the morning was lucky I hadn't raced upstairs and slapped the hell out of 'em. They knew Grant and I had recently broken up. I didn't need to hear that depressing-ass music right now. The feelings of rejection palpitating in my heart fluttered up to my throat, suffocating me. Fanning myself, I could hardly breathe.

"Damn," I whispered, wishing I had the courage to hop a flight to D.C., show up unannounced at Grant's front door, and make him talk to me. But I didn't. What if a woman opened his door? I'd kill 'em both. For real.

Clenching my teeth, I scratched my neck. I was so frustrated, I felt like taking my damn iPhone, raising my arm high above my head, then slamming the iPhone on the ceramic floor and watching it shatter, like my heart, into tiny splintered pieces. What good was a communication device when I couldn't get a response from the main person I wanted to hear from? Trembling, I exhaled heavily, then quietly sat my PDA on the counter and resumed cooking breakfast.

Flipping bacon in the frying pan, feeling lonely, I stood in my new home, inhaling the sweet aroma of thick strips of sizzling pork and watching grease specks splatter onto the stove. I hadn't had a normal appetite in almost two weeks. The burning energy in the pit of my stomach had melted away ten pounds in the fourteen days that I hadn't seen or spoken with Grant. I had gone from a size ten to an eight.

Outwardly, I struggled to appear calm so my girls wouldn't think I was going crazy, but inside, I'd lost control of the hatred raging through my body, knowing I could easily slap or curse, for no rational reason, the first person that said, "Good morning."

Onyx, my personal assistant, peeked her head inside the kitchen. When my eyes narrowed and shifted to the corners, I caught a glimpse of her disappearing into the foyer.

"Let me know when breakfast is ready," she blurted, quickly trotting upstairs.

After my favorite escort, Sunny, Onyx, with her sweet black-cherry pussy, had earned me the most money when I was their madam. Men of every nationality had lost their fucking minds when they saw Onyx in my lineup of whores. I was glad I wasn't exploiting women anymore.

I wasn't proud of my past, but I was one of the few lucky ones that had got out of the escort business before it was too late. I was thankful that I hadn't been arrested, like my ex-boss Valentino James, who was awaiting sentencing in a Nevada prison for thirteen counts of pimping and pandering, plus one count of first-degree murder. That could've easily been me sitting behind bars, facing the same charges.

There was such a thing called luck. With the help of a woman I barely knew, undercover police officer Sapphire Bleu, I'd escaped the prostitution arena in Las Vegas, and I'd avoided incarceration for the horrible things I'd done. Why she decided to help me, I wasn't sure. But I'd learned never to question where my help came from. Sometimes the person I least expected to help me helped me the most.

Footsteps crept over my head, reminding me my girls were safe upstairs in the entertainment room. I prayed none of them would ever have to revert to prostitution. Girl Six was my only escort who'd remained in Las Vegas. She was reluctant to come live with me in Atlanta. Couldn't say I blamed her, considering I'd kicked her in her stomach and fractured her ribs for showing up at work one day with a pimple on her ass.

Bam!

"Madam! Please stop! Don't! I'm sorry! I won't let this happen again," Girl Six had cried. *"Pleeeeaaaseeee, Madam, stop!"*

Wham! Bam! Stomp! Kick!

Girl Six had balled up into a fetal position, holding what I had hoped was a few broken ribs.

"You are costing us fifty thousand dollars a night every time I have to send your ass home. You've got one more time to have a rash, a cold sore, or a pimple, and I will beat your ass into the ground, then fire you. Put your clothes on, and get the hell out," I'd said, dismissing her.

Valentino had trusted me to run his multimillion dollar business, and the johns who paid ten grand an hour had demanded flawless women with beautiful bodies. At that time, my reputation meant more to me than sparing Girl Six's life. Today I felt remorseful. In my heart, Girl Six was now family, and I'd given her a one-way airline ticket to Atlanta, the same as I'd done with all my girls. I wasn't going to call her. She didn't need another invitation when she already had a standing welcome to join us.

Thinking about my top-producing escort, Sunny Day, I whispered, "I couldn't save them all."

CHAPTER 4

Grant

"I'm out. Bye, Dad. Bye, Mom," I said.

"Bye, bro. I'll see you later," Benito's sorry ass said, gnawing on a piece of my bacon.

Stopping in the restroom adjacent to the foyer, I took a piss, shook my dick, washed my hands, then left my parents' house. I got in my car. "Ooh-wee, I wish he wasn't my damn brother," I said, checking my messages. Honey had texted again, at nine o'clock. *I give. You win.*

"Good. No, great. Me too. I hope you mean it this time," I said. "I hate when Benito's fucking ass is right." I was angry at Honey. She had made me look like a fool in front of my parents. Wasn't she obligated to disclose beforehand situations that could embarrass us?

I pulled into Starbucks to get a grande soy White Chocolate Mocha Expresso, no whip, extra hot. I'd stopped adding the whipped cream after Honey and I broke up. The things she could do with whipped cream made me shiver. *Damn.* The line was long. I'd wait. Give myself time to cool off before getting to my office. I swear, I wished I could've hit Benito's ass one time, right in his big mouth.

"Ooh, he's got a nice big one," I heard the woman in front of me tell the lady she was with.

Frowning, I thought, *Is she talking about me within listening range?* D.C. women didn't hold back on anything, particularly on pursuing men.

Her friend turned around, looked at my dick, smiled, then nodded. "He sure does, girl. Good looking out. You don't miss anything. That's big enough to share. We could double-dip fuck him at the same time."

The woman who'd checked me out first handed me her business card. "Call me, on my cell. We're having a private party tomorrow night. We'd love for you to *come* with us."

I didn't want to embarrass her by saying, "I'm not interested," so I took the card and said, "Thanks," putting it in my pocket.

Her opening line reminded me of a cheerleader I'd met in Las Vegas damn near fourteen years ago. I was fourteen years old at that time.

"Ooh, you got a nice big one. Please let me suck this pretty dick," she'd pleaded. "That is why you invited me over, isn't it?"

"Yeah, but—"

"No buts, silly. Come here and shut up," she'd said, peeling the plastic off of a small square pack of . . . peanut butter?

Frowning, I'd stood by the edge of my hotel bed, looking down at her. "What's that for?"

"It's my favorite," she'd said.

A devious grin had crossed her face. She'd scooped the peanut butter onto her tongue, smeared it all over my dick, then jokingly asked, "Got milk?" Then she'd opened a small packet of strawberry preserves. Layering the preserves over the peanut butter with her wet tongue, she'd put both of my nuts in her mouth at the same time.

"Ooh, my lord that feels good," I'd said, trying to control my shaky teenage legs.

Gripping my dick like a microphone, she'd spat on it, started singing like she was on stage, then licked everything off, including my cum. I'd recalled thinking, Girls in D.C. don't swallow.

"Sir, you're holding up the line," the cashier said. "May I please"—her eyes darted down to my dick—"take your order." She smiled a little too hard.

"Oh, sorry," I said, ordering my drink. I had to see what they were seeing. Damn! Those freaky-ass women. I had to start wearing underwear. One of them could've told me my dick was out. Tucking myself away, I dug into my pocket and pulled out a twenty.

The cashier held her hands up in the air. "Uh, that's okay. The ladies in front of you paid for whatever you wanted," she said, grinning. "Here's your Starbucks card. You have a ninety-five-dollar credit."

I was flattered but not convinced to call. Waiting for my mocha, I continued thinking. I'd never forget my first blow job. That shit felt ooh-wee! incredible, but I couldn't say I loved, strongly liked, or even knew the girl who'd done it. In fact, I lost respect for her because she didn't respect herself by going around and sucking dicks for fun while all the guys on our sophomore field trip in Las Vegas talked bad about her.

"Man, she'll suck your dick in the bathroom, in the hallway, in the stairway, anywhere you want," one guy had said. "All you have to do is pretend you like her ass, give her a few compliments, and that trick will drop to her knees and let your nuts bang against her chin until you cum in her mouth."

To see if they were telling the truth, I joined in the experience. I felt like shit immediately after I'd cum in Tiffany Davis's mouth. I doubted the other guys even knew her name. From that day forth, I promised myself I'd never disrespect another woman. If I didn't care anything about her, I wasn't putting my dick inside any part of her, no matter how attractive she was.

Tiffany was definitely not the type of woman I wanted to call my own or invite to my house to meet my parents. Damn! What made that girl do that shit? At times I wondered who or what had made Tiffany that way. What was she doing now? Probably somewhere prostituting. What had made my Honey fuck strange men for money?

"I guess I'll never know," I said aloud.

CHAPTER 5

Red Velvet

The only thing better than having sex was getting paid to have sex. I lived for the next orgasm. Cuming, squirting, and sucking dick was my natural high. Masturbation was a satisfactory last resort. I was born that way. Sexy. Sexual. Overachiever. I had shown my cleavage the minute I grew big, beautiful, perky breasts, had worn the shortest shorts I could find to show off my boo-tee-licious ass, which made me popular with all the guys, and had experimented with make-up until I found the products that were a perfect blend for me.

A few months after I started stripping for Trevor Williams, all the men wanted a stroke of my Red Velvet pussy. Trevor had propositioned me, offering me a special relationship with unique benefits. Our agreement was I kept him and his clients happy, and he made certain I got compensated with movie auditions, clothes, jewelry, and some cash.

"Velvet, image is everything," Trevor had said. "If you look like money, people treat you like royalty. If you look poor, people ignore you. I'm going to make sure you have the best opportunities to become a star. Remember good pussy ain't never broke. You're a complete package."

No, I wasn't a complete package. No one was. But I did have big dreams and high hopes. After I graduated from high school, my mother paid for me to attend a one-year hands-on program at the New York

Film Academy. At one of the workshops, I met an agent based out of Los Angeles who said I had tremendous potential. I felt good saying, "Call my agent."

I visualized myself on the big screen one day. Not as a porn star. I was destined to become a famous movie star. All of my sexual freelancing would help me get my big break, meet the right producer, and become huge in Hollywood. I wanted celebrity neighbors, limo drivers, and I wanted never to have to show ID again, because everyone would instantly recognize my face and they'd know my name. Trevor had promised to help me if I helped him.

On a day like today, I couldn't say no to Trevor, so I begged my mother to keep my son for a day while I accompanied my boss from Atlanta to D.C. on a business trip. Our two-hour direct flight arrived at Dulles Airport at about eight in the morning. It took almost another two hours to get our luggage and for the driver to get us to our hotel on Connecticut Avenue. The lobby was huge, with an elegant circular bar centered underneath the largest chandelier I'd seen.

"Have a seat while I check us in," Trevor said to me, handing the receptionist his credit card.

Browsing the lobby, I peeked over my sunglasses and into the gift-shop window. On every trip, after I got paid, I bought something for my mother for watching my son. Usually nothing over a hundred dollars. I usually got her a nice scarf or a black figurine to add to her collection.

Trevor walked by me, dialing his phone. Motioning for me to follow him, he handed me my room key while speaking into his Bluetooth. "Yeah, Grant. How far is your office from Dupont Circle? Meet me at my hotel for a cup of coffee. Twenty minutes." He repeated the time, then said, "Perfect."

"So what does this one look like?" I asked.

"You'll see in a few minutes. I need you to take extra special care of my man. I have a lot of money riding on this deal."

"So he's already said yes?"

"Velvet, if Grant had already signed the papers, you wouldn't be here."

"I thought I was his congratulatory present. You sure you want me to do this before you get a commitment?" I asked him. I was going to have fun regardless, but I knew pussy didn't persuade every man. In fact, my fucking this Grant guy might dissuade him from becoming Trevor's partner.

"Give him the Red Velvet special," Trevor insisted. "Be ready in thirty minutes. I don't want to keep my man waiting."

I held out my hand for my money. If this deal fell apart, Velvet was getting paid. Whatever other perks I'd get would be lagniappe.

Trevor handed me five one-hundred-dollar bills while the bellman unlocked my door and handed me back my key. I followed the bellman, watching him place my suitcase on the luggage rack. Then he took the other bag inside Trevor's room next door.

Locking the door to my room, I unlocked the connecting door between the two rooms, so Trevor could eavesdrop on his client. Trevor opened his side, peeked his head inside my room, and said, "Hurry."

"You can't rush good pussy," I said, picking up the phone. "Yes, I'd like a bottle of champagne, a pitcher of freshly squeezed orange juice, fresh red grapes, and plain yogurt."

"We'll have your order up in thirty minutes, Mrs. Trevor," said a room-service attendant.

They should train hotel staff not to make assumptions. I had no desire to be Trevor's wife. "There's nothing to cook. Have it here in five minutes, or keep it," I said, hanging up the phone. I couldn't wait to become a celebrity and have someone else order for me.

Waiting for room service, I debated whether to wear my leopard-print bustier and black boy shorts or my red outfit. "It's too early for leopard," I said, walking to the door. "That was quick. Thanks," I said, adding the attendant's tip to Trevor's bill.

Quickly, I smashed the red grapes, mixed them into the yogurt, then stood in the kitchen smoothing the mixture all over my body. I let it dry for ten minutes, then headed to the bathroom. I enjoyed a hot, steamy shower. I stuck my finger deep inside my pussy, making sure she was extra clean; then I rinsed with cold water to tighten my skin. While my body was still dripping wet, I saturated my skin with almond oil, lightly toweled off, then slipped into my red silk lounging halter and my stripper pants with the breakaway sides. Sitting in front of the vanity mirror, I applied fresh eyeliner, eye shadow, and my special glossy, red, velvet lipstick.

I heard a tap on the door. I smiled. "He's here," I sang. I slipped on my red, furry high heels. I knew it was Trevor's guest. *Lord, let this one look good. My pussy is percolating. It's too early in the morning to fuck an ugly trick.* I took a deep breath, then opened the door. "Ah yes," I said. A tall, handsome man stood in the hallway outside my door. *Thank you, Jesus!* I wanted to snatch his ass inside, throw him on the floor, and ride him righteous.

"Excuse me, but I must have the wrong room," he said, smiling at my breasts, then my lips.

"Are you Grant? Trevor's partner?"

"Yes, I am. But, uh—"

I flashed a sexy smile. "Come on in here. Trevor had to go out for a moment. He'll be back," I lied.

"I don't have a lot of time. I'm on my way to my office. Tell him to call me later. Our meeting isn't until tomorrow."

Later my ass. Hell to the motherfuckin' no. This man was unbelievably fine, and he wasn't going nowhere. My eyes lingered on his too-big-to-hide dick, making my mouth water. I wasn't fucking him for Trevor; I was going to ride that dick Red Velvet style for myself.

Gently grabbing his arm, I politely ushered him inside. "Have a seat on the sofa. Make yourself comfortable. Here's the remote," I said, smiling at him as I handed him a magazine. Clipping on my Bluetooth, I pretended to call Trevor.

"Trevor, Mr. Hill is here. He said he has to go to his office," I said, leaning over the sofa, pretending to reach for the *Black Enterprise* magazine. Intentionally, I put my breasts in his face. "Trevor is on the phone with his broker," I lied, sitting really close to Grant. "He said for me to make you comfortable until he gets here."

Tap. Tap.

Grant looked toward the door. "Oh, good. He's here."

Who was that? I hoped Trevor hadn't reconsidered what I'd said earlier about him getting the deal first. I hurried to the door. My heels clicked against the bottom of my feet. I peeped through the peephole. Who was she? I cracked the door open about an inch. "Can I help you?" I asked.

"Oh, sorry. I was looking for Trevor. Is he here?" the woman asked.

She needed to get her room right. Poking my hand outside the door, I pointed next door, then locked my door.

"Who was it?" Grant asked, looking over his shoulder. "I thought I heard her ask for Trevor."

"She was lost. Would you like a mimosa, a glass of orange juice, or champagne?"

"No, thanks. Maybe I should wait downstairs," he said as he headed for the door.

Only if he could get past me first. Untying my halter, I removed it and placed his hands on my firm tits. "It's okay. I work at Stilettos for Trevor, and from what I'm told, I'm going to be working for you, too."

Leading Grant back to the sofa, I sat sideways, facing him.

"So Trevor sent you, huh?"

Kneeling before his dick and unzipping his pants, I answered, "Sure did." Grant wasn't giving it to me, so I had to take his dick. Easing out the most beautiful dick I'd seen in my life, I gave him a mini dick massage, then placed my juicy lips over his bulging head.

Grant's thick, long, smooth dick throbbed in my mouth. "Stand up for a minute," I said, squeezing his ass. I leaned my head back, then made him fuck me good in my mouth.

"I can't believe this is happening," he moaned as precum oozed down my throat.

His was the sweetest vanilla-cream cum I'd ever tasted in my life. I wanted him to shoot a heavy load in my mouth for breakfast, but I had to feel him inside me before he released the big one.

He unbuckled his pants. I pulled them down to his ankles, helping him undress while sucking his head and massaging his nuts. Everything about this man was to die for.

Slowly, I eased his dick out of my mouth, holding him with my hand. "Don't move," I said, picking up my purse and pulling out a Magnum XL. Putting the condom on the tip of my tongue, I sucked the tip, kissed his dick, and rolled the latex down his shaft, all the way to his nuts.

"Now, that's quite impressive," he said.

I slid my pants over my ass, then said, "You ain't seen nothing yet."

I raised my right leg and rested it in his left hand, then lifted my left leg and rested it in his right hand.

His strong arms then hugged my waist. Locking my ankles behind his back, I rolled my sweet pussy Red Velvet style up and all the way down his dick, making sure he felt my ass squeeze his nuts on the way up and my pussy tighten around his dick all the way down. He held me tight about my waist until he lowered himself to the sofa and sat me on top of him.

"What the hell. I'm in it now," he said. "Ride this dick, baby."

"Uh," I moaned. "Uh, uh, uh, uh, uhhh. Hell, yes." Exhaling, I started singing to him. "Cum for me, Daddy."

I was grinding my big, sweet behind so hard, my booty damn near disappeared inside his ass. My middle finger circled my clit. His face tightened, his eyes closed, and his mouth opened. "Oh yeah, Daddy," I cried and went for it. Passionately, I pressed my mouth against his and kissed him Red Velvet style, inserting my tongue in his mouth, softly sucking his tongue, then easing my tongue back into his mouth. I kissed him the same way he came inside of me—nice and slow.

"Aw, fuck. Who are you again?" he asked, holding my wet ass in the palms of his hands.

Seductively, I winked, then whispered in his ear, "I'm Red Velvet, but you can call me Honey."

CHAPTER 6

Honey

Gazing out the kitchen patio window, I decided that today seemed like yesterday. But it wasn't. I realized another day had gone by and there were a few differences. Today I removed a bag of diced potatoes from the freezer, selected a package of chicken apple sausages, and placed a loaf of wheat bread next to the toaster. A dozen brown eggs—a standard breakfast item—were in a large, clear bowl next to the salt and pepper.

I wondered what ingredients of life created the greatest love of all. I felt unjustifiably abandoned and ostracized by Grant. This shit wasn't right. One day my life seemed perfect; I'd finally met a decent man that I actually enjoyed spending time with. Wasn't it out of love that the Creator took a rib from a man and gave it to a woman? Well, right about now I could rip through Grant's abs, snatch out one of his ribs, and beat him over the head with it.

Relentless, I texted him again: *Hi, baby. I miss you.*

I tried analyzing the anger that had suddenly brought me to tears again this morning. I jabbed my index fingers into my temples to suppress the painful throbbing that was exacerbating my frustrations. "I'm ready," I whispered, placing the chicken apple sausages in the skillet before spreading the potatoes on a cookie sheet and placing them in the oven. "I'm ready to settle down."

Could Grant invest so much time into our relationship, then say, "I love you," and not mean it? "Nah, I don't think so. He still loves me. He just needs a little more time to come to that realization," I said aloud. Closing my eyes, I sniffed the long-stemmed white roses centered on my island. The scent reminded me of Grant's favorite Sean John cologne, Unforgivable.

I placed the cooked sausages in a Pyrex dish, then covered them with the glass lid.

Was true love solidified by sex, material possessions, or unconditional acceptance by the beholder? Did love beget happiness? When and how did I fall in love? Out of love? How could love or the lack thereof fester into a hate so volatile the burning sensation could emotionally cremate human beings with suicidal or homicidal thoughts? And how could a deranged person be resuscitated within seconds by one compassionate kiss on the lips? I longed for Grant to kiss my neck, right behind my ear, hold me in his strong arms, and slide his big, thick chocolate dick deep inside my wet, creamy pussy.

I turned off the oven, leaving the potatoes inside.

Struggling to maintain my sanity, I picked up a champagne bottle, pressed the opening against my mouth, leaned my head back, then took a huge gulp. I filled a flute to the rim with champagne, sipped, picked up my phone, then somberly made my way to my bedroom. My girls could scramble, fry, poach, or boil their own eggs this morning. I needed time alone to let go of the pain that was killing me slowly with the nonstop dialogue racing in my head.

"Breakfast is ready," I shouted from the foyer and up the stairs before quietly closing my bedroom door. Turning on the flat-screen television mounted on the wall across from my bed, I reclined on the white suede chaise beside the sliding glass door leading to my patio, forcing back my tears.

"Dammit, Lace! Not again today," I scolded myself.

My head rested against the back of the chaise. I closed my eyes. I was no longer that teenage girl with blossoming breasts that my mother envied or the innocent virgin adolescent that my father disowned. I was a thirty-year-old woman who'd only had one person tell me, "I love you." I was a woman who couldn't bring her only sister back from her grave or win back the heart of the only man she'd ever loved.

Sitting up, I texted Grant again. *I'll tell you anything you want to know. Please speak to me. I need you.*

Tossing my iPhone onto the floor, I curled my fingers into fists, then knelt beside my chaise, crying profusely into the cushion. "Out of the billions of people in the world, why can't I find one somebody to love me? My God, is that too much to ask for? Is it? Huh? You've given me pain, misery, disappointment, abusive husbands, dysfunctional parents, and you can't give me one, not one, somebody who truly loves me? Why?"

Sniffling, I stood in front of the freestanding mirror, staring at my tattered reflection through my sad green eyes. My purple lace boxer panties barely covered my ass. My hair was gathered into an uncombed ponytail. My breasts sat high and firm. My nipples hardened. Goose bumps invaded my pale skin. Despite the way I appeared at the moment, I knew I was gorgeous. Maybe this time my good looks had gotten me into a situation that my heart couldn't get me out of.

"Stop taking Grant's rejection personally," I said aloud, trying to convince myself. "I am good enough for him. Our breakup isn't about me."

I had never had a positive role model in my life, and my inability to trust men had carved permanent scars into my psyche, leaving me fucked up . . . in the head. I'd done the unspeakable. A voice whispered in my ear, "Hush, you're a good woman."

Clinging to the hope that we'd get back together, I wanted Grant to love me, yet somehow a part of me felt unworthy of his love. Of any man's love. If Grant could see me from the inside out, he'd know my truth. I was afraid to become completely vulnerable. What if I told him the whole truth and he turned me in to the police?

Swallowing the tears that had spilled into my half-filled flute of champagne, I decided I was much better off when I wasn't in love. My feelings for men were strongly guarded, and the self-centered men I'd encountered were purely sex objects. When I met Grant, I was focused on the grand opening of my counseling agency, eager and ready to provide resources to help as many women as I could get out of abusive situations. If I didn't pull it together before I walked through the doors of Sweeter Than Honey, I'd be my first and last client.

My finger circling the rim of my flute, I said aloud, "I've got to stop pitying myself." But I couldn't let go of the pain. I didn't know how to let go of the hurt inside of me.

Unexpectedly, this breathtakingly handsome man had stepped out of my blind spot and into my spotlight, and instinctively, I'd known he was different from the rest. Within a few hours of having met Grant, I'd learned he was intelligent, wealthy, and an excellent kisser and lover. More important, he had a gentle soul that connected to my pulse.

Once upon a time, he'd cared about me. Wasn't that love? I hadn't thrown caution to the wind. I'd thrown my heart in his hands when he'd said, "I want you to meet my mother."

Fuck Grant Hill. His ego wasn't more fragile than mine. How could he ignore my voice mails and text messages? Did two wrongs make him right? Wrong or right, my heart ached. A flat line of disappointment stretched the corners of my mouth toward my ears.

Three decades of living on this planet called Earth and I had nothing and no one that I cherished, not even myself. The glass for me wasn't always half full. In fact, for most of my life, my glass had been dry until I suppressed my emotions and took charge of fulfilling my material needs. Having money to the tune of fifty million dollars didn't make me happy, but it sure as hell enhanced my lifestyle.

CHAPTER 7

Grant

*D*amn. *I can't believe I let Red Velvet ride my dick like that yesterday. That shit was fucking cosmic. That woman's pussy was certifiably a lethal weapon. Aw, man, it's a good thing I have a healthy heart, or she could've fucked me into an early grave. And the way she swallowed my dick . . .* I had to stop thinking about her.

Sitting in my car, parked outside my parents' house, scrolling through the extensive list of text messages Honey had sent, I squeezed my hard-on, trying to make my erection subside. Since my breakup with Honey, I'd kept every single one of her messages. My voice mail was always a few messages away from full. I'd saved Honey's messages so I could hear, "Hey, baby. I miss you," anytime I wanted.

Damn! Out of all the respectable, beautiful black women in the world, why did I have to fall for her? Couldn't she see how much I cared about her? I seriously wanted to press the CALL BACK button to talk to her. "Damn, that Red Velvet pussy was sweet and exactly what I needed to take the edge off. Trevor was the man for that one," I said aloud.

If Honey would've whispered in my ear, "Grant, I used to be a whore," I could've eased out of her bed, gotten dressed, and never seen her again, instead of holding her in my arms and falling in love with her. I hated to admit it, but I'd been more than pussy whipped. I had put my business on hold for two straight weeks to help Honey find both a place to live and a great location for her business. I'd introduced her to my personal banker so she could open her accounts. I didn't lay up with women after sex, sharing my goals, my dreams, and my fantasies, the way we'd done. Honey had had plenty of time to tell me the truth. Whatever her truth was.

I'd known immediately that Red Velvet had been paid to fuck me. That was obvious, and I'd treat her as a paid client if I ever decided to call her up. Good thing she'd left last night. Said she had to get back to her son. I respected a woman who kept it real up front.

Looking at my parents' large pale blue Victorian with royal blue trim, I couldn't believe my father refused to sell that house and move out of D.C. There were lots of nicer and newer developments in Virginia and Maryland. I shook my head, thinking I'd actually invited a hooker to meet my mother. I laughed. Man was I a fool for that one. "Next time . . . Nah, forget Honey. There won't be a next time for her," I said aloud.

Looking up from my phone, I smiled hard. My dad was standing in the front door, waving. "Son, come on in here. Breakfast is almost ready," he called.

"In a minute," I called back, wondering if my mother had ever cheated on my father.

The heart of a man wasn't hidden; it was ripped out of his chest, then buried six feet deep, the minute his heart was broken by a woman for the first time. For me, that woman wasn't Honey, but Honey reminded me of Valerie Jamison. Experiencing such excruciating pain was something I'd never forget. No matter how hard subsequent women strived to eradicate the pain or kindle the pleasure, only one woman had been sweet enough to penetrate that barrier.

Other women I'd met thought that they knew every damn thing and that the ex-lovers they complained about were all idiots incapable of making good decisions. What women didn't understand about black men was that we suffered in silence with major discontentment with ourselves for countless reasons, including a lack of financial stability; but being illiterate, unemployed, racially profiled, incarcerated, taken for child support, wanted for alimony, and verbally castrated by white men and black women; feeling inadequate; and being unable to support our families. The number one reason was that, like most black women, the majority of black men were fatherless. Men were tired of living up to the unrealistic expectations of women, who were never satisfied. The black man wasn't trying to get over; he was trying to get by. I knew Honey was pissed off at me, but did she once stop to consider how I felt? I doubted it.

Opening the front door, Dad waved again, this time frantically.

"Okay, old man," I called, getting out of my car. "Calm down."

I had been living on my own for ten years, and my parents were always happy to see me. My dad was the greatest father. He did his best to ensure I never became a statistic. I couldn't lie; I was fortunate to have him in my life. I vividly recalled my dad being present at every stage of my life, beginning with him videotaping me being born.

"You're looking mighty sharp in that button-down shirt, son. If I didn't know any better, I'd think you were trying to outdress me," he said, running his hands down his sleeves. Then he fingered his cuff links and smiled. "I bet you don't have a set like these. Your mother gave them to me this morning. An early thirtieth-anniversary present."

Damn. That's right. How could I forget? Honey had my mind so preoccupied. I'd order something extra special for my parents later today. Dancing my way into the living room, I stopped in front of Mom, hugged her, and said, "Good job." Then I glanced at my cell phone before silencing the ringer. "Where's Benito?"

Dad shook his head. "We had to put him out this morning. I'm sure he'll show back up, complaining he's got no place to go. Son, is that woman still calling you?"

I couldn't lie to my father. I nodded.

"Did you ask her to stop?" my dad asked.

"She'll get tired eventually," I said, following my dad into the dining room. I sat in my seat, the same seat I'd sat in since I was a kid.

Dad got quiet for a while. Then he said, "Son, I raised you better. She deserves closure. I hope you're not one of those men that enjoy having women chase you." He stared at me, peering above the rim of his black-framed eyeglasses. "When it comes to relationships, women are smarter than us. She might stop calling for a week, a month, maybe even a year, but trust me, if she stops, it won't be because she got tired. Forget about Honey for a minute. Isn't your big meeting about partnering with Trevor Williams today?

I smiled, thinking back to yesterday morning. Wonder-pussy was not going to influence my decision. I had my professional reputation riding on the merger, not to mention the ten-million-dollar preapproved business loan I was prepared to take out for my half. If I followed through with the plans, I couldn't afford to lose, either. The real-estate deals with Trevor appeared solid, but I wasn't sure what was going on with that strip club Stilettos. That was the part that didn't feel right. I knew sex and strip clubs were lucrative, but they were also seedy. One bad decision or incident at Stilettos and the Atlanta city government would place a moratorium on the development of all our hotels and condos. If that happened, we could lose hundreds of thousands of dollars each day.

Shaking his head, my father stared at me. "Son, never make a business decision or a marriage proposal based on emotions. It always seems good on the surface. Take time to scratch a little."

On high school graduation day, my friends got keys to cars. My father handed me the deed and the keys to my first home. I continued making sound real-estate investments. Every income stream from every piece of property I owned was attached to the 411-unit condo building and hotel I was developing in Atlanta. Partnering with Trevor would give me collateral leverage to build additional properties.

Mom entered the dining room. She stood behind Dad's chair, as she often did to quietly show her support of my father.

Dad said, "Back to Honey. Son, your mother came to me. Ain't that right, baby? But . . ." Dad paused, then continued. "I chose her. Not because she's beautiful. Not because she's white. I chose your mother because she has a loving heart." He turned around, slapped Mom's behind, then said, "And a big booty. Son, never marry a woman who believes you are responsible for her happiness."

I watched my mother massage my dad's shoulders. He stretched his neck side to side. Mom scratched his back.

"I love you, Ma," I said, easing out of my chair to kiss her cheek. My mom was my number one lady, and my dad was my hero. "I disagree. I am supposed to make and keep my wife happy. Isn't that right, Mom?"

Mom's eyes widened, and she looked toward Dad. "I'll be back. Tell him," she said. Leaving the room, Mom glanced over her shoulder at dad. "Tell him now."

Dad exhaled. "Yes. But deep down inside, an unhappy woman is bitter about something someone else did to her, and she expects you to make up for it," he said. "You can't make a fractured woman whole. Honey wasn't prostituting because a hooker showed up at her high school on career day, telling her about the benefits. Something happened to her. That's not your fault. Let her go. Please, son, marry a good woman, one with a loving heart and a big butt like your mother, and notice whether her eyes light up for you so bright that you can feel the goodness resonating from within her. That is the woman who will never forsake you. It's better to learn to love a good woman than to fall in love with a bad one."

I heard my mother yell from the kitchen, "Baby, snap out of it. She's got you in a trance." Reentering the dining room, Mom insisted we eat. She placed hash browns topped with sautéed onions, fluffy scrambled eggs, turkey sausages, and wheat toast, neatly arranged on a plate, in front of me and another plate in front of my dad.

She placed my plate down first. Oh, oh.

"Grant, your father is right. She's not the one, baby," said Mom, placing her hand on Dad's shoulder. "Go on and tell Grant the truth. If you don't tell him before I return, I will. I've got to go to the hair salon. Call me later and let me know how things went."

I was grateful my parents had taught me how to be a good man before becoming a father, lover, friend, or husband to a woman. I knew the woman I wanted to marry was Honey. Hopefully, my dad wouldn't try to decide for me. Despite her lies, Honey had a sweetness I couldn't deny. I just prayed she didn't hurt me like Valerie had.

"Uh, uh." Dad cleared his throat, looked directly into my eyes, then said, "Son, why are you still worried about that woman? Your brother already told you she's bad news. Besides, if for no other reason, you don't want to date a woman who's dated your brother."

"Not date, Dad. Marry. I want to marry Honey."

A man never forgot his first love, and I'd never forget Valerie Jamison. In Economics 101, I fell hard for her the moment I saw those never-ending legs reaching from her ankles to her torso. We dated our freshman and sophomore years, but I couldn't give Valerie enough of me no matter how hard I tried. Valerie lived for the spotlight. Depending on what sport was in season, she fell in love with the most popular athlete on campus.

A puff of air shot out of my nostrils. Placing a forkful of hash browns in my mouth, I tried eating my breakfast. "Since he has so much to say, let him say it to my face. Where is he?" I asked.

"I already told you I put him out," my dad said emphatically. "He's trouble. You made up your mind about that merger?"

Nodding, I said, "I'ma go for it."

"Don't. You're not thinking clearly. Give it some time. Take every detail under consideration, and then consult with your lawyer for a month or so."

"But—"

"But nothing. This Trevor guy needs you, dammit. You don't need him. Just like Honey. You don't need her, either. You're wealthy, smart, successful, young, and good-looking. The right woman will come along."

Yeah, right. What made any woman the right woman?

I never expected Valerie or any other woman to want me solely for my physical appearance. What if I got hit by a car or disfigured in a fire? What if my dick stopped working? Would the woman I loved still love me? I wanted the woman who would unequivocally answer yes, without hesitation.

I was no athlete like my brother, but my body would beg to differ. I worked out five times a week. The definition from my Adam's apple to my dick formed a straight line; I had no bulging belly like other guys. My smooth six-pack abs were accented by parentheses. And my tight ass sat high above my thighs. I knew women wanted to fuck me before finding out I had a big dick. Damn. Where'd I put that card I got yesterday? Had I missed the party?

Biting my bottom lip, I couldn't get Valerie off of my mind. When she'd said she was pregnant with my first child, the first words out of my mouth were, "Will you marry me?" I didn't ask her to marry me before our baby was born because I felt obligated. I loved Valerie with all my heart. I wanted to do all the right things for and with her. But when Valerie said that she couldn't keep my child, and that she'd had an abortion the day before she'd told me we were pregnant, I felt like my heart had stopped beating. I couldn't breathe.

My dad picked up his plate, then said, "Keep thinking about everything, son. That's good." Then he walked into the kitchen.

I sat at the table, stirring my eggs in with my hash browns.

A few months later, Valerie got pregnant with the star quarterback's baby. I'd never seen her so happy, until she discovered four other women on campus were also pregnant by him at the same time. Valerie ended up joining the seventieth-percentile ranks of those girls and black women who were single parents, while the quarterback walked down the aisle with his high school sweetheart shortly after going pro and clinching a thirty-million-dollar contract.

Valerie dropped out of college, and I couldn't say I was sorry that I didn't see her again. Why did black women claim they wanted a good man, then carelessly and continuously give themselves to men who were unworthy of them? If I ever saw Valerie again, I'd ask her one question. "Who's loving you?"

My dad walked back into the dining room, placed his hand on my shoulder, and said, "Son, stand up and look at me."

"All right." Slowly, I pushed back my chair.

As requested, I faced my father and listened. "Son, your brother says she's a murderer. That she killed a man," said my dad. "Your mother and I are afraid that she might kill you, too. I hope that's convincing enough. If you don't let Honey go for yourself, do it so you won't kill your mother. I can't live without my wife."

CHAPTER 8

Red Velvet

Whoever believed sex was overrated must've been asexual. I wished I could've stayed in D.C. another day with Grant, but after our fuck session, I had to fly back to Atlanta and go straight home so I could care for my son. This morning I fed him instant oatmeal with strawberries and walked him four blocks to his kindergarten class. Then I walked back down those same four blocks, bypassed my house, and walked three more blocks to work at the hotel. I stood on my feet from eleven to seven, with no break.

"See you tomorrow, girl," one of my coworkers said as we walked in opposite directions.

"Not if the movie producer calls me, you won't," I said, checking my text messages.

We weren't allow to text or make personal calls while working. I smiled. I'd missed one voice mail from Grant, or G, as I'd started calling him, and he'd sent four texts: *Velvet, thanks. I'd love to see you again. I'll call you again later. I want to take you to dinner when I get to Atlanta.* Grant was so nice, but I wasn't confused. Grant wanted to hit this good pussy again, and I wanted him to.

I texted him back: *G, can't wait 2 c u ... miss u already.*

The sun was setting. I didn't mind walking the three blocks to get home. I hated that there was no time for me to rest my tired feet. I wanted to take off my shoes. The balls of my feet stung; the heels of my feet ached. My mother thought it was a good idea for me to work at this hotel since it was close to home and my son's school.

"Velvet, take that job, because you need to be close to home in case anything happens to Ronnie," she'd said. "I'll pick him up for you. I'm not going to sit at home worrying about how to get to him if something bad happens."

The day I was born, I was naked, pure, and innocent; I wasn't put on this earth for my mother to validate my existence. Control what was between my thighs. Constantly tell me how I should live my life. Give me advice, knowing at some point in her own life she'd been exactly like me: undereducated about her body, inexperienced with sex, and clueless about love. My mother was thirty years older than me.

While raising me, all she could say was, "Velvet, keep you legs shut. Stay a virgin as long as you can." Why? Who was I saving myself for? She had made wrong choices for the wrong reasons, and she'd survived. Why couldn't I do the same? If she'd wanted me to make smart choices, why hadn't my mother taught me about sex? About my body? Probably because she still hadn't figured it out for herself.

All the women I knew chose guys who didn't love them. If they did love them, it didn't last long. My mother had had her chance to screw up; now she wanted to preach what she hadn't practiced. I wasn't trying to impress my mother or be a role model for younger girls. I was going to continue taking risks and fucking up until I got tired, 'cause nobody I knew had gotten love or sex right.

I unlocked my mother's door with my key.

"Hi, Mama," I said, giving her a hug.

"Hey, baby. How was your day?" Mama asked, opening her mail while looking at me.

"I'm tired," I answered, pouring a glass of cranberry juice.

"I have just the break you need," Mama said, nodding.

Uh-oh. Here we go. Reluctantly, I said, "Tell me what you've come up with this time."

"Baby, it's sweeter than honey. Honey Thomas is helping women empower themselves, and I figured if you could start getting child support, you could stop stripping at night."

"Mama, I don't know this Honey Thomas woman you're talking

about, and neither do you. I like stripping. I don't like standing on my feet for eight hours."

Sitting at my mother's glass-top dinner table for four, I removed my shoes, then rubbed my tired feet. "Ronnie, you've got fifteen minutes to play video games. Then we have to go home."

Mama said, "Stripping doesn't have health benefits for my grand-son."

Working in customer service, I'd learned that people were fucking selfish and rude, just like my mother. They didn't give a damn. I could be puking up my guts, and in the middle of heaving, they'd ask, "Can you give us directions to Atlantic Station?" They wouldn't even apologize for interrupting me. One day soon I wouldn't have to answer to those your-mama-should've-raised-you-better tricks or my mother.

"Okay, Mommy," my son yelled from the living room. In an hour he'd be right back at my mom's, 'cause I had to be at my second job by nine.

"Baby, she's new to Atlanta, and her commercials are on Michael Baisden's show all the time. Honey is going to help women get out of abusive situations," said Mama.

I didn't know that woman and had no desire to. "Anybody can advertise on the radio, Mama." Honey was probably a rip-off chick, out to make a quick hustle by preying on desperate women. The fact that my baby's daddy had never seen our son or paid a penny of child support wasn't abuse; that was neglect, and I didn't want to see his trifling, rusty, married behind ever again.

"Ronnie," I called out to my son, "let's go!" Looking into my mother's eyes, I said, "Ma, please. This one time listen to me. Don't contact that woman."

Picking up my shoes, I left my mom's house and went next door to mine. If I didn't need my mom to keep Ronnie so often, I'd encourage her to go back to work. She'd taken an early retirement buyout from her federal government job to help me out.

"Hey, Ronnie. Hey, Red. That sure is another nice suit you have on today. They have any more of them concierge openings at that new fancy hotel you been working at?" Mrs. Taylor asked as she sat on her porch. "I could use me some new clothes, too. Never mind, chile. I'm just dreaming out loud. They probably ain't got no positions for a sixty-year-old woman. Besides, I can't walk all them blocks back and forth like you do. You sho' look good, Red. Them Hollywood producers call you yet?"

The heaviness weighing down my heart was invisible. No one, including Mrs. Taylor, could look beyond my sexy smile and big booty to see that my fucking feet were hella tired from standing all day, exotic dancing all night, and running to or from men that didn't deserve me.

Some of those lazy Negroes wanted me to cook, talkin' 'bout, "My mama cooked, cleaned, worked two jobs, and took care of us. That's the problem with y'all black women. Y'all don't know how to keep a man happy."

Fuck that. I wasn't doing that domestic bullshit. I told that nigga, "Yeah, your mama did all that for you, and look at where it's gotten you and her. She still doing the same shit, and your ass ain't shit. Get the fuck outta my face. And before you leave, if your mama is such a good woman, let her suck your dick! Trick!" I got mad just thinking about how stupid and lazy some black men really were. Bunch of underachieving sons of bitches! "I'm handling mine. Stay your black ass out of jail, and get a real job," I added.

If it weren't for my child, only God knew where I'd be. I smiled. Probably in Hollywood, starring opposite Denzel or Jamie or opening up for Steve Harvey or Mo'Nique. Everybody I talked to knew how badly I wanted to act. I was super-talented and eager to launch my career. My last audition, for the movie *Something on the Side*, was six weeks ago. I'd auditioned for the part of Coco Brown. But I hadn't heard anything. Maybe they thought I didn't weigh enough. I'd gladly gain weight if I had to.

I stopped smiling.

Single parenting was so hard. I hated it. If it weren't for my unconditional love for my child, I would've killed myself immediately after giving birth to him. Alone, in a cold operating room with a doctor and strangers poking, probing, and pulling between my legs, I'd cried. Not for joy. I'd cried because I wondered where my baby's father was. Probably out raping somebody else with his nasty fifty-plus-year-old dick.

When a woman was twenty (the age I was when I met him) and a man was forty-five, they didn't seem so far apart in years. But now that I was twenty-five and he was fifty-one, his ass seemed hella ancient. He hadn't showed up at the hospital, and I hadn't seen Alphonso Allen since I told him I was pregnant.

Standing by my side, my son said, "Hello, Mrs. Taylor."

Mr. and Mrs. Taylor's porch was separated from mine by a waist-high white wooden fence. Mrs. Taylor still believed in knowing her neighbors and keeping watch over our block. The suits I wore were different styles, but they were the same navy-colored, mandatory hotel concierge uniforms. Still, Mrs. Taylor liked them.

"Baby, your cell phone rangin'," Mrs. Taylor said, staring at my Sidekick like it was a foreign object.

"I know. I'll call 'em back later," I said, silencing the ringer.

I doubted Alphonso ever told his wife about our five-year-old son. The day we met in Los Angeles, I'd just finished auditioning for a lead role in a movie called *Married Men*. I was going to play Jay's girlfriend. That opportunity was long gone, I guessed. I hadn't heard anything yet, about any part, but each day I held on to hope.

"You okay, chile?" Mrs. Taylor asked. "You'll get the part, Red. Don't worry. Worrying ain't never done nobody any good, anyways."

I dug in my purse for my keys, answering, "Yes, ma'am. I'm good."

That day Alphonso was driving the bus route along Wilshire Boulevard. I'd gotten on, and he'd given me his cell phone number when I got off at my stop, promising to take me to dinner that night. I showed up at Harold & Belle's on West Jefferson Boulevard and waited for hours. I told myself that maybe he was in one of L.A.'s traffic jams I'd heard about or had to work late. I sat at the bar, by the door, drinking Patrón Silver margaritas with salt on the rim. I speed dialed his cell every half hour, in between drinks, but after six failed attempts, I gave up and left the restaurant.

I knew I was too fine for him to pass on this ass. I was looking forward to making a friend that could help me out if I ever got in a bind. The next day he called me back, and we met up. No lunch or dinner. I had a one-night stand with him on Venice Beach on a wild, hot summer night, and my whole life changed. But not his. To this day, I regretted opening my legs in hopes of getting a sugar daddy to give me some money. I hated that I opened my legs and encouraged a man I didn't know to penetrate me. Maybe I should've listened to my mother when she tried to warn me about men. Why did I wrap my legs and arms around him? Kiss him? Go down on him? When I didn't even know him. *Whateva.*

Glancing at Mrs. Taylor, I said, "You don't need a fancy suit to make you look beautiful. You're gorgeous." I wondered if Mr. Taylor still loved Mrs. Taylor, or if he stayed with her to honor his commitment to God or to protect his assets.

"Baby, yo' phone," she said, pointing this time.

I silenced it again. I had to quit giving up my number so easily, but these older men weren't into texting, and the younger ones wanted their dicks sucked for free. Not by Velvet.

Depending on which direction you traveled, our row of town houses sat on State Street, two blocks away from Interstate 85 and walking distance from the hotel where I worked. My mother lived next door to me, on the opposite side of Mrs. Taylor's. My mother was the main reason I couldn't commit suicide. Burying me would kill her, and then who'd take care of my son?

"I'ma go on inside and get ready for work," I said, unlocking my front door and throwing my shoes on the floor. Ronnie raced inside to his room, then turned on his Nintendo Wii, as I threw my purse on the sofa, headed to the refrigerator-freezer, removed the bottle of Pa-trón Silver, poured two shots into a glass, then went to the bathroom and turned on the shower.

Mistakes happened, but why was I the only one who had to pay for our mistake for the rest of my life? I hated to think that way, but honestly, Ronnie was a mistake and a constant reminder for me not to make the same mistake twice. So when I got pregnant the second time, by a different man, one who had no intentions of marrying me or being with me, I had an abortion.

My dreams were deferred, not abandoned.

"One day," I whispered. I sat on the toilet, massaging my toes. "Damn, my feet hurt."

I'd believed Alphonso would pull out after we realized the condom was stuck inside of me, and when he didn't, I'd suddenly realized I was having sex with a rapist. He'd penetrated me as deep as he could, and then he'd grunted, "Velvet, your young pussy is tight like my little princess, Tiffany Davis." He'd thrusted deeper, then said, "Velvet, your pussy is better than Tiffany's baby. If my stepdaughter hadn't run away from home, I wouldn't be here with you. Thanks, bitch."

That motherfuckin' trick was driving teenagers around on his bus every damn day, and his employers didn't know he was raping women and girls?

I tossed back one shot as I started peeing. "Why me?" I cried.

I'd yelled, "Get the hell up off of me, nigga!" as I felt his pulsation pumping semen inside the walls of my vagina. He called me a bitch? Was he telling me he'd molested his stepdaughter? Shaking my head, I got sand in my eyes and my mouth. I tried to move from underneath him. I couldn't see. My legs were over his shoulders; he had intentionally locked his arms around my thighs.

Covering my mouth, he shivered and said, "I'm almost done."

I managed to grab a fistful of sand and throw it in his face. That was when he punched me in mine. That was the worst encounter of my life. I couldn't move. All I could do was cry and pray. But I endured nine long months of denial and daily wishing. Each night I said, "Now I lay me down to sleep. I pray the Lord my soul to keep. I pray to die before I wake, and I pray the Lord my soul to take." Each day my prayers were unanswered. I went into labor, and one bad decision to open my legs for the wrong man changed my life forever . . . forever.

Finishing off the Patrón, I removed all of my clothes. A hot shower always felt good, and I took three a day to make sure my pussy stayed fresh.

The demanding chores of single parenting left little time for me to sleep. A facial, a massage, a hair appointment, a manicure, a pedicure, shopping on the weekends, flying to the All-Star weekend, the Essence Music Festival, and the BET Awards with my girls were all the things I'd done to get a man, until I got fucked over by a man. Now I struggled to keep my appearance up. All of my girlfriends had had babies before me by black men who'd moved on with their lives. I'd sworn to them, "Whatever nonsense you guys are listening to, Velvet ain't hearing it."

Now I had to find time to let my nail polish dry while microwaving dinner. Sew in my own tracks to save a few dollars to pay the rent, utilities, after-school care expenses, and my Sidekick bill, and to compensate my mother for graciously watching my son all the time. Not one penny of child support did he have to pay. I had no idea where to find Alphonso, nor was I about to try. I didn't have an address, and I'd erased his cell phone number shortly after I told him I was pregnant. Determined to make it on my own and provide a decent life for my son, I'd taken on a second job, working nights.

Toweling off, I wanted to cry, but I didn't. What good would that do?

I was tired of living dollar to dollar and struggling to take care of Ronnie. He deserved better. Hell, I deserved better, too. Mrs. Taylor was retired, and if she knew the truth about her husband, who had offered me money in exchange for letting him taste my pussy, Mrs. Taylor—married to her husband for forty years—wouldn't have thought my suits were beautiful. Instantly, I would've become the whore, slut, and tramp next door. Women of all ages were ignorant like that. Always blaming other women for the affairs their husbands had.

"Damn. Can I wash my ass in peace?" I said, making my way to the living room. "If one mo' horny motherfucker calls me when I'm already running late for my second job, I swear I'ma scream at the top of my lungs."

Every Friday, Saturday, and Sunday night, I barely made it in the door before the men started calling. John always tried to beat the rest and convince me to hook up with him after I finished stripping. I tried telling John's cheap ass that being with me was a relay race, not a marathon. Until I found the right man for Ronnie and me, all men were a financial means for me to quit stripping. Pressing the button on my Bluetooth, I didn't bother looking at the caller ID. I went into my bedroom, opened my lingerie drawer, then placed a soft, red, furry bra with strings and a matching thong in my oversized purse before answering. "Make it quick," I said.

"I want to know if you sucked my husband's dick," a female voice yelled in my ear.

"What! Who in the hell are you?" Moving the earpiece away from my ear, I shouted, "Ronnie! You hungry, boy?"

"No, Mama."

"I'm walking you over to Grandma's in exactly twenty minutes. Go make yourself a sandwich."

"Okay, Mama."

"Where's my damn boots?" I said, placing the earpiece back on my ear.

"You gon' answer my question or make me show up at your ho job tonight and beat your ass? The choice is yours," said the female voice.

Working at Stilettos was getting old quick, but I hung in there because the money was decent. And Trevor gave me a bonus whenever the bar broke six figures. A few rappers and high rollers, men and women, dropping credits cards and offering to buy a few rounds of drinks or a case of champagne, and I was on my way to making some extra change.

What I couldn't stand was the guys who claimed to have their shit together, begging to take me out for a drink, translation, sex, and they couldn't even keep their women in check. I had picked up a few "friends with benefits" to fund my emergency savings account, but whosoever the fuck this chick was who was challenging me, she was way out of line. I wished she would show up tonight at Stilettos, talkin' that shit to me. She'd end up with this heel right in the middle of her damn clit. I picked up my spike-heeled boots, then put them in the bag with my outfit.

I had to ask her, "Who are you, and why are you wasting my damn time?"

"Don't worry about who I am."

"Okay. Then who's your trick?"

"My what?"

"Your man, bitch! Who's your fuckin' man?"

"Oh, Tolliver. But you probably know him as T."

I had to smile. T was my favorite. We were cool and had fun kickin' it at the movies and hotels and shit. T was the bomb, or so I'd thought until I heard him get on the phone and say, "Velvet, tell my wife that we're just friends and we're not fucking, because she's tripping. I told you, woman, I go to the strip clubs to relieve my stress. What's wrong with that?"

No, this too-dark-to-be-white, too-light-to-be-black, punk-ass, biracial motherfucka wasn't pleading with and lying to his wife and asking me to have his back. He must've forgotten Red Velvet was the one on the other end of the damn phone. *I swear, I gotta stop fucking these trifling-ass men,* I thought. He was probably taking her money and giving it to me, but that wasn't my concern.

"Yeah, Velvet, tell me, because Tolliver claims you're just a sleazy stripper begging to ride his dick," said Tolliver's wife.

No, those fools did not put me on speaker. This bitch was checking the wrong person. She'd asked for it.

I took a deep breath. "Look, bitch," I said. "I did not say 'I do' to you. Someone else walked down the aisle and said all that for better or for worse shit to you. That's the bullshit *you* signed up for. Listen up and you tell me if you think I fucked your *husband* or not. Tolliver's dick is eight and a half inches long, it's thick, it's circumcised, and it's beautiful. The lips around his opening, when you look at his dick sideways, are shaped exactly like those succulent lips on his face. He has four flat chocolate moles, one between his nuts and three in a row on the underside of his dick, so when I play connect the dots with the barbell in my tongue, I draw a straight line. He shaves his pubic hairs down to a shadow. His favorite color is blue. Favorite movie, *American Gangster.* And his favorite pussy is Red Velvet. Hope that helps both of you sick-ass tricks the fuck out. I gotta go. And, T, don't call me no fuckin' mo'!"

That bitch didn't know who she was questioning, and I didn't know what in the hell Tolliver was thinking by trying to check me. I hated men who couldn't keep their nosy bitches in check. *Let that bitch show up tonight,* I thought. *I've got something for her ass.* And T, with his big-ass, country-sized dick could still hit this pussy, but first he'd have to pay for every dollar I'd missed tonight for being late. Plus I was gonna charge him a hundred dollars extra for being stupid. After throwing my fiery red human-hair wig into my bag, I slipped into a green velour jogging suit and flat shoes, just in case I had to kick that bitch's ass. The last thing Red Velvet did was run from any motherfucker.

"I'm ready," my son said, walking into my bedroom, with his Spiderman backpack strapped tightly over his shoulders. "Mommy, who was that on the phone?"

"Nobody, baby. Nobody important. At least not anymore. Let's get you to Grandma's."

CHAPTER 9

Honey

My pussy. My pleasure.

Fucking Grant was my preference, but having a man penetrate me wasn't necessary in order for me to have a satisfying orgasm. I spread a black mink throw on the patio beyond the sliding glass door outside my bedroom. The stars surrounded the moon as I inhaled the cool midnight breeze.

"Ah, every night should be this peaceful." I bet God got upset whenever He blessed us with a beautiful day that we didn't take time to appreciate. It was up to me to take advantage of each minute. Tonight, right now, I was doing me. *Forget about Grant*, I told myself. I wasn't thinking about the girls. I declared this Honey time.

My pussy was so starved that it felt like she'd eaten my labia minora, sucking it inside my vagina, and like my labia majora had closed, the way a *Mimosa pudica* flower closed when touched, when cold, or when put in the dark. My pussy trapped and stored the chi energy inside the walls of my uterus. The combustion was going to erupt into an orgasm so explosive, all of Atlanta might get swept underground by my fluids.

I had to stop suppressing and ignoring my sexual feelings. I could go out, find a charity dick attached to a man, fuck him, then forget about him, or I could please myself. Opening my mint green pleasure chest, which I kept at the foot of my bed, I pushed aside my vibrating rabbit. "Nah, fuck that. You'd better come with me," I said, putting the rabbit on the bed.

I moved my ruby glass slipper aside. Not the kind of slipper Cinderella had, my glass dick was twelve inches long and heated up nicely in the microwave, or I could chill it in a bucket of ice. The extreme sensations inside my pussy felt fantastic. I didn't want to go into the kitchen. Any room other than the kitchen would've been okay.

I buried the slipper at the bottom of the chest, then scanned the edible panties, pleasure pearls, my remote-control egg, and a whole lotta other stuff. I came up holding a silver bullet, dangling from my cyber-skin vibrating tongue, in one hand, and in the other hand was my pink pocket rocket. The toys that solely focused on clit stimulation made me cum in less than two minutes, so I tossed the pocket rocket back into the chest and kept the tongue.

Sitting on the black mink throw, I squeezed a few drops of lube onto my tongue, attached the silver bullet, then put a few drops of lube on the bullet. Lying back, I bent me knees upward, spread my thighs, slipped the bullet in my ass, then turned the vibration on high. The tongue fluttered against my clit, almost feeling like the real thing. At the same time the bullet shot vibrations inside my ass.

Sometimes I'd put the bullet in my pussy or in my ass while fucking Grant. He enjoyed the feel of the vibration. "Ooh-wee! Damn, this shit feels good." But not good enough. Leaving the bullet in my ass, I placed a condom over my vibrator, lubed the shaft and the rabbit ears, then powered on my fucking rabbit.

Inserting the rotating dick into my pussy, I let the pearls vibrate along my G-spot. The rabbit ears teased my clit. My ass felt wonderful. Gazing up at the moon, I moaned, "That's it. That's the spots."

Thirty minutes later I'd given myself explosive pleasure that made my pussy wet inside and out.

I tossed the toys aside, stared up at the stars, and relaxed for a moment. Fucking myself felt good. Fucking Grant felt great.

Exhaling, I thought, *Maybe I'm not good enough for Grant.* If he wouldn't give me the decency or respect I deserved and allow me to explain my side of the story, perhaps Grant was the one who wasn't good enough for me. The time had come for me to let go.

CHAPTER 10

Grant

Entering my D.C. office at 8:00 a.m., I paused in front of my receptionist long enough to say, "Good morning, Beverly. Hold all my calls until eleven a.m."

Beverly was five feet eight. Her short brown hair was neatly tapered to accentuate her beautiful, big brown eyes. The mesmerizing curves of her hips matched those of her lips each time she smiled, which was often. She held a broker's license but didn't like sales or managing people. Beverly was dependable and flexible. She'd visit a few properties when I needed her to. But generally, I had other employees handle on-site management.

"Certainly, Mr. Hill, and good morning to you. You have—"

Walking away from her not-so-bright smile, I said, "I know. Another message from Ms. Honey Thomas. Trash it."

If my wanting to be with Honey was worrying my parents, I had to do the right thing. Why did this woman repeatedly call me at home, at work, and on my cell, then text me in between? Didn't she get it? She was a murderer, and I was done with her, and thankfully, I'd found out the truth before making the same mistake I'd made with Valerie by giving my heart to a black woman who didn't know how to care for me.

Clicking on her computer, Beverly dragged a file to her trash can, smiled, then said, "She hasn't called you today."

Oh, she must be still sleeping, I thought, feeling embarrassed.

"What I was getting ready to say was you have a visitor, who invited himself into your office."

"What! She showed up instead! She had the audacity to show her face without my—"

Holding her open palm toward me, Beverly slowly said, "Hold up. Calm down. No, Mr. Hill. I said, 'Himself.' Actually, it's a man, and he refused to give me his name."

Frowning, I felt like a fool this time. I wasn't listening well, and I was hurt that Honey hadn't called or texted since the day before yesterday. Maybe she had sensed I'd let Velvet fuck me. Had she found another man to replace me? Or was it like my dad said? Would she call in a week or a month? I wanted her to call this morning, like she'd done almost every day for the past eighteen days.

"Is it one of my evicted tenants? Did you call the police?"

"I wasn't sure what to do. He wasn't unruly. He just invited himself into your office."

Banging my fist on her desk, I yelled, "What! You should never allow anyone to invite themselves into my office! Ever! You got that!"

Beverly's eyes widened. "Mr. Hill, I apologize. I'm sorry. You want me to call the police?"

"Yes," I said, slowly approaching my office. People who had nothing to lose sure as hell didn't mind taking other people down with them. What was Honey's fucking problem? *Fuck her!* She was probably laid up with some other man.

Peeping through the crack in my door, I saw it was trifling-ass Benito. "Beverly, never mind," I yelled over my shoulder. "I can handle him."

"Who is he?" she asked.

"My brother."

"I didn't know you had a brother," Beverly replied and waited for a response, which I refused to give.

But I did give her what she deserved. "Beverly, I apologize. I overreacted."

She smiled. "It's okay, Mr. Hill. I know you're under a lot of pressure with the merger. It won't happen again. I'm getting a lock put on your door today."

Standing in my doorway, I watched Benito browse the hundreds of architectural design, real estate, and law books on my wall-to-wall customized shelves. I slammed the door. His ass didn't flinch. He nodded as he looked over the encased model of my newest 411-unit hotel and condominium building, which was under construction across the street from Trevor Williams's hotel and condos in Atlanta. I glanced around to see if any lightweight items were missing, like my Montblanc pens or my platinum golf balls. Nope. They were there.

"Hey, bro. I apologize for imposing on you like this, but we need to talk about Lace," said Benito. "You should thank me for saving you. She was getting ready to fuck you blind."

First my dad and now this asshole wanted to tell me how to live my life. Lace, Honey, whatever her real name was, I wanted no parts of that pathological prevaricator.

Oh my God. Looking at her picture on my credenza, I'd been sure that woman was amazingly beautiful both inside and out. Her silky skin, juicy lips, perfect figure, sculpted legs and thighs, and those incredible crystal green eyes had commanded my attention the second she sat next to me on the plane, in first class.

I'd pretended I wasn't impressed with her when we first met, but I couldn't lie: she'd had my undivided attention the instance our eyes met. I smiled on the inside, remembering how she'd made me laugh off and on the entire trip. Honey was easy to talk to. I'd felt like we were two old friends getting reacquainted after a long period without contact.

On our first date, she'd looked and felt ravishing on my arm, making me the proudest man alive. Men and women had stared at her, and all I had thought was, *She's spoken for. Yes, this is the woman I'm going to marry one day.*

"Man, she whipped that red, snapping pussy on you, too, huh? Consider yourself lucky, G. You only put in two weeks. I'm telling you," Benito said, puckering his lips like a baby getting ready to cry.

Exhaling, I cut him off and said, "Yeah, I guess, but don't compare me to you, ever."

What had impressed me the most about Honey wasn't her ability to sex me senseless; it was the business objectives for her company. After becoming successful, I wanted what my parents had. I wanted some-one special to share my life with. I truly wanted to marry a black woman like Obama's wife, a woman who would dedicate her life to improving the community in a huge way. A woman who knew her self-worth. A woman who would stand by me and be a wonderful mother to our children.

I had to stop thinking about Honey . . . but I couldn't. With all my investments, I could have sex with practically any woman I wanted, in-cluding those two women I'd met at Starbucks, but the only woman I desired to make love to was Honey.

"Give me a job," Benito blurted. "I can handle things here in the office while you travel, or I can manage one of your properties, for a good salary and a free apartment."

I shook my head. "Outside of football, you don't have any employ-able skills. Besides, I don't trust you," I said, suppressing my memory of Honey drizzling hot chocolate syrup on my chest, abs, dick, and balls, then smearing it all over me with her pussy.

I'd grown tired of sharing my bed with strange and estranged women. I no longer wanted to pretend I enjoyed the company of highly intel-lectual women who didn't realize they had four holes between their thighs that could generate orgasmic pleasure, from clitoral orgasms to vaginal orgasms to ejaculating secretions produced by the Skene's glands—which they squirted from the urethral canal, the same way I shot cum from my nuts through my dick—to anal orgasms. Those women made me impervious to their empty promises of giving me unforgettable sexual pleasure. My eyes closed for a few seconds as I relived some of those disappointing situations.

"Okay," Benito said. "Is it the silk scarf tied around your nuts while you're fucking her doggie style, and just when you start cuming, she tugs your balls, and you screaam like a bitch because that shit feels so fucking good. Or—"

Opening my eyes, I felt my forehead buckle as I stared at that fool. "I'm not giving you a job, nor am I going to sit here and swap X-rated stories with you."

Yeah, I knew exactly what Benito was talking about, and that shit had felt fucking fantastic. I needed to release the backed-up cum building inside my nuts. If I had sex tonight as planned with those two ladies I'd met, fine, but if I didn't, that was okay, too. I'd stroke my own dick. But either way, I was busting a big one tonight. Since my breakup with Honey two and a half weeks ago, my encounters had been dreadful: I had to do most of the work, and I'd get dressed immediately after cuming and go home.

In my desperate search for an experienced woman like Honey or Velvet, I had reneged on my promise never to stick my dick inside a black woman I didn't care about. Before I could make it to my house, my cell phone would ring, and the woman I'd just finished fucking would ask, "Grant, what's wrong?"

How could I respond, "Take time to learn your own body. Open your mouth and tell me what pleases you. Move your ass. Suck my big, beautiful dick like you enjoy that shit. Hell, learn how to please yourself," without insulting a woman? So I gave my canned response, "Nothing," followed my unconscious lie, "I'll call you later," which meant nothing to me before or after I'd said it.

Money couldn't buy experience. Earning a degree didn't educate women about sex. Either a woman had it—knowledge about her body—or she didn't. Ooh, Velvet could teach classes on how to suck a dick the right way.

Benito stood in the middle of the floor, bobbing his head. What was fucking wrong with him? Was he retarded or something? I wanted to see how long he would stand there before opening his mouth or, if I was lucky, leaving.

Honey knew all of her spots and all of mine, too. She was perfect, or so I'd thought. What I knew for sure was I needed someone to share my life with and somebody who loved me for me. I still wanted Honey. I picked up my iPhone, hoping I'd missed a voice-mail message or a text. Nothing.

Honey was the last person I thought about at night and the first person I thought about in the morning, but I was afraid of learning the truth about her. Or perhaps I was afraid of learning the truth about myself. What really attracted me to her? Either way I'd rather hold on to the best memories of my life and let her go than take her back and have regrets for doing what I knew I shouldn't have done. Honey was a former prostitute and madam, but I had to prove to my parents that my brother was lying about her being a murderer.

Swallowing the lump in my throat, I said, "Benito, seriously, you've got to go. Now. I have a client arriving shortly."

Trevor had delayed our meeting by a day. He wanted me to go forty-nine to his fifty-one on purchasing land instead of fifty-fifty as originally agreed. And he wanted to add in designing the layout and constructing the improvements for an upscale gentlemen's club in order to get a jumpstart on professional basketball player Darius Jones-Williams, who was reportedly getting ready to open up several multilevel mega strip clubs, which would put Trevor's and all the other Atlanta strip joints out of business in less than a year.

Against my dad's recommendation, today I was partnering with Trevor in his strip club, Stilettos, and our developments already under construction. I could hold off on partnering to develop a new strip club. Maybe we could consult with Honey on finding the hottest female exotic dancers. That would give me a reason to call her.

"Your client can wait, man. I'm your brother. I'm homeless. I've got no place to go," Benito confessed. "I have no money. Dad said I couldn't stay at the house, 'cause Mom is afraid of me. Like I'd ever do anything to hurt her. You can at least let me stay in one of your apartments in Georgetown until I get on my feet. I promise to pay you back every penny with interest."

I chuckled, then said, "I see you and Honey have something in common. Deceiving people. No can do. Like Dad told you, call your baby mama. I'm sure she'll be happy to have you spend time with your son. Considering that you've screwed everybody who's tried to help you, this is a perfect time to do right by her and your son."

"I don't owe that bitch nothing! She turned her back on me."

"Yeah, by taking care of your son by herself. I get your point," I said, shaking my head. "Look, seriously, my client is here from Atlanta to meet with me. I won't waste his time or mine trying to solve your plethora of problems."

The sight of Benito's unshaved face and his stained jeans, and his stench, hit me all at once, making my stomach churn. How could a black man who was abandoned by his birth parents be so ungrateful all of his life?

My mother adopted him while she was a single parent, then struggled to take care of him until she married my father. My parents had given him every luxury they'd afforded me, including a house, after he graduated from high school, which he'd immediately sold. Then he'd pissed off the money trying to impress his college teammates.

Did Benito think he won four college-football championships on his own? He should've been grateful, but, no, he was never satisfied, and what disgusted me the most was nothing was ever his damn fault. Nothing anyone did for him was ever enough. He'd earned millions playing professional football, and what did he have to show for it? Not a damn thing.

Looking at Honey's picture on my credenza, I said, "Get out."

"Forget that bitch. She's a ho, man. And she stole my money. Okay. I'll leave, but you're the only one who can help me get my money from her ass. Help me, and I promise I'll never ask you for anything else. I swear."

Benito was pathetic scum. Whatever Honey took from him, I was sure she deserved and then some. "You've got ten minutes to say what's on your mind," I said, sitting on the corner of my desk, hoping to hear something redeemable about Honey.

His ass descended toward the seat of my camel-colored leather chair. "Oh, hell no," I said. "Don't get comfortable. Keep standing up, look me in my eyes, and tell me what you have to say about Honey. I've terminated my relationship and all communication with her, so don't infringe upon my time by trying to convince me to contact her on your behalf."

I checked my phone again. Still no messages from Honey.

"Man," Benito exhaled, scratching his ear like a monkey. "So much shit happened over the three years I lived with her, I don't know where to start."

I couldn't believe she had let this bum leech off of her for three years. I'd thought she was smarter than that. Thank God this ignorant idiot wasn't my biological brother, or I'd have to petition him for a DNA test. Standing tall, I said, "Then leave and call me when you get your lies together."

Benito's lips tightened. "Man, I'm not lying. Okay. Here's the truth. Lace worked for my boy Valentino James. Valentino is in jail because Lace let him take the rap for killing one of her bitches. She did it. Now I can't go back to Las Vegas to bail him out and prove he's innocent, 'cause I don't have any money. That and that undercover bitch police officer Sapphire Bleu told me, if I ever stepped foot in the state of Nevada, she'd personally arrest me. I ain't letting another woman stick a gun in my ass the way Honey did after she tied me up. Forget that." Benito swiped the back of his hand across his sweaty forehead. He frantically shook his head, and his sweat landed on my face as he said, "Whatever you do, man, don't ever let Honey tie you up."

Wiping my face, I repositioned my thigh on the corner of my desk. I bit my bottom lip to keep from laughing at that fool. I asked my brother, "What the fuck have you done? This isn't about Honey. You're involved in something illegal. What is it?"

Benito's face was drenched in sweat, as though someone had dowsed him with a bucket of water. His dingy white cotton T-shirt stuck to his chest as he exclaimed, "Wasn't my fault, man. I didn't kill Sunny. I didn't pull—"

"Wait a minute. You mean Sunny Day? That gorgeous young girl who was on the national news a few weeks ago? The twin who was murdered in Vegas the day before her twenty-first birthday? All of this shit you're telling me is recent?"

"I guess you heard about that, huh? Yeah, that's the one. Like I was saying, I didn't pull the trigger. Valentino did. But he made me bury the body. But I didn't bury her body. I left it in Sunny's condo back in Vegas. Her twin sister found the body, and they had a funeral and all, but you can't tell nobody I had anything to do with any of that shit. That's all over, man. What I need you to help me do is find out what happened to the hundred million dollars I heard Lace stole from Valentino's mansion so I can get Valentino out of jail and get my share for saving his ass. I know you don't need my money, but I'll break you off a li'l something when I get paid."

Okay, I thought. *First he said Lace killed Sunny. Then he said Valentino killed her, but he disposed of the body. Then the money was his. Now it's not his. It's Valentino's, but Lace has got it. A hundred million dollars? Damn, if Benito is telling the truth, Lace, Honey, whosoever she is, she is smarter than I thought.* I was greatly intrigued. *So that's how she paid cash for her mansion. With that amount of money, Honey would need some legitimate invest-*

*ments in addition to her business. Perhaps she could partner with us. Hmm.
I'll propose the idea to Trevor.*

I looked at Benito. "First off, none of the money is yours," I said.
"Second, you're fucking crazy if you think you're going to make me a
conspirator to murder and money laundering, and third, take this
five hundred dollars, get the hell out of my office, and don't ever
come near me or my parents again."

Benito stood there dazed and confused, like he didn't know if he
wanted to beat my ass or cry. But I could tell he was happy as hell to
have a few dollars.

I went on. "Invest it wisely. I thought my father was overreacting,
but he's right. You're endangering all of our lives. What if this pimp
Valentino James has a hit out on your dumb ass, thinking you set him
up and stole his money? You ever contemplate that? I'm going to ask
you politely one more time. Leave."

Benito pleaded with me, gesturing with his hands. "Valentino is my
boy. He wouldn't do that to me. But look, you have to help me. We're
blood, and I don't have anywhere else to go. Five hundred dollars
won't last long in D.C. You want me to sleep under the freeway again
with those homeless people?"

"Here. Take this card. Maybe this woman can help you," I said, giving the number for the lady I'd met at Starbucks. My blood pressure
must've shot up fifty degrees as I yelled, "We're not blood! Get the
fuck out!" This time I snatched opened the door and waited for this
ignoramus to leave.

"Aw'ight. That's cool. But you'd better pray Lace doesn't have my
money, or she's one dead bitch," Benito said, walking out.

I yelled, "You're so stupid, you'd probably shoot yourself, and you
don't have any money, you dumb ass!" Then I slammed the door.
"The nerve of him."

Sitting in my chair, I exhaled heavily and stared at the amazingly
beautiful woman in the picture. I wondered who in the world she was.
Loose curls framed her flawless face and dazzling smile, but there was
no sparkle under her long eyelashes, although I could picture how
Honey's eyes did light up for me whenever we were together.

I had to find out for myself who she really was. But I wasn't going to ask her over the phone. I had to look deep into those captivating green eyes. After questioning Honey, I was taking a trip to Las Vegas to find that police officer, Sapphire Bleu. Surely, she knew everything about Honey, Benito, and Valentino. Picking up my cell, I began dialing Honey's number, then hung up. I blocked my number, then redialed hers.

"Mr. Hill, Mr. Williams is here," Beverly said on my landline at the same time Honey answered, "What's sweeter than honey and more valuable than money?"

Damn. Her voice was soft and so succulent, I could taste her pussy on the tip of my tongue. My dick got so hard, it throbbed against my zipper.

"Mr. Hill?" Beverly chimed in my right ear.

"Hello," Honey spoke in my left ear.

Intentionally, I said, "Beverly, send Mr. Williams in."

Honey said, "Grant?"

I whispered, "You are. I'll call you back." Then I ended our call.

CHAPTER 11

Honey

I'd brought my girls from Las Vegas to Atlanta, and it was my responsibility to make sure no man ever exploited or violated them again. Thus far, it'd only been a few weeks, but they were becoming bored being at home most of the day. I was, too. And a few of them had added on a few pounds. I was not going to have a house filled with overweight, unhealthy women. They'd already eaten breakfast, but come lunchtime, I was ordering Subway sandwiches. I was the only one with transportation, and Onyx was the only one allowed to drive my car. Maybe I should hire a personal trainer to work them out in the morning and an intake specialist to train them on how to properly document cases in the afternoon. Then they could practice interviewing one another in the evenings.

Sitting downstairs, in the family room, which I'd converted into my home office, I turned on my laptop. I positioned my hand above the keyboard, daze at the peach trees in the backyard. What would I say to the women who walked through the doors of Sweeter Than Honey? What were my beliefs?

Just as I began typing, the phone interrupted my thoughts. Checking the caller ID, I saw it was a 404 area code, but I didn't recognize the number. Was it Grant? Oh, my, God. I should be pissed at him. But I wasn't. My heart started racing. I took a deep breath, exhaled, then answered. "What's sweeter than honey and more valuable than money?" I was hoping to hear the same response he'd whispered in my ear earlier.

"My daughter," a woman replied.

Frowning, I replied, "Of course, she is. Is she in trouble?"

"How much?" the woman asked flatly.

My eyebrows stretched toward my forehead as I shifted my thoughts to business. "Excuse me?"

"I don't have a lot of money. How much will you charge me to find her son's father?" The woman began crying. "It's not fair that she has to work a second job at a strip club to take care of her son. We've got to find him, and you've got to help us."

Wasn't this why I had decided to start my business? But I had never envisioned tracking down deadbeat dads. "What's your daughter's name, and what club does she work at?"

"I named her Velvet Waters. Her stripper name is Red Velvet. She works at Stilettos. Her son's name is Ronnie Allen. His no-good daddy's name is Alphonso Allen. Oh, and Alphonso is a married man. We live in Atlanta, but my baby, Velvet, met him almost six years ago in Los Angeles, when she was auditioning for a movie. How much?"

I had no idea how much to charge this woman. "Pro bono," I said. "E-mail me right away with the details. Include your contact information, and we'll handle the rest. Have a sweet day."

Wow, my first case, I thought. I had to make a good impression. Actually, I was rather excited about finding this Alphonso guy and hearing what his excuse was for not taking care of his son. And if his wife didn't know about Ronnie, she was about to find out.

I believed women deserved to have their fathers and the other men in their lives lift them to the highest heights, not deny, degrade, or disrespect them. What happened to the women who were repeatedly stampeded for years, were fucked for free, with nothing invested in them, and then were dragged through the venomous quicksand of deception? If they survived before turning stone-cold, were they living or simply sustaining themselves on an invisible respirator, or had they become mush, like those rotten peaches soaking up the soil in my backyard?

They say tears cleanse the soul, giving clarity to new beginnings. Suddenly, raindrops the size of silver dollars pounded against my patio window. Yesterday the weatherman had predicted clear skies for today. Grant had promised he'd never leave me. I rolled my computer chair to the window, then watched the wet circles until they either disappeared or were replaced by new raindrops, kind of the way I'd seen men treating women. Beyond the patio, a barrier of Georgia peach trees secluded me from my neighbors.

Oh, I didn't need to go out in the rain to witness what was on those trees, just like I didn't need to travel the world to know millions of women were suffering in silence from neglect, abuse, rape, postpartum depression, and the blues. Not the kind of blues that Barbara Morrison imparted in her lyrics to "You Don't Know What Love Is."

Women were suffering from the kind of blues that made the marrow in their bones shrivel; the kind of blues that twisted already-driven stakes deeper into their broken hearts; the kind of blues that scarred from the inside out, aging them seemingly overnight; shoeless blues that left footprints in the icy snow; the kind of blues that didn't make the headline news until they killed themselves, their mates, or, even worse, their children. I knew those things were real because not so long ago, I was a blue woman.

Not anymore. Now I was plum purple, with the kind of bruise that temporarily clotted the blood but would fade with time and eventually heal. My problem was I couldn't purge myself of the beautiful memories I had of Grant. I was determined to get my man back while rescuing as many suffering women as I could.

Each of those peaches clinging to my trees represented beautiful women, bruised women, succulent women, spoiled women, sexy women, ripe women, and premature women. The fruit that had fallen from those trees, decomposed, and returned to the earth, were the women I wanted to help the most, before they let go of life. No man should ever savor a bite of a precious peach without first caressing her in the palms of his hands, cleansing her soul, appreciating her, and giving thanks for all that she'd given him, especially if she was his mother, daughter, sister, significant other, wife, or friend.

Ka-boom!

Backing away from the window, I gasped at the crackling thunder, which shook my mansion from the ground up. I beheld a ray of sun-shine beaming brightly through the pillows of dark clouds. It left a warmth across my face, and a remnant of the one woman I'd never forget appeared in the silhouette of an angel. With just a few blinks of my eyes, Mother Nature had shrunk the raindrops to speckles and dissolved the black clouds, clearing the way for blue skies. I guessed the weatherman was right, after all.

Closing my eyes and then slowly opening them, I glanced at Sunny's picture resting on my desk, accepting that I was the reason my fa-vorite escort had been shot in the head the day before her twenty-first birthday. I couldn't bring Sunny back, but I felt obligated to keep a close watch on her identical twin sister, Summer, who was pregnant with Valentino's twins. Looking out the patio window and admiring the green leaves, I squinted and noticed the streaks remaining on my windowpane, which were as visible as my flaws. That was a good thing. No longer would I hide my past from anyone, especially Grant.

Peaches couldn't grow on trees that had no roots or had roots that had no soil, or in soil that had no nutrients or had nutrients but no water, or with water that had no clouds or under clouds that couldn't give way to the sunshine warming my face. Like those peach trees, a woman without the basic elements of life would die before she blos-somed.

I'd heard that people who were too proud, too embarrassed, or too afraid to cry in front of others were hiding something. Shame. Guilt. Insecurities. Vulnerabilities. Secrets even. At one point in my life, I had experienced all of that and added a few more reasons why I in-carcerated my salty sadness. I'd turned away from life, not wanting anyone to look into my eyes. I was afraid they'd see I'd been molested, abused as a child, beaten by my ex-husbands, and assaulted by some of my johns.

The real reason I killed Reynolds wasn't because he'd raped Onyx. I shot that motherfucker in the head because I was tired of men who felt justified forcing their dicks inside of women to bust a fuckin' nut or to establish dominance. Punk-ass, bitch-ass men deserved to die. If I saw Reynolds in the afterlife, I'd kill his ass again.

Women weren't put on this earth for men to control them. God gave men women to love. For Reynolds's death, I had no remorse. I had no blood on my hands or my conscience. If I ever got arrested, my trial would undoubtedly empower women everywhere to stop hanging their heads and stand up for themselves.

You could tell a lot by looking into a woman's eyes, especially if that woman had low self-esteem or if she was smiling from her nose down, struggling to keep from crying. There'd been a haziness obstructing my judgment of others. At first, all I'd wanted to do was please people, hoping that would make them like me and, if I was lucky, love me. The harder I tried, the less they cared about me.

The men, oh, how the men had loved the way I circled my juicy tongue around their dick heads, letting them shoot cum in my mouth. For eleven years, I had been their fantasy come true, granting their deepest desires, the ones their wives or girlfriends wouldn't. My pussy had possessed the kind of power that made men sign their names to payday loans so they could experience my unforgettable lingam massage.

Unconsciously, I'd picked up Sunny's picture and placed it inside my top desk drawer. Before closing the drawer, I took it out and put it back. Today was as good as any day to stop living inside my head, to stop agonizing over Grant, to stop dwelling on depressing memories, to get off of my ass, and to go out into world and save Red Velvet.

I went upstairs to the entertainment room, where the girls were gathered, and announced, "I have a surprise!"

They all stopped watching *Oprah* and stared at me. "This had better be important," Onyx said.

"Forget it. I apologize. I shouldn't have interrupted," I said. "Go back to watching television. I was going to buy each of you your own car today and give you each a million dollars as I'd promised, but *Oprah* can do that for—"

"Aaahhhh!" they all screamed at the same time. Titties and asses joyfully bounced up and down.

It wasn't the money or the materialistic luxury cars I was giving them that excited me. I was giving each of them their independence. Having enough money to enjoy life did good things for women . . . Money empowered women. If women had the right amount of money, they could buy themselves a few good men. But the one thing money couldn't buy was love.

"Oh, shit," I said, laughing. Instantly, I found myself buried under eleven very excited women. For a moment, in that moment, I couldn't say we all loved one another or that we had anyone out there that loved us, but I knew in that moment, we were all truly happy.

CHAPTER 12

Sapphire

Tiffany Davis . . . runaway, abducted, kidnapped. Height: five feet six. Weight: 135 lbs. Eyes: brown. Hair: brown. At the age of sixteen, I was listed as everything except voluntarily missing. *Last seen on Broadway, near Lincoln High School, in Los Angeles, California. If anyone has any information or has seen Tiffany, please call your local police department.*

How ironic that as an adult, I had ended up working for an agency that couldn't find me when I was a minor. When I was growing up, my family wasn't rich or affluent, I didn't live in an upscale neighborhood, and the public high school I attended wasn't famous for anything positive. I wasn't born with natural blue eyes or blond hair. So I wasn't surprised that the police department didn't find me. They probably never tried. Or perhaps the underlying reason my mother never found me was she cared more about her husband than she cared about me. I'd been missing from home for fourteen years.

Now I was thirty years old, with the perfect career, but I still missed my mother every day. I was passionate about my job, but in my personal life, I'd never had a man who loved me for more than sex, so I married my job to keep my mind off of wanting a husband and a family. Being an undercover cop in Vegas, working the Strip a few days a week—some days solo, others on a sting operation—arresting guys who solicited sex was what I wanted to do. But what had thrilled me most recently was busting Valentino James and taking his money.

I dialed my associate's number.

"Hey, lady. What's up?" she asked.

"You keeping track of my client?" I asked her.

"But of course, and the status remains the same. I'm starting to hear some rumors, though, about it being a summer day in springtime. I'll keep you updated if the weather changes."

"Peace," I said, ending our conversation.

I jotted my phone number on a blue sticky, then sealed it inside of an envelope addressed to Valentino. He hadn't received any mail, but his baby mama, Summer Day, was working to get him out on bail. It looked like I'd have to pay her an unexpected visit.

After I'd arrested Valentino, I'd made certain he had no viable contacts outside of prison. I'd encouraged Lace to take all of Valentino's girls to Atlanta. I'd threatened Benito to keep his dumb ass out of Nevada. Valentino's security staff had become unemployed the second I put the cuffs on Valentino. No pimp that I'd ever arrested had been released on bail or had made parole. My intent was to make sure Valentino wasn't the first.

Walking into the living room, I asked Girl Six, "You good?" I lounged on my blue sofa, next to her and stared at her, waiting for a response. "You good?" I asked again.

"Yeah. Yeah," she said, rubbing her thigh. "I've been here for nearly three weeks, and I don't understand why you keep asking me the same question every day. That's all."

Whenever I wasn't sure of what was on a person's mind, I frequently engaged them in conversation. I put *The Pimp Chronicles* on mute. I eased my hand into hers. I needed to persuade her to trust me, 'cause I didn't trust anybody, including my mother. I'd never intended for Lace to keep the money I'd given her. The fifty million I was letting her hold for me was a decoy to lure Valentino straight to her, that is, if Valentino's public defendant couldn't be bribed to misrepresent the case.

Lace had no idea she was the scapegoat, but she was about to find out. Girl Six wasn't my girl. She could never be my girl after working for Lace. I had no idea if Girl Six was loyal to Lace or me. It didn't matter. I was sending Girl Six where she belonged, with Lace. But I was sending her with my agenda.

I questioned her. "Who killed Sunny?"

"I told you I don't know. Lace sent me home that night." Scooting away from me, Girl Six added, "Look, if you want me to leave, just tell me. I hate being drilled every day."

I didn't want her to leave. I needed her to get the hell out of my house. I'd delayed important job-related matters to baby-sit Girl Six. My arrests of pimps and johns could no longer wait. Valentino's hearing was coming up soon, and I had to find out what Summer was up to. I'd missed out on arresting a few other pimps because I wasn't leaving Girl Six in my house overnight while I was at work. In a few days, I planned on visiting Valentino, and I couldn't take Girl Six with me.

I asked Girl Six, "Are you happy living here with me?"

My place was casually decorated, with little more than the necessities of life. It had a moderate two thousand square feet, two bedrooms, two baths, a living room, a kitchen, and a dining area and was tucked away in a gated community on the outskirts of Las Vegas. Before letting Girl Six move in, I was seldom home at night.

"Yeah, I think so," Girl Six answered. "I don't know what I want to do with my life. Prostitution is all I know."

Girl Six was of the majority. Most prostitutes, especially the young ones, didn't know what to do outside of selling themselves. "You miss the life? You regret not going to Atlanta with Lace and the other girls?"

"Definitely not. She's a bitch. The worst kind. One of these days she's gonna kick the wrong person," Girl Six said, staring at the flat screen.

We'd watched this DVD together at least five times. Picking up the remote, I turned off the mute feature to hear Katt Williams say, "It's called self-esteem, bitch. Esteem of your motherfuckin' self. How am I going to make you feel bad about you?"

Ordinarily, this was one of the funniest parts, and we'd laugh out loud, but this time we didn't. Lifting my leg onto the back of the sofa, I said, "Here. Play with my pussy and talk to me."

Girl Six didn't mind getting me off whenever I asked her to. Gently, she parted my lips. Up and down, she massaged my pussy. Her touch excited me. I'd been so busy working sunset to sunrise, I hadn't realized how much I'd missed having someone, anyone, to talk to or to touch me.

I enjoyed the pleasure. "I'm sending you to live with Lace," I told her.

Girl Six shook her head. "You can't make me. I'm not going."

The hell if I couldn't. "Yes, you are."

Girl Six sprang from the sofa. Tears streamed down her cheeks. "I'm not, and you can't make me. I'm getting my things, and I'm outta here. I'd rather live on the street!"

Following her into my guest bedroom, I forced Girl Six onto the bed. Grabbing her biceps, I asked, "What the hell is wrong with you? Are you crazy? You can't stay here, and you have no place else to go." I wanted to slap her but didn't. "Get yourself together, because, yes, you are going to Atlanta."

Frantically, Girl Six shook her head. "Every time I get close to someone, they leave me. I've only been here two weeks, and now you're putting me out."

Almost three to be more exact. I had never told her I was putting her out. Had I? Well, maybe I had, but . . . Was she serious? Could a prostitute suffer with abandonment issues? Or was Girl Six faking it? "You had your chance to go with Lace. So what's the real reason you asked to move in with me instead of going with her?"

"Sapphire, I'm in love with you. I knew I was in love with you the minute you walked into that hotel room to say good-bye to Lace. If it hadn't been for you, I probably would've gone to Atlanta."

Okay. I must be stupid. Am I supposed to believe her? "We can talk about this later." I didn't believe a word of what Girl Six had said, and I wasn't finished cuming. She might as well relieve my frustrations since she'd created the tension. Opening the dresser drawer, I pulled out my dual dildo. "Here, lick the head," I said, easing it in her mouth. "Now lie down and lick this end."

Easing seven inches of one end inside of Girl Six, I positioned myself missionary style on top of her, then inserted the same amount of inches inside of me. With four inches of the eighteen-inch dual dildo between us, Girl Six wrapped her legs around my hips. My pussy tightened. Slowly, I thrust my pelvis into hers as she tilted her ass upward.

Our rhythm was in sync. "Aw, yeah. You feel great," I whispered in

Girl Six's ear. "I'm not abandoning you. I need you to do this one favor for me. And I promise when you're done, if you want, you can come back here and live with me. But right now, I want you to cum for me, baby."

Sex always made women vulnerable. Tears rolled from the corners of her eyes. I kissed them away, then held her closer. I did all the shit I knew women liked. "Let it go. Whatever is bothering you, release it and let it go," I said softly. "You're beautiful. Letting all of those strange men fuck you night after night made you feel bad about yourself. Don't. I know they didn't love you. They only wanted to use you for their pleasure."

Her lips quivered. "You don't love me, either?"

She had put me on the spot with that one. Should I tell her the truth or tell her what she needed to hear? "I do love you," I said, thrusting a little deep. My nipples pressed hard against hers.

Did we crave compassion so deeply that we were willing to have sex outside of our preferences to feel the power of love? I had plans for Girl Six, but what I hadn't planned on was developing feelings for her. Not sexual feelings. The human emotions drawing us closer disturbed me.

She was nineteen; I was thirty. Maybe this was all a façade, and all Girl Six needed was to be held by someone who cared about her. Maybe our connection had nothing to do with me or my emotions. Maybe I was the one with abandonment issues. It didn't matter. I sincerely enjoyed her as much as she appreciated me. Kissing her lips, I said, "Lie here and relax. You're going to be all right."

Gently, I removed the dildo, went into the bathroom, placed it on a towel, sprayed it with sex-toy cleaner, scrubbed it, rinsed it, then dried it off. I'd been sidetracked for a moment, but it was time to get back to business. I put on a pair of shorts, then sat on the sofa in the living room, holding my cordless phone.

Lace had taken her deceased sister's name, Honey Thomas, to escape the morbid prostitution arena, and I'd selected the identity of Sapphire Bleu when I was hired as an undercover cop. My new name best described my personality. Sapphire fit because I was hot-tempered, and I had no problem shooting a rapist between the eyes if I had to. Bleu suited me because I had never known the meaning of the word *love.* Next to Sunny, Girl Six was the closest I'd come to caring for anyone. Sunny and I had shared a different kind of love. We'd been emotionally intimate, with no desire to become physical.

The time to make my phone call to Lace was now. The difference between us was Lace's mother had kicked her out the day before her sixteenth birthday, whereas I had tired of crying myself to sleep at night and had left home, refusing to return to parents who'd fought and argued more than they'd displayed affection—that, and the fact that my stepfather, Alphonso Allen, had raped me more than he'd had sex with my mom. Running away from home hadn't allowed me to escape the haunting memories I fought daily to suppress.

What had made him do that repeatedly to me?

After I ran away from home, I learned that I was one of several million teenagers that had run away that year. I was certain each of us had had a valid reason—primarily abuse of some sort or depression—that most of our parents had ignored us until we'd left or turned up dead, and that our parents were then the depressed ones. Did my mother miss me at all?

How had Girl Six ended up in this lifestyle? What was her story? Every woman had one. I peeked in the bedroom. She was underneath the covers. Her eyes were closed. The covers were up to her shoulders. Quietly, I turned off the light.

I went back into the living room and replayed *The Pimp Chronicles.* As a teenager I'd been trapped in a society that was apathetic to my generation, unwilling to embrace our freedom of expression, and unable to recognize, and protect us from, sexual predators in our own homes. I couldn't believe how many mothers had allowed their family members, boyfriends, and husbands to rape their daughters—until I'd seen the stats.

My parents had been chronic complainers, had lacked effective communication skills, and had seldom talked with me. "Didn't I tell you to shut up? Don't say another word," my mother would say. "I've heard enough." Nothing could have been further from the truth. Problem was my mother hadn't heard a word I'd said when I'd cried to my stepfather, "Please don't rape me again." That was enough of thinking about my childhood. What I was really doing was procrastinating about making that call.

I reached for my cell phone, and I dialed Lace's number.

If my mother had listened to me or tried to understand me, maybe I would've felt safe telling her the truth. I was too young to protect myself. Once my mother married Alphonso, he changed, acting as though he owned everyone and everything under our roof, including my mom's house, her car, her money, and me. Their certificate of marriage was more like his fake-ass license to manhood, making his spine straighten and his voice escalate with authority as he looked down upon us. Because of my stepfather, I swore I'd never get married or have children. Did I have any sisters? Brothers? Only if my mother had more kids. I had no idea who my real father was or where he was. I sure as hell wouldn't lay claim to any children Alphonso or my father had.

Lace eagerly answered. "Hello. Grant, is this you?"

Did she respond that way to all blocked callers? "No, it's not. It's Sapphire Bleu, and, bitch, I'ma kick your ass, and then I'ma kill you." I knew I'd caught her off guard by sounding crazy, but that was my intent. Most people were easily manipulated.

"Say what? Who the fuck you think you talkin' to? I've been trying to reach you. Where the hell are you?" Lace asked. "We need to talk."

Addressing the real reason I'd called, I said, "I need you to chill on spending my money until I get to Atlanta. I'll be there as soon as I finish handling Valentino."

"I don't have any money for you," Lace countered.

"The fifty-million-dollar cashier's check I asked you to hold. That's mine. Not yours. I hope you didn't deposit it."

"Deposit? Wait one minute. I never asked you for anything. I've spent half. Put a few million into my business, and I have eleven girls living in my house with me, and I have plans for the rest of the money, too. We need to live—"

"You'd better think and think fast, because you were the one who bought their airline tickets from Vegas to Atlanta before I gave you the money, so obviously you had that part covered, right? I know that after working an entire year for Valentino, you have your own money stashed. Where is it? In your North Las Vegas house? I could go over there right now and find out. And don't forget you are an ex-madam

and a murderer. Don't force me to have you arrested. I can have Atlanta PD all up in your ass in a matter of minutes."

"Arrest me? Your lying ass don't work for the police department.
Who in the hell are you?" Lace yelled.

She shouldn't be upset. The point of being an undercover cop was
to keep my real identity a secret. "Better question. Who in the hell are
you, Lace?" I replied calmly. "Oops, I mean Honey. I'll call you when
I'm on my way. And, bitch, you'd better have my money."

Ending the call, I smiled. Actually, I liked Lace. She wasn't afraid of
me, and I knew that. I wished more women were like Lace: not afraid
to shoot an abusive man, yet caring enough to support other women.
That was enough of a threat to keep her guessing about what she
needed to do next and what my next move was. Didn't she know?
Cops craved control.

My threat wasn't about the money; it was about maintaining power.

CHAPTER 13

Honey

Every woman needed a sabbatical for reflection. A day, a week, a month, each morning or night, at some point she had to make time to revisit her childhood, her adolescent period, turning twenty-one, and beyond. Her nectar, sometimes bitter, often sweet, lingered in eyes that she seldom looked into. Her own. A glimpse in the mirror to wash her face, brush her teeth, apply her lipstick, and she was on her way out the door to please everyone except herself.

Did she enter a room with wide strides that showed those watching her she was confident? Or did she drag her tired feet, not even noticing her heels were worn to a slant? Were her shoulders straight? Was her head high but her self-esteem low? Or was her body slumped, leaning toward a pit she found the strength never to fall into no matter how weary she was?

Driving along West Peachtree, heading toward downtown, I passed the Fox Theatre. One block beyond Gladys Knight and Ron Winans' Chicken & Waffles, I observed groups of homeless black men. On one side of the street, some gathered at the bus stop; on the opposite side of the street, others stood in line, waiting for a handout. Those men sure as hell weren't the pick of the litter, but they were part of the litter black women had to choose among. Had their fathers forsaken them? Had their mothers given up on them? Did those men have children? Wives? Girlfriends? Family?

Glancing through my windshield, I saw a small-framed woman cross the street, shoeless. Her blackened feet were covered with scabs. What was her story? Was she on crack? In search of food? Sex? Shelter?

Beep. Beep.

Motioning to her, I pulled over, then stuck my hand out the window and said, "Come here. Take my card."

"Is that a dollar?" she asked, slowly approaching me.

"Call me tomorrow. I want to help you," I said, handing her the card and a fifty-dollar bill. Not knowing her situation, I didn't tell her what to do with the money. The tears in her eyes spoke the words *thank you,* and that was my satisfaction.

Hmm, obviously, that woman and I had taken different paths, but I bet we'd overcome similar obstacles. Rape. Molestation. Abandonment. Did she have children? A lot of women had experienced some form of abuse. Some worse than others. Maybe that was why women didn't take time to stare into their own eyes. Best to leave the hidden pain dormant behind each beat of their heart. Besides, who cared about abused women, anyway? Most men were preoccupied with their problems or focused on their personal gain. Women preferred to turn their heads rather than say, "Hi. How are you?" to a woman they didn't know. But their heads would linger in the direction of a man, and they'd hope he'd acknowledge them.

I merged into traffic, continuing to my destination. Forgiving my past, I realized there was nothing to atone for. Sapphire didn't scare me. Guilt held women prisoner in their minds. It was time for women to stop apologizing for things that weren't their fault. Certainly, some of the decisions I'd made were heartless, cold, insensitive, and ruthless; I didn't deny that. But the suffering I'd endured had allowed me to forgive myself, my mother, my father, all the people that had abused me, including the men.

Parking in my personal space, I smiled. "Yes! I did it. This is my business, and no one is taking this away from me except over my dead body," I declared.

Glad I'd come in a day early, I stood outside, staring at the embossed gold lettering of SWEETER THAN HONEY on the fuchsia awning. Preparing to launch my company overwhelmed me. I felt like Whoopi

Goldberg in *The Color Purple*, when she inherited that money. I didn't dance on the outside, but my insides were doing flips.

Unlocking the front door, I locked the door to my heart. I'd dialed Grant's number almost twenty times. Not once had he answered. He knew what he was doing when he called me. Grant was trying to fuck with my emotions. I refused to let him.

You are, resounded in my head. *I'm done with Grant.*

Sitting at my desk, I listened. There was silence. When was the last time I'd been physically alone, with no one under the same roof? Certainly not when I'd been on my patio, having an orgasm. When I came, I think I awakened all of my neighbors and the girls, too. Turning on my computer, I opened the results to my background investigation of Alphonso Allen and dialed the first number listed.

"Yes, bitch. What do you want?" a woman answered.

Ooh, somebody had mad drama in their household. "Hello, this is Ms. Thomas. I'm trying to reach an Alphonso Allen. Is this the right number?"

"So now you tryna sound all professional and shit. I know it's you."

"Let me reassure you, this is business. Is this the right number or not?"

She screamed in my ear, "Alphonso! Another one of your bitches is on the phone!"

The next voice I heard was that of a man. "Who is this?"

"If you want to avoid a warrant for your arrest for nonpayment of child support, you'll listen carefully."

"What!" He laughed nervously. "You must have the wrong number."

"Are you Alphonso Allen?" I asked him.

"Yeah, that's me, but there's lots of Alphonso Allens, you know?"

"You work for the transit department? You live at thirteen twenty-four . . . Los Angeles, California? You drive a black Benz with the license plate number 6UF . . . ?"

He never repeated the reason I was calling. I imagined whoever the woman was who had answered the phone was standing near. I went on. "You remember raping a young lady by the name of Velvet Waters on Venice Beach about six years ago? She called you and said she was pregnant." I wanted to curse that motherfucker out. He knew damn well it was him. That was why his ass got quiet.

"Uh, I can't talk right now, but I am interested in the supervisory position. Call me on my cell in about an hour. It's three-one-zero . . . ," he said, then hung up.

Oh, he was definitely getting a call back and a visit from his son. I called Velvet's mother and told her to prepare Ronnie for a trip to Los Angeles. Hanging up the phone, I began developing a blueprint of my life. Column one was my past, column two was my present, and column three was my future.

Prostituting for eleven years (past), and being a madam for one year (past), I was eager to settle down and become a supportive wife and a loving mother (future). I wanted happiness, and I needed to surround myself with happy people (present and future). I was tired of the invincible shield encasing my heart (past and present). What was I truly afraid of? Rejection? I'd been there before, and I prayed Grant didn't take me there again.

In my first two marriages, I wasn't a wife. I was a licensed whore, a human sperm bank, and a built-in maid. That was my past, but it wasn't my future. Thanks to Officer Sapphire Bleu, I had money, which I wasn't giving back to her or Valentino. Were Sapphire and Valentino trying to set me up?

I typed *thirty million* under ASSETS in my present column. I had a seven-figure stash of my own, but I didn't need to list that. The only picture I had of Sapphire was etched in my memory, but I could definitely spot her within seconds in a crowded room. Sapphire Bleu was stunningly beautiful.

I didn't have any woe-is-me stories, but was this the life God had planned for me or the life I had chosen for myself? Either way, I was fucked up, pissed off, disappointed, hurt, and lonely. Finding my way back to the front door, I stood staring out the window, wondering what tomorrow would bring. The day was clear.

How in the world could I have possibly fallen in love with a man I'd spent only two weeks with? Before we'd had a chance to really get to know one another, Grant was gone. Actually, I was the one gone after he'd dismissed me. Couldn't say I blamed him. I was gonna tell him the truth . . . eventually. On my terms, turf, and time, I would've said, "Grant, there are some things you need to know about me."

No man wanted to marry a former prostitute—once a prostitute, always a prostitute. Ignorant men believed that. I didn't. I'd changed for my personal best. I hummed, "Silly of me to think that I could ever have him for my guy. Hm, hm, hm, hm." I'd prayed Grant was the one man who wouldn't judge me. If I had a chance to give him all the facts, I knew he wouldn't hold against me the promiscuous things I'd done before meeting him. Especially when I told him my mother had kicked me out of her house when I was sixteen, so I'd married the first man I'd met. What about the things Grant had done? Was that important?

Hurrying back to my computer, I continued categorizing my life. It wasn't my fault both of my ex-husbands had beaten me worse than my mother had. Prostituting had been more about survival than a desired occupation. Maybe I had drawn the abusive men to me. Back then they didn't love me. I didn't love myself. What was worse?

Given all the unspeakable things men had done to me, I had every reason to hate them, and a few women, too, but I didn't. Hating people meant I hated myself. Instead of hating others, I suppressed my hurt, ignored my feelings, and numbed my pain by having sex for money. Some of my johns had sexed me good, but taking their money had made me happy. No matter how great I fucked my johns, at the end of the night, I wanted a man of my own to hold and to love. While other lonely women dried their eyes with tissues, I wiped away my sorrow with hundred-dollar bills.

Glancing at my watch, I said, "Oh, damn. It's been an hour already." I dialed the number Alphonso had given me.

He answered right away. "Hello."

"Yes, Mr. Allen. What I have to say is straightforward. You owe back child support in the amount of seventy-two thousand dollars, and your future monthly payments are a thousand dollars. You can take out a personal loan or a line of equity on your home if you have to and send the full amount to this address. You ready?"

"Bitch, you crazy! Stop playing games. I thought you were serious," he complained.

"Oh, I'm very serious."

"You don't even know how much money I make, and you already got this shit figured out on what I'ma pay that sleazy bitch."

That's it! I snapped. My patience was done with this bastard. "Look, motherfucker, the choice is yours. I can have the police on your motherfuckin' ass in two minutes. I can have you arrested for rape, then have your fuckin' ass raped before you close your bitch-ass eyes tonight . . . or you can have a cashier's check in the amount of seventy-two thousand dollars delivered to three-two-one . . . Atlanta, Georgia, in two days. A rapist never rapes once, so I'll dig up every female you've ever stuck your nasty-ass dick in without her permission just to make sure you die in jail, motherfucker! Oh, and your son is coming to Los Angeles to meet your sorry ass, so you'd best figure out how you're gonna tell that crazy-ass wife of yours the truth. Your forty-eight hours start right now, motherfucker." I hung up in his face. That nigga didn't know who he was fucking with.

How many women's lives had that one man ruined?

I took the good along with the bad; I wouldn't trade a single moment of my life. Well, that wasn't completely true. Even if it meant no one in the world loved me, I wished my mother had loved me. I wished my father hadn't shut the door in my face when I confronted him about whether he was my real dad, and it bothered me every day that my sister was dead and I'd killed my favorite prostitute.

I didn't pull the trigger, but I might as well have. Instead of showing up on time for work, I'd been laid up with my deadbeat, throwback ex-quarterback boyfriend Benito, who'd lived in my North Las Vegas home for years. His jealous ass had set back the time on my clock, because he wanted me to put him first.

Put him first? I listed his name twice under PAST. Make that three times.

Benito had been unemployed, hadn't been trying to find a job, and had wanted me to put him first. The fact that I hadn't put his ass out meant I'd put him first every damn time I went to work while he laid up in my bed. Changing that clock that night had made me late for the first time since I'd worked for Valentino James. If I had been on time, Sunny Day would be alive.

I hummed, "I can't make you love me if you don't." Bonnie Raitt's lyrics played in the background, on my iPod. I'd listened to her songs each morning, seeking clarity with regard to the love I'd lost.

Grant Hill personified perfection, with his strong cheeks, thin mustache, firm yet tender touch, and succulent lips. Perched in his eight-by-ten photo hanging on my wall, he brought a melancholy smile to my face. What could I do to make things right between us after his brother showed up at their parents' home, blabbering like a fucking idiot? Why couldn't I have met Grant first?

The difference between Benito and Grant was Benito wanted a mother and Grant wanted a woman. Now I presumed some other lucky woman was getting the love that should've been mine. Good pussy did strange things to men. Problem was, I didn't have an exclusive on good pussy. But what I did have was undeniable love for Grant.

I'd kissed Grant until I heard the words *I love you* roll off the tip of his tongue. No man, not even my ex-husbands, had invited me to meet his mother. His father? Yes. Mother? Hell, no.

Of all the orphans that could've been adopted by Grant's biological mother, what made her choose Benito, and what made him refuse to speak of his family over the three years we dated? Maybe she'd adopted Benito for the same reason I'd dated him. I felt sorry for Benito.

My cell phone rang. "Aw, damn. I talked his ass up," I said aloud. "What, Benito?"

"I'm in Atlanta. I just left the bus station, and I'm a few blocks away from your house. I need a place to stay for a couple of weeks. I know you're in love with Grant, but help a brotha out. Will ya?"

"If you show up at my front door, I'm going to neuter you and shoot you. Then I'ma drag you inside, call the police, and have you arrested for breaking and entering," I said, then hung up. What the fuck was wrong with black men, thinking black women were supposed to bail their asses out? I had no love for any of them, except Grant.

Love. That one emotion had fucked up my head while crushing my heart. Lonely. Sad. Angry. Disappointed. Sick. Overjoyed. The lack of love as a child had made me suicidal. The lack of love as an adult made me angry. Love was the feeling that had made me the happiest and saddest person.

"Fuck love!" I yelled. "I hate you! Leave me the fuck alone! No, I can't make Grant love me! Go fuck up somebody else's life!" Stomping over to the wall, I snatched Grant's picture, then threw it in the trash.

I'd definitely sat in the wrong seat on that plane. All the other window seats in first class had not been next to Grant. *Better to have loved at least for a little while,* I thought. Was that true? I kicked the trash can. "Hell no, that shit ain't true!" Whosoever believed that must've been happily in love. No one in a fucked-up relationship would say such a thing.

Picking up my business phone, I dialed Grant's number, the same as I'd done almost every day since Grant and I had broken up. Maybe this time Grant would answer, and I could curse his ass out, too, while I was on a roll. Get it off my chest. Fuck explaining that I wasn't a bad person.

My cell phone interrupted my thoughts. A gentle voice resonated from the opposite end, interrupting my pity party. "Hello, Lace? This is Girl Six. I'm coming to live with you."

CHAPTER 14

Valentino

"Number two-one-three-six-five-four," the warden called out.
For real, I had never been no fuckin' number before. And no
matter how long I was up in this bitch-ass correctional institution, I'd
never get used to being no fuckin' number. Correctional institution?
More like a fuckin' concentration camp if you'd asked me, 'cause a
nigga could die or get killed or rise up outta this bitch-ass place being
ten times worse off than when he stepped foot in this motherfucker.
Especially if a nigga was entrapped, like me.

My mother named me Anthony Valentino James. That was what the
fuck I repeated in my mind whenever I heard *213654*. Thanks to
those bitches Lace and Sapphire, I was facing death row or life without the possibility of parole if I entered a plea for killing a bitch who
had pulled the trigger her damn self. But how was I going to prove my
fuckin' innocence when I couldn't afford my own goddamn attorney?
I didn't know where my money was, and I had no one on the outside
to figure that shit out for me. But one thing was sho'. Whatever bitch
stole my money was one dead motherfucker when I got out. Straight
up, I was definitely getting outta here, even if I had to break outta this
bitch.

Fuck!

Why had I relied on my damn cell phone to remember all of my
phone numbers? I hadn't made a single call since I'd been locked up.

I couldn't even call Benito's ig'nant ass. I had no idea where Lace was, and that was 'bout the extent of my contacts on the outside, because my parents were deceased. I should've been more like that elephant memory–ass, don't-forget-shit bitch, Lace.

Angrily, I answered, "What you want this time?"

I'd been locked up and locked down for 'bout a month now. The only time I heard my number called was when some bullshit had gone down overnight, like a nigga gettin' fucked in his ass, or like the night I'd stabbed that nigga in his throat with my fingernails. Seventy-two hours in solitary confinement had been hell and well worth it. I wasn't volunteering to be nobody's fuckin' girlfriend. I tried keeping to myself and wished these niggas would just let me be. I knew I had a big, beautiful dick, a nice ass, and naturally wavy hair, and my flawless caramel complexion was tempting to these gay-by-default niggas. "Listen up, motherfuckers!" I'd told them when I first got here. "Let no nigga try to run up on me or inside of me unless he wants to die on the motherfuckin' spot. I ain't no snitch, and I ain't nobody's bitch."

The warden held up two envelopes, waving his hand back and forth. For a few seconds, all I could do was stare at him. Breaking my silence, I asked, "For me?" Then I turned to my cell mate, who was sprawled across his bed, clenching his Bible, his head resting on the mattress.

"It's not for him. This time it's for you. For the first time, you've got mail," the warden said.

My cell mate sat up as I faced the tall, muscular man in uniform. I'd packed on a few solid pounds myself by pumping iron every day. There wasn't much else to do. On the under, I'd started loving the way my new body was developing. I didn't give a fuck if a lump of shit was inside one of those envelopes. Yes! I finally had outside contacts. Trying to conceal my excitement, I frowned. Me? Was he sure? "Give it to me," I said, reaching into the rectangular slot in the bars, where they made us turn around, put our hands behind our backs, then put our hands through before handcuffing us. "Y'all need to rehab and upgrade this hellhole, man. Give us some of that Oz shit," I told him. There was one blue, letter-sized envelope and one of those yellow five-by-sevens.

I peeked inside the already peeled-away edge of the blue letter first, then stuck my fingers in. "What is this? A fucking joke? Where is the damn letter? No fucking return address, either." I ripped that shit in half, balled it up, then tossed it in the trash.

Fucking trick!

Squeezing the edges of the yellow envelope, I peeked inside, praying to see something. Were my eyes deceiving me? I pulled out a five-by-seven photo. I pressed my fingers deep into my sockets to force back the tears, but I couldn't. I started crying like a li'l bitch.

"Man, what's up? Cut out that fucking babyfide bullshit," my cell mate said, leaning over his top bunk, staring down at me.

"I'm straight, man. This shit caught me off guard."

"Yo, that's your son and your girl?"

She wasn't my woman, but I lied. "Yeah, man. I thought they'd forgotten about my ass." Gasping for air, I couldn't take my eyes off of Summer and what could only be my son. That li'l nigga looked dead-on like me when I was about his age, which I guessed was five or six.

Sitting on the edge of my bottom bunk, I removed the letter, then silently read.

Dear Anthony,

I love you. (She did? Why? Wasn't like I'd done right by her. My heart thumped.) *I don't know what happened to you after we stopped seeing each other, but I've always loved you. I apologize for not telling you about our son for five years, but my parents didn't want me to have anything to do with you. Actually, they still don't want me around you, and I don't have their blessings for contacting you. They don't hate you. My parents dislike your ways. But you are the father of our son, and no matter where you are or what really happened for you to be in prison, you are Anthony Valentino James the second's father, and I shouldn't take that right away from you.* (Damn. Summer named my li'l nigga after me.)

I pray you didn't kill my twin sister, Sunny, who was also my best friend. But I'm sure you had something to do with her death. When I first met you, I should've told you I had a twin. What exactly did Sunny do every night while working for you? I have so many questions I need answers to. There were so many conflicting stories in the newspaper, I stopped reading them.

I guess you've heard they paid me for the rights to my story, and they're going to do a movie and a book that will highlight the days I spent with you before Sapphire busted you. I'm ashamed to admit, I was bribed into being a part of the sting operation to bring you down, and, yes, I'll testify to that fact. I don't know much, but Sapphire told me she gave Lace fifty million dollars of your money, and that Lace was taking care of your escort girls and they were all living in Atlanta. Buckhead, to be exact.

What does all of that mean? Your girls? Sapphire mentioned that Benito couldn't come back to Nevada or she'd arrest him. She also gave me ten million, but I'm afraid to deposit the cashier's check. I mean, what if they think I did something illegal and I get arrested? I know my parents would take care of our son, but what I haven't told you is . . . I'm pregnant. This time with twins. Remember that night during the sting operation when you thought I was Sunny and you made love to me? I'm so sorry I let them use me to get to you, but we're having two more babies. More than anything, I want us to be a family. But if you really killed my twin sister, I could forgive you, because that's what God would want me to do, but I'd never forget. I need some answers from you.

Today our pastor said, "The present is a gift of happiness. In order to be unhappy, you must relive the past." With or without you, I choose to be happy. Anthony, what's done cannot be undone. No matter what, I will always have a place in my heart for you.

Your Summer Day

Now I wasn't sure if I should jump for joy or be pissed the fuck off at that bitch. Summer had set me up? She was the fuckin' reason I was behind bars. That was a hard one to deal with. I cried on the inside, wondering what my life would've been like if Summer's father hadn't single-handedly taken away my parental rights. What in the fuck had made him think he had the right to tell Summer not to tell me she was pregnant with my fuckin' kid? That wasn't his fuckin' right! That was my fuckin' seed, not his!

My cell mate dug into the trash and pulled out the blue envelope. I ignored him.

Who knows, my entire life could've been different. I could've gotten out of the pimping game early. I'd only been less than two years in when I met Summer. She was a senior in high school, still a virgin, and naturally beautiful. I loved Summer for letting me be her first. Even a hard-core nigga like me, along with all the pimps and gangsters in the world, needed love. What was it about fuckin' women that could soften the heart of the hardest motherfuckers? Even Frank Lucas loved his mother and his wife, and he was the smartest and hardest straight, hard-core, capital *G* gangster.

I needed Summer to deposit that ten-million-dollar check and hire the best attorneys in the fucking country so I could get up outta here. That was my fuckin' money. I'd have more than enough money left over for me to settle down with Summer and my kids. I had to get out before she gave birth to . . . twins? But first I had to find those bitches Lace and Sapphire. Summer probably had their numbers. I prayed Lace hadn't plotted this shit to get my money, because if she had, I might just end up right back in this bitch, because sure as my name was Anthony Valentino James the first, I was gonna put a bullet in her head, then her ass, in that order.

"Man, there's something written inside here. You just ripped it," my cell mate said, leaning against the wall.

"For real? Let me see," I said, reaching for the wrinkled halves of the blue envelope.

Piecing the envelope together, I discovered a blue sticky inside with a number written on it but no name. "What the fuck am I supposed to do with this shit? Ain't no fuckin' name on it."

"Blue, man, blue. Didn't you say the cop that got your ass was—"

"Yo, I'm ready to make my phone call," I yelled out to the warden. "Now!"

CHAPTER 15

Honey

Stepping between the ladies that were standing tall in sexy high heels and the men posing in their new tennis shoes, Onyx and I strutted across a thin gray Berber carpet sparsely covered with single dollar bills. There were two women abandoning a high table with two bar stools near the stage. Swiftly grabbing the stools, we sat, then crossed our bare legs underneath our baby doll–length dresses and began watching amateur strippers bounce their booties, some firm, others soft. I'd touched enough asses during my days of being a madam to distinguish between soggy, soft, or supple with just one look. Three mediocre girls were performing on stage at the same time. Humph. No wonder the patrons seemed more interested in entertaining one another with conversation than making it rain. None of those supposedly exotic dancers could have worked six seconds for me.

Hm, six. Girl Six. I was happy she was finally on her way to Atlanta. Then we'd all be family again. I couldn't change what I'd done to her, but I was going to do my best to take special care of Girl Six. She deserved that much from me and had it coming.

I stretched my neck, then stood up in hopes of locating another stage. *This can't be what all the hype is about,* I thought. I wasn't remotely impressed. Any one of my eleven girls could take over that stage and put these out-of-shape dancers, who were probably college students by day, on the unemployment line before the end of the first song.

Whosoever owned this placed needed an ass whipping. "Onyx, you know what?" I said.

"What's that?" Onyx asked. "You ready to get up?"

"No, not yet. Velvet's mom asked us to come check out her daughter, but I got one better."

"And?" Onyx said. "You're not thinking about having us work this spot, I hope, 'cause—"

"Hell, no. I'm going shut down this strip club. I bet half the men in here have babies and baby mamas they don't give a damn about, and they're up in here, waving money at these strippers, hoping to get their dicks sucked."

Glancing around the room, Onyx asked, "How you plan to do that?"

"You know me. I'll come up with something, and I'll tell you later," I said, watching the women on stage.

The crowd was comprised mainly of men dressed in denims and long T-shirts and resembled the gathering you'd see at a hip-hop concert featuring Chris Brown. A few of them wore striped, button-down, collared shirts. Butch women sucking on cigars and dressed like the majority of the men were sitting in corners, with naked strippers giving them either a lap or private dance.

Sitting back on my stool, I overheard one of the two young men standing behind us say, "Man, I'll be glad when Darius Jones does his thing and opens up his FL strip clubs for men only. D is clever, man, naming all of his clubs FL for 'Flawless diamonds,' then putting the cut on the end, like Princess, Radiant, Emerald, Marquise. And that FL HeartBreakers location opening downtown is gonna be the shit!" The guy started grinding the air behind me to the beat of, "Come, girl, let me get your pussy wet. Work that, let me see you drip sweat."

None of those tired girls were working hard enough to break a sweat. They need to play "Peep Show" by Joe, "Taking you from the bed, to the walls, to the floor. Sexing you, sexing me, freaky freak, behind closed doors. Nobody else can know . . ." because these girls were seriously barely moving their asses. I was sure no one would have RSVP'd if they'd known what they'd be getting in advance.

"That's what's up. Me, too, man. Can't wait," the other guy replied. "I heard gymnast-type dancers that are top-notch models, like women we ain't never seen before, gon' be in D's club. These honeys are going to be imported and shit, flown in from Brazil, Trinidad, England, Africa, and Spain. I'ma spend my whole paycheck up in his joint, 'cause I swear, man, I'm tired of competing with these lesbians for a ten-minute lap dance from a stripper who acts like she hates her job. Red Velvet is the hottest dancer up in here, and they say she quit giving lap dances after she had that abortion. What I really hate is these lesbians and bisexual chicks are making it rain up in here harder than us."

"Yeah, but I heard DJ gon' make us put on Steve Harvey suits and Sean John button-ups and slacks and shit, and no tennis shoes are allowed up in his spot," the first guy commented.

"That's what up. You can't get no fine-ass woman dressed like this here," the other guy said, smoothing out his T-shirt. "Check out them two honeys in front of us. Long, sexy, shiny legs. Pretty, soft hair. Nice skin. Especially that black one, man. We can't get no women like them dressed like this. We gotta step it up."

Well, I'd overheard enough about Darius Jones to add him to my list of club owners not to shut down but to partner with. He sounded like my type of man. I wasn't into basketball, but I was definitely going to a game or two before the season was over.

Returning my attention to the stage, I realized the upbeat music was great, so I ordered a bottle of champagne while we waited for this round of dancers to clear the stage. My stiletto touched Onyx's as I nodded, indicating she should look over her shoulder.

A stripper with fiery red hair stopped beside Onyx and shook her breasts, hoping to get a reaction. Onyx turned to face her, checked her feet, and then scanned up to her face. Then Onyx said, "You got it. Do your thing, girl."

The dancer was a woman of average height, with striking features—perfectly lined almond-shaped eyes, high cheeks on her face. and damn!, an incredible ass. She had long, luscious lashes and flawless make-up. Dressed in a leopard bustier, black boy shorts, and thigh-high stiletto boots, she made her way to the stage as the other girls picked up the last of their few dollars, then exited the platform.

The lights dimmed. The men and women gathered around the stage as the announcer said, "Ladies and gentlemen, every damn body up in this motherfucker, get the fuck up out of your seats, get on your feet, and make some noiseeeee! Welcome Red Velvet up in this bitch! Aw, it's about to sizzle up in this joint."

Red searchlights bouncing off of a huge disco ball centered above the stage beamed across the room, then froze on Red Velvet. The crowd went wild as Red Velvet dropped to the floor. Her legs were spread east and west as her pussy rolled north and south. The red lights vanished, and the crowd was engulfed in darkness. When the lights flashed on, Red Velvet was hanging upside down from the top of the pole. She was so far up that it looked like she was hanging from the ceiling. Gracefully, she slid down, clenching a banana peel between her teeth.

Where was the rest of the banana?

That was the woman's daughter. Damn. I needed to call Alphonso and make his ass pay a hundred and fifty thousand. I could easily see how Alphonso had lost his damn mind, but how could he ignore his fatherly obligations to a woman that beautiful?

Crawling on the stage, Red Velvet perched in front of a man standing in front of the stage. Slowly, the skin of that damn banana came out of her mouth, like a lily blossoming, and the longest banana I'd ever seen eased out of the banana skin and fell right between another stripper's titties. Dollar bills rained like a thunderstorm had hit, flooding the entire stage. Looking at the money, all I saw were ones. *These cheap assholes.* I was stunned.

Amid the dollars in the middle of the stage was a sixteen-ounce water bottle. Red Velvet took her time sqatting on the bottle. She inserted the top, picked up the bottle, then put it back down. Each time she squatted, she inserted the bottle a little more. The crowd lost all composure.

"Excuse me. Excuse me," one woman said, forcing her way through the applauding crowd, trying to see the performance.

I guessed she was a fan.

Red Velvet squatted down on the bottle again, and this time it disappeared inside of her pussy. She climbed up the pole, then slid down, and repeated this several times. Standing tall, with her legs spread wide, she squatted on the floor, bounced her ass, then rolled her pussy while spreading her thighs like a butterfly. Suddenly, she stood, then dropped her ass to the floor. I swear, I was kneeling on top of my table, next to Onyx, trying to figure out what had happened to that water bottle.

The red, swirling lights zigzagged around the stage. I frowned as I caught a glimpse of the side profile of the woman who'd made her way to the front. Her behavior was different. Her body was twisted. Above the cheers and clapping, I couldn't hear what she was saying, but she definitely wasn't cheering. Seemed like she was yelling at Red Velvet.

"Aw, shit," I said and nudged Onyx. "Cover me."

Hell, I was missing the act by trying to keep an eye on the deranged woman, but I felt some shit was about to go down harder than it was raining. Briefly turning to watch Red Velvet end her performance, I saw the water bottle hit the stage. She picked it up, then tossed it in the air to Onyx. Onyx caught the bottle, which probably smelled as sweet as honey. The cap was on, and Onyx yelled, "It's empty, y'all!"

Well, her last name was definitely appropriate. Shaking my head, trying to comprehend how Red Velvet had done that shit, I caught a glimpse of the deranged women. I stared at her lips, reading each word. "I warned you, bitch!" she muttered as her eyes, nose, and mouth shriveled.

I saw her hand ball into a fist, gripping a sharp object. Leaping from my stool, I parted the crowd. When Red Velvet turned her back to exit the stage, the deranged woman raised her arm above the still-cheering crowd. Standing directly behind the woman, I grabbed her wrist when she lowered what was clearly a knife toward Red Velvet's back. I made her drop the knife, then proceeded to choke the shit out of her from behind so she couldn't grab me.

"What kind of trick are you?" I yelled. "If you hate Red Velvet so much, why didn't you confront her face-to-face like a real woman would?"

I tried to strangle the life out of that bitch. I didn't want to kill her, but she needed to think about what the fuck she was trying to do. Then I felt a strong arm choking me from behind. "Bitch, let go of my wife!" a man snarled. A few seconds later, he yelled, "Uhhh!" Then he released me.

The music stopped; the crowd parted as Onyx pulled her spiked heel out of the man's neck. I refused to let go of whoever this bitch was.

Red Velvet left her money on the stage, walked over to us, and looked at the woman. "You're a day late, aren't you?" she said. "You seriously tried to stab me in my back over a dick, and now your husband is the one bleeding to death, and you're going to jail. You're one dumb bitch to be that possessed by something you can never control. When are you going to get it? Tolliver does not love you, you stupid bitch. I don't even feel sorry for your ass."

After sticking her middle finger inside her pussy, Red Velvet smeared her juices all over the woman's face, and then *bam!* Red Velvet kicked the woman in her clit, returned to the stage, gathered her money into a large clear-plastic bag, and made her way back over to me. "Thanks for saving my life. Here," she said, handing me the bag.

For a moment I thought about what Red Velvet had said to the woman, who I was still holding around the neck. Velvet was right. Any man who knew his woman was mentally capable of killing another woman over him, and voluntarily stood by and watched his wife stab a woman, didn't love his wife. Maybe he was hoping he'd get rid of his wife, that her dumb ass would end up behind bars. That would allow him to fuck whomever he wanted whenever he wanted. A part of me felt sorry for the woman, so I let her go when the police arrived, because now she was going to jail for attempted murder, smelling like Red Velvet's pussy.

I couldn't believe that that woman, whoever she was, loved her man so deeply that she'd willingly take another woman's life. What was that dumb bitch going to do? Go around killing or stabbing every woman her man fucked? If only she could've dealt with her emotions in a positive way and left her husband before she'd gotten to this point.

I stared at her as the police placed her hands behind her back, then snapped the handcuffs around her wrists. Her husband was nowhere in sight, but my guess was Tolliver was on his way to the nearest hospital. Exhaling, I looked at the overstuffed bag of money Red Velvet had given me. If Sapphire was serious about getting her money back from me, I might need Red Velvet's cash. Pushing the bag back to Red Velvet, I handed her a business card. Before I left home I'd already written a note on the back: *Meet me at my office tomorrow at six p.m. You need to get out of this business.* That was her mother's request.

"Let's get out of here," I told Onyx as we headed toward the door.

A tall, charming gentleman dressed in an expensive suit blocked our path. "Excuse me, ladies. Let me give you my card," he said. "I'm Trevor Williams, the owner. Thanks for protecting Red. She's a good young lady. Hard worker. Don't know what I would've done if anything had happened to her. Next time you come, please call me first. I want you to be my personal guests." He paused. "Better yet," he said to me, "I'd like to take you out. Call me."

Firmly shaking his hand, I looked deep into Trevor's eyes and said, "You'll definitely see us again." Then we left his club. I shoved his card in my purse, thinking if I got tired of fucking myself, he was doable, but I'd have to beat his ass into submission first.

Onyx and I got in my car and headed toward Buckhead. "You know what I despise about Mr. Williams?" I said.

"No. What?" Onyx asked, wiping her heel with a towelette. "This was one helluva night. That trick Tolliver made me fuck up my brand-new slides. Oh, he's definitely buying me a new pair of Jimmy Choo shoes for sho'."

"That's why I really want to shut Trevor's strip club down now . . . for exploiting women. I could fuck him, then fuck him over the same way he's doing to those young girls. Trevor doesn't care as much about Red Velvet as he does his income stream. He didn't even bring his punk ass over to see what was going on until the police arrived. If Red Velvet wasn't working for him, that club would be empty every night. And there's no way Red Velvet should've had a stage covered with one-dollar bills. I bet she barely made two hundred. As talented as she is, she should've had all one-hundred-dollar bills on that stage."

When Onyx didn't answered, I glanced over and saw she was asleep. I tuned my radio to 102.9, then set the volume to low.

"I can't make you love me if you don't," streamed through my speakers.

Tears clung to my eyelids as I thought of Grant. With the exception of the last day I spent with Grant, all of my memories of him were good. What I wouldn't give to hold him in my arms again.

Tapping Onyx on the shoulder, I whispered, "We're home, baby."

Entering through the garage, I helped Onyx upstairs to her bed, then went downstairs and opened the door to my room. I flicked on the light. "What the hell!" I yelled, quickly drawing my gun from my purse.

"Whoa, it's me, baby. Put that away. I thought you'd be happy to see me," Grant said, frowning, with his hands held in front of him.

I wanted to say, "You could get a bullet in your head doing some unexpected shit like this." I wanted to wake up each of my girls, except Onyx, make their asses come downstairs, and seriously beat all of them for letting Grant or any man into our home without calling me first. But all I did was place my gun on my dresser, quietly close the door, then stand in the middle of the floor, waiting for Grant to come to me.

CHAPTER 16

Sapphire

There were no accidents in life. Some men were unarguably mentally fucked up, and they needed to be put to rest for the greater good of womankind.

A husband dehumanizing his wife, a pimp mercilessly beating into submission women he claimed as his whores, and a whole gang of evil men who raped women and children had one thing in common, a disillusioned desire to control females by any forceful means necessary. What gave any man the right to abuse women? His dick? His balls? His barbaric strength? His inability to maintain or obtain what he desperately fought to acquire, namely power?

Standing over my king-sized bed, which was covered with a blue comforter, blue silk sheets, and matching pillows of different shapes and sizes, I stared at Girl Six. She was a true sleeping beauty, but I wasn't going to miss her. I tapped her shoulder. "Get up. It's time to get you to the airport."

After hanging up with Lace, I'd booked Girl Six a red-eye flight that would get her into Atlanta in the morning. I had to sever her emotional attachment to me; Girl Six had to go.

"Huh?" She yawned, stretching her hands toward the wooden headboard. "What? I'm leaving right now? What time is it?"

I peeled away the covers to take in the image of her perfect body. This was probably the last time we'd see one another. "Come here," I said, opening my arms to her. "You know I'm going to miss you terribly. I promise not to leave you in Atlanta one second longer than necessary." I held her chin so it faced mine. "If any one sneezes on you or looks at you the wrong way, you'd better let me know."

I tried to give her the reassurance she needed to get on that one-way flight to a place she'd never been. I imagined that could be frightening for any nineteen-year-old.

Smiling, she made her way to the edge of the bed and hugged me. "Go," I said, ushering her into the bathroom. I poured myself a goblet of merlot, then sat in the living room, on the sofa. My body shivered when I saw what was on television.

The commentator said, "More than four million women in the Democratic Republic of the Congo have been massacred. Millions more have been raped in front of their powerless husbands and their empathetic brothers, who have died for refusing to follow military orders to rape their wives or sisters."

Oh my God. Women were being raped by one bitch-ass man after another after another after another, gang-raped every day for months and months, and somehow they managed to survive. Ejaculating inside of a woman's uterus as target practice for her unfertilized eggs wasn't enough for these men. I heard the commentator say, "After raping the women, the men take machetes and slice the women's vaginas. Or even worse, these military men shoot the women between the legs, leaving them for dead, or they impregnated and abandon the women."

I turned off the television. I'd heard enough. Like many of the African women, some of the prostitutes in Las Vegas would end up carrying, from conception to birth, a child conceived in hatred. And if the children weren't taken away, or given away, they'd end up at the bosom of their mothers, fatherless.

I knew what I had to do. I'd been contemplating this way too long. Their time had come. I was going to kill each pimp that I had on my list to arrest. I knew exactly what I was doing. In the line of duty, I was getting ready to save generations of women from suffering. A part of me wished I could journey to the Congo villages, with war paint splashed across my face and semiautomatic weapons strapped across my back. With tears of blood streaming down my cheeks, in broad daylight, I'd wrap my fist around the handle of the sharpest machete, the same machete they'd used to slice those beautiful women's vaginas, and I'd cut off the dicks and sever the balls, one at a time, of every man that had raped or mutilated a woman or a little girl. Then I'd cast their naked, dickless bodies into a venomous-snake pit laced with gasoline and burn them like trash, because they were the filthiest kind of trash, and they would leave an unforgettable stench embedded in the hearts and souls of innocent women and children.

A flutter in my heart made me pick up my home phone and dial a number I hadn't forgotten in more than a decade. Waiting for someone to answer, I wondered what I would say. Where would I begin? How could I explain the things I'd done? Why should I have to? So much had happened since the last time we'd seen one another. I couldn't deny or confirm that I was a cold-blooded killer preparing to kill once more. But killing was in my job description.

I had a reason and had to exercise my license. The strange thing was, I knew I'd kill again tonight, but I couldn't harm the person I was calling in any way. I'd die first. What made me capable of taking a person's life without remorse yet love someone I didn't truly know with the same heart? The dichotomy of my heart and my brain terrified me. Perhaps I'd come back home after dropping off Girl Six. Maybe I wouldn't kill anyone tonight, that is, if the right person picked up the phone.

"Hello," a deep voice answered.

Speechless, I froze. Instantly, my feet and my hands felt like they had been soaked in gasoline and then had accidentally touched a flaming match. Heat raced up my arms, all the way to my face, my brain. Hot flash! No, I was too young. I was mad as hell. Sweat beaded at the crown of my skull, wetting my hair, neck, and shoulders. My dress clung to my body.

"Hello," he repeated.

It was him. I hadn't wanted him to answer. Ooh, if I could have killed him through the phone, I would have. I wanted to hear my mother's voice. I opened my mouth. Not even air escaped my lips. All I could think was I shouldn't have called. Racing into the kitchen, I grabbed the entire roll of paper towels, turned on the cold water, held the roll under the faucet, then pressed the clumped, cool, wet towels against my forehead.

Click.

He'd hung up. *Probably best,* I thought. I didn't know why I'd called my mom, but I regretted it the moment I heard Alphonso's voice. Turning on the shower in the guest bathroom, I removed my wet clothes, then stepped in, letting the cool stream soothe my body.

"Ah, cold water feels so good. Oh, damn," I said aloud. Stepping out of the shower, I stared in the mirror. "Wait a minute. Had Lace answered her phone, 'Grant, is that you?' She had. Couldn't be. There is no way she could know the same man. I sucked his dick twelve years ago. No fucking way."

I wanted to call Lace back, but how could I ask her if she was referring to Grant Hill? I didn't have enough information to track him down. Then again, if he still lived in D.C., maybe I did know enough to find him.

"I'm ready," Girl Six said, standing in the doorway, dressed in a sharp all-black pantsuit, white stilettos, and a matching bustier. Her hair was partially up, with the hanging portion flowing down her back.

"Damn, you clean up good. Let's get outta here before I change my mind."

The drive to the Las Vegas airport was less than fifteen minutes, but it gave me time to lay out my instructions.

"When you get to Lace's house, act normal," I said, glancing at Girl Six. "Do not tell her you ever stayed with me. Pay attention to everything, but pretend not to. Don't ask too many questions. If you get a glimpse of a bank statement, a deposit slip, or anything pertaining to where she keeps her money, memorize the name of the bank and, if you can, the account number. Oh, and if you hear her mention the name Grant Hill, call me immediately."

Shaking her head, Girl Six said, "You want me to be your spy. Is that why you're kicking me out?"

"Our spy. You're doing this for us."

"But why? I know she treated me bad, but what are you asking of me? To get myself killed?"

"I'm asking you to do as I say. I can't explain all of this in fifteen minutes. Get out. And call me when you get into Atlanta," I said, softly kissing her on the cheek.

I watched Girl Six until she disappeared behind the sliding glass door and into the ticketing area. Her walk wasn't as confident as her wardrobe. "For her sake, I sure hope she doesn't fuck up," I muttered. Neither Lace nor I would show her mercy if she did. No matter what side of the prostitution game a pimp, a hooker, or a cop was on, one mistake could end up deadly.

Before I could change my mind, I headed to the Strip on my way from the airport. The casino I stopped at was sparsely crowded. Half of the crap tables were empty. The slot machines were quiet. Taking a seat at the bar, I greeted the bartender. "I'll have a double Hennessy straight up, heated," I said, keeping my eyes on everyone around me. I glanced over my shoulders frequently.

I couldn't stop thinking about Grant and wondering if he was the man Lace knew. Part of me hoped it was him. Every time I ate peanut butter and strawberry preserves, I thought about him. We'd been young and foolish. I hoped he didn't think I was a slut for sucking his friends' dicks, too. Grant didn't complain when I did him. I'd do him again in a minute, except this time, if I had the chance, I wouldn't do any other man. My heart raced with each thought. If that was him, what was his connection to Lace? Hopefully, he wasn't one of her clients.

Black Jack, an amateur pimp, sat across from me with his whore. Peripherally, I observed him schooling his whore on how to approach certain men. His whispering and nodding gave him away. How any woman would work for him was beyond my comprehension. The fact that Black Jack didn't recognize me meant he was a wannabe pimp who looked like a college dropout. He was a total misfit.

"Here you go, beautiful. Compliments of Black," the bartender said, sitting my drink in front of me.

Acknowledging my appreciation, I held up a glass, then took a sip. Black Jack had more than twice the number of prostitutes as Valentino, but Black's tricks were cheap, raggedy chicks from small towns. From their paid-less shoes to their frail, dollar-store outfits, those women could've done better by working for minimum wage. Word was Black would make them suck a dick for a dollar if that was the only dollar they'd bring him.

"Yo, Black," Long Money yelled, walking up to the bar. Then he tried to whisper, "A busload of Little Bo Peep–looking high school students just hit Tropicana. You in?"

If Black said, "Sho' nuff," it might prove his best decision of the night. Looking at me, he said, "I'll catch up to you." Then he pushed his trick off the stool. "Take this bitch with you. She can lure a few pretty young things to you. Drug them. Then bring them to my place at midnight."

Dirty bastards. That was exactly how he had so many young girls. The sapphire in me came out. I despised the way these pimps kidnapped and drugged these young, innocent females, and then put them on the stroll. This was why I'd gone undercover as a police officer, and now it was time for me to avenge these women.

Picking up his drink, Black Jack came and sat next to me. "I see you here and there. What's up with you, oldie? You got a pimp?"

"Of course," I lied. Not anymore, anyway. Once upon a time, about twelve years ago, Pretty Ricky was my pimp.

I started out sucking dicks for fun. Then, after I ran away from home and ended up in Vegas with Pretty Ricky, I had to do whatever a paid client wanted me to.

Putting a little bass in his voice, Black Jack said, "You know the rules. Give me yo' money, bitch."

The unspoken rule was if a prostitute spoke one word to a pimp who wasn't her pimp, then she had to give that pimp every dime she had in her possession. Reaching into my top, I handed Black Jack three hundred-dollar bills. He was lucky I didn't pull out my badge and gun instead and shoot him in the head. In time. Three hundred dollars didn't mean anything to me, but it was probably the most money he was going to make tonight.

Black Jack squinted and stared at me before asking, "Haven't I seen you around before?"

"Obviously not," I snapped. "I wouldn't be the same fool twice. You wanna take a ride?" I licked my lips.

"You that cop Bleu I heard about?"

"Who's that? You wanna ride or not?" I asked him, rubbing my nipple.

"For sho'," he said, pushing back his stool. He tossed back his double, ice and all. "Damn. You sho' all you got is three Cs hidden underneath those big-ass titties?" Black Jack asked, massaging his dick.

"That's it, Daddy. Where to? I ain't got all night to entertain you."

"Bitch," he said, slapping my face. "Don't ever question me again. Shut the fuck up and let's go."

Throwing one of the hundred-dollar bills I'd just given him onto the bar, Black Jack led the way, trying to walk upright, with his shoulders back. The tip was a payoff for the bartender not to kick Black Jack out of the casino and not to report his illegal activities.

I followed Black Jack to his car, which was parked out back. I hopped in on the passenger side and kept quiet.

"You gon' make me some money tonight, but first you gon' suck my big-ass dick," Black Jack demanded, pulling into a vacant parking lot off of the Strip.

The rip of his zipper reminded me of the first time Pretty Ricky recruited me as one of his substitute prostitutes, sending me out on the stroll when one of the other girls was too badly beaten.

Leaning my head on his lap, I reached for his little dick with one hand and for my gun with the other. He motioned for me to wrap my lips around his swollen head. I moaned, right before swiftly wedging the barrel on my gun between his nuts. *Pow!*

I pulled the trigger with no remorse. Blood splattered across my face. Calmly, I propped his body up straight, then stepped out of his car and walked away, refusing to look back. Eventually, someone would realize he was dead. Black Jack wasn't the first pimp I'd killed. Long Money was next. I was saving Pretty Ricky for last, the pimp that had personally beaten my ass for fun.

CHAPTER 17

Grant

Honey stepped into her bedroom, looking ravishing enough for me to drop to my knees and press my drooling lips against her hot, sweet pussy. She came through that door the same way she had each time I'd laid eyes on her; Honey was mesmerizing. Her short dress exposed her sculpted thighs, shapely calves, and diamond anklets. Honey was one sexy-ass woman. The type of sophistication Honey exemplified, a woman couldn't buy or be taught. I wanted to grab her, throw her on the floor, and make love to her all night long. When I saw that gun, I did not move, not even after she placed it on the dresser.

Honey rolled her eyes long and hard. "Grant," she said, staring at me. If she hadn't spoken my name, the livid expression on her face would've kicked my ass and thrown my behind out of her house, headfirst.

I should've been the one who was pissed off. Opening my arms, I stood before my angel. "Baby, you don't look happy to see me. I do understand I should've called, but, baby, I needed to see you. I was hoping you'd be home when I arrived, and if I'd left before you got here, chances are I wouldn't have had the fortitude to return. At least give me a hug." Stepping closer, uh, uh, uh, I got a whiff of her captivating Prada perfume.

She didn't move, so I accepted that as an unspoken yes.

Slowly, I embraced her shoulders, leaning her head against my chest as I exhaled. "Honey, I miss you so damn much, baby."

Silence followed our magnetic reunion and lasted for at least fifteen minutes, allowing our body language to confirm we were overwhelmed holding one another. I loved the way her body quivered.

Gently pulling away, Honey said, "So what do want from me? Why did you show up at my house unannounced? You didn't return any of my calls or respond to my text messages. Didn't you get any of them?"

Whenever a woman was calm on the outside, she was capable of bursting into a rancid rage without notice. I wanted to do my part by not aggravating Honey. Kissing the crown of her beautiful head, I answered, "Yes. I got every single one. Each and every day. And, I did call you once."

"You consider that a—"

"See? Look," I said, scrolling through her text messages on my phone. "I wasn't ready to confront you but knew I had to at some point. So I was in town on business and tried convincing myself to leave, but I couldn't board my plane to D.C., because I kept thinking of you. So I left the airport, and here I am."

"So you think you can show up at my home any time you feel like it. Don't ever step foot on my property without my consent. How would you feel if I showed up at your front door without calling first? And what do you mean by confront?" Honey walked away. "What the fuck do you have to confront me about, huh?" She turned on all the lights in her bedroom.

The huge white canopy bed was illuminated. It complemented the chaise. The bed we'd made love in the two weeks we were together was tempting me to forget about talking, remove my clothes, undress Honey, and feverishly fuck the shit out of her until we were raw and exhausted and our bodies felt paralyzed. I wanted to say, "Quack, quack, quack," but somehow I didn't think she'd find my humor amusing.

Rubbing my eyes, I asked, "Is it necessary to have all the lights on? It's brighter than a sunny day up in here." No sooner had I said, "Sunny day," than I regretted it.

Tears filled Honey's eyes, swarming between the red veins zigzagging across her corneas. When she blinked, I watched the drops fall to her breasts and disappear into her cleavage. "What the hell did you just say?"

I wanted Honey to clarify whether or not she'd killed Sunny, like Benito alleged, but truly I had more tact than to slip in a question on the under. "I don't want to bicker over my callous choice of words. I apologize for that. I came here hoping you'd tell me the truth about who you are and why you lied to me." Patting the chaise, I gestured for Honey to sit next to me. I had to look into her eyes when she explained her side of the alleged criminal acts that had transpired. I prayed what she had to say was different from Benito's confession.

Honey sat next to me, exhaled, then removed her stilettos. As she thumped her left shoe in the palm of her hand, for a moment I became fearful that she might try to nail me in the forehead with her spiked heel, then bury me beneath the peach trees in her backyard, which I'd admired earlier, before the sun had set.

"Where do I begin?" she asked, placing the shoe beside the chaise.

Her question was obviously rhetorical. Patiently, I remained quiet.

"Grant, I miss you, too. I don't offer any excuses. My past is unchangeable, and my future is unpredictable. My mother kicked me out of her house the day before my sixteenth birthday. I've been on my own ever since. Two failed marriages led me to eleven years of working at a brothel and—"

A brothel? Benito was right? I did not want to believe that Honey was a whore. There was no reasonable explanation for any woman pathetic enough to sell her body. Not Honey. No way. Looking deeper into her eyes, I sought clarification. "In what capacity, exactly, were you employed?"

Staring into my eyes, Honey never blinked as she answered, "Prostituting. I was a prostitute for eleven years and a madam for one year afterward. I worked for Valentino James. At first I thought being a madam was above being a prostitute. I was wrong. It wasn't. It was different but definitely not better. In some instances being a madam was worse. As a prostitute, I degraded myself. Being a madam . . ." Honey's words trailed into thoughts. Silence pierced the air between us.

Honey's honesty definitely wasn't what I'd anticipated hearing. "So why did you do it? Why did you feel you had to do any of it?"

"Grant, look. I have trampled through way too much bullshit in my life. I don't give a damn about what you think of me. Do I make myself clear? I wasn't put on this earth to prove myself to you or anyone else," Honey said, with tears in her eyes. "But since your world seems to be so fucking perfect, let me ask you a few questions." Honey sat on the edge of the chaise. "Have you ever slept in a doghouse just to live another day? Have you ever been homeless, Grant? Huh? What about hungry, not knowing when you'd eat again? Have you ever been so afraid that when you lay your beaten and bruised body down to sleep, you're too frightened to go to sleep, so you lie awake all night, praying for God to rock you into heaven? If you've got all the fucking answers, Mr. Perfect, open your goddamn mouth and say something. If you don't like what you just heard, you get the hell out of my life. But this time you stay gone."

Instead of being the teacher who'd helped my dad show young entrepreneurs how to make wise investments, today I was experiencing a paradigm shift. I'd become Honey's student. "No, baby, no. Oh my God, what happened to you?" I asked, forcing back my tears. Wrapping my arms around Honey, all I could think was, How could anyone hurt someone as beautiful as Honey? Then I asked, "So what's your real name?"

"My birth name is Lace St. Thomas. My deceased sister's name was Honey Thomas. When Honey passed away, I accidentally gave *my* birth certificate, not Honey's, to the guy at the funeral home. With so much going on, Valentino getting arrested, and Sapphire giving me a cashier's check for fifty million, I decided to leave Vegas and take all of my escorts with me in hopes of giving these brilliant young ladies a better life than the one I had. Then I got sideswiped when Sapphire called and said she didn't *give* me the money and that it was hers, but I can handle her. When I realized I had buried myself on paper, I figured it was best to leave the old me dead and start anew with the name Honey Thomas."

Honey was right. She, like the women she was now trying to help, including Red Velvet, deserved a fresh start. And I wanted to help them, not hurt them. I reassured her. "Honey, there are no accidents in life, just lessons to be learned," I said. Then I kissed Honey on the nose, her small, adorable nose.

"Thanks for believing me," she said, resting her head on my chest.

Believing? I wouldn't take it that far just yet, I thought. Curious, I asked, "How do you define the word *love?*" I ran my hand through her hair.

"As something I've never had," she said as she began to cry on my shoulder.

Whoa. That was devastating. Continuing to stroke her head, I said, "See, that's where you're wrong. I love you. Despite what my father, my mother, and my brother had to say about you. I'm here because I love you."

Honey exhaled. "If that's true," she replied, "then tell me how you define *love.*"

The answer for me was easy.

"Love is what my parents have. Love is everlasting. Love is the genuine giving of oneself, with the intended purpose of uplifting, embracing, and improving another, for the advancement of another. Love makes us smile. Love makes us happy. Love makes us cry, and underneath our sadness, love brings us pure joy. That's why we can love so many people in so many ways. Our needs are uniquely different. A man desires a love that reassures him that his woman needs and respects him. That she's going to be there for him through his toughest times. A woman craves a love that constantly shows and tells her she's appreciated. True love is painless. I want what my mother and father have."

"That sounds so scripted," she said, staring at me.

I chuckled. "I know, and you're right. What can I say. I'm starting to sound like my father."

"No, it's not painless," Honey countered, shaking her head. "Love hurts like hell. It makes you feel like you're dying. While you've been away from me, not calling me, I've been upset, sick, even angry at you. But I never stopped loving you."

I held my angel closer to my heart. "You know what's ironic? The desperation to be loved can come through the deepest expressions of hate, and if you think about it . . . we hate because what we honestly need is love. Don't get me wrong. Oh, I am concerned about the things you've done, but I care more about you. No woman has ever made me feel the way you do."

Cutting her eyes at me, Honey said, "You sure about that?" She looked down at my dick.

I gazed out the window and into the darkness of the night. For the quickest second, I thought about Red Velvet. "Let's not go there. Whatever happened while we weren't together is irrelevant."

Honey whispered, "You haven't asked me why I killed Reynolds."

Since she was volunteering, I said, "I'm listening."

"He raped one of my girls."

"Well, there you have it. It was self-defense. Or somebody's defense." Honey was strong in so many ways, she scared the hell out of me. "Damn, compared to what you've gone through, my life is squeaky clean, and you might get bored with me. I'm in no position to judge you. That's God's job, baby," I whispered, pausing for a moment.

"Yes," she answered, her nails meandering along my spine. Her touch was incredible.

"Baby," I repeated.

"Yes?" she answered slowly.

"Let me make love to you."

CHAPTER 18

Red Velvet

What had made Tolliver's wife so insanely jealous that she actually showed up at my job, with the intention of stabbing me in the back? She could've killed me! Surely, she must've known I wasn't the only woman Tolliver had fucked. But after seeing her overweight, out-of-shape, too-many-rocky-road-ice-cream-cones behind wobbling out of the club, in handcuffs, I understood how she'd turned him off. Damn, picturing her naked made me want to throw up.

What made some women think a marriage license gave them permission to neglect themselves? If I got married, I would work out twice a day. Once at the gym, and once a day, every day, I was going to ride his dick. Besides, what was Tolliver's wife going to do? Assault all the women Tolliver had stuck his dick in? I had no remorse for her serving time in jail. At least she would have time to reflect on what she'd done, and I wouldn't have to wonder if she'd show up at either of my jobs, acting a fool.

Entering my mother's kitchen, I heard Mama say, "Ronnie, chew your food really good before swallowing." Then she covered my son's hand with hers. "Slow down, sweetheart. Your mother isn't going to leave you again."

"Yes, ma'am," my son answered politely and nodded, with his jaws stuffed. When I Joined them at the table, his brown eyes connected with mine, seeking reassurance that I'd take him with me this time.

Ronnie didn't care where I went. As long as he could go with me, he was happy. "Mommy, here. You eat this," Ronnie offered, handing me half of his turkey sandwich.

"No, baby. Eat your lunch. Mommy ate already," I lied.

"Velvet, you have to spend more time with Ronnie. I can't raise him for you," said Mama. "I've taken him to the King Center, the Coca-Cola factory, the Georgia Aquarium, and you've taken him where?"

"Ma, don't say it like that. I do spend time with my son." Why was my mom having this conversation in front of my baby?

I flipped open my Sidekick and smiled. Grant had texted: *Are you available for dinner tonight?*

"When?" Mama asked. "You're either working or hanging out. Ronnie didn't ask to be here, you know. You're going to start showing him some motherly love right now by spending quality time with him," Mama said, cupping Ronnie's face in her palms as though he was two years old. "I'm going shopping with my friends today."

I texted Grant back. *Yes. When and where?*

"Not today, Ma. Can't you shop tomorrow? I have to meet someone in a few hours. I promise I'll make it quick. Just watch Ronnie until I get back."

Ronnie sat there, pivoting his head back and forth from my mom to me and eating his potato chips. He was saving his carrot and celery sticks for last to dunk in his ranch dressing.

"Nope. I'm not asking you. Take him with you. That's my final decision," said Mama. "He needs you. Look at his plate. If I hadn't slowed him down, his plate would be empty, and he just sat down right before you walked in. You don't realize why he eats so fast?" As soon as I opened my mouth to answer, my mother interrupted. "He's afraid that if he's not finished eating when you get ready to walk out that door, you'll leave him. And he's right. Changing the subject, what's this I heard about you having a physical altercation at that place?"

Grant texted: *Two Restaurant @ 6.*

Damn. What had struck a nerve with her? "Mama?" I said. I tilted my head toward my son, then demanded, "Ronnie, go in the living room and play video games."

"But I'm not finished eating," he whined.

His inquisitive behind wasn't fooling me. He wanted to hear what my mother would say next. Firmly, I told him, "Now, Ronnie. Take your plate with you, boy." I knew my mother didn't like anyone eating in her contemporary-style living room, with expensive chinchilla throws draped over the edges of her customized pineapple-colored leather sofa and mocha chairs.

Staring at me without blinking, my mother overruled me. "Ronnie, leave the plate on the table, sweetheart, and go read a book."

I texted Grant: *Can't wait!*

"Okay, Grandma," my son said, dashing off to his personalized bookcase, which my mother had designed and engraved with his name on the day he was born. I must admit that having his own book collection—some autographed—and having my mother read with him every day for twenty minutes had made Ronnie more eager to read than to watch television, like he did at our house. I'd noticed that being able to spell words and read complete sentences made my son proud to be smart.

Tilting my head sideways, I wondered how long it took my mother to teach Ronnie how to read a book on his own.

Observing the expression on my face, Mama said, "I taught him in six weeks. Children like consistency. But what they don't like is having their mother consistently gone. Now, Velvet, tell me what happened last night." Mama clamped her hands on top of the table, then stared at me.

Closing my Sidekick, I said, "Ma, it was nothing really." Actually, it was none of her business, but I wasn't bold enough to say that.

"Velvet, when are you going to stop lying to yourself, to me, to Ronnie? From what I was told, that woman showed up at Stilettos to kill you because you're sleeping with her husband."

As usual, my mother knew more than I'd figured, and I had no idea how she'd found out, but I couldn't lie to her. I was grateful for that woman who'd saved my life. I vaguely recalled her handing me a business card, which I'd stuffed in my bag, without looking at it.

"She's the stupid one. She's in jail, and I hope she rots there," I told Mama. "I didn't do anything to her. The person she should've checked was her cheating husband, not me."

"Velvet, look at me. She's a woman."

"Yeah, a crazy woman."

"Be quiet and listen. Haven't I taught you how to respect yourself? I don't approve of you working at that place, but I can't make you quit. You don't know everything, sweetheart. That woman undoubtedly has marital issues that need to be resolved with her husband, but that's her husband. When you become involved with a married man, you're putting yourself in the middle of their problems. It's easier for the other woman to attack you, because no matter what that man has done or continues to do, she still loves him. Whether or not he loves her is irrelevant. What's real is neither one of them loves you."

At that moment I received another text message . . . from Tolliver. *I need to see you. Call me.* No way was I going to call him. Was he fucking retarded?

Go fuck yourself! I texted him back, then laid my phone on my lap, out of my mother's reach. I didn't care if she got a hold of Grant's messages, but no way was I letting her read what Tolliver had texted. Some of what Mama said might've been true, but Tolliver's wife was wrong for trying to hurt me. I picked up my phone and texted, *Well, now she has time to think about what she should've done, because I'm pressing charges against her.*

Tolliver texted again. *Velvet, don't do this to me.*

Under the table, without looking at the keyboard, I texted him back. *What part of go fuck yourself didn't you get, trick?*

Slap! My mother's hand landed across my cheek as if she were clairvoyant.

"Ow!" I rubbed my aching jaw. "Ma, that's not fair."

"Don't you tell me what's not fair. What's not fair is Ronnie doesn't know his father, and if I leave it up to you, he never will. Honey Thomas found him. We found Alphonso Allen."

Frowning in disbelief, I said, "You did what?" My burning cheek hung low. "Ma, no," I whispered, with tears running down my face. She had no right to do that. Especially when I'd told her not to.

Tolliver texted a third time. *Velvet, don't make me come to your house.*

My fingers ran across the keys of my phone. *Try it and you'll end up behind bars like your crazy-ass wife. Leave me the fuck alone!* What could he possibly want from me?

"This isn't about you, Velvet. It's about Ronnie. He has a right to know, and like it or not, I've arranged a date for Ronnie to meet Alphonso."

Frantically, my head swung from side to side as I told Mama, "You have no right to do this!"

Slap! My mother's hand landed across my opposite cheek.

This was quickly turning into one of those days when I should've gone the fuck about my business without stopping at my mother's house. "Stop it, Ma. I'm twenty-five. I can make my own mistakes. I'm not your little girl anymore. I'm a woman. And what if they call me for a second audition and my face is messed up because of your misdirected anger. Stop it."

"You are not your priority. Ronnie is your priority. Ronnie deserves to judge his father for himself. Just because you opened your legs without thinking first and conceived my grandson doesn't mean you have the right to decide whether or not he gets to know his father. And you're not running off to Hollywood and leaving him for me to raise by myself."

I looked down at my phone. No text from Tolliver. I worried that he was serious about showing up at my house. I started crying. "Alphonso made it clear he wanted no parts of us. Ma, my God, you know he raped me."

Mama's lips tightened. She exhaled. "If you hadn't carelessly gone to the beach late at night with a stranger, that wouldn't have been an option for him, now would it?"

My mom couldn't say the word *rape*, because that was how she'd conceived me. Just because she loved me and had raised me by herself, she felt I was supposed to do the same with Ronnie. But I couldn't. I wasn't strong like my mother. "So you're still blaming me?"

"The us part could be true, baby, but Alphonso has an obligation to Ronnie, and he needs to pay you child support so you can stop struggling, working two jobs, and sleeping with married men for money, and start investing time in your child. I'm trying to get you to see the bigger picture. Let him pay for his mistake. The time has come for you to handle yourself and your son differently."

Conceding to a competition I hadn't signed up for and couldn't win, I asked, "So what should I do?"

Another text popped up from Tolliver. *I'm on my way.*

Then another from Grant. *Are you on your way?*

Suck your own dick, trick! I texted back. *I'm calling the police right now, and I'm going to show them your messages. I don't give a fuck about you or your crazy-ass wife!*

"Oh, shit!" As soon as I hit the SEND key, I'd realized my last message, intended for Tolliver, had gone to Grant.

"You'll start by dropping all charges against that man's wife," Mama said.

How in the hell had we gotten back to Tolliver's wife? Backing away from my mother's reach, I shook my head. "No, I'm not. Ma, she deserves to do time."

"Who in the hell are you to determine if that woman deserves to do time? What she deserves is not to have women like you fucking her husband. Taking money from him is the same as taking her money. How would you feel if someone took your money?"

Suddenly, I remembered my mother's husband had divorced her for another woman. This was another battle I was destined to lose, but I had to defend my position. "I didn't take Tolliver's money. He gave it to me," I said, trying to think of an explanation to text to Grant since he hadn't texted me back.

"In exchange for what, Velvet? Don't you see those men idolize what's between your legs, not what's between your ears? What did you have to give him to get a few dollars? Huh? What? Pussy? Suck his dick? What?"

Actually, yes, I did want to suck a dick. Grant's dick. But he hadn't texted me back. *Fuck! Mama, shut up!* I thought. I decided to pretend the previous text message hadn't been sent at all. I texted Grant: *C U @ Two in 30 mins.*

I couldn't change what had happened to my mother. She was forever going to be a bitter woman. That was why no man, not even the ones at the church she went to, wanted to spend time with her. She couldn't let go of her pain. I knew she lived her life trying to do the right things, but she'd made her mistakes, and I wished she'd leave me the hell alone and let me make mine! Angrily, I exhaled and became quiet. This was an argument I was not going to win, and the reality was I needed my mother more than any other person in my life, including my son.

"Fine. I'll have Honey call Alphonso and confirm our meeting, and I'll let you know," Mama said. "If you don't want to go with us, I'll take Ronnie to Los Angeles to meet his dad, and then I'll take him to Disneyland."

I was not amused about my mother's attempt to get me excited about going back to Disneyland. We'd had so much fun when she'd taken me that I still had my Minnie Mouse ears in my bedroom. Ronnie was going to literally do flips when my mother told him they were going on vacation and he'd get to meet his dad and Mickey on the same day.

"Are you done telling me what to do with my life? If so, I have someplace to be."

My mother walked away from the table. "Ronnie, it's time to go," she called. Looking over her shoulder at me, she said, "Baby, you've got to learn to let love . . . love. Take your son with you."

"Fine." Yanking Ronnie's hand, I tugged him straight to my car. I was trying to figure out what my mother had meant when she said, "Learn to let love . . . love."

I texted Grant: *I'm on my way.*

"Ronnie, sweetheart, go tell Grandma to pick you up some undershirts while she's out," I said, sending Ronnie back to my mom. When her door opened, I drove off.

CHAPTER 19

Grant

Texting was not my thing, but Red Velvet loved it. Maybe I'd call or respond to her some other day. Honey and I had made love all night long, and when I got that strange text from Red Velvet, I decided not to show up at Two Restaurant with a stripper who half of the male patrons had probably fucked. What was I thinking, offering to take her to a nice public place? I bypassed the restaurant and drove straight to Honey's house instead. I had enough strange things happening. Plus, I wanted more of my sweet Honey love. We'd had a fucktastic time last night, this morning, both.

En route to Honey's house, I called ahead. "You sure you're up for company again tonight?" I sure hoped so. My dick had got hard off and on all day, whenever I thought about how Honey had me pulling toys out of her pleasure chest. I think we used the whole tube of Sweet 'N Blow.

"I was just about to call and confirm. You know you're flakey. If you're really coming, come on. Hurry up," Honey said. "If you're not here in an hour, don't come tonight."

I didn't want to argue her point, but just because I didn't do what she wanted, when she wanted, did not make me flakey. My comprehension was good and my vocabulary somewhat extensive, but that wasn't even a real word. I refused to spoil our evening. To add a little fun to our sexcapades, I stopped off at Best Buy and repurchased *The Boondocks* series, went to Albertsons and got one pint of Cherry Garcia, then headed to Honey's. That woman made me feel so alive, I felt like I was having an out-of-body experience.

Honey greeted me at the door, dressed in a long, black, sheer lace gown with a split from the center of her tits to the floor, so I could see that her Brazilian wax was fresh. I didn't care who saw us. I knelt in the doorway, before her pussy, then kissed her soft lips.

Bracing her hands on the opened door, Honey spread her legs and sat her pussy on my face. Ducking underneath her legs, I lifted her onto my shoulders, braced her back against the door, and began eating her sweet pussy. I eased her clit between my teeth and sucked her into my mouth.

Honeysuckle oozed onto my tongue. Lowering her to her feet, I unzipped my pants, pulled out my dick, turned Honey so she faced the door, raised her lace gown over her firm ass, then penetrated her nice and slow, so deep my nuts sandwiched between her lips.

"Grant, yes. Fuck me, baby," she moaned. Her body remained motionless, letting me take the lead.

I had no problem with that. I wanted to please Honey every chance I could. "Get on your knees," I told her. I knelt behind her. I grabbed my dick, rubbed my head all over her wet pussy, then glided deep inside of her. Holding her shoulders, I slammed my dick hard against her ass.

We fucked our way onto the porch and damn near into the driveway, like two dogs stuck together. I never wanted to pull out. "Damn. How could I have ever stayed away from this sweet pussy?" I said. "Damn, baby."

Honey reached behind her head, snatched off the ribbon that held her ponytail in place, then reached between her legs, tied her ribbon around my nuts, and pulled me closer to her while she stroked her clit.

"Baby, cum with me," I whispered in her ear. Honey's body trembled. I collapsed on top of her. Watching the sunset fade into night, I kissed Honey's lips. "I think we'd better get inside. Where is everybody? It's awfully quiet."

"All the girls have cars now, so they're out. I think they're at Atlantic Station, shopping, but who cares. What's in the bags?" she asked, closing the front door.

"Damn. I forgot all about those bags," I said, picking them up off the white-marble, million-dollar floor. I loved Honey's flooring so much, I'd decided to do the same at my hotel and condo building downtown. I grabbed two spoons from the kitchen, then followed Honey into her bedroom. I pulled out the DVDs and the ice cream.

"That's why I love you," she said, softly gripping my hand. Honey moved my hand to her pussy and her hand to my dick. "We need to shower."

After fucking outdoors, I knew we had to wash up. I thought she just wanted to feel this big dick again. I got into the shower first and lathered my body. The hot water felt good. Being back in Honey's house with her was where I belonged. Hm, she'd never spent the night at my house. We'd have to change that. As I stepped out of the shower, Honey said, "Leave the water on."

I kissed her, then made my way to the bed and lay down. What in the hell was I doing? I only had a fraction of the information I'd come for. I'd forgotten to ask her about Sunny and to clarify the story behind all the money. Wasn't like she'd offered to bring up the conversation again, either. I had to know more about my Honey love, or else my ass might end up behind bars with Valentino, whoever he was.

Honey's cell phone chimed, interrupting my thoughts. The shower was going, so I imagined she couldn't hear her phone. Walking over to her dresser, I picked up her iPhone. Blocked call. *Why not?* I answered. "Hello," I said.

"Who's this?" a woman asked. Before I answered, she demanded, "Put Lace on the phone."

Okay, this person must've known Honey for a while, because she'd used her real name. I replied, "Lace, is not available. I can give her a message."

Silence followed.

"Hello?" I said, trying to speak low so Honey wouldn't hear me talking.

"Grant Hill, is this you?"

Fuck! How'd she know my name? "Yeah. Who's this?"

"Tiffany Davis. Remember me?"

"Naw, I don't remember you. Help me out."

"Excuse me for being so blunt, but do you remember the cheer-leader who covered your dick with peanut butter and—"

"Strawberry preserves. Goddamn." My mouth hung open for a few seconds. "No way. Is that what you do for a living now? Are you one of Lace's prostitutes?" I had to ask her but couldn't believe I was having this conversation. Was I dreaming?

"Not hardly, sweetheart. I'm an undercover cop, so I arrest guys who solicit for sex. My undercover name is—"

Finishing her sentence, I said, "Sapphire Bleu."

"Now how did you know that? Don't answer that. Can you come to Las Vegas? I'll get you a ticket, and you can stay at my place. I want to see you ASAP."

And I needed to see her, too, to get the truth behind what was hap-pening with my brother, Honey, and that Valentino guy. "I'll make my own reservations. Give me your number." I gave her my cell phone number, then said, "I've seriously got to go," when the shower stopped.

"Grant?" Tiffany whispered.

"Yes?"

"I want you to know, I never forgot the way you respected me back then. It's because of you that I know there are good black men out there. I just haven't found one yet. I want to say thanks."

"I gotta go." Fearing Honey would catch me on her phone, I hung up, tossed her cell phone on the bed, got dressed, and left. There was no way I could make love to Honey again tonight. Maybe a different night. But not tonight.

Cruising out of Honey's driveway, I mumbled, "Goddamn, Tiffany Davis." They said bad luck came in threes, but three outstanding dick suckers in a row? That was all good.

CHAPTER 20

Honey

Too much was enough. What sick-ass game was Grant playing? I was not giving him any satisfaction. I had other things to do, and if I met an interesting man, I was adding him to the top of my to-do list.

Folding three pairs of fitted jeans, three tops, a professional suit, and a few casual things, I packed for my trip to Los Angeles with Red Velvet, her mother, and Ronnie. I glanced around my room, wishing I could dispel Grant's energy. Hopefully, his scent would dissipate before I returned in two days.

Six degrees of separation cut in half. What Sapphire had told me was beginning to bother me, but I had other things to do. I'd visit Sapphire on my way back from L.A. I showered, got dressed, then called Onyx downstairs to take me to pick up Velvet and her family and drive all of us to Hartsfield-Jackson Atlanta International Airport.

Handing Onyx the keys to my car, I said, "You drive."

"You good?" Onyx asked, with concern, as she picked up my suitcase. She put it in the back of my SUV.

"I'm good," I said, staring out the passenger window. I didn't want to look into her eyes. She'd see my sadness. Quietly, I took a few deep breaths. Continuing to stare out the window, I told her, "I'm going to Los Angeles, and I'll be back in a few days. You're in charge. I want a full daily report on everybody. No overnight guests are allowed. And if Grant shows up here, do not let that motherfucker in, you hear me?"

Onyx said, "Everything will be okay. I'm sure he has an explanation. Maybe he had a family emergency and didn't want to alarm you."

"Yeah, right."

"You just handle your business, and I'll make sure everything here is taken care of to your satisfaction." Onyx parked in front of Velvet's house.

Getting out of the car, I wanted to scream. How could I fall for this bullshit-ass nigga? Walking up to the front door, I felt like a private investigator instead of the president of my own company. I was supposed to open the doors to my business today. Best not to. I was so pissed off with Grant, my clients would've been counseling and consoling me. I was glad I was going across country to L.A. today. I needed to occupy my mind with something productive and get far away from Grant before I seriously hurt him.

I rang Velvet's mother's doorbell.

An older woman opened the door, then called out, "Ronnie, Velvet, let's go. Honey is here."

This woman actually had faith that I could successfully arrange for her daughter and grandson to meet this Alphonso guy. I sure hoped she was right. Onyx helped them put their bags in the back of my SUV.

"You," Velvet said, standing in front of me. "I should've known. That's how my mother found out what went down at the club."

"Velvet, get in the car," Velvet's mother said. "Honey didn't tell me anything. Mrs. Taylor did."

Stch. "Whatever. I'll be glad when all of this is over. And I need to stop by and see my agent while we're in L.A.," Velvet said, getting in the car. "Ronnie, get in and move over. Sit in the middle. Grandma's going to sit on the other side of you." Velvet fastened his seatbelt. "I hope this trip satisfies everybody so I never have to do this again."

"Let me speak to you for a moment," I said to Velvet's mother, who was standing outside the car. We walked a few feet away so no one could overhear our conversation.

"What? Is something wrong?" she asked.

"No, no. Before we leave, I just want to make certain you fully understand this trip may not produce the outcome you expect," I told her. 'Cause I didn't want her looking wide-eyed at me if shit didn't go the way she'd expected.

"Yeah. Yeah, I know. But we have to try. Right? For Ronnie?"

"Whatever you want to do is right. Right?" I said, reaching into my purse. I handed her the envelope I'd received with Velvet's name on it. "Open it."

"What is it?" she asked quizzically, staring into my eyes.

"You won't know unless you open it. Whatever is inside will determine how we approach Ronnie's father." If Alphonso had sent the seventy-two thousand dollars, everything was good. If not, he was going to wish he had.

"Shouldn't Velvet be opening this? It is addressed to her."

"I don't want Velvet to be disappointed if it's not what we expect. If she never knows, then she can't be. Go on. Open it. We've gotta go. Please," I said, looking at the envelope, anxious to find out if my efforts had been successful.

Sliding her finger inside a hole on the side of the envelope, she carefully tore the seal. She removed the contents. "Oh my God, dear Jesus," she cried, stumbling into me.

"What is it? What?" I asked, reaching for the papers she was waving. I read the first few lines of Alphonso's letter.

Stay the fuck away from me and my wife. Velvet is lying. I never touched her. There's no way Ronnie can possibly be my son. I feel sorry for her. . . .

"Could this be true?" I asked Velvet's mother. "You think she made this up?"

A person's first reaction was usually the real one. I believed Velvet. What I didn't want was to get to L.A., confront this man, then have Velvet's mother make me look like a damn fool, the way Grant had last night. In my line of work, many people got a bullet in the head for taking on a fight that wasn't theirs.

"You still want to go? It's not too late to change your mind if you're unsure," I said.

"Velvet wouldn't lie about something like this. I say we go," she answered.

Handing the letter and check back to her, I said, "Go put this inside. And whatever you do, don't tell Velvet or Ronnie about this check until we return."

Alphonso was trying to buy his way out of something. He might not have been sure about Ronnie being his son. Neither was I. But the thing Alphonso knew for sure was he'd raped Velvet. That was why he'd sent the check for seventy-two thousand dollars. There was more to this situation; I still didn't know the real reason he'd tried to bully us into not coming. I got in the passenger seat and buckled up.

"Where's Grandma going?" asked Ronnie.

"We're not leaving your grandma. She forgot something," I said, looking in the rearview mirror at Ronnie.

"Grandma never forgets," Ronnie said. "Huh, Mommy?"

Velvet seemed preoccupied. She was working her thumbs like crazy, sending text messages. "Who are you texting like that?" I asked her. "Girl, you're working them thumbs into a frenzy."

"Yea! Grandma's here. Let's go," Ronnie said cheerfully. "I'm going to Disneyland."

Laughing into her Sidekick, Velvet said, "You are so stupid." Then she typed some more. "Oh, I'm sorry." She chuckled. "Just this guy I met the other day. G seems different. But they all do when I first meet 'em. He wants to make up for standing me up yesterday. He's taking me out to dinner when I get back. Maybe if you're not busy, Honey, you can join us and give me your take on him. I really like this one."

I was the wrong person for Velvet to ask an opinion from. What was Grant's problem? Damn, he was Benito's brother. Both of those bastards were missing a few links.

"Well, he probably is. Different, that is. Just make sure he's not you know what," Velvet's mother said.

I kept quiet and tried to map in my head how to proceed when we got to L.A. If what we had read was true, our visit could be disastrous.

CHAPTER 21

Valentino

Incarceration was the absolute worst kind of motherfuckin' confinement for men, not women. Women could cope better with their feelings and shit. They were born that way. For men, being locked up was an emotional fuck. In or out of jail, women enjoyed talking about their problems, but men didn't give a fuck about hearing another nigga's headaches, especially if he was bitching about being in love.

Man, shut the fuck up, handle yours, and keep your bitch-ass problems to yourself, or get your ass kicked or beat down . . . That was how men were raised, not by their parents but by niggas on the street. Niggas to me didn't come in colors—black, white, or other. A nigga was any ig'nant motherfucker who couldn't handle his women, his money, or his business. Like that bitch Benito. Hadn't heard from his ass since I'd been put in this hellhole. I should've been his priority. Let me find out that punk went back to Lace, with his tail tucked between his nuts, and I'd kill him myself. Women weren't good for much. The shit they called spending quality time was a waste of a man's time.

Women liked cuddling. A real man didn't give a damn about holding no bitch before or after he'd cum. Women looked forward to shopping; men hated that sissy-ass bullshit. I'd slash my wrist before tagging along with some bitch to the mall, holding her fuckin' bags.

So let me get bitches right. I was supposed to spend my money on them and be their fuckin' gofer? No way.

What really pissed me off was the women who craved monogamy and voluntarily committed themselves to celibacy. I needed a ride-or-die bitch who was willing to turn tricks to fast-forward my mission of regaining my hundred-million-dollar status. Men just wanted to fuck as many bitches as possible or get paid to let another nigga fuck his bitches. Love the game or hate it, that was the real motherfuckin' deal. I could find a straight-up whore or a woman who was one paycheck away from prostitution on every, I meant every, damn corner of the world.

The animalistic behavior niggas exhibited behind bars—they'd shank an Italian, poison a Muslim, put a hit out on a snitch, start territorial gang wars to demand respect, stick a dick in any hole, including another man's asshole, to bust a nut—was fucking me up. I'd learned you never said what the fuck you wouldn't do to survive until you'd been in compromising positions. I got tired of beating my shit two, three times a day. That was right. I did what I had to.

"Bend your punk ass over, and spread your motherfuckin' ass," I said to the new inmate.

My cell mate had gotten transferred to the hospital. He was lucky I didn't have him killed for watching me jack off every morning before taking my piss. Turned out he'd made several enemies. So I'd chilled and let someone else do additional time for cutting his throat. My intent was to get out on bail. Receiving that letter from Summer was my ticket. The letter I wrote telling her what she had to do was going out in today's mail.

I considered myself lucky to have a first timer in my cell. Fucking him first gave me less of a chance of contracting HIV or some other sexually transmitted disease. It didn't make no fuckin' sense that these trick-ass guards didn't pass out condoms when they knew what we were doing and sometimes watched us shit packing. That punk-bitch guard just stood in the shadows outside my cell. I guessed he'd seen so many rapes while working here that he knew he'd have to place 98 percent of the inmates in solitary confinement to prevent us from fucking or getting fucked.

I swore I'd never do this, but a nigga was tired of waking up under a pitched tent, with his big-ass dick hard as cement. Gurgling up a chunk of spit, I let it drop dead on his asshole, then slid my dick all the way in. Imagining I was making love to Summer, I ignored him. He was yelling like a bitch.

"Shut the fuck up," I said, forcing the cum from my nuts. "Damn!" I didn't want this homo shit to last any longer than it had to. I wasn't gay, 'cause I'd never been penetrated.

At least there was a code of ethics that meant this kind of shit stayed inside the prison. Once I was free, never again would I fuck a man. I didn't trust these niggas sucking my dick. I knew a few guys had, ha! yah!, gotten their shit bitten straight the fuck off alligator and snapping turtle style.

The second after I finished cuming, I was sick to my damn stomach and started throwing up all over his back. Pushing him into the wall, I became angry with that nigga, angry at myself, knowing I was straight. He'd seemed straight, too, until I'd taken his manhood. I should've had the willpower to suppress my sexual urges.

Lying on my top bunk, I clamped my hands behind my head, then stared at the ceiling. Felt like that cement motherfucker was closing in on me one inch at a time. I couldn't breathe. Day started feeling like night, and night like day.

"I've got to get the fuck up outta here before I go fifty-one fifty," I muttered. The outside world had no idea how many niggas committed suicide or homicide in this bitch. Not me. I refused to go out either way.

Instincts were straight weird. The phone number on that blue sticky I'd received, I'd never called. Obviously, it was some anonymous trick trying to play me . . . but who? Why? They probably thought that because I was confined, they had the upper hand. I'd find them after I got outta here, and if their intentions were ill, I'd kill them. With so much shit on my mind, I lay awake for hours, until the sun crept through the window and the lights came on.

Laughing, the eye-spy, bitch-ass guard who had watched me earlier stood outside my cell and said, "Number two-one-three-six-five-four, your balls, I mean your bail, has been posted."

"Man, that shit ain't funny. Stop fucking with me," I said. *Punk ass!*

Pulling out his handcuffs, he unlocked the door. "You know the routine. Get dressed, then put your hands behind your back," he instructed.

Slipping into my jumpsuit, I realized I needed to wash my dick, but if he was telling the truth, I could have my dick, ass, and balls in a hot tub of water before sunset. I turned away from him, put my hands behind my back, then waited for him to secure the cuffs. After we stepped out, he locked the cell. I wanted to say bye to my cell mate but couldn't look him in his eyes. *Fuck it.* What was done couldn't be undone. Maybe when he got out, he'd learn to work for himself, instead of selling some other niggas crack.

I didn't believe this guard. Something underhanded was about to go down. Constantly checking my surroundings, I put one foot in front of the other, heel to toe "Who bailed me out?"

"You'll find out soon enough. Relax. You're going home. For a short while, until your hearing. So don't fuck up, or you'll be back in here before your hearing." Shaking his head, the guard laughed. "Man, you should've saved that nut. Why you break down like that, Valentino man?"

It felt great. Not busting the nut. Hearing him call me by my name. I wasn't no fucking number anymore? I was a free man? There wasn't a reason to answer him, but I asked, "Why you didn't stop me instead of watching?"

The guard answered, "The best advice I can give you is to make sure you get tested before fucking anybody else, male or female."

What? "I ain't gay, man. You know something I don't?" I asked, staring at him. "You saw me. I was in and out in less than five minutes."

The guard shook his head. "Don't matter. That shit happened for a reason. And too many black men leave here infected and pass that shit along to women. Get checked. If not for yourself, for her. The beautiful woman waiting out there for you."

Beautiful. I smiled, knowing that could only be one woman. The one I should've married. Processing out, I thought they were going to give me the clothes I was arrested in, but I ended up with a fresh pair of black slacks, new shoes, and a black button-down shirt that fit perfectly. I took the fastest shower ever before putting on my new clothes. After soaping up the crack of my ass and my private parts, I rinsed off, got dressed, signed my papers, and got the hell up out of there. I yelled, "Valentino James ain't never coming back up in this bitch!"

As I exited the gate, my heart stopped. I stood still. What was happening to me? I was really outside. No bars. No handcuffs. Damn. Walking toward the parking lot, I saw a platinum Bentley first. Then I saw her red stilettos, her bare legs, the hem of a red, flaring dress, and her face, beaming brighter than the sun.

Summer ran to me, and I knew she was the one. Her hair danced in the wind. She jumped in my arms, wrapped her thighs around my waist. The rosy scent of her perfume made me forget for a moment where I was. What had I done to deserve Summer? That shit felt ridiculous. On the one hand, I was the happiest motherfucker. On the other, I was fucked up. Was that her car? Summer was the image of her sister, Sunny. Summer was simple sexy, and Sunny had been spicy sexy. But Sunny was dead, and her death wasn't my fault. I had to make certain I didn't get convicted of a crime I didn't commit. Every nigga in prison was innocent if you let them tell their stories, but my shit was real. Sunny had pulled the trigger and put a bullet in her own head. Not me.

Spinning with my woman in my arms, I whispered, "Hey, baby." Hugging Summer tight, I stood still. When she lowered her feet to the gravel, I stepped back, placing my hand on her stomach. "You don't look pregnant at all, baby."

"Well, I am. I'll show you the ultrasound when we get home. Anthony, I love you so much."

A tear fell from her eye. Softly, I kissed it away. "I love you, too, baby."

"When I found out where they'd transferred you, we had to come and get you out."

"We?" I asked, trying to see through the tinted windows of the Bentley.

"Yes, we. I brought Anthony with me."

Raising my eyebrows, I sought confirmation. "My little man, Anthony?"

"Yeah, silly. Our son."

"Let's get the fu . . . I mean the hell away from here." I had to work on not cursing so much. Summer always made me want to be a better man. There was something sweet, innocent, and pure about her intentions. I never had to wonder if she was plotting against me. We got in the car.

"Hey, Daddy," Anthony said, tugging on my shoulder.

"Hey, man. What's up? You good?" I replied.

Fuck. I was so happy to get out, I'd forgotten my family's pictures. But my son seriously looked dead-on like me. Wavy black hair, light complexion, light brown eyes.

"Yes, sir. I'm doing well," Anthony answered cheerfully.

A puff of air exited my nostrils. *Damn.* My parents had raised me the same "yes, ma'am, no, sir" way. I was gonna do right by my seed. Summer shouldn't have to raise him by herself. "Where're we going?" I asked Summer.

Keeping her eyes on the highway, she answered, "Well, you have to stay close until your hearing, if you know what I mean, so we're going to my place until the charges are dropped and the case is closed. Then we're moving far away from Vegas. Somewhere in the south, where we can buy a bigger house, give birth to these two babies in my stomach, provide a safe environment for Anthony, go to church every Sunday, and settle down."

Settle what? Buy what? Have who? Go where? What the hell? What if those twins weren't mine? Why didn't she throw in a wedding date, too, while she was plotting a nigga's life?

"They have to drop them. You're no good to us being locked up, and nothing can bring my sister back," she added.

Pointing, I said, "Take this exit by In-N-Out Burger. I need to stretch my legs for a moment. Shit is happening too damn fast."

Summer disobeyed me. She bypassed the exit.

I stared at her, then yelled, "What? Are you deaf! Bitch, take this next exit!"

"Stop yelling at my mommy!" Anthony cried, covering his face.

Summer's hands trembled. Her voice quivered. "I never take that exit. That's where my dad and I pulled over the night Sunny was killed. I knew she was dead, because I felt like I'd been shot in the head, too. I wasn't ignoring you. And please don't you ever call me the B word again."

A stream of tears rolled down her beautiful face. What the fuck was I doing? "Baby, I'm sorry. Keep going," I said.

The next half hour I gazed out the window, happy that thanks to Summer, I was free. She was right. I shouldn't have called her a bitch. Was that bitch threatening me on the under? I watched cars pass us on the highway. Summer exited in Henderson, drove into one of those new developments, and pressed the garage button. The garage door lifted. Inside the garage were a new luxury sports utility vehicle and a new, expensive four-door sedan. I walked into the house. Everything was so new and, I swear, so perfect that it looked like nobody lived there. Standing in the living room, I realized it wasn't the money, the cars, the house, or Summer that excited me. To the core of my existence, till the day I'd die, Valentino James was a pimp. I couldn't wait to hit the Strip tonight. *Maybe I should lay low for a while,* I thought.

"Anthony, go play in your room. Sweetheart, Mommy needs to talk to Daddy."

"Yes, Mommy," Anthony said, running upstairs.

I followed Summer upstairs to her bedroom. A king-sized bed, surrounded by dressers, mirrors, and nightstands, was decorated in all white.

"I'ma take a bath," I said, closing the bathroom door. Taking off the clothes Summer had bought, I filled the tub, stepped in, and relaxed. A nigga was so glad to let his nuts float for an hour. Enjoying the sunshine on my face, I scrubbed my dick a million times over, or so it seemed, trying to get rid of any disease. That bitch-ass guard had me paranoid.

After drying off, I wrapped a fresh towel around my waist and joined Summer in the bed. She cuddled me from behind. Her breasts, her nipples, her stomach, and her pussy hairs felt amazing against my back, spine, and ass. Her thighs caressed mine. Her knees touched the back of mine. Her legs overlapped mine. Her toes fondled mine.

I'd done pretty good suppressing my sexual urges until Summer caressed my dick, then whispered in my ear, "Anthony Valentino James, make love to me," before kissing my earlobe.

Instantly, my dick got hard as a fucking rocket. "You got a condom?" I asked, praying she did.

"Do we need one?" she asked.

Thinking about the babies growing inside of Summer, the word *yes*, was on the tip of my tongue, but my throbbing dick answered, "No, we don't."

CHAPTER 22

Sapphire

I was excited about a man. When was the last time that had happened?

Nervous, I stood near the luggage carousel closest to Starbucks, waiting for Grant. Peeping in the window, at my reflection, I wondered if my hair looked good. Spreading my fingers, I inspected my natural nails. I couldn't risk wearing acrylic or gel nails and having one to break as I pulled out my gun to shoot somebody. My French manicure was immaculate.

Did I wear the right dress? I covered up my cleavage. I didn't want his second impression of me to be the same as the first. I couldn't believe, here I was, acting like a giddy teenager in love, when I had seen this man only once, hadn't seen him in more than ten years, and had never been in love. Maybe he could be my first.

My cell phone rang. Eagerly, I looked at the caller ID. This would be a quickie.

"Hello," I said, listening for my associate's update.

"Hey, springtime came early. Yesterday to be exact," she said.

"Peace," I said before ending the call.

I'd gotten so excited about Grant, I had forgotten I was supposed to visit Summer. I hadn't made time. Guess I'd underestimated her ability or the system's capability to process Valentino out. I had to find time to get to Valentino before he made time to get to me.

Wringing my palms, I shifted my weight from one leg to the other, wishing I could bum a cigarette. I wasn't a smoker. I had to calm down. Inside I was jittery. My nerves were bad. "Okay. I'll walk around the carousel a few times. Damn. I still want to smoke," I said aloud. What if he smelled nicotine on my breath and hated kissing smokers? Just about everybody in Vegas smoked something. Why shouldn't I?

My cell phone rang again. Happily, I cheered, "He's finally here." Checking the caller ID, I saw it was Girl Six. Damn. Her timing was bad. "Hey, make it quick," I said, looking into the crowd for Grant. "You made it in safely?"

"Yeah, but I saw Lace, two women, and a little boy boarding a plane to Los Angeles. They were in the same terminal with me."

"Are you smoking what I should be smoking? Are you sure? That red-eye flight has you jet-lagged. Lace with a little boy? That doesn't sound right. Your driver should be waiting for you when you exit the terminal. He'll be in front of the rental car area, holding a sign with your name on it. Call me back when you get to Lace's house." I quickly ended the call. I didn't want Grant's call to bypass the ringer of this possessed cell phone and go straight to voice mail. Technology these days had all kinds of quirks the manufacturers hadn't figured out how to resolve. Sometimes the malfunctions, like dropped calls, worked to my advantage.

"Wait a minute," I said out loud. Girl Six got in to Atlanta yesterday, not today. What took her so long to call me? Something was up. I'd get back with her later.

A half hour had passed since Grant's flight had landed. I was beginning to wonder if Grant had changed his mind. Couldn't say I'd blame him. Wasn't like his visiting me was business. For me, it was all pleasure. If he hadn't answered Lace's phone, eventually I would've contacted him. I'd checked his background from my office computer. There were several Grant Hills, but only one was twenty-eight and extremely wealthy. His GH Property Management and Development business license and portfolio were impressive. That had to be him. I imagined Lace fucked only the best. I didn't care what she'd done sexually with Grant. I had no loyalty to her.

I'd changed my linen, cleaned my entire house, and freshened up the guest bedroom, and I'd cooked a delicious seafood pasta in Alfredo sauce, with sun-dried tomatoes, pesto, and a few capers. My melt-in-your-mouth garlic bread was ready to go in my oven, which was already preheated to 350 degrees. It had been a long time since I'd invited a man over for more than a meal, and I found that having a hot, home-cooked dinner on the stove increased a man's appetite for sex.

Searching the crowd for Grant, I couldn't believe . . . What the hell? Was that who I . . . I moved closer, praying he didn't turn around before I made certain my eyes weren't deceiving me. Standing three feet behind him, I pulled out my handcuffs, then said, "Looking for someone?"

His head jerked in my direction; his body froze. "Aw, shit. I'm not who you think I am," he exclaimed. "Uh, I'm a hologram. I mean, I'm a ventriloquist. I can explain." He started moving his hand like a talking puppet, trying to speak without moving his lips. "I had to come back. In fact, I was looking for you. There you are." He started backing away.

I moved closer, listening to his act. I wanted to bust out laughing, but I didn't want to encourage him.

He said, "You know, Lace has got your money. And I can help you get it back, 'cause my brother is crazy in love with her. And—"

"And shut the hell up!" That "in love" shit pissed me off. Flipping open my handcuffs, I said, "No need to explain anything to me. Obviously, you thought I was kidding. Turn around. You're under arrest." I snapped on the cuffs.

"Ow! That's too tight," he said seriously. "I wasn't even supposed to be here. I was headed to Arizona, and I got confused. The Amtrak, I mean Greyhound, you know, the bus stop outside. I thought I got off in Scottsdale. I was going to the spa. Please, lady, that's too tight."

I ignored his protests. "You have the right to remain silent." I glanced around for Grant, but no luck.

"What am I under arrest for? I'm not even on probation," Benito said, staring off into the crowd, hoping someone would hear and help him. "I'ma have your badge taken away. Oh, shit. You don't have your gun on you, do you? You don't own this city."

That was where he was right. I didn't own the city. I owned the entire fucking state and everyone who crossed the state line. I could justify arresting any person in Nevada, including those cyber-bully, no-home-training, wanna-hide-behind-a-computer minors threatening their peers over the Internet.

That shit had gotten out of control. Parents needed to investigate every little thing their children did. I was outraged that a twelve-year-old had hung herself because another twelve-year-old had instant messaged her, demanding that the girl commit suicide. Now the offender had to do time in juvenile. They should've tried her as an adult. Maybe I wouldn't have any kids for Grant. Raising children these days was worse than doing twenty-four-hour surveillance.

Benito's neck kept snapping left to right.

"Who you looking for?" I asked him, turning him so he faced me.

"Valentino," he answered. "Can you take these things off of me? I didn't do nothing."

"Oh, you looking for Valentino James? I'll show you where he's at. You can be his cell mate." I was testing him to see how much he knew.

Benito laughed at me. "You don't know everything?"

I did not have time to entertain this idiot. When I did find Valentino, Valentino was gonna be locked up so long, Benito might have to pay him a conjugal visit. Maybe a guardian angel had sent me here not to meet Grant, but to catch this fool. Obviously, he hadn't taken me seriously when I'd let him go a month ago. I could detain Benito and wait for Grant, or I could take this hysterical hyena in and miss out on the best sex of my life. Or I could let Benito go with a warning. What if Grant had gotten fat? Or what if he'd let himself go and had one of those beer guts that hung over the belt?

"I see you're not the only one who doesn't like my brother," said a voice behind me.

I turned around, and my world stood still. What cloud did this Mandingo god fall from? "Grant?"

"Tiffany?" Grant said, with the brightest smile.

"Tiffany? Who's Tiffany? That ain't no Tiffany," Benito said. "That's Officer Sapphire Bleu. Man, you'd better not let her handcuff you, I'm telling you. How do you two know each other, anyway?" Benito babbled on. Neither of us paid any attention to him.

Damn. Grant was fine! "Is he really your brother?" I asked, staring at Grant's dick. I knew I was being rude, but I couldn't help myself, Lord, Jesus!

Smiling, Grant shook his head, then said, "No blood relation, but I'd be lying if I said he's not my brother."

"What do you think I should do with him?" I asked. For all I knew, Benito could've been halfway back to where he'd come from. I refused to take my eyes off of Grant.

"You can start by taking off these tight-ass handcuffs. You women have a problem trying to tie a good-looking brotha like me down." Benito started singing. "We shall overcome some day-ay-ay-ay. Oh, oh, oh." With each *oh*, he got louder. "Deep in my heart!"

Grant started laughing. "Please, spare us. Let him go. He's only harmful to himself."

I didn't have time to debate the issue. I unlocked the handcuffs. "It would behoove you to get back on Amtrak or Greyhound and get out of Nevada," I told Benito. "If I see you again, your brother won't be able to save your ass."

"Be who?" Benito said, rubbing his wrist. He held out his hand. "Thanks, bro. You heard what she said. I used all my money coming here. Can I get another five hundred? Mom wouldn't want me in jail."

Grant reached into his pocket and handed Benito five one-hundred-dollar bills. "Now you have no excuses," he said.

Skipping away and fanning the money in the air, Benito didn't look back.

Grant smiled, took a step back, and checked me out. "Well, Tiffany Davis, how are you? I really don't need to ask that question. You've taken excellent care of yourself. I would've never guessed, as pretty as you are, that you're a cop. I see you don't mind using those cuffs, either."

There was so much I wanted to say. Speechless, I stood staring in amazement. If anyone had told me I was going to reunite with this man, I would've arrested them on the spot for lying to an officer. "You know you look better than good," I said, trying to maintain my composure. "Let's get you to my place."

"I have a room at the Wynn," Grant said.

"And?" I'd already told him where he was going.

Thank God the ride was short. I parked in my garage. Opening the door, Grant followed his nose to the kitchen. "Wow. You can cook, too. That was a long flight, and I'm famished."

"I figured you would be. You can put your bags in my room. The bedroom to the right. I'll fix you a plate."

I watched his ass until it disappeared out of my sight. After placing the garlic bread in the oven, I warmed the pasta. It wasn't long before we were breaking bread and talking like we'd known each other for years.

"How do you know Lace?" I asked him, watching him eat and wishing like hell I was a shrimp or scallop.

"I didn't fly all this way to be interrogated. You first."

"Okay, I knew of her before I actually met her. I could've arrested her for pimping, pandering, and for killing my best friend, Sunny, but I spared her because she seemed a lot like me. We weren't hard because we wanted to be. Men made us this way."

"Okay," Grant said, biting into the garlic bread. "Oh, this is so good. Thanks."

"You're welcome." *Now get to the point of how you know her,* I thought.

"I've heard Honey's story. That's what I call her. She didn't kill Sunny Day. Now what's your real reason for giving her fifty million dollars and keeping her involved in this? I want to help clear Honey's name. Seems like you want to have everyone around you on a short leash."

Clear her name. I started laughing like Benito was laughing earlier. Grant's fine ass was now on a shorter leash. He just didn't know it yet. *Clear her name. Get the fuck outta here.* Officer Sapphire was runnin' this, not Grant.

CHAPTER 23

Honey

Spending time with Ronnie made me want to have children. I started missing Grant all over again. Right before the announcement of our flight's departure to Los Angeles, I texted him. *Miss you. Don't know what happened last night. Care to explain?* I touched SEND, then powered off my iPhone.

Ronnie was so sweet and easy to please. He was the kind of child I'd clone if I could. Flying first class, he sat next to his mother on one side of the aisle, and I sat in the aisle seat across from them, with Velvet's mom next to me in the window seat.

During our short time together, Ronnie had become adultlike. He watched his mother while Velvet went to sleep on takeoff. Ronnie's love and happiness were genuine. I watched him bounce up and down each time we experienced turbulence. He was smiling, laughing, and singing out loud.

At one point, his little mouth opened wide, he clapped his hands hard, and then he launched into song. "Woke up this morning with my mind stayed on spirit. Walking and talking with my mind stayed on spirit. All day long I keep my mind stayed on spirit. Hallelu, hallelu, halleluuuu-jah." Then he said, "Mommy, wake up and sing with me." He grabbed Velvet's hands, making her clap.

Pulling away, Velvet said, "No, baby. Mommy's tired. You go ahead."

Velvet seemed lost without her Sidekick to text message G or anyone else.

Frowning back at the people seated around us in first class, I clapped along with Ronnie. "Who taught him that song?" I asked Velvet's mother. "Isn't that a bit too old school for such a young child?" The overstuffed business shirt–wearing men seated behind us in the other eight seats, rattling their newspapers, could have used some spirit. I ignored them.

"My mom taught him," Velvet mumbled. "She sings that song religiously each morning, and he hears it again on Sundays at one of those scientology churches my mother takes him to. Are we almost there yet?" She leaned her head against the window and dozed back off.

Church? Hm. That was a place I'd never been. "Do you go, too?" I asked Velvet.

Her mother answered, "She used to, but not anymore."

Velvet was sound asleep and Ronnie, too, now. Me, I never slept in public places. I was happy to engage Velvet's mother in conversation. She seemed wise, and I bet she had one incredible story she could tell. "Have you ever been in love?" I asked her, hoping she could help me understand why I was still in love with Grant when I knew I could offer no logical explanation.

"Hm, in love? I don't think so. If he loved me, he would've never left me for another woman."

A man leaving didn't mean he didn't love the one he left. "You think he left because he stopped loving you, or do you think he loved her more than he loved you?" I asked as respectfully as I could.

"Both, and you can throw in convenience, too. Whatever he wanted she did. Not me. I used to, but all that cooking, cleaning, and taking Velvet everywhere I had to go got old. He wasn't her father, and he acted like she wasn't his child. Before we were married, that seemed okay, but after we got married, it wasn't, but I still couldn't leave him. I didn't want to be alone, on my own again, struggling financially. That's why it hurts me to see my baby work so hard. I help her all the time, but I've raised her. I don't want to raise Ronnie, too." She stared out the window.

"Hm, well, Ronnie is blessed to have you for his grandmother. You did an excellent job raising Velvet. She's a wonderful woman."

Velvet's mother shot me a look that said, "I'm not so sure about that."

Finally, after five hours in flight, we landed at LAX. Now the real journey was about to begin. We headed to the baggage claim. Ronnie's suitcase came first, then mine, and then Velvet's and her mom's. I went to pick up the rental car and then met them curbside at terminal one.

After I programmed the address Alphonso had given me into my iPhone, we were in transit to Lincoln Heights. The neighborhood was rather quiet for a sunny afternoon. Parking in front of Alphonso's home, I checked our location twice, matching the address on my paper to the one on the house.

"Who lives here?" Ronnie asked.

Velvet was quiet. I guessed G wasn't returning her text messages. Funny how a man could easily create mood swings in a woman. One phone call and she was happy. No contact and she got upset. If a man started out unpredictable, he'd be that way forever. Damn, she probably wasn't tripping on G at all. Alphonso was the bastard that had raped her, and she was on this trip because of her mother.

"Let me see if this is the right place. Y'all wait in the car," I said, then walked up the stairs to the front door. Unexpectedly, my legs got weak. I was remembering the day I'd walked up the stairs of my house in my hometown of Flagstaff, Arizona, hoping my father would be happy to see me. He wasn't. I hadn't seen my father, my mother, or my mother's trifling-ass husband since my sister's funeral.

Before I rang the bell, a tall, heavyset man opened the door. "We don't accept solicitations," he said, eyeing me up and down. "You don't look like any Jehovah's Witness I've seen. Damn, girl, you look good."

Already he had it twisted. I was a woman, not a girl. Glancing at his first name on the tag pinned to his transit department uniform, I said, "Hi, I'm Honey Thomas. We brought your son Ronnie to meet you." I moved to my right and pretended to let him look at the parked car, but I was trying to peep through the cracked door.

He stepped outside of his house, closing the door behind him. He grunted, "Didn't you get my letter?" Grinding his teeth, he stared at the car. "I told you I didn't want that lying bitch coming to my house, and I don't want to meet her son. He's not mine. I'm done with this bullshit."

"Then you won't mind consenting to a paternity test while you're behind bars serving time for rape, will you?"

The door to the house opened, and a woman came out and stood beside him. "Alphonso, who in the world is this woman?" she asked, looking up at him.

"She has the wrong address," he said, deepening his voice.

Extending my hand to her, I said, "Hi. I'm—"

"What's all this chatting about?" Velvet's mom said as she walked up the stairs with her grandson. "Alphonso, this is your son, Ronnie. Ronnie, say hello to your father."

"Wait, wait, wait, wait. Hold up one fuckin' minute," the woman said. "*This* is why your ass kept peeking out the fucking window. You thought I'd be at work today. You had these people show up on my doorstep with an illegitimate child? I can't take any more." She shook her head. "Is he yours? You'd better open your damn mouth and answer me, 'cause if he is, you can go wherever the hell he's going."

The woman disappeared inside.

"See what the fuck you've done?" Alphonso said, raising his voice. "I told you bitches not to come here."

I looked at Ronnie, then back at Alphonso. "No, I don't. But I see what you've done. Do you have any idea how what you've done has ruined all of these people's lives?" I said, pointing toward the car. "Especially hers."

The woman returned with an armful of men's cotton boxer briefs. Bypassing us all, she marched across the lawn and threw the underwear in the middle of the street. She stomped her way back into the house, and Alphonso followed her. "Baby, please," he pleaded. "You're embarrassing me."

Quickly, I stepped inside the house before the door closed. Ronnie and his grandmother were right behind me. We stood in the living room, listening to them argue. I was surprised they didn't put us out, but Alphonso was too busy trying to cover up his shit.

"Baby, please, my ass. Alphonso Allen, as sure as I'm your soon-to-be ex-wife, I will hurt you if this boy is yours," yelled the woman. "How old is he? Six?"

"No, ma'am," Ronnie said, blinking away his tears. "I'm five. Why are you so angry at my daddy? Are you mad at me, too?"

Children had a way of calming the most enraged adult.

Placing her hand over her heart, the woman said, "Everybody sit, and, Alphonso, you be quiet. I want to know exactly why y'all came here today. Start from the beginning, and explain it to me like I'm his age." She pointed to Ronnie.

Opening the front door, I motioned for Velvet to get out of the car, but she wouldn't. "I'll be right back," I said, going to get her.

Velvet opened the car door. "I don't want to go in his house. I can't do it. Just make sure nothing happens to my mom or my son, or else I will be in there all over his rapist ass," she said, closing the car door.

I went back inside and stood by the door, with Ronnie, just in case some shit broke out. If it did, I could push him out of the house.

The woman calmly said, "Child, what's your name?"

"My name is Ronnie. Ronnie Allen."

"Alphonso, you care to explain how this child is yours?" the woman said, patting her foot.

What a fucked-up way for a kid to have to meet his dad. Next time I decided to help someone find their father, I sure wasn't listening to the grandmother unless she was the legal guardian. I felt sorry for Ronnie and Velvet. Velvet's mother seemed quite content as she eagerly awaited Alphonso's response. I looked at the picture above the mantel, and my eyes froze. The face looked familiar.

"I don't think he's mine," Alphonso said quietly.

"Think or know? Which one is it, dammit?" his wife demanded.

Alphonso grimaced. "Well, he—"

"Oh, my gosh," I said, not realizing I'd spoken out loud.

"What? You know her?" the woman asked. Her tone went from pissed to hopeful. "Do you? Do you know her?"

"No, I don't think so," I said. The girl looked familiar, but I wasn't sure. We were in deep enough already. We didn't need more drama.

"Think or know?" The woman pressed me for an answer.

"What's her name?" I asked.

"Tiffany Davis," said the woman.

"Then, no, I don't know her. She just looks a lot like someone I know," I replied.

Velvet's mother said, "Ronnie, go get in the car with your mother, sweetheart."

Squinting at Velvet's mother, I tightened my lips, signaling her to keep quiet. I opened the door and watched Ronnie run to the car. Velvet opened the car door, then stared at the front door. I closed the front door to indicate we weren't done talking.

The woman's eyes shifted to the corner, and she stared at Alphonso. Then she looked at me. "Well, if you showed up at my front door, claiming my husband is this kid's father, then maybe you can help me find my baby," she said, crying.

Easing toward her, I kept my hand on my purse. Then I said, "I can help you. If you want."

"That's an old picture of Tiffany. She's thirty now. Here. Take this picture of her," the woman said sadly, handing me a flyer from the stack of newspapers piled against the wall. "Oh, let me write my other cell number on there just in case."

Why anyone needed more than one cell phone number was beyond me.

My world couldn't possibly get any smaller if the girl on the flyer was Sapphire Bleu. Naw, couldn't be. Could it?

Handing the woman my business card, I glanced at Alphonso. The eerie look on his face sent chills through me, which Velvet's mother must've felt, too.

It was time for us to leave. I offered a closing statement. "Mr. and Mrs. Allen, we don't want to impose on you any longer. We're in town for a few days, and we'd like to arrange supervised time for Ronnie to spend with his father. Oh, and thanks for the seventy-two thousand dollars in back child—"

"What the fuck did you just say?" the woman yelled. Her neck must've done a 360-degree turn. "How much? What? Alphonso Allen, your broke ass don't have that kind of . . ." Picking up the phone, she pressed a few buttons. She pressed a few more. "Here I was believing the bank made a mistake, and you took the money. That's what I get for opening a joint account with you, you bastard! You know I struggled to save that money. Now how am I supposed to pay a reward if someone finds Tiffany?"

A reward? Hm.

The telephone that was in her hands landed against Alphonso's forehead. *Damn, she's good.* I wanted to throw something at his sorry ass, too.

Alphonso bit his lip, then rubbed his head. Exhaling, he swallowed hard, then said, "This shit ain't my fuckin' fault! What the fuck you hit me for?"

Velvet's mother walked up to Alphonso. What the hell was she doing? Trying to get all of us killed? I wasn't sure if I should walk up to him. Nah. I stayed back, holding my purse closer. I couldn't bring my gun with me on this trip, but I had a piece of steel the size and shape of a hot dog, and if I hit that big-ass motherfucker in his temple hard enough with it, he'd die or black out.

"Velvet says you told her you raped that girl. You even told Velvet her name was Tiffany Davis. And if Tiffany hadn't run away . . ." said Velvet's mother. She started crying. "You said you wouldn't have raped Velvet if Tiffany hadn't run away. I hope you go to jail and those men gang-rape you so you can see how it feels to be raped. I've changed my mind. Velvet was right. I don't want you anywhere near my grandson. We won't be coming back here ever."

I'd seen that evil, burning look before in the eyes of my ex-husbands. I ushered Velvet's mother out the door. I was right behind her, and Alphonso was right behind me.

"You lying old bitch!" he yelled, slamming the door.

Turning the key in the engine, I heard someone scream, "Aaaahhhh!" Quickly I drove away, pretending not to hear the scream. I dialed 9-1-1.

Ronnie asked, "What was that?"

Immediately upon getting a response, I gave the 9-1-1 operator the address, told her there was a 217 in progress, then ended the call.

Velvet looked at her mom, then flatly said, "Told you so. Satisfied? Now can we stop by my agent's office?" Velvet started text messaging again.

I was speechless. I wanted to go back to help Alphonso's wife, but somehow I didn't think she was the one who needed help. Hopefully, she was kicking his ass, and it wasn't the other way around. Size didn't matter when a person was outraged or in fear for their life. I knew the remarkable strength a person could conjure up in heated confrontations. If I were her, I'd shoot him first, then pistol-whip his ass. I should've let her borrow my steel hot dog. The only reason I didn't stay was because I couldn't live with myself if anything had happened to Ronnie, his grandmother, or Velvet.

We heard screams a block away. Desperately trying to see out of the back windshield, Ronnie kept asking, "What is that?" None of us answered.

Somebody was either going to the hospital or the cemetery. Hopefully, the police would respond to my 217 call, assault with the intent to murder.

CHAPTER 24

Sapphire

What the fuck? Had Grant come all the way to my house to protect his Honey? "You don't know me," I said. "I'm just doing my
job. And Honey isn't the only one who's had it hard. I've been through
a lot, too."

"Really?" Grant said like he didn't believe me.

I'd prove it to him and make him love me more than her.

"When I was sixteen, my stepfather gained my trust by showing interest in my cheerleading competitions and my academic achieve-
ments, which made my mother extremely proud. Perhaps it was my
full splits or my high kicks or my voluptuous tits or my ability to do
multiple flips without using my hands that excited him below his
waist. When I was fourteen, he started touching me in places that made
me feel weird, but at the same time, it felt kinda good. My breasts tin-
gled. My pussy twitched with excitement. When I was fifteen, he began
fondling me, probing a little deeper into my vagina, and pressing
against my hymen, and when I turned sixteen, he stole my innocence
and began fucking me more than he fucked my mom."

Grant sat there, staring at me.

Uh-huh. Told him so. I knew he was feeling sorry for me now, so I
kept talking. "Desperately, I wanted to tell my mother the truth, but I
wasn't sure whom she loved more. Him? Or me? Plus, I felt guilty for
having allowed him to do all the things he'd done before he started

raping me. Plus, my mother was so in love with Alphonso, she couldn't look into my dilated pupils and see the iris of my pain, and she was struggling, like me, to stay out of his way when he was angry, which progressively became all the time. I never could figure out what or who had made him so angry, seemingly for no reason. Maybe he resented all females because of something unforgivable a woman from his past had done to him."

Grant interrupted. "Tiffany, I'm really—"

Oh, you're going to listen to me. I didn't give a fuck what he was getting ready to say. I was talking, and it was rude of him to try and change the subject. I bet he didn't interrupt his little Honey.

I continued. "Whatever happened to him, it wasn't my fault or my mom's. I didn't bother telling my mother about the sexual abuse, and I didn't know how to make him stop, but I knew there had to be a better place somewhere out here for me. The day I ran away, I caught the bus to Wilshire Boulevard; walked into an expensive hotel's restroom; changed into a short, sexy dress and high heels; put on tons of blue eye shadow and red lipstick; then sat high upon a stool at the bar during happy hour."

"Aaahhh," Grant yawned, covering his mouth.

He had one more time to interrupt me, and he was going to regret it.

"Frowning, the bartender asked, 'Can I see your ID?' just as I opened my mouth to order an Amaretto and pineapple."

Grant cracked a smile, nodding. "I remember that drink. I didn't mean to interrupt," he said, raising his brows. He looked at me this time, giving me his undivided attention.

"Embarrassed, I chuckled, then lied. 'I lost my driver's license. But I really am eighteen,' I said. The bartender didn't believe me. 'Well, your license wouldn't do you any good at any bar anywhere. You have to be twenty-one, and you can't sit here,' he said. 'Make it easy on yourself, young lady. Leave. And if you are as smart as you are beautiful, you'd go home. Dressed provocative like that, you're headed for nothing but trouble.' Damn, What was I thinking that day?"

"I have no idea," Grant commented. His eyes were halfway closed.

"I'm almost done," I said, continuing. "As much I'd talked to my girlfriends about not being able to wait until we turned eighteen to be legal and twenty-one to drink legally, I knew that shit. I couldn't call my best friend to tell her I'd run away, because she would've told her mother, and her mother would've told my mother. I've been gone fourteen years. Did my parents have hope that one day they'd see me again, or did they think I was dead? After that bartender kicked me out, I picked up my bag, left the hotel, and headed to Sunset Boulevard. I figured I'd have a better chance there of meeting a nicer bartender who'd believe I was twenty-one, and I prayed I'd meet a rich, handsome man who'd invite me to his house.

"I was somewhat experienced. I'd learned how to give pretty good blow jobs to my mother's husband, and I'd tested my skills on a few of the high school boys from D.C. who were staying in the same hotel as my cheerleading team while we were in Vegas. That summer we won the cheerleading competition. I guess I was proving I was more experienced than the other girls on my squad. I sucked eight dicks on that trip, including yours. Each of those boys lied to me. All except one. You."

Grant was silent.

"Grant, are you listening to me? This is the part about you," I said, shoving his forehead up from the table.

"Huh? What? Yeah, sure, I heard you," he said, nodding.

"You were tall and handsome. Sometimes I'd fall asleep pretending you were my boyfriend. I never forgot the look in your eyes after you came in my mouth. A teardrop fell. Not because you felt good. You honestly apologized. 'Tiffany, I'm so sorry. You're so beautiful,' you said. 'And obviously you're popular. Save yourself for a guy that cares about you. All guys aren't dogs. Please forgive me.' While I was still on my knees, you kissed my forehead, then walked away. I remember that day like it was yesterday.

"The saying 'Be careful what you ask for' quickly became my harsh reality after this charming man by the name of Pretty Ricky approached me on Sunset and offered to take me on a trip to Las Vegas. Unfortunately, I was still in search of a place to call home, a boyfriend to claim as my own, and someone to love, so I went with him, thinking if I was lucky, maybe I'd see you again."

Grant's shoulders and head slumped. His eyes were closed. He was probably one of those people who could listen in his sleep.

"I was so damn naïve, but I grew up fast when Pretty Ricky drugged me and beat my ass on the regular, and he actually enjoyed that shit. If I didn't suck enough dicks or fuck enough tricks or steal expensive jewelry or things of value to increase his bottom line, bam, right in my face. Pretty Ricky didn't give a fuck about me. To my pimp, I was a means for him to maintain his big house, his fancy cars, his designer clothes, etc. In exchange for what? Nothing. I had to give him all of my money.

"A busted lip or a bruised hip didn't warrant a trip to the hospital. A cotton ball drenched with witch hazel and held against the purple swelling, followed by make-up, and I was back on the stroll to get his money, and if I showed up without it, bam, another ass whipping was guaranteed. The best thing for me was I never got arrested.

"When a john stabbed me in my side, then pushed me out of his car, my pimp left me for dead. Standing over me, staring down at me, Pretty Ricky uttered his last words to me. 'Tiffany, you're one dumb bitch. No, you're the dumbest bitch. You're not worth beating. I hope you die.' He reached toward me, and when I held out my hand to him, he snatched the two hundred dollars I had in my bra. Then he walked away as though he'd never known me, as though I hadn't made hundreds of thousands of dollars for him by fucking filthy, doggish men for an entire year.

"After being released from the hospital, I hitched a ride with a stranger I'd later discover was a youth counselor. The elderly lady drove me from Vegas to the small town of Henderson and dropped me off at a nice home. She said, 'Go inside, my child. You'll be safe here.' I was fortunate enough to get taken in by a family that owned a restaurant. They helped enroll me in adult night school, let me live with them until I graduated from the University of Neveda, Las Vegas, and employed me part time as a waitress during the evenings and weekends. There were nice people in the world, but I couldn't say they loved me. I think, like you, Grant, they felt sorry for me.

"Determined to survive, I started by keeping my legs shut. I saved every dime, including my tips, until I had my college degree and enough money to move out. Returning to Vegas, I applied for every available undercover cop position until I was hired. I insisted on working the Strip. Most johns coming to Vegas to get laid thought getting their dicks sucked was part of the perks. I showed them how wrong they were. I enjoyed being part of the sting operation that arrested their dumb asses and listening to them plead for me not to take them in while they quietly offered me bribes. Right when they were on the verge of pulling their dicks out of their pants, I'd flash my badge and say, 'You're under arrest for the solicitation of sex.' 'They'd all say, 'I thought this was legal in Vegas.' Tightening the handcuffs to cut off their circulation, I'd reply, 'You're dead wrong.' I wish I could've castrated them all.

"Sitting at my dining table one night, sipping on diet cola, I decided I was going to shoot every pimp. Execution style. Until I killed every pimp alive or died trying. I scribbled names on a napkin. Alphonso Allen was on my hit list, right before that sorry-ass pimp I'd worked for. I was saving Pretty Ricky for last. Valentino James was a different kind of pimp. If he hadn't killed Sunny Day, he wouldn't be on my list at all. The year before she was killed, Sunny had become my only friend. I didn't approve of her working for Valentino and Lace, but I couldn't force her to quit, so I stayed close enough to watch over her. Never in my lifetime did I think Valentino would rape then shoot any of his escorts in the head, especially a nice girl like Sunny.

"Stealing one hundred million dollars from Valentino would've been sufficient, but I won't be done with him until I shoot him in the head in broad daylight and watch him take his last breath. How quickly society forgets the women and children, like Sherrice Iverson, a seven-year-old, who are raped and then killed by men like Jeremy Strohmeyer. Does the Bible not dictate an eye for an eye? Iverson is dead, and Strohmeyer escaped death row by pleading guilty and received four consecutive life sentences without the possibility of parole, *life* being the operative word. Strohmeyer, soon to be thirty years old, is alive. He probably thought that because he had Leslie Abramson, the lawyer who also represented the Menendez brothers, he'd get off by claiming he was high on alcohol and drugs and didn't remember committing any crime.

"Generously, I gave Lace half of Valentino's stash but quickly changed my mind. She doesn't deserve half until I am convinced she is on my team. Since I'm killing pimps, eventually, my counterparts will catch up with me, and I need an ally with enough money to bail me out. That's why I need Honey."

As I relived my past with Grant, he pushed his half-empty plate aside. "Wheeewww!" Grant exhaled so loud, I stared at him.

What was his problem? "You okay? I didn't mean to spoil your appetite, but having someone to listen so attentively to my problems for once without changing the subject has moved me to tears." Sniffling, I wiped my nose. "I'm sorry. I didn't mean to break down like this. I'm really a strong person."

Holding me in his arms, Grant said, "Yes . . . indeed. Yes, indeed. And you are special. You are a true survivor."

Gazing up at him, I asked, "So how well do you know Honey?"

With firm conviction, Grant said, "It's simple. I'm in love with her, and I want to marry her."

Not at all what I wanted to hear. Easing out of his arms, I went to the cabinet and removed dessert. I sat the jar of peanut butter in front of him, alongside the strawberry preserves.

Shaking his head, Grant reached into his pocket and pulled out a handful of small packets. "Just in case, I brought my own. But this time I'm gonna make a sammich."

He liked me. He wanted me.

I unbuttoned Grant's shirt, and I swear, I'd never seen a chest so defined. I was tempted to rub my hands all over him, until he removed his pants and I saw his perfectly muscular ass. His dick hung with thickness over his large nuts. Ooh-wee! My pussy pulsated with joy.

I guessed he was lying about marrying Honey, but I wasn't about to bring her ass up again.

We went into the bathroom. Handing him a set of towels, I removed my clothes. I saw his eyebrows rise with approval as he closed the shower door. I stepped into the tub and sat facing him. He lathered his body. I bet those were the happiest suds sliding over his nipples, down his navel, and between his thighs. Grant faced me, lathered his face. Then he leaned his head under the flowing water. Aw, damn. I started cuming as I watched the water glide over his forehead, his eyes, his nose, in and then out of his mouth, over his succulent lips.

Grant stepped out of the shower. I got out of the tub and began drying his body with my tongue, licking the wetness from his dick and his balls.

"Tiffany, we really shouldn't do this. I really am in love with Honey."

"And I'm horny as fuck, and, yes, you are either going to fuck me or I'm going to rape you. The choice is yours."

Ignoring Grant's weak protest, I straddled him, rotated my pussy, then eased his dick inside of me. That shit felt incredible. I didn't need him to move, but I was delighted when he did.

Grant's strong hands gripped my ass tight. He started slamming me down on his dick. "Get up," he said.

"What?" Was he serious? I was on the verge of cumming all over his dick.

"Get up," he repeated.

This time I got up.

"Come here," he demanded. "Bring that pussy over here."

Grant barely finished the sentence before I made it to the foot of the bed.

"Wrap your arms around the post, and spread your legs," he ordered. "I'm about to get deep in this pussy."

Aw, shit. I felt every inch of Grant's dick sliding inside of me. My body trembled with orgasmic pleasure. His arm embraced my waist, and he dug deeper inside of me. It had been a long time since I'd let a man penetrate me. The pain reminded me. The pleasure reminded me, too.

"Grant, don't ever stop loving me," I moaned.

"I don't love you, Tiffany. I'm fucking you. There's a difference," he said. His sweat rolled down my spine and between the crack of my ass.

He was right. But sooner than he could imagine, I'd be right.

CHAPTER 25

Grant

Ooh-wee. I wanted to stab Tiffany in her side and push her to the floor. My God, that woman was crazy. I figured I had to fuck her to shut her the hell up. Tiffany needed a real good fuck to clean out her pussy, and she needed to see a shrink. The bitch was on one helluva whirlwind psychological tour.

I would never fuck Honey the way I was fucking the shit out of Tiffany. I ain't gon' lie. Tiffany's pussy was good. But she couldn't compete with the love of my life. Honey deserved all of me, emotionally and physically. I knew Tiffany wanted more, but she got what she deserved, a straight fuck, and she should be grateful.

I wasn't eating her pussy or licking her ass the way I'd done each time I made love to Honey. Going down on a woman for me was personal. I regretted leaving Honey's house after violating her privacy by answering her cell phone. If she'd done that to me, and I'd found out, I'd have cursed her out. Our trust bond was already broken, but a move like that would've severed our relationship for good.

In less than twenty-four hours of my being at Tiffany's, we'd run out of peanut butter and strawberry preserves, milk, honey, and anal lube. The sheets on her bed were sticky. My nuts were stuck to my ass, and her hair was matted. That was how we ended up in the shower.

"Haaaa, haaaaa." I exhaled. "Turn your ass around." Spreading her cheeks, Tiffany tilted her head backward, letting the hot water beat against her face.

"Grant, you're everything I imagined," she moaned, thrusting her ass onto my dick. "I just can't get enough of you."

I'd had enough of her hours ago. Other than sex, we had nothing in common. Her past was a sad one. Her stepfather was one dirty son of a bitch that deserved to have his ass beaten beyond recognition. Sapphire was a cop. Why didn't she go after him? She knew where he lived. I think she wanted to go home to see her mother and would have, without hesitation, if she knew he wouldn't be there. Or maybe the fear was so overwhelming, nothing could make her step foot back in her mother's home.

Pressing my hands on her lower spine, I dug deeper into her pussy. "Aw, Tiffany, I'm getting ready to cum. You ready, baby?"

She reached between her legs and mine. She grabbed my nuts and held them tight. I didn't know what felt better: my dick deep inside her pussy or the way she kept massaging the spot between my dick and my balls, stimulating my prostrate.

"Aw, shit." Pussy was a man's best friend. "It's right there, Tiffany. That's the spot. Press harder," I said. I inhaled, and steam raced up my nose, then down my throat. I didn't care. I kept digging deeper in her tight pussy. Tiffany's ass was nice and wet. I slipped my thumb all the way inside her ass.

"That's it. Yeah," she moaned, backing me into the wall with her ass.

Turning around, Tiffany squatted in the shower. I slipped my dick into her mouth, and franticly she stroked my shaft. "Give it to me. Cum on, Daddy," she moaned. Water flowed in and out of her mouth along with my dick.

She was forcing another load out of me. What the hell. I was ready to be done a long time ago. I grunted as I spit out the few seeds I had left to give. My legs became weak. "That's it," I said, stepping out of the shower. "You are not going to have me limping back to Atlanta. No more dick for you, insatiable lady."

I wrapped a towel around my waist, went into the guest bedroom, and stretched across the mattress, sideways. A few minutes later, Tiffany came in. She cuddled beside me.

"Thanks for giving me the best orgasms. You sure you can't stay another day?" she said.

Moving away from her, I shook my head. I didn't want to cuddle with her. "I came here to find out your connection to Honey. Now I know." I rolled over, hiding my dick. "But every time I say I'm leaving, you beg me to stay. You want to have sex. I'm all sexed out. So can we talk about my brother now?"

"One question. I'll only answer one. What do you want to know the most?"

"Did you really find him with a gun stuck in his ass?"

"Yes, in the house that Honey still owns."

"Did Honey stick the gun in his ass?" I needed to know for personal reasons.

"That's two questions," Tiffany said, rolling her eyes at me.

"No, it's part two to one question. So answer me."

"He said she did, and I believe him. Look, Grant. Honey is holding my money for you and me. For us to be together. Not for you to be with her. I'm so glad I found you. How's your four-hundred-eleven-unit development in Atlanta coming along?"

What the fuck? She was investigating me? Frowning, I sat on the edge of the bed, then said, "There is no us." Was she hearing impaired, or like most women, did Tiffany only hear what she wanted to hear?

"Why can't you give us a try? I could move to D.C. or Atlanta. I know you didn't spend the last twenty-four hours making love to me while you were thinking about her. I made you forget about her. Admit it," she said, grabbing between my legs.

Swatting her hand away, I said, "Leave my dick alone. Damn." I pushed her arm away again and again. "Fuck! Stop it, will you!"

"Grant, no man has made me feel this way. We have to be together. We will be together whether you like it or not."

That statement confirmed my thoughts that the woman was stone crazy. "Why don't you go cook us breakfast while I think about it," I lied. Whatever happened with the fifty million was between them. At least Honey was honest about what she'd done. Tiffany wanted to play head games and live in some make-believe world in which she made me make her happy.

"That means you're considering my proposal. Make the right decision, baby. I wouldn't want to have to arrest your sweet Honey for murdering Reynolds to have you all to myself. But I will do whatever it takes. I don't want you going near her again." Tiffany left the room.

Decisions. Decisions. For me, shit like this only happened in movies. The sun started shining through the window. The problem I had was Tiffany actually believed, with a badge and a gun on her side of the law, she could make me do any damn thing.

"Tiffany!" I yelled, sitting up in her bed. "You can't be serious. Forget about us!"

"Of course, I am, sweetheart, and I need an answer from you before you leave." She paused. "Or you're not going anywhere," she sang.

"What do you want?" I heaved, then swallowed the bile sliding up and down my throat. "Fuck it. Your ass is sick."

"You haven't seen sick." Tiffany returned, clicking a nutcracker. Ripping away the edges of a plastic bag, she scattered walnuts all over the bed.

Crack.

Casually, she asked, "Want some?"

I'd never made a bad choice, one where I felt there was no redemption. I hadn't planned on letting Tiffany control my life. Since breaking up with Honey, I'd fucked Velvet and Tiffany, but my dick had done most of the thinking. It felt fucking fantastic in the moment, but sitting here right now across from this crazy bitch, I regretted it. That was why I'd stopped texting Velvet. She wanted a relationship, too. She was a stripper, for God's sake, traveling around the country with Trevor to seduce his business partners. I was glad I'd listened to my father about the business deal. Women who were looking for a man to take care of them weren't the kind I wanted to commit to. And I wanted kids, but not some other man's kid, like Ronnie.

"I can't do it," I said. Irrespective of how my parents felt, what my brother had said, and what Tiffany said she was doing, my heart had never wavered. Honey was the one I wanted to have a family with. My cell phone had died during the night. I left Tiffany on the bed, unzipped my suitcase, and plugged in my phone.

"Can and you will," she said, picking up her cordless phone. Tiffany dialed eleven digits, then said, "Here."

Crack. She busted another walnut.

I pushed her hand away. There was something forgivable about Honey that made it impossible for me to give up on her.

"Grant! Have you heard a word I've said?" Tiffany yelled.

Ignoring her, I quickly dressed, then started packing my things. I'd rather wait at the airport than endure several more hours of her insanity.

"Grant! I'm sorry!" A walnut hit me in the head. "I'm sorry!" Another walnut hit me in the face. "I said I'm fucking sorry!" she yelled. I had to block about a half dozen walnuts. "How many times do you want me to apologize? Please don't leave me," she pleaded, pacing in front of me, with a mouth full of walnuts, looking like a chipmunk.

One of us had to be calm and sensible. I knew she wanted me to give her a reason to take this confrontation to a higher level. I refused to hit her or raise my voice. I had no intention of ever seeing Tiffany again, but there was no way any man, including me, could make that woman happy. My father was right again. Tiffany had allowed her stepfather to rape her happiness away from her, and there was nothing I could do to change that.

"Fine. Then let me cook you breakfast. You said you were hungry," she said, leaving the bedroom.

Unplugging my cell phone, I placed my charger in the side pocket of my suitcase. I dialed the 800 number for free directory assistance. My call dropped. I dialed again. The call dropped again. I tried a third time. I swear, some days I wished I could put this phone on a little yellow bus and roll it into the cell phone store! I picked the cordless up off the bed. Pressing the green button, I heard Tiffany talking to someone.

"Where's Lace?" she asked.

"I was right. She's in Los Angeles," a woman answered.

"What's she doing there?"

"Per Onyx, she's accompanying one of her clients on a child-support case."

Overhearing that confirmed my love for Honey.

"So how are the other girls treating you?" asked Tiffany.

"I'm good. I'm glad I came. I wanted to let you know, I can't keep spying on Lace for you. This is my new family, and I want to help them help other women. You'll have to find another way to get your money back. Why don't *you* ask her for it?"

"Bitch, I will hurt you," growled Tiffany.

Here we go with threats again, I thought.

"Do whatever you want. I'm happy here," said the woman.

"Girl Six, don't you hang up on me."

"Good-bye, Sapphire."

Girl Six. I had to remember that name. I waited until I heard Tiffany hang up. Rolling my suitcase to the front door, I looked at Tiffany. "You're worse now than the day I met you."

"Grant, I'm done fucking with you. Go ahead. Leave." Picking up her phone, she dialed a number. "Yeah, this is Officer Sapphire Bleu," she said into the phone. "I have a break in the Valentino James case. Put out an arrest warrant for Honey Thomas. She's reportedly in Los Angeles." Tiffany proceeded to give a physical description of Honey.

I had to change my strategy. Sitting on the sofa, I read Honey's text message from yesterday, then texted her. *Where are you?*

She texted back: *Oh, so you're not dead.*

Tiffany said, "Send all the text messages you want. Unless you want to change your mind about us, it's too late."

Ignoring Tiffany, I replied to Honey. *Almost, but not quite. Seriously, where are you?*

L.A.

Get out now! I texted.

She texted back: *Why?*

Be careful. The police is looking for you.

How do you know this? she texted.

Please just trust me on this one. Don't go to the airport. Drive the speed limit, and meet me in Vegas, at the Wynn.

Who is this? she texted. *Is this a joke?*

I wish. Help me out here. I'm trying to save you, I texted. Immediately afterward, I deleted our text history. Smiling at Tiffany, I said, "I just told Honey I don't want to see her anymore. I'm staying here another day. Maybe we can come to a better understanding."

That sicko smiled, then came to me. "Grant, I promise you, you won't regret it."

"But first you need to make a call and tell whomever you just called you made a mistake."

"I didn't call anybody, silly. I was joking. Let's eat."

CHAPTER 26

Valentino

Summer was the most beautiful woman. Natural. No make-up. No weird colors in her hair and shit. Now that was the way a woman should look, the same at night and in the morning. All that wig wearing, red and fake blond coloring in the hair, and tons of stuff smeared all over their face to try to look like somebody else was ridiculous, 'cause they had to wash it off at some point, and when they did, goddamn, I could jab two forks in the sides of some women's necks, and abraca-motherfuckin'-dabra, I swear, some of those bitches were uglier than Frankenstein, but a nigga would've licked their pussies dry if I could've gotten a conjugal visit while I was in jail. A nigga didn't appreciate pussy until there were zero pussies around.

Summer made a motherfucker like me soft and shit. Being around her a whole day, knowing she was carrying my seeds, I tried to become a family man by playing with my son and having dinner together. That shit was cool for one, maybe two, hours max. What the fuck did a stay-at-home dad do all damn day was beyond me, unless he was an entrepreneur, finding and managing fine-ass females for his clients to fuck.

"Come here, ba," I said, grabbing Summer by the arm. "I got some shit I have to say that can't wait."

"What is it?" she said and smiled. "You're ready to make love to me.

You didn't give me any last night. I'm going to bust if I don't get some dick." Summer's smile was that of a woman with a little girl trapped inside. Her parents hadn't let her grow up and shit, but that was cool. I could change that in a few weeks.

What the hell had she done for sex before I got out? My dick got hard. I wanted to fuck Summer so bad. Exploding inside of my lady was worth the wait. There was always another opportunity to run up in some other pussy or maybe some nigga's ass. I couldn't chance getting down again without wrapping my shit up. I was a hard motherfucker, but I didn't want a sick-ass dick hanging over my nuts.

Damn, I wished I hadn't fucked that nigga in his ass! I hated to admit that shit was bigger than busting a nut. I felt empowered. For me, fucking a female was stress relief. Fucking a man in the ass, I felt like the alpha male, the lion king of the motherfuckin' jungle. I wanted to beat my chest and beat his ass at the same time. I ruled my domain. Any nigga could control a bitch, but making another man my bitch, that was power.

"Naw, that ain't it," I told Summer. "I promise to get us some condoms while I'm out. Sit next to me." I was sitting on the edge of the love seat inside the bedroom. Holding Summer's hand, I faced her, then looked into her eyes. "I want you to listen carefully. This here shit I'm about to say is for real. Summer, you know me better than anyone else. I love you, girl. I thank you for bailing your nigga out. When we go to court, you are going to testify on my behalf. You have to be a believable character witness for me. You're all I've got. When all of this here shit is over, we're fuckin' getting married."

I was sincere about the marriage part. My being associated with Summer would look good for me. And if, for any reason, I got arrested for some of the shit that was about to go down, I knew Summer would bail me out again.

Summer's eyes beamed with joy. Smothering me with kisses, she said, "Why wait, Anthony? If you love me, and I do love you with all my heart, let's go to Chapel of the Bells right now and get married today."

What was the rush with her tryin' to tie a nigga down instantaneously? "Tomorrow," I said. I had shit to do today.

"Okay. I won't take Anthony to see my parents today, 'cause they won't approve of us getting married, and I can't lie to them. That wouldn't be the Christian thing to do. Seriously! Tomorrow?"

"For sho'. Go get any dress you want, and we'll get married in the morning. Seriously."

Shit. Summer's idea was better than mine. Once she said, "I do," I'd have total access to everything Summer owned, 'cause there'd be no time to draw up a prenup. I would not sign that shit, anyway. I bet her dad, old man Mr. Day, was going to feel like Old Man River, wishin' he could roll down the muddy Mississippi, when I called him Dad. Mr. Day was gonna shit cement bricks. I didn't give a fuck.

"Come on, baby. A quickie for your bride," Summer said, rubbing my dick.

That shit felt good. She was making it hard. But I could wait a few more hours. "Later," I said, going to the kitchen.

"You gon' eat breakfast with us before you leave?" Summer asked, trailing behind me.

Back in the day, when my parents were alive, sitting at the table together was special. I wanted to be there with Summer and my son, but I had so much shit on my mind, mentally I'd be elsewhere. I had to keep moving. But when it came time to relax, home with my new family was where I was gonna be. Every man wanted a place to call home.

"Keep it hot for me, baby. I'll be home for dinner." I was not thinking about food. When I did get ahold of Summer, I was going to fuck the hairs off of her pussy. Summer would be so sore, I might have to take her vows and mine or teleconference her in on our ceremony. "Let me see the car keys to the Bentley and the bank card. What's the pin again?" I was double-checking to make sure I'd memorized it right.

"Eighty nineteen," Summer said.

"Oh, and let me use your cell phone until we get me one, and I need you to write me out a blank check. I might need a few extra dollars to get you that special ring," I said, kissing Summer tenderly.

Summer signed and dated a check, made it payable to me, then handed it to me. "Don't write it for more than ten thousand. I don't need an expensive ring."

I took the check, glanced over it to make sure she hadn't left anything out or filled in an amount, then folded it and placed it in my pocket.

Racing to my side, li'l Anthony said, "Daddy, I wanna go with you."

"Anthony James," Summer said sternly, "sit your behind down in that chair right now and be quiet. I don't ever want to hear you say that again. You hear me?"

"Dang, he is *my* dad," Anthony mumbled, slouching in the chair.

Damn. Like that? I looked at Summer, walked over to her, took the keys and the bank card, then left. I didn't bother saying bye or kissing her. She acted like I was gonna get my seed killed or some shit. Fuck that bitch! She could marry her damn self!

I headed straight to the bank. I wrote out the check for ten million dollars to open up my own account with my own money. The banker left me sitting at her desk for fifteen minutes. Then she came back.

"I'm sorry, Mr. James. This check was not honored by Ms. Day. We just called her. She did approve ten thousand, and I can give you that if you'd like."

I sat there staring at that bitch, trying to figure my next move. "But it's signed by her. She owes me this money. You have to honor it."

"Sorry. How would you like the ten thousand dollars?" she asked.

"Cash, bitch. Cash," I said, folding my arms across my chest.

After escorting me inside the private room for merchant account holders, she counted out my money, then put it in an envelope. I went straight to the ATM and withdrew one thousand, then another one thousand. I tried for another, but the fucking machine kept the card. Was two thousand dollars all she had authorized for her daily limit? Bitch!

I drove down Paradise Road, off the Strip. A nigga sure felt good being back on the streets. I stopped off at Terrible's casino. Ordinarily, I'd valet park at the casinos on the Strip, but under the circumstances, every minute was a state of a motherfuckin' emergency. I had to maintain access to all my shit while watching my own back. I didn't even have enough cash to hire bodyguards.

I browsed around to see if I saw anyone I knew. "Well, I'll be goddamn," I said aloud. I thought Vegas was bigger than this here. Was that dat nigga sittin' by the door, playing the penny slots? That was about right. I walked up on him and said, "What's up, motherfucker?"

"Hey, yo, I knew I was going to see you, man. I just knew it. I felt that shit, V," Benito said, hugging me. "That's why I waited for you right here. Been at it all night. I'ma hit big. I can feel it, man."

"Nigga, stop lying. You are not going to hit that million-dollar jackpot on no fuckin' penny machine. Cash that bitch out, and let's go."

Shaking his head, then covering his grin, Benito said, "You just don't know, man. So much shit has happened since—"

"Shut up and let's roll," I said, taking six steps back from his ass.

"Wait, V! Don't leave a brotha. I'ma get my ticket out of the machine," he said, standing up.

I couldn't believe I'd graduated from high school with that nigga. What I truly couldn't believe was he'd actually graduated and gone to college.

An old lady walked up, put one dollar in the machine, hit the spin button one time, and I'd be damned. That old, wrinkle-ass bitch hit the jackpot. Benito lost it. Pushing the woman aside, he said, "That's my money. That's my machine." I had to drag that nigga away before that old lady knocked him upside his head again.

"I told you, man," Benito said, holding his ticket so tight, it crumbled.

"Let me see that," I said, snatching the ticket out of his hand. "Five dollas?" I tore up the ticket. "Nigga, you can't do shit with five fuckin' dollars. You can't even guess the letter *r* for five dollas. Don't even bother cashing this shit in. Let's go."

"Man, why'd you do that shit? I just lost a million dollars."

"Then you can get another million. As soon as you help me get my money back," I said as we headed to my car. I cruised along the Strip to let it be known I was out. That shit only meant something to me because outside of my former empires in North Las Vegas, I didn't hang around creatin' no friction with other niggas who wanted to be like me. All of my headaches had been brought on by one bitch or another. I missed my mansion, but I wasn't dumb enough to drive by it. What I really missed was my customized aquarium built underneath my glass floor. A nigga like me walked on water every day. Those bastards had probably let my sharks die. That or sold them.

I got straight to the point and questioned Benito. "You know who got my money?" I asked to see if his answer would match what Summer had told me.

Benito nodded. "Sapphire and Lace, man. I tried to tell Lace she needed to give it back, but she threatened to shoot me if I stepped foot on her property. I know where she lives. I followed my brother to her house. I know where Sapphire lives 'cause I had a taxi follow her home when she picked up my brother from the airport. Valentino, I been thinking, man. We drive to Atlanta first thing in the morning—"

"No can do. I'm getting married in the morning. In fact, I need to go buy my girl a big-ass rock before the stores close and shit."

Benito chuckled. "That's a good one. As if you would ever get married. Like I was saying, we drive to Atlanta first thing in the morning, get our fifty million from Lace, then tie her up, stick a gun in her ass, and leave her for dead, and then we drive back here and hire somebody else to take care of Sapphire, 'cause I'm scared of her ass. Once we get our money from her, we buy us an island in the Caribbean, cruise over to our new spot, and get us some new hos."

"Nigga, first, it ain't our money. It's my money. And all this driving and cruising bullshit is for bitches. How the fuck you get here?"

"Leave the driving to us. Greyhound," Benito said, nodding.

"You took the fucking bus all the way from D.C.? I oughta bust you in your head for lying."

"I barely had enough money to do that. Plus, it's cheaper than flying. I rode the dog from D.C. to Atlanta to Las Vegas, and I ain't gettin' on no plane. We're driving to Atlanta, right? Remember, I've got a plan to get all of our money back. We need to be on our way to Atlanta right now, but we gotta drive. I'm afraid to fly."

"Nigga, your big ass played pro ball. How you afraid to fly?"

"Valiums, man. I was knocked the fuck out."

Nigga, your ass is broke, I thought. That was what I'd ordinarily say, but I wasn't no fool. I didn't have shit to go on, and for the first time, I needed Benito more than he needed me. That was fucked up. I refused to invite his ass to my wedding.

"I'm out. I gotta get my girl a ring. Meet me back at this casino at noon tomorrow. Don't be late," I said, dropping him off on Tropicana.

"I'll be sitting right back where you found me until tomorrow."

"Nigga, get a room."

"With what? My good looks?"

I tossed Benito three hundred dollars and left.

Driving to the jewelry store, I thought about what lie I was going to tell Summer when I got home. I had to go to Atlanta but wasn't supposed to leave Nevada. "Wait a minute," I said aloud. "Benito told me he ran into Sapphire at the airport. What the fuck was he doing at the airport if he came in on the dog?"

If that nigga was trying to set me up, I was gonna kill his ig'nant ass. "I got one better," I said aloud, then headed back to Tropicana, where I'd dropped Benito off. "Fuck going home. I'ma spend the night with Benito."

CHAPTER 27

Honey

Any type of contact with Grant excited me. That texting thing took me forever. He was firing back so fast, I wanted to ask Velvet to type for me, but she was inside the building on Sunset Boulevard, meeting with her agent. Velvet had insisted on us not joining her. Couldn't blame her after the ordeal with Alphonso.

I sat in the car with Ronnie and his grandmother, waiting and texting. Initially, I wanted to be tough with Grant and tell him off and make him feel the pain I was feeling, but I couldn't. We'd put one another through enough. Either we were going to be together or we weren't, but the least we could do was be friends.

It was time for me to accept my accountability, get real with my feelings, and the first opportunity I had, I was laying my heart in his hands once more. Didn't most relationships deserve at least a second chance? Then the choice would be his to either handle me with care or let me go. Grant was the only man I wanted to marry and have kids with. I didn't know what made me so sure. But I was. It wasn't hard to meet men. Meeting a nice man and then getting to know him was the challenge, and meeting one with character and substance . . . Lord, a woman's chances of winning the lottery were greater. Sad but true.

Velvet came running out of the building. "Aaahhhh!"

I got out of the car along with Ronnie and Velvet's mom. "Don't tell me you got the part!" I said. I was so happy for her.

Velvet picked up her son. "I didn't get the part yet, but it's between me and one other person! Oh, my, God!"

"Mommy, that's great. We're moving to Hollywood," Ronnie said, hugging his mother's neck.

"Not just yet, baby," said Velvet. "We'll know for sure in a few days. They're going to review the test film, then decide."

"Velvet, baby, calm down," her mother said. "I don't want you to be disappointed."

"There's nothing to be disappointed about," I said, giving Velvet a big hug. "She's one of two finalists. That's a major accomplishment. Okay, everybody in the car. Something important came up. I have to drop you guys off at the airport." I reached into the cup holder for my iPhone.

Driving down Century Boulevard, I intentionally went slow so I'd have to stop at the red light. I texted Grant. *Where are* was all I typed before the light turned green.

"Why?" Ronnie protested. "Grandma promised to take me to Disneyland."

Oh my, the disappointing look on his face made me sad. I even felt guilty. "You can go to Disneyland, but I can't take you," I said, pulling into the Sheraton's parking lot. "You guys decide if you want to stay or go back to Atlanta, but I need to go to Vegas, and I have to leave now."

I finished texting Grant, adding *you?*, then pressed SEND.

"I'm rolling with you," Velvet said, as though her decision was final and she didn't need my permission.

Actually, it wasn't a bad idea to have Velvet ride along. If anything happened to me, at least she could tell Grant. "Fine. You can go, but this isn't a trip for Ronnie," I said.

Velvet's mother chimed in. "I guess since I started all of this, I can finish it. Ronnie, it's me and you, baby, once again. You can let us out here. I'll check into one of these hotels."

"Aw, don't say that. I'd never dump you out on the curb with your bags. I'll make you a reservation at a five-star hotel on Wilshire Boulevard, take you there, and get you and Ronnie settled, and then Velvet and I will leave," I said. I tapped a few buttons on my iPhone. Seconds later several hotels popped up. I selected the best and my favorite, the

Beverly Wilshire. I called for reservations and booked a double queen suite with two bathrooms.

I drove to Beverly Hills, checked them in at the hotel, and paid cash for the room. Velvet's mother could use her credit card for incidentals. I couldn't chance being tracked by the police if any of what Grant had texted was true. Maybe he was just trying to get me to spend the weekend with him. I handed Velvet's mom a thousand dollars cash, and Velvet and I were on our way to Vegas.

I merged onto the interstate. "Now I don't want you getting caught up in Vegas," I told Velvet. "Stay off the pole, off the stage, off the corner, off the streets, out of the alleys, off the stroll, and out of strange men's hotel rooms. Got that?"

"You're starting to sound like my mother," she answered, never looking up from her Sidekick.

"Well, I'm going to Vegas to meet with a friend, and then we're headed back home. I may have to drive back to Atlanta, but I'll put you on a direct flight out of LAS. I'm not sure yet. We'll have to see once we get to Vegas. Atlanta, damn." I speed dialed Onyx's number.

"Hey," Onyx answered. "Is everything okay?"

I exhaled heavily into the receiver. "We're good, but there's been a change in my plans. You wouldn't believe the turn of events. I'll fill you in when I get back in a few days. How's everything there?"

This time Onyx exhaled. "Where do I begin?"

Oh no. Turning down the radio, I braced myself for the worst. "What's happening?"

"I didn't want to bother you, but I'm glad you called. First off, Girl Six came back the same day you left."

"What? That's good news. Didn't I tell you she called me? She said she was coming." Had I forgotten? How could I expect Onyx to stay on top of things if I couldn't remember to tell her the important things?

"No, you didn't, but yes and no to the good news," Onyx said, sounding as if her eyebrows were raised above her forehead. "Girl Six wants to stay, but I overheard a conversation between her and Sapphire. Seems to me Girl Six was sent here by Sapphire to spy on us."

Immediately, I answered, "Let her stay. At least we know where she's at. I'll deal with Girl Six when I get back. What else?"

"I'm thinking about going back to my husband. I'm not happy in Atlanta." Onyx started crying in my ear.

No way. "Give it some time. Promise me you won't leave before I get back. If you still want to go after we have a chance to talk things over . . ." There was no way I was letting Onyx go back. "First let me decide on another personal assistant to replace you."

"If that's a job opening to work for you, I'll take it," Red Velvet said while texting.

"You're going to Hollywood, and Onyx is irreplaceable," I said into the receiver, trying to let Onyx know how much I needed her.

Onyx didn't understand that she couldn't disappear and leave her husband, then suddenly show up at their home again. What if he'd moved another woman in or rented the house? Onyx had mentioned her husband only once, on the day she started working for me.

"Did you contact him?" I asked.

"No, I know better than to do that," Onyx said.

"Good," I replied. "I'll call you back tonight so we can talk. In the meantime, keep an extremely close watch over Girl Six, monitor all of her calls, and give me a full report. Bye."

"You sure have a lot on your plate," Velvet said. "How do you do it?"

"This is nothing. Nothing I can't handle," I said, sounding confident. I wasn't the norm, and what made me exceptional was I was willing to give my all for a cause I believed in, while others gave lip service about what they were going to do with their lives. "So tell me about this G, this man you keep texting," I said, driving the speed limit.

I knew we had to talk about Alphonso, but that entire situation was depressing, and there wasn't anything we could do to change it in a few days. Velvet, not her mother, would have to decide if Ronnie and Alphonso should meet again. Ronnie was such an intelligent and happy child. Introducing him to a loser like Alphonso, even if Alphonso was his dad, had been a terrible idea.

Velvet smiled. "Trevor, my boss, introduced him to me. He's considering being Trevor's new business partner."

I'd forgotten all about my plan to shut down Stilettos. "Yeah, Trevor gave me his card that night. You ever heard from that woman's husband?"

"He texted me a few times, trying to hook up again, but I don't know where his wife is. Obviously, he doesn't care about her, or he wouldn't keep sending me texts."

Velvet was a smart girl, but I had to say, "Stay the fuck away from his ass. What's his name?"

"Tolliver."

"Stay the fuck away from Tolliver. Let that bitch flash on somebody else. You have a son. Always put Ronnie first. I did a little research on your boss. Do you realize that Trevor offers you up like a two-dollar ho to suck his clients' dicks? Stilettos is in financial trouble. I bet Trevor bought and paid you like a prostitute, for less than a grand."

Velvet stared out the window. Was she smiling?

"It was worth it because G and I connected. I'd never seen a man that fine in my life." Velvet crossed then uncrossed her legs. Then she squirmed in her seat.

"Trust me, he's only interested in what's between your thighs. You're the best stripper Trevor has. Ever think about getting your own studio and teaching women how to pole dance? Pole dancing is extremely popular. You could even teach celebrities' women and wives in the privacy of their homes. The income could allow you to live in L.A., keep your schedule open for more auditions. You could make a lot more money working for yourself."

The smile on Velvet's face got bigger. "I hadn't thought about that. But where would I get that kind of money to get started?"

Oh, she already had more than enough and didn't know it. "We'll do your business plan, find you a good location, and I'll help you get set up when we get back. That's what I do; I help empower women. Trevor will be coming to you for a job. And you'd better put his ass on the pole."

We laughed at that one.

My iPhone chimed twice, indicating I had a text message. It was Grant. *? x will u get here?*

2 hours. ? r u ? I texted back while driving. I was getting better, but driving while trying to text with one hand was difficult. Swerving into the next lane, I let my phone drop into my lap.

"Ooh, you want me to do that for you?" Velvet offered.

I wanted to say no, but by the time I finished texting back and forth, we'd be in Vegas. Handing her my phone, I said, "Ask him what room he's in at the Wynn."

Velvet texted my message in five seconds.

The phone chimed again. "What'd he say?" I asked.

"Sixty ninety-eight," Velvet said, handing me back my phone.

"The sixtieth floor? That's perfect in case I need to push him out the window. By accident, of course," I said, thinking about how Grant had disappeared the last time we were together.

"Just curious," Velvet said slowly. "Is your Grant, Grant Hill, six-five, about two hundred thirty pounds, gorgeous, to-die-for body and booty, from D.C., and owns his own real-estate development company?"

My eyes left the road. My neck turned in her direction. "Bitch, you'd better not tell me that's your G man."

"I didn't know you knew him. What's the big deal? We're all sharing, anyway. That just shows we have a similar taste of and in men."

I slammed on the brakes, going from ninety to zero in thirty seconds. Cars behind me skidded to the side. A few of them crashed, but I didn't give a fuck. I looked at Velvet and said, "Bitch, you fucked my man?"

"Not knowingly," she said. "Wasn't like his dick had your name written on it."

That bitch had no fucking idea who she was dealing with. I drew my hand back. . . . *Whack*! I slapped that bitch as hard as I could.

Thump! Thump! Thump!

No, that bitch did not punch me back. No woman had ever hit me. I unbuckled my seat belt. Reaching over her lap, she punched me in my back, my head. I didn't give a fuck. I opened her door and tried to push that bitch out of my rental car. Starting the engine, I drove ten miles an hour, then twenty, then sped up to thirty. Blasting the radio, I pressed down on the accelerator and sped all the way up to sixty miles an hour, ignoring that bitch and her screaming as she gripped her seat belt.

"Stoooooop! I'm soooorrrryy! Pleeeeeaassseee stoooop!"

Bitch should've unbuckled her seat belt when I unbuckled mine and got out before I took off. I pulled over when I got ready, not because her ass was screaming like a li'l bitch. I turned down the radio and stared at her, daring her to open her fucking mouth. Fuck! Once a madam always a madam. Velvet reminded me of the way I'd treated Girl Six. Once I was in that anger zone, whoever pissed me off could end up dead. Why did that bitch have to fuck Grant?

Velvet sat in her seat. The bitch didn't even cry. If she made it back to Atlanta alive, I was definitely offering her a spot on my team if she didn't get the part in *Something on the Side.*

I kept quiet, and if the bitch was smart, she'd shut the fuck up, too. I couldn't wait to show up at Grant's room; his fucking ass had a lotta explaining to do. But first I was going to open his window and get a little fresh air so I could cool the fuck off.

CHAPTER 28

Sapphire

Grant left me.

I'd done all I could to make him stay. Once we talked, I realized he was right. A woman could never keep a man who didn't want her. Either way, with or without that man in her bed, she'd end up sleeping alone at night. After we showered, Grant wouldn't caress, touch, kiss, or make love to me. Maybe he needed time to reconsider his decision not to visit me ever again.

I decided to take the night off from work and have a few drinks at a bar, but first I had to make a quick visit. I stopped at the gate of Summer's community. I hadn't been here since her twin sister's funeral a month ago. Flashing my badge, I lied to the security officer, telling him I had an emergency from this area and needed to patrol the premises. I drove around the perimeter first, gradually making my way to the rear of the complex, where Summer lived. It was eight o'clock at night. Driving by her house twice, I saw a light on upstairs and one downstairs. I tucked my gun in my bra.

I parallel parked in front of her home. I was proud of Summer for moving out of her parents' home. I knew she loved them, but the Days were too protective and extremely religious. Everything that happened in life wasn't a sin governed by the King James Version of the Bible.

I rang Summer's doorbell, then stepped back. I didn't care if Valentino was there or not. Yes, I did. I wanted to stare into his cowardly eyes. Valentino wasn't a man. He was a mutt.

Slowly, Summer opened the door. She stared at me for a moment, then said, "Sapphire, hi. I wasn't expecting you."

I invited myself in. Standing in the foyer, I said, "This is official business. I know my timing isn't great. Neither is yours. You shouldn't have bailed Valentino out of jail. Where is he?"

Summer frowned at me, then said, "He's not here, but why not? No one told me I couldn't."

She was so innocent and naïve. What did she see in Valentino? Why did women spend their money bailing out men who didn't give a damn about them? Now Summer had to pray Valentino did the right thing, or she'd lose a million dollars. That was her concern, not mine. I had to keep things moving.

"You'll find out why," I said. "But I promised your sister I'd take good care of you and Anthony. Have you deposited the cashier's check I gave you?"

"No. Why?"

"For your safety, I need it back."

"I planned on giving the money to Valentino for his attorneys' fees."

How many ways could I spell *stupid?* "Don't. Give it to me. You won't be able to use the money, anyway," I lied. "It'll hurt his case. The check is linked to Valentino for prostitution. Whoever cashes the check goes to jail." I said that only because she'd told me she hadn't cashed it.

"Oh my. Wait right here." Summer ran upstairs. She returned, holding the check in her hand.

"Thankfully, you and your son won't be associated with this check," I said, taking it from her. "I've got to go, and if I were you, I'd put Valentino out."

That was easier than I imagined. Driving to the casino, I missed Girl Six. Not in a sexual way. I missed having someone to talk with, or as Grant had said, someone to listen to me while I was at home.

Was he serious? I thought I was a good listener. Grant had told me a dozen times in every way he could imagine that he loved Honey. "I love Honey. My heart is with Honey. Honey is the woman I want to marry. Honey is the sweetest woman I've ever met," he'd said, and I'd heard him each time. He'd gone on and on until I went to my kitchen, opened the cabinets, and threw out my bottle of honey, my honey sticks, my honey-flavored cough drops, and the empty containers of peanut butter and jelly, too. A man that in love with a woman couldn't fake being in love with another. Damn, maybe one day I'd be lucky like Lace. I wondered if she loved Grant as much as he loved her, or if she even knew how much he loved her.

Some men could articulate their feelings to everybody in the world except the one person they loved. Oh, I'd heard it all. "Please don't arrest me. I love my wife and kids. I'll lose them if I go to jail for soliciting sex." Those men would break down, crying like babies. I could imagine that their expressions of love probably hadn't escaped their lips before they'd left home in search of a blow job, free pussy, or a prostitute. In search of a woman that would do to them all the things they'd fantasized about. Men who were unable to communicate the freakiest sexual desires burning inside them to their wives, fiancées, or girlfriends somehow could show their alter ego to a complete stranger. Suddenly, they'd become Superdick, able to satisfy any woman with multiple orgasms. Any woman except their significant other.

That was what Grant did with me. He fucked the shit out of my pussy. If he loved his Honey the way he professed, then why did he call me baby sixteen times. Hm, guess the word was meaningless to him. Definitely not to me. Men did those types of things. They lured women in with the one thing women desired most, not sex, affection.

My cell phone rang.

I debated about checking the caller ID. I never answered blocked calls, but something urged me to touch the answer box.

"Hello," I said.

"Tiffany?" a woman asked.

"Who is this?" Only people from my past knew me by my real name.

"Tiffany Davis?" she asked.

"Yes," I responded. "This is Tiffany."

I heard a female in the background ask, "Is it her?"

What the hell difference did it make what my name was? At this point in my life, I was miserable without Grant.

Silence followed. I waited a few more seconds, then hung up and headed inside the casino to watch folks with problems far worse than mine. With all the money I had, plus an added ten million, I contemplated turning in my badge and finding my own Grant Hill. Every woman should be so fortunate as to have a Grant Hill of her own.

CHAPTER 29

Grant

There were casual relationships, and then there were committed relationships. In the eyes of men, the two were definitely not the same. For women, the two were exactly the same.

"So why in the fuck did you do them, man, after professing you'd never stick your dick inside of a woman you didn't care about?" I asked myself.

Standing alone in my suite, I mused about the people strolling along the Strip. Like me, each of them was in search of something or someone, or else they'd be at home. No one ended up on Las Vegas Boulevard by happenstance. The men handing out postcards plastered with gorgeous women; the men holding, folding, or gawking at the cards; and the women hoping to get paid from a slot machine or a john were strolling along, with an agenda.

Sex. Money. Food. Companionship. Fun. They made potent concoctions, with everything except the main ingredient of life. Love. I bet none of those thousands of people were looking for love. They'd gamble their life savings in hopes of experiencing instant gratification, lust, explosive orgasms with strangers, and winning the big jackpot.

Fucking Red Velvet and Sapphire was my way of releasing my frustrations. Masturbation was not my preferred way to ejaculate. Masturbating was a temporary fix for my voracious sexual appetite. A warm, juicy pussy felt better and sustained me longer than the palm of my hand pumping up and down my shaft. I refused to stick my dick inside one of those silicone pussy pockets Honey had in her pleasure chest, but I'd thought about it for a second. It was clear I didn't love either Red Velvet or Sapphire. I loved Honey.

A man knew exactly who he loved, and that was why he'd let other women do exactly what they wanted to. Nothing that those women did or said would change his mind. His dick could easily be persuaded to slip up or slide into a woman's pussy. A rest stop or detour of sorts. The scenic route en route to his, not her, destination.

Red Velvet was one sexy young woman who knew how to, ooh-wee! fuck a brotha right. She had an incredibly supple body. Sapphire thought putting her lips or her pussy on me was the same as fucking me. Red Velvet fucked me with passion. Red Velvet enjoyed getting both of us off. That shit was exhilarating. Sapphire fucked me with feverish determination to make me cum until I couldn't cum anymore. That shit was exhausting. I was convinced she didn't know how to enjoy herself while having sex. Doing me seemed more like a blue-collar job than an explorative adventure. But I caught all the pussy they willingly, voluntarily, and deliberately threw at me.

"So what's the real reason I fucked them?" I asked myself.

Because I was a man. Because I could. Because Honey had hurt me. I had no idea if I was going to get back with Honey or if our relationship was over. Fucking took my mind off of things. I didn't go out searching for pussy; pussycats landed in my lap at times when I happened to be idle. If I were in a relationship with Honey and had fucked Red Velvet and Sapphire, that would constitute cheating.

My father once told me, "Son, you can't divorce a woman you're not married to, and you can't cheat on a woman you're not in a relationship with. Never let a woman convince you otherwise." Dad was right. But somehow women didn't see it that way.

Women didn't see a lot of things the way men did. I bet if Honey ever found out about Red Velvet and me, she'd get pissed off. But why? I wanted to be her man, but I wasn't her man, and she wasn't my woman. Honey had the right to fuck whomever she wanted. I just hoped that she wasn't fucking any other men. Men were selfish and inconsiderate of women's feelings that way, too. I was predatory and wanted it all. Love. Sex. Money. Not necessarily in that order.

Communication was important. I couldn't assume Honey was mine. In fact, she'd never been mine. We fell into a casual relationship of convenience without a commitment. Hanging out for two weeks, making love every day, helping her find a home and a location for her business did not mean we were a committed couple.

I smiled, inside and out. Honey had called, saying she was a few minutes away. I felt sorry for Tiffany, but I was glad I'd told her the truth with respect for her feelings. In a way, I was flattered that an undercover cop wanted me. That was my ego kicking in. Sapphire didn't love me any more than that super-pussy stripper Red Velvet. I bet she could spread her lips and charge by the lips. Men would stand in line to taste her. Not me.

I hooked up my iPod to my portable speakers and selected R. Kelly's greatest hits and started singing as I stepped into the shower. "Aw, yeah, come inside. Now turn the lights down. Don't be scared, touch me. Tonight is your night for the rest of your life . . . Give me that honey love . . ."

Slicking my wet body with baby oil, I admired myself in the mirror, trying to see what the women saw in me. "Oh, yeah." My eyes lowered to my dick, which damn near touched the vanity. 'Ah, don't be scared. Touch me.' " I had to smile. I shaved, slipped into a fresh pair of black silk pajama pants, put a splash of Unforgivable in the crevice of my abs. I lit a few vanilla-cinnamon candles, double-checked the ice in the bucket to make sure it hadn't melted. The champagne was nice and cold. I had the Wynn's lobster special for two in a warming tray beneath the table covered with a white cloth and topped with red and white roses. The bananas Foster dessert tempted me. I wanted to taste something sweet before Honey arrived.

I dipped my finger in the sauce, eased it into my mouth. "Ummm, ummmm. That's good shit right there," I said aloud.

The doorbell rang. "Perfect timing," I said. I smiled from ear to ear. Taking a deep breath, I exhaled, then opened the door and almost shitted on myself when I saw Red Velvet. "Hey, how'd you get here?" I mumbled. "Trevor, man, fuck. Not this shit again. Look, Velvet, I apologize for standing you up the other night, but you can't come in. I didn't invite you here. You've got to go back to wherever you came from. And my God, what happened to you?"

Red Velvet's acrylic nails were chipped on each hand. Her hair was all over her head. Her T-shirt was partially torn. She looked a mess.

"She's with me," Honey said, appearing in front of the door and standing beside Red Velvet.

"What kind of sick-ass shit is this? You two in cahoots? Setting me up?" I said, motioning to close the door. *Why'd I do that?* I thought. *The two of them together in my bed at the same time? Would probably kill me!*

Honey pushed against the door before it locked. "Grant, wait. It's not a setup."

Walking away from the door, I removed the lobsters from the warmer. I was not about to let a five-hundred-dollar meal go to waste. I opened the champagne and poured two glasses. I didn't want to be impolite. At that moment, Honey and Red Velvet entered my room.

"Honey, you can share what was supposed to be your meal with Red Velvet since y'all came together," I said, slamming a whole glass of champagne down my throat. I refilled my glass.

"I'm not hungry. She can eat if she wants to," Honey said to me. She could've told Velvet directly.

There went my efforts and hopes for an intimate evening. I watched Honey walk over to the window. Red Velvet rolled the dining table toward the door. What were these two up to?

Velvet quietly ate the lobster, texting me while she was eating. *Don't go near Honey. She is pissed. She tried to kill me. We had a fight. I hit her ass back.*

What the hell? I texted back, keeping my eye on Honey. Finally, I asked, "Is there something you two want to talk about? If not, I'd appreciate it if you'd both leave." I hated playing mind games with women.

"Grant, why? Why did you have to fuck Velvet?" Honey cried.

Damn. Here we go. Tears and all. I knew the guilt trip bullshit was coming. I wiped my mouth, sucked in my lips, and exhaled heavily. "Haaaa," I said. Why did I have to explain myself? I was a grown-ass man, not a child. I hadn't been in a relationship with Honey at any time. I loved her, but I wasn't obligated to be with her. "What difference does it make who I fucked? We are not together."

Red Velvet's eyes widened. "That's the same shit I said in so many words."

Calmly, Honey replied, "Okay. That's cool. The two of you are absolutely correct." She stared out the window. "Grant, can you come here for a minute, please, dear?"

Red Velvet texted: *Stay the fuck away. Don't move.*

Instinctively, I took Red Velvet's advice. Whoever invented text messaging had just saved my life.

Honey stood by the window, watching the bright lights on the Strip. She walked over to me. Softly, she said, "The next time y'all decide to make a fool outta me, motherfucker, don't!" *Slap!*

The word *motherfucker* hurt more than the slap. Actually, the slap turned me the fuck on. My dick stood the fuck up. Fortunately for Honey, my father had taught me never to hit a woman, so I grabbed her wrists, threw her sexy, heated, emotional ass on the bed, then straddled her. I knew what she wanted. She wanted this big-ass dick gliding in and out of her sweet pussy. Otherwise, she wouldn't have come here. And she definitely wouldn't have stayed. I was burning up inside, ready to dig deep in her pussy. My dick was so hard, I could drill a hole in a piece of steel. I pressed my stiff shaft against her and kept it there. My dick throbbed against her clit. I unleashed it, letting just the head press her thong inside her pussy.

Honey panted. "Oh, Grant."

Red Velvet said, "I'ma go out for a walk and leave you two alone before I end up on that damn bed, fucking both of y'all. Oh, by the way, I need some money."

Say what? Like that? She was bi? Damn! What was I thinking? Atlanta was the bi capital of America. Having Red Velvet join us would've been a fantasy cum true for me, but I didn't want to fuck up a sure thing with Honey. I nodded toward my wallet on the nightstand. "Take a thousand dollars."

Burying her face in my chest, Honey said, "And get the key to our room out of my purse. I'll see you in the morning." Honey wrapped her legs around my waist, then hugged me tight. Flexing my muscles, I leaned my nipple into Honey's mouth.

Red Velvet eased my pants over my ass, her tongue circled my ass-hole, and then she squeezed my ass. I moaned the words *oh fuck*, hoping Honey would think I was responding to her nibbling on my nipple. That shit felt good, too. Precum oozed onto my silk pj's. I thought Velvet had left, but then her finger penetrated my rectum, making me thrust my pelvis into Honey's pussy.

Squirming, I tightened my ass. Velvet sucked my big toe, and I damn near came in my pants. "Take two thousand," I said, hugging Honey so she couldn't look over my shoulder.

Then I felt it. Red Velvet slid my dick out of Honey's pussy. Red Velvet's mouth sucked my head three times.

Honey screamed, "Oh, fuck! Damn, girl. Stop," Honey paused, panted. "Stop finger fucking me. Get outta here."

"I was just tryin' to add a little something extra for the two Gs. Y'all have fun," said Velvet. When the door closed, we heard her say, "Damn, this is the easiest money I've ever made. Look out, Las Vegas. Here comes Velvet Waters."

Waters? Red Velvet Waters. What a nice sound. "Goddamn!" I yelled. *That girl ain't no joke.*

I snatched Honey off the bed, stood her up, and ripped off her pants, tossing them aside. Moving her thong aside, I slid my silk pj's to the floor, picked Honey up, sat her on the windowsill, and I swear, I made love to her like the song playing in the background . . . like I'd never see her again. My dick entered her, and I felt her pussy explode. Within five minutes, we both had experienced orgasms more powerful than the fireworks bursting outside our window.

"You'd better hold on tight," I said, kneeling between Honey's legs. I kissed her clit. "Damn, I miss you and my sweet pussy," I moaned. I slid my tongue along the inside of her lips, lingering in the upper left crevice and applying pressure. I sucked her shaft. "I miss my sweet pus-sy, damn!"

Honey screamed with pleasure. "Oh, Grant. That feels so fucking good. You gon' make me cum again."

"Not yet. Hold on to this one for Daddy," I said, easing my finger inside her wet pussy. I stroked her G-spot while teasing her clit with my tongue until Honey gushed like a water fountain.

Honey's body relaxed; she leaned backward. That was when we heard a crowd of people scream, "Ahhh! She's gonna fall!" They weren't screaming for Honey.

Honey was on the edge, but she wasn't falling, because our window wasn't open and I wasn't letting Honey go. My baby was squirming. Pulling her in, I carried her to the bed and cuddled behind her the way Tiffany had wanted me to cuddle behind her. I held Honey in my arms and whispered in her ear. "You're the only woman I want. Welcome home, baby. In my arms is where you belong."

CHAPTER 30

Red Velvet

Every man was available.

The question wasn't if he was available outside of his relationship; it was a matter of timing. Right place. Right time. He was there. His woman wasn't. His dick was hard. The pussy next to him was wet. No one was watching. No strings attached. It was on. Any woman could entice a man on any given day. It didn't take stripping for me to learn there were three easy, real simple steps to luring a man.

Men were visual creatures.

While I was thinking of men, my phone rang. I answered. "Hey, Trevor. What's up?"

"What's up? Where the hell are you?" he asked.

This was the first time I'd heard Trevor obviously upset. "I'm in Vegas. I'll be back at work tomorrow," I said apologetically.

The woman who showed the most didn't necessarily get the most attention. A woman had to learn how to tease, how to please, and how to position herself with patience. The first time I met Grant, I did what I was paid to do: pounce on his dick right away. But if I'd met him on my own, I would've given him my confident one-second glance. Looking at a man for three seconds or more and then looking away gave two impressions, desperation and insecurity. I would've gotten close enough for him to smell me and get a close-up view, which would've given him time to figure out his approach. Then I would've slowly strutted away, shaking my big-ass, juicy booty, as if to say, "You know you want some of this. Don't be scared. Come and get it."

"What the fuck you doing in Vegas? I'm losing money over here. My clientele left early last night and even earlier tonight. Stilettos is empty," he said, as though it was my fault. "I want you here at eight o'clock tomorrow. I'm tripling your shows, and I'm taking every dollar I lose out of your tips. You hear me! Are you down there working? Are you fucking somebody else?"

If I wanted to fuck Grant again, I could. Believe that.

I wasn't jealous of Honey or her wannabe relationship with Grant. I did want to join them, though. My pussy had been percolating so fucking hard, I'd swallowed some lobster and I'd come by myself. Watching Grant straddle Honey and hearing them breathing heavy and shit had got me all excited. I loved having sex. I coulda made both of them scream, "Velvet!" At the same time.

Trevor yelled, "Do you hear me!"

I was grateful Honey had saved and spared my life, and had I known Grant was her man, I would've fucked him, anyway, 'cause that was how I got down. And it was like I said: I didn't see her name tattooed on his dick. Plus, wasn't like I'd thrown that big, fine-ass man down and taken his dick. He was the one trying to get back at this velvety pussy, until I messed up and texted him that crazy message that was intended for Tolliver's punk ass. That was when Grant changed up on me, giving me the black man's silent treatment and shit, like his fingers had gotten jammed from texting or he'd gotten a sudden case of lockjaw.

Softly, I said, "You don't own my pussy. You don't own me. I'm hanging up my stilettos. Trevor, I quit."

Couldn't say I blamed Grant, but I hated that noncommunicative, immature behavior black men exhibited. I was glad I'd had the opportunity to suck Grant's dick. A dick that beautiful should be in some woman's mouth all the time, like a pacifier. The only times he should pull out were to take a piss and a shower.

"You can't quit on me. I made you," Trevor shouted, then went on about paying me more money. I was done listening to him.

"Um, um, um." I smacked my lips, then slapped my ass. Lord, that man was fine and a skilled lover, too! As sexy as Grant was, there was nothing for me to be jealous of. Sure I'd daydreamed about a life with Grant, texted him like crazy, but what woman in my position wouldn't have done the same? Wasn't like I knew him, or like we were making wedding plans and shit. But he did have a pretty-ass dick. I should've taken a picture of it with my camera phone, then saved it as my screen saver.

"Huh, what did you say? We have a bad connection," I said. The call dropped as the elevator doors closed. "Thank, God."

Strolling through the hotel lobby, I went inside one of the nail shops and got a fresh set of French-manicured, solar nails that lasted, like my individual eyelashes, up to three months. Then I went to the gift shops, bought me a fifteen-hundred-dollar outfit, charged it to Grant's room, and went back upstairs. That was the least Grant and Honey could do for me.

I headed to my suite on the fiftieth floor, showered, put on my new little short black halter dress, then sat on the side of my bed, texting Tolliver. *I'ma drop the charges against your wife when I get back home tomorrow.*

I was too happy to make anybody else miserable. Tolliver was tired, anyway. He texted back: *Thank you, Velvet. Thank you so much. I'll break you off when I see you.*

"I'm already broke off, fool. I don't need you anymore," I said aloud. "I'm starting my own business, and I'm moving to Hollywood. You don't owe me nothing." I knew his promise to take care of me with a few dollars was Tolliver's way of apologizing and hitting this pussy one more time, but that was what was not gon' happen.

I stroked on my eyeliner and red velvet lipstick. "Watch out, Vegas! Here comes the hottest, the finest, the sexiest, the prettiest bitch in town . . . Make some nooooooooise for Reeeeddddd Vel-vet!"

Slipping on my iridescent stilettos, I decided I could star in my own Vegas show, with bright lights swarming around me, Oscar style. Forget that. One day I was going to become an actress. Bouncing to the floor a few times to warm up, I strutted out of my room like I owned the entire casino. I saw a couple guys I could get down with on a one-nighter, but they were busy shaking dice while watching me shake my ass. Damn. Having a bank to build a spot like this was seriously what was up. I browsed a few more of the designer stores, peeked inside the club, then I headed to the bar for a drink that somebody else was going to buy. I was banking that two grand I'd gotten from Grant. Did he always keep that kind of money on him?

I wanted a man like Grant. If he were mine, Grant could fuck whomever he wanted whenever he wanted and wherever he damn well pleased. If the chick was badder than me, I'd break her off for keeping us happy. The worst thing a man could do was creep with a chick that gave him stress. That meant she was wearing both of us out when he came home unhappy. What was the big deal about women double-dunkin' dicks?

Monopolizing men like Trevor and Tolliver couldn't do shit for me no more. Thinking of Tolliver made me think about his wife, and thoughts of his wife reminded me to call my mother to check on her and my son.

"Velvet, where are you?" Mama asked, sounding worried. "Did you turn off your phone?"

"Chill out. I'm fine, Ma. I'm at the Wynn. This place is fab-u-listic!"

Quickly, Mama said, "Stay off the pole, Velvet."

"Yeah, yeah. You still trying to tell me how to live my life? Honey already told me to stay off of everything." *Except a dick.*

"She's right, and you're right. I owe you an apology, sweetheart. You were right. I should've listened to you. I never should've found Alphonso."

"It's okay, Ma," I lied. No, she shouldn't have. It was my life, not hers. It was my mistake, not hers. And she never should've gotten involved. Clearly, she'd made things worse for all of us, including Alphonso's wife. "Where's Ronnie?"

"Sleeping. He passed out in his clothes the minute we got back to the hotel. He had a ball at Disneyland. We'll sit and talk with him about what happened when we all get back home. Okay?" Mama said, almost asking for my permission.

Whatever my mom wanted to do was good with me. She was and always would be my rock. I knew she had our best interests at heart. "I love you, Ma. I'm gonna enjoy. Viva Las Vegas, yeah! I'll call you in the morning. What time does your flight get in?"

"Six in the evening."

"Honey and I get in at three. I'll pick you guys up. Oh, and Ma, I quit stripping." I blew my mother a kiss into my phone, then hung up. A guy next to me caught the kiss in midair.

I snatched it back. "That was not for you."

Smiling, he asked, "Can I buy you a drink?"

Mission accomplished. "Sure. What's your name?'

Thrusting his chest forward, he said, "Pretty Ricky," as though I should've known who he was. Wasn't everybody in Vegas famous for something? He had nice, large teeth. Bleaching would've made them shine like diamonds.

"Where you from?" I asked him.

"Wherever I'm at." He flipped open a stack of hundreds, spread them like a fan, then tossed a hundred-dollar bill on the bar. "You got a nice li'l frame there," he said, leaning back and looking at my ass, which was hanging over the edge of the bar stool. "You out to make some change? I can make you famous." He started fanning me with his money.

I ordered a double Patrón Silver, chilled. "You didn't know?" I politely moved his arm out of my face. "I'm already famous," I said. Checking him out, I fanned my twenty one-hundred-dollar bills in his face. I felt good having that much money to flaunt.

He was fine, but he had *pimp* written all over his half-perm, half-fake-ass, synthetic, silky, straight weave, which flowed midway down his back. His acrylic nails were longer than mine. His too-tight jeans, cowboy snakeskin boots, and button-down, collared shirt, with a T-shirt underneath, gave him away. All Pretty Ricky could do for me was buy me a drink or two. Regardless of whether or not a woman planned on having sex, a lady always ordered a double shot straight, because the drink lasted longer than the man.

"You good. I got you. Put that away before I break you." He stared at me. "What's your name?"

If he thought about touching my money, he'd have a stiletto up his ass and coming out of his balls before my money reached his pocket. "Red Velvet."

He covered him mouth. "Damn. I heard about you. My boys told

me about Red Velvet. Stripper, right? Stilettos, right? You outta the
ATL, right?"

"Told you I was famous."

"That ain't you, bitch. You lying."

I didn't have shit to prove to him, but I felt like having a little fun.
"Bartender, give me an unopened bottle of water," I said, smiling at
Pretty Ricky.

The bartender placed the bottle on the bar. I told Pretty Ricky,
"You might wanna hold your glass. Here. Hold mine, too."

I stood on the bar in my ankle-strap heels, squatted over the bottle,
moved my thong aside, then eased the plastic sixteen-ounce bottle inside my pussy. I reached for Pretty Ricky's hand, pushed out the
empty water bottle, then sat back on my stool. I did that shit so quick,
the bartender asked, "What happened?"

"Damn, baby. That's what's up," said Pretty Ricky. "You gotta be on
my team. I ain't taking no for an answer. I'll pay you double. Triple
whatever I pay my other bitches."

I wasn't stupid or impressed. Pretty Ricky needed me more than I
wanted him.

A woman sat next to Pretty Ricky and said, "She's a bad bitch, huh?"

Pretty Ricky scrambled out of his seat and vanished. No comment.
No bye. And he'd left his change on the bar.

I was still feeling upbeat and wonderful. I didn't know what made
me say to the woman, "You look like you could use a friend. May I buy
you a drink with his money?" Perhaps I was in search of companionship above the waist, but I had nothing to lose. The people in Vegas
made Vegas exciting. The dicks weren't leaving the casino in droves,
so I had time to pick a decent man to drop this pussy on.

"No, thanks. Let me get yours," she said, looking at the bartender
and nodding in my direction. "You're new. What's brings you here?"

"You're a regular. You tell me," I said, not willing to divulge that
level of personal information. She could've asked my name instead.
Damn.

She hunched her shoulders. "Not really sure. I guess I'm here because I didn't want to be home alone, and I decided to quit my job
tonight."

"You too. Dang. I just quit my job, too. I'm Red Velvet. I have had an unbelievable night. Last few days actually," I said, thinking about my son's father.

"I'm Tiffany. Tiffany Davis. Pleased to meet you, Red Velvet."

I sat there, with my mouth hanging open. I texted Honey: *You won't believe who I'm having a drink with at the main bar, near the waterfall. Come down here now!*

CHAPTER 31

Sapphire

The world, my world, couldn't possibly get any smaller. I hadn't seen Pretty Ricky in years. Funny how time brought about a change. Pretty Ricky had never imagined he'd be running scared from me. After my return to Vegas as a cop, he'd successfully managed to stay out of my way. Seeing him and recalling how he'd abused me made me angry, but seeing him run made me smile on the inside. I held the power over him, and he knew it. I wished I had that kind of control over Grant.

Ordinarily, I wouldn't have shown up at this casino, but I wanted a different venue, a place where I could relax and feel like I wasn't in work mode. I was glad I'd gotten the money back from Summer. For the love of money, Valentino would come running to me. Valentino loved money more than Summer, more than life. Any man that would kill for money would also die for money. For Valentino, which one would it be? There was no way I could ever kill all the pimps or save all the prostitutes, and honestly, I'd gotten tired of trying to help people who didn't want my help.

Prostitution for some women was a preferred way to make a living. Wasn't as though they couldn't go out and get a respectable job. Prostitution wasn't a living; it was an addictive lifestyle that endured because of the possibility of making a fast dollar—by the minute, not the hour—by making a man cum quickly. Virtually a same time exchange of money and the blow job was done. Wanna cum again?

Got more money?

Tonight I had no desire to arrest or shoot anyone. I'd simply planned to have a few drinks while reflecting on my life. I had to uncover the real reason I was unhappy. Why did I want Grant to make me happier than I made myself?

"I know you don't know me," Red Velvet said. "But you do know the person I want to introduce to you. Come upstairs with me for a minute."

Was this overly hyper woman deranged? She'd just finished talking to Pretty Ricky. I knew why he'd left abruptly, but was Red Velvet one of his new girls? Why did she offer to buy me a drink? Now she wanted me to go upstairs with her. Where? "Why don't you have your people come down here? I'll wait."

"I tried. She doesn't want to. But you have to go up with me. Okay. I'll let you hold my purse with my money and my identification just to prove I'm being honest."

I took her purse, handed it to the bartender, then said, "Hold this until I get back."

Red Velvet protested. "I don't know him. You can't give my purse to him to hold. I gave it to you."

Opening my hand, I wiggled my fingers at the bartender. "Give it back," I said. After handing Red Velvet the purse, I sat on the stool and continued sipping my drink.

Red Velvet opened her purse, stuffed her money in her halter, and tossed her purse on the bar. "You'd better not open my purse, or I'ma beat your ass when I get back, you hear me?" She looked at me, then said, "Let's go."

She could be my replacement. That was if she wasn't afraid to kill. I had to have lost my damn mind. Why was I following this lunatic, big-booty chick to the elevator? Obviously, she didn't really know who she was dealing with. If I decided to shoot her, I would pull my gun from between my titties and pow! I didn't care how beautiful she was. I'd let her have it. I relaxed. What was the worst that could happen? I was inside the most secure hotel on the Strip. Even on the sixtieth floor, security observed everything.

"Step back," Red Velvet told me as she tapped on the door. "Open up. It's me, Velvet."

The door opened a crack, and I heard a man's voice. "What is it? Do you need more money?"

My heart stopped; my jaw dropped. I couldn't see his face, but I'd recognize Grant's voice anywhere.

"No, I need to talk to Honey," Velvet insisted.

He said, "Honey went to sleep."

"No, she didn't," Red Velvet said. "She just texted me to come upstairs. Let me in." She motioned for me to come in, too.

Once I was inside the hotel room, my eyes widened. Honey's eyes widened. We stood across the room from one another. This was the first time we'd seen one another since the day I'd given her the fifty million.

"Is this who you met at the bar?" Honey coyly asked Red Velvet. "How? Did you go looking for her? I didn't ask you to do this, now did I?"

"No, she didn't come looking for me, and I wasn't looking for her. I don't even know her," I said in Red Velvet's defense. Looking at Grant as he walked away without seeing me, I asked, "Why does she want us to meet?"

I couldn't believe my eyes. Grant was fuck-tas-tic. My eyes lingered on his back as he disappeared into the bathroom. I couldn't believe my ears. Was Honey pissed off with Red Velvet for bringing me to her room?

Honey smiled at me. "Come sit on the sofa for a minute. We have a lot to talk about."

"We sure do," I said, sitting across from her and wedging my back into the side of the sofa. I heard the shower going. I pictured the day Grant and I were in the shower. I relived how I'd dropped to my knees and sucked his big, beautiful dick. I wished I could go get in that shower with him right now and leave Honey and Red Velvet where they were. Why shouldn't I get up and go in the bathroom with Grant, instead of looking at Honey, who was sitting across from me, with his pajama shirt on. It would be nice to feel Grant inside of me again.

"Have a seat," Honey said to Red Velvet, motioning toward the chair across the room. Ignoring Honey, Red Velvet stood by the window.

Biting my bottom lip, I wasn't amused with Honey's attempt to control the tempo. Seriously, I asked her, "Where's my money?"

"I'm not playing games with you, Tiffany," said Honey. "You were the one who came to me, offering the money and claiming you wanted to help. I didn't solicit it in any way. Stop acting like you didn't give me that money. And this is the last time I'm having this conversation with you. I don't know what made you change your mind, but I'm not giving it back. Read my lips. I am not giving the money back, not one penny." Honey reached into her purse.

I reached into my bra.

"Here." Honey handed me a folded piece of paper.

Whew. She almost got shot in the head on that one. Then I could have had Grant to myself.

"This is why Velvet invited you up," said Honey.

Maybe I should shoot her. Glancing at the paper, I became speechless. Tears flooded my eyes. It was hard to swallow the lump in my throat. "Where'd you get this?"

Red Velvet stood quietly, gazing out the window.

"Your mother gave it to me," Honey said softly.

"My mother? Yeah, right! How would you know my mother?" I said.

"I don't," Honey said.

Sadly, Velvet said, "Honey was looking for my son's father. He just so happened to be married to your mother." She never stopped staring out the window.

I asked Red Velvet, "You know Alphonso? How?"

Red Velvet kept staring out the window. "He raped me. I got pregnant. Had a baby. And he's the father. I really don't know him, but I do hate him. Men are fucking irresponsible liars who will say whatever to fuck whomever they want. Dirty old bastard. When they finish cuming, they act like it's all our fault, like we got pregnant on our own, or we tricked them. And the reality is, whether what happened to me is my fault or not, I'm the one stuck with the responsibility of raising Ronnie. I don't know what I'd do without my mother. Sometimes I wanna die so I don't have to work so hard. Alphonso is the lucky one.

He doesn't have to do shit! He hasn't served time in jail. He has not even paid child support. I haven't figured out how to explain this to Ronnie. Maybe he's better off not knowing."

"He raped me, too," I said. "Every day he came to my room, and he raped me." I didn't want to cry, but I couldn't hold back the tears. This was the strangest thing that had ever happened to me.

Never did I think I'd meet a woman that Alphonso had raped. And she had his baby. There was something sad underneath Red Velvet's words, the same type of sadness that plagued me. I didn't know how to rid myself of the stigma. Red Velvet kept staring out the window.

"I'm going to kill him," I said.

"What good would that do?" Red Velvet asked, still staring out the window.

Honey answered, "He won't stick his dead dick in another woman without her permission, that's for sure. I'll help you kill his ass."

"I got a mama and a baby to take care of," said Red Velvet. "Otherwise, I would've shot that sorry motherfucker the day I found out I was pregnant. That's how I felt. Still do. I just can't do it."

Honey scooted closer to me. "It's okay. Both of you have to move past that. Tiffany, your mother told us she's looked for you every day. She never stopped. You have to call her. You can have the same loving relationship with your mother that Velvet has with her mother. But I have to warn you. When we left your mother's house yesterday, we heard screams. We don't know if she was kicking Alphonso's ass or if he was beating hers, but I did call in a two seventeen."

Damn. Honey had love like that? For me? I had to leave tonight for Los Angeles. What I needed was . . .

The bathroom door opened. Grant entered the living area, dressed in a silk pajama bottom. When he saw me sitting on the sofa, next to Honey, and staring at his dick, he froze. He probably was having a *Fatal Attraction* flashback and thinking I was scheming against him. I knew how much he loved Honey. And I wasn't trying to put him in a compromising position, but I needed him to hold me. Standing up, I walked toward Grant. He shook his head, then said in a normal tone, "Don't do it, Velvet."

Turning toward the window, I saw that Red Velvet was sitting on the ledge, with her feet dangling out the open window. I didn't know what made me want to push her off the ledge instead of pull her in. Yes, I did. I wanted Grant to hold me, not her, in his arms.

Honey was faster than Grant. She hugged Red Velvet's waist and pulled her inside and to the floor. I hugged Grant, then said, "You saved her life. Mine too. Thank you."

"What? Y'all thought I was going to jump? Please! Not over some shiftless nigga. Y'all were acting all depressed and stuff. I was watching the fireworks," Red Velvet said, smiling. "I'm tired of crying over what happened to me. I was imagining the fireworks were for me. I imagined I'd gotten that call I've been waiting for. 'Red Velvet, we're calling to offer you the role of Coco Brown in *Something on the Side.*' My first leading role in a movie, and the stars bursting in the air were all for me. I was pretending I was on the red carpet, smiling for the cameras like Jennifer Hudson, taking pictures, giving interviews, sitting on stage with Oprah. Y'all sure know how to mess up a girl's fantasy. Let me go. I'm going to my room." Red Velvet stood up, then walked to the door. She squeezed Grant's butt, then said, "Good night."

What the hell? I stopped hugging Grant and looked at him. Why had Velvet done that to Grant? I made my way to the door, too. I said, "Thanks, Honey." Then I walked up to Grant and said, "I'm Tiffany, and you are?"

Grant pivoted, with his back to Honey, so she couldn't see his face. He closed his eyes, opened them, shook his head, then said, "Grant. Pleased to meet you, Tiffany."

I couldn't resist. I hugged him again. I nestled my cheek on his bare chest, softly kissed his nipple, then quietly left. I wished I knew what room Red Velvet had disappeared into so I could thank her and confront her. I needed to talk with her to find out more about her encounter with Alphonso. More important, I wanted to know why she'd squeezed Grant's ass in front of Honey and me.

Waiting for the elevator, I wasn't sure what to do next. But I was happy to learn that after all these years, my mama hadn't given up looking for me. Maybe nobody else loved me, but I now knew without a doubt that my mother did. Her search was over.

Tiffany Davis, who had been missing for fourteen years, was going home. I prayed that Grant was right. Maybe now I could find true happiness within myself.

CHAPTER 32

Valentino

A nigga didn't have a choice.

What the fuck was I gonna do with less than two thousand dollars to my name? That was all I had after stopping at the pawnshop and spending ten fucking grand on a round-cut solitaire. The five carats were worth every penny. I'd heard that when niggas bought marquis diamonds for their fiancées, the marriage didn't last worth a shit, but when they bought the round rock, the shit was like infinity, solid forever. Unless Summer died or was killed, I was getting married one time.

I'd put Benito on hold last night, put his ass up in a cheap motel, and left. First off, I'd never sleep in a two-star hotel. And it was best that I took my horny ass home to blast inside my girl this heavy load weighing down my nuts. The thought of fucking Benito didn't empower me; that shit scared me, because fucking him would've been the same as fucking a bitch. As soon as I married Summer, I was out . . . on my way to Atlanta in this Bentley to collect my fuckin' money from Lace.

I parked in the driveway at my house, walked up to the front door. Quietly, I slid my key in the lock, but it wouldn't turn. I took the key out, put it back in, and tried that shit again, and it still didn't work. I speed dialed Summer's home number, and the bitch was temporarily suspended. Not the home phone, but the fuckin' cell phone she'd given me. I knew money wasn't the issue. That bitch was trying to control me? With a damn phone? I hurled that motherfucker like a football into the middle of the street and started banging on the door.

"Summer! Summer, you hear me, bitch! Open this fuckin' door!" I yelled, trying to knock the door in. I didn't give a fuck if her nosy-ass neighbors across the street did call the fuckin' cops. Disturbing their motherfuckin' peace was the least of my concerns.

"Summer said to tell you she left you a note," a lady yelled from next door. "It's in the mailbox!" Then she shut her door.

I walked to the edge of the driveway, opened the mailbox. "Well, I'll be damned. A fuckin' note addressed to me in my own mailbox. What will this bitch think of next? Why didn't her ass just send me a homing pigeon?"

Stuffing the note in my pocket, I got back in my Bentley and took off. "Bitch!" I yelled. I'd spent ten grand that I couldn't get back on that fuckin' ring. That left me with seventeen hundred after breaking off Benito's broke ass. What the hell was I gonna do with that? Wipe my asshole? I tried to calm down. I hadn't read the note yet. Maybe she's at the chapel. "Yeah, that's it. Why hadn't I thought about that?"

I changed my course and drove to Chapel of the Bells. After parking in the small lot, I went inside. A woman was standing at the altar. Her back was to me. The dress was white, some bland shit that Summer would wear. The veil covered her face. I straightened out my tuxedo as I approached her. Slowly she turned around. Lifting the veil, I uncovered her face, then exhaled. "Summer, baby. Why didn't you wait for me? Where's my son?"

Summer opened her mouth and said, "Summer is dead, motherfucker!" I didn't know who that possessed bitch was who was cocking a Beretta double-action semiautomatic pistol and pointing it at my face.

"Oh fuck!" I yelled. Of all the fuckin' times for a nigga to trip. I fell straight on my ass, shielding my face with my hands.

"You shot my sister in the head at point-blank range. Summer is dead. I'm Sunny. How does it feel having a gun in your face, Mr. Badd Ass? Huh? Exploiting women. Making money off of women's pussies while you sit on your dick! I should put your fuckin' ass on a stroll. Make you suck a couple of dicks and take it in the ass. The money is not yours! The money is not yours! It's not yours! None of it belongs to you!"

She pressed the barrel hard against my temple. The same way I'd done to Sunny. But I didn't pull the fuckin' trigger. She did. Sunny killed herself. I swear. "Don't shoot! Don't shoot me! I didn't mean it! It was an accident! I swear!" I yelled, scurrying backward on the floor, wishing I had picked up Benito before coming to the chapel. That nigga was a guaranteed fuckin' distraction.

I felt a tender hand nudging me in the side, and I heard a sweet voice in my ear. "What was an accident? Wake up, baby. Wake up."

My chest heaved. I was drenched in sweat. My body was freezing cold. I looked at the woman in the bed with me and screamed, "Bitch, who are you?"

Reaching for me, she said, "It's me, Summer."

I pushed her arms away; I didn't want that bitch touching me. "Prove it. Prove that you're not Sunny. Tell me something only Summer would know," I said, sniffing the bedroom air. "What's that fuckin' smell? Damn! Damn! Damn!" I was losing my fuckin' mind.

Summer shook her head. "That's frankincense. My mother told me to burn it to rid the house of evil spirits. Anthony, are you evil? Who was haunting you in your sleep? Was it my sister? You did kill Sunny, didn't you?" Summer asked me these questions like she was fuckin' working for Dr. Phil.

I got out of the bed, got on my knees, and lift the covers. I didn't see anyone under there. I frisked Summer's body for wires, then ripped off her gown. Was Summer trying to get a confession from me? "Bitch, you setting me up again?"

Scrambling out of the bed, Summer said, "Anthony, I have no reason to set you up. Besides, if you didn't kill my sister, you have nothing to worry about. Was Sunny haunting you?" Summer stood on the opposite side of the bed.

I sat on the edge of the bed, out of her reach. Trying to calm down, I said, "Nah, nah. Just some shit that happened in prison. Nothing I want to talk about. I'll be okay." As soon as I got the fuck outta this haunted house and away from this possessed bitch.

"Is that why we had to wait to make love? Did some man violate you while you were incarcerated?" Summer asked, sounding like Barbara fuckin' Walters.

"Who the fuck are you!" I screamed, covering my ears. "No, nobody touched me." That answer was . . . false. What did this bitch think we were doing? Playing *The Moment of Truth?* "Look, stay the fuck away from me. I'm going to shower and put on my tux," I said, going into the bathroom.

"Okay," Summer said. Then she started singing, "Going to the chapel, and we're gonna get ma-a-a-ried." She danced her way into the bathroom with me. "I'm going to get ready, too."

"I'll use the other bathroom," I said, not wanting to be in the same space with her cheery, spooky ass.

I wasn't sure if I should leave or follow through with our plans or kill Summer. That way I wouldn't have to worry about whether she was Sunny or not. They'd both be dead. I was tripping over my own guilt. I decided to go ahead and marry my girl.

I went into Anthony's room, woke him up. "It's time to get ready to be a family, li'l man," I told him.

"Daddy?" Anthony said, sitting up in his superhero pajamas.

I was changing his room and his wardrobe when I got back. I didn't believe in all this false sense of heroic power.

"Yeah, man. What's on your mind?"

"Do you love us?" he asked.

His question caught me off guard. "Of course. Otherwise, I wouldn't be here."

Anthony hugged my neck super tight. "I love you, too, Daddy."

This li'l nigga was making me tear up. "Let's get ready. We don't want your mother to get upset."

I took Anthony into the shower with me in case that demonic bitch planned on resurfacing in the mirror like Candyman. We showered together. Summer came busting into our bathroom.

"I was looking all over for Anthony! Why do you have him in the shower with you?" she asked, snatching open the shower door. "Come with Mommy, baby," she said, leading Anthony out of the bathroom.

Damn. Who in the fuck did she think I was? Did she think I was going to fuck my own seed? Summer's paranoia and shit were getting old real quick.

I dried off, then slipped into my monkey-ass tux. Summer looked great in her white, ankle-length dress, but she looked more like a Muslim than a bride with her veil, which covered her head while revealing her face. In a few hours all of this shit would be a done deal. I checked my pockets to make sure I had my house keys, car keys, and driver's license.

"Let's go," I said. I went to pick up Anthony. I pulled back when Summer's lips tightened. "Are you sure you want to marry *me*?"

"Yes, don't be silly. I love you," she said, getting in the car.

Driving to the chapel, I reminded myself that our getting married was a straight convenience. I knew what I wanted. Financial security, a woman to love me, and a safe, quiet place to sleep at night. I was clueless about what Summer wanted from me, but she was up to something.

Parking in the lot in front of the chapel, I got out of the car. Summer just sat there, and Anthony remained in the backseat, behind her. If she didn't let my son grow up to be a man, he'd sit behind every woman he met. What was her problem? Why was she motioning for me to come to her?

"What is it? You changed your mind?" I asked her through the cracked window.

"No, silly." She smiled. "You're supposed to open the car door for us."

Damn. A nigga wasn't no slave and shit. All this female liberation and she expected me to open the car door. Who opened her damn door before I came home? I pulled the handle on her door first, then Anthony's. He actually needed me to let him out, 'cause the child safety lock was on.

"Daddy, I'm your best man today," Anthony said, with his chest stuck out.

"You're my best man every day," I told him. I meant that shit. I didn't have any best buddies, brothers, or sisters. It was just me.

Summer held her stomach.

"What? What's wrong?" I asked, staring at her stomach.

"Nothing. I'm good," she said, walking inside the chapel.

What if her twins weren't mine? I was not raising some other nigga's kids. First we signed a few papers, then we made our way to the altar, and Summer pulled that veil over her fuckin' face. She knew I had just had that damn nightmare. Actually, she didn't know it had been about her sister. I'd lied to her.

I took a deep breath. We exchanged vows. The reverend said, "You may kiss the bride."

I was not lifting that veil over Summer's face until she said something. Summer removed the veil, and I exhaled. "Thank, god," I murmured, then gave her a peck on the lips.

Before getting back in the car, I opened her car door, then Anthony's door. Then I drove Summer straight to the bank at ten in the morning.

"Baby, why are we here?" Summer asked.

"I got some things to take care of, and I spent all the money I had yesterday on your ring." I went to pull the ten-million-dollar cashier's check from my tuxedo jacket pocket. "Where is it?" I turned every pocket inside out. "Where the fuck is it? Summer, where is the check?"

Summer's eyebrows lifted. "What check? Oh, you mean that check. Sapphire stopped by, asking for it, so I gave it back to her. She said we would've gone to jail if we'd deposited it."

I did a three-sixty in the middle of the bank parking lot. "You did what! You searching through my shit? Are you fuckin' retarded?" I yelled, wanting to go off on her.

"And so? You found the key to my safe, and you went in it without my consent and took the check."

"You gon' give me my money. All of it!" I bellowed. "I want you to add my name to your bank account right now."

A woman came out to our car and knocked on the passenger window. "Ms. Day, are you okay? Do you need assistance?"

"No, bitch. She does not need assistance," I yelled. "If you're the fuckin' wizard, give this bitch a brain."

"I'm calling the police," the woman said.

"It's okay. We'll be fine," Summer reassured her.

"And she's not Ms. Day. She's Mrs. James to you, bitch," I yelled. "Don't you see me in this monkey suit?"

"Anthony, you're embarrassing us," said Summer. "Look at your son sitting back there and hiding on the floor. Is this the type of role model you want to be for him? That's not nice."

I swear, I wanted to cry. I sat there, shaking my head.

"Why don't I get you a cashier's check, and you can open your own account?" said Summer.

I'd been expecting more of a protest, but Summer went inside the bank with me, went into the merchant room, and came out with a cashier's check for one hundred thousand dollars made payable to me. She handed it to me and went back to the car with our son.

I wanted to complain about the amount, but it would do for now. However, she was not putting me on no fucking allowance. When I opened up my account, they put the whole fucking cashier's check on hold.

"Wait one damn minute," I told the teller. "Go get your boss. I need some money now."

The manager came over and stood there explaining the matter to me like she was talking to my son. "Mr. James, this is an astronomical amount of money," she said.

No, bitch, ten million is astronomical, not this measly amount, I thought.

"And your account is new," she argued. "It'll take fifteen business days for us to release the funds. If the check clears, the full amount will be available to you."

"Bitch, it's a fuckin' cashier's check!" I wailed. "The same as cash! Drawn against your fuckin' bank."

"Not all cashier's checks are honored, Mr. James."

"Ain't this a bitch? That's bullshit, and you know it!"

"Is there anything else we can do to assist you? If not, do have a good day," she said, walking away before I answered.

Fuck this! All I had was seventeen hundred dollars for fifteen fuckin' days. I got in the car, drove Summer and Anthony home, and sat on the couch, in my tuxedo, until I could figure out my next move.

CHAPTER 33

Honey

The time had come to get back home to Atlanta and get back to my business. Getting to normalcy wasn't part of my life. Some people could project with a good degree of accuracy what tomorrow might bring for them, but not me. I had no idea. There was no predetermined to-do list I could sketch and follow. I'd missed the grand opening of Sweeter Than Honey, kind of. Being out and actually pursuing my objectives was more productive. The first thing I had to do when I got home was check Girl Six's ass and find out what she was up to.

My trip here to Las Vegas had been successful. I had reunited with Grant and had got to know Red Velvet. I was happy that Sapphire was going home to her mother. Not to visit. To stay. At least until Sapphire decided what was next. I'd gladly have her on my team. And I'd called her this morning to reassure her I was serious about taking out Alphonso if that was what she and Red Velvet wanted.

Nah, she probably wouldn't work for me. I couldn't quite get a read on why she'd hugged Grant for so long. He'd said the saliva on his chest was from her runny nose. Anyway, hopefully, her mother was doing well, and if her mom was smart, Alphonso was long gone, never to return. I couldn't comprehend mothers who'd put their man before the children. My mother, Rita, had treated me that way, but she'd favored my sister, Honey.

"Baby," Grant said.

"Yes?" I answered.

"Baby."

"Yes?"

"One quickie before we go our separate ways," he said, spreading my thighs.

We both had flights to catch in two hours. It could take one of those hours to get through security at the Las Vegas airport. But flying first class had its privileges. We could all move to the front of the line if we wanted.

Flipping into a sixty-nine position, I straddled his dick, wrapped my fingers around him, squeezed him, then eased the most delicious dick in my mouth. I felt his lips caress mine, making me sit closer to his mouth, to his face. The more he sucked my clit, the firmer I sucked his dick, until my jaws caved in around his shaft.

I moaned, "We're going to miss our flights."

"Who cares? There's always another one," Grant said, circling my shaft with his tongue.

His ass tensed as he thrust his dick deeper down my throat.

Not for me, there wasn't. A few weeks ago I would've missed a flight for Grant. Not today. I was genuinely happy to have spent a whole day with Grant, virtually uninterrupted, but I'd be lying if I said my feelings were the same as before. His promiscuity concerned me. I stopped sucking his dick, turned to face him, then sat my ass on his dick, sandwiching his erection between my butt cheeks.

I exhaled, gazing into his eyes. "We need to talk."

"Now? Can't we finish first? We can talk later. I promise to give you my undivided attention."

Truthfully, there might be no later. Men thought relationships revolved around them. Grant couldn't honestly think everything he'd done was fine.

"Baby, I was so close," he said, making his dick throb. "Five more minutes and I'm done. I promise. Don't leave me like this."

"Okay. Answer one question for me, and then we can finish." Of course, it all depended on his response. "Did you fuck Sapphire, too?"

Grant's eyes penetrated mine. "What? Are you serious?"

"*What* is not an answer. Did you fuck Sapphire?"

I'd learned a woman had to be direct. I refused to give him an out by asking, "What's your relationship with Sapphire?" Hell, it would've been easy for him to respond, "I don't have a relationship with her." Relationships and fucking were two entirely different things.

"Well?" I asked.

"Honey, move. Please," Grant said, "You've ruined what could've been a good moment. At least you're consistent. I've got to go. I don't know why you have to keep going there. It's like you're looking for a reason for us not to be together. It's like you want to find a reason to be miserable. If that's how you want it, fine. But you can ride the misery train solo."

Grant balled up his pajamas and shoved them into his bag. I walked over to him. "Why can't you answer a simple question? The answer is yes, isn't it?"

"Yes, Honey. The answer is yes," he said, being sarcastic to throw me off. "What difference does it make if I'm telling the truth or lying? We were not a couple. I wasn't in a relationship with you. I have never been in a relationship with you. Therefore, it was impossible for me to cheat on you."

Zippp! Angrily, he'd closed his bag.

"Grant," I said, packing my things. "There is such a thing as emotional responsibility and emotional infidelity. You fucked me every day for two weeks straight. That constituted an emotional relationship. An emotional bond. You invited me here to your hotel room. You fucked me like you were a dog in heat. You cuddled with me last night. You said in your arms was where I belonged. What did all of that mean to you?"

"You were a prostitute, for God's sake. You've fucked more men than I have women. You sucked my dick when you were sixteen. You fucked a different man every day and probably sucked their dicks, too. I've never thrown any of that in your face. But you feel justified in drilling me on fucking a few women. Go fucking figure! So you're a prosecuting prostitute now. We never made a verbal commitment that we were a couple. Is that what you want from me? Do you want to be with me?"

Picking up the flower vase with the red and white roses, I hurled it at Grant, then rolled my teary eyes. My lips tightened; I squinted my eyes. I wanted to slap the fuck out of him! "I didn't know you when I was sixteen!" A part of me had become angry at him for being right. His words hurt me. "Why are you fucking with my emotions? If you don't want a relationship, say so. Don't stand there condemning me and then ask me what the hell I want from you."

"I love you, Honey," Grant said, walking over to me. "I love you, and I do want to be with you. This doesn't have to be difficult. You're making it that way. Just relax, baby. We'll be okay."

What was I to say? I did want Grant. But I didn't want a man who could stick his dick in any woman who opened her legs for him, then cum inside of me, without a fucking conscience. "Why don't you seriously take some time to consider what you truly want. I'ma do the same. And if you want to talk about us being in a committed relationship, call me in a few days. If you decide I'm not the woman you want, don't ever call me again."

"In a few days? So you're putting me on hold, like my feelings don't fucking matter to you? You want it like that? Fine, Honey." Grant exhaled. "Fine."

I tried blocking his path. "Grant, you don't know what you want. If I called Red Velvet in here right now and told her to join us in a ménage à trois, you'd do it. Your fucking her is not my concern. My concern is you'd do it without any forethought or afterthought."

Going to the bed, I picked up my bag, kissed Grant on the cheek, and said, "I love you, too. But sometimes love isn't enough." I turned away, then opened the door.

"Baby," he said.

"Yes?" I answered, holding the doorknob.

"Baby."

"Yes?"

"Love is always enough," Grant said, opening his arms to me.

"Not always," I replied, then walked out.

CHAPTER 34

Red Velvet

Fuck. Fuck. Pass. Fuck. Fuck. Pass.

The principles of fucking were synonymous with smoking weed. All dicks were used, never pre-owned, with at least a hundred thousand strokes on them, and not a one came with a warranty for shit, not even a good fuck. That was why I couldn't take men seriously. Men wanted women to fall in love with them. Then what? They wanted women to be faithful while they fucked every trick they wanted. Not this Velvet pussy.

I was in control of my pussy. I didn't always make the right decisions, but I made my decisions about the men I fucked, when, where, and why. Sometimes I just wanted to have fun. Releasing my pent-up sexual tension drove me to find and ride an available dick. Having sex was as important as excreting toxins. Velvet was not going to walk around with a toxic pussy.

Tap. Tap.

I opened my hotel door. It was Honey. "Why you looking so sad?" I asked. "Oh, Grant. You don't want to leave him, huh? Trust me, I understand."

My bag was packed. I double-checked my room and the bathroom to make sure I wasn't forgetting anything; then I picked up my bag and closed the door.

"I'm happy to be going home," Honey said.

"That's not your happy face," I said, pressing the button for the elevator. Had I seen Honey's happy face? A little. On our way to L.A. I couldn't see her face last night when Grant was on top of her, but I could tell she was happy to kick me out. All that dick-a-licious good loving should've had her dancing all the way to the airport. When the doors opened, Grant was inside the elevator.

Honey stepped on. She stood so close to the buttons, her breasts pressed a few, I guess by accident. Maybe she was trying to give Grant time to say something to her. I had to look up at Grant. His eyes darted away from mine. Oh, I'd seen this egotistical attitude before.

"I hope y'all are not tripping over me. Y'all should've invited me to stay," I joked, but neither of them cracked a smile. "Anyway, I like you," I said, hugging Grant. "And, I love you," I said, hugging Honey. And that was the truth. Honey was a wonderful person, and I didn't know much about Grant's character, except that he was a kind man.

Our rental cars were waiting for us at the valet. Grant got in his rental car and drove off. He never looked back or said bye. Were these the same two adults who were fucking each other's brains out last night? Now both of them were so stubborn, neither could say good-bye? I didn't get it. I mean, I did but didn't at the same time.

The ride to the airport with Honey was short and quiet. If I'd learned only one thing being with Honey that one thing was when to be quiet. We got through the security checkpoint rather quickly, but we still had barely enough time to board our flight.

"This is sweet," I said, sitting next to Honey in first class. "I'ma travel like this all the time when I start acting."

Ever so gently, I covered Honey's hand with mine. I spoke to her as my mother had often spoken to me. I felt sad for Honey. Of course, she had a mother, too, but I'd never heard her mention her mother. Many of us lived our lives without the presence of our fathers. That was sad, too. But very few people—male and female—experienced life without a mother.

"It's okay," I said, with patience, with love, with a calm spirit. "Either you want him or you don't. You're a proud, successful woman. Not to mention wealthy. Do not allow your pride, your ego, or your expectations to deny you what could be the best man of your lifetime.

If you really want him, it's okay, because you don't have to live up to anyone's expectations but your own. I saw in his eyes, he loves you. And your eyes say you love him."

Honey sighed. "Sometimes," she said. Then she leaned her seat back and closed her eyes. Trapped tears escaped from underneath her lids and glided down her cheeks, cleansing her soul.

I'd never been in love before. I hoped one day some man would have for me the look I'd seen in Grant's eyes for Honey. Obviously, being in love created an inner struggle that made people not want to cope with their emotions. So they'd eat or sleep or drink their feelings away. Seemed as though the more they tried to dismiss their true feelings, the more they hurt themselves. I'd watched my mother struggle with accepting the fact that her husband had left her. After years of separation, she still hadn't recovered completely. I thought keeping Ronnie gave her someone to love, but in a very different kinda way.

I wasn't sure how important being in love was. What did love mean? My generation of men seemed to want all the conveniences of having a woman, but they didn't want me. Not if it meant buying flowers, taking me out on a real date, holding hands, and kissing affectionately in public.

Guys were into groping, shoving their tongues down my throat, showing me off, and constantly proving their manhood to themselves, not me, by trying to knock the bottom out of my bottomless pussy. I was tired of saying, "Slow down. Hold me. Listen to me. Talk to me, not at me." The one thing I'd never say to any man ever was, "Do you love me?" If a woman had to ask, the true answer was obvious.

Men wanted children, but they didn't want a family. They wanted sex, but they didn't want a commitment. Basically, men didn't want to accept responsibility for their actions. Watching Honey sleep away her pain to avoid deciding whether or not she wanted Grant, I decided that maybe I'd be better off never falling in love.

I watched a few movies, took a short nap, and was glad when we landed. Onyx was at the airport, waiting for us. The ride from Atlanta's airport took forever. There was no place like home. I was happy to see Mrs. Taylor sitting on the porch. I was gonna miss her.

"Hey, Red. Where's your mom and Ronnie? That sure is a fancy jogging suit you have on. You think they make them in my size? Probably not," Mrs. Taylor said, answering her own question.

"I'm going back to the airport in an hour to pick them up," I told her.

I went inside my house, locked the door, undressed, and showered. It felt soooo good to be home. I wished I didn't have to run out the door. I sat still for a moment. Sitting in my living room, I exhaled, wondering if I'd go to Stilettos tonight as a patron or a stripper.

"I can't trip off of this crap. I gotta go get my mom and my baby," I said aloud.

As I was locking my front door, Mrs. Taylor said, "Red, that thing. It's ringing again."

Lord, please don't let this be Tolliver's relentless ass. I glanced at my caller ID. My heart stopped beating for a few seconds. It was my agent.

"You never answer it," Mrs. Taylor said. "Why you have it?"

My phone kept ringing. Should I let it go to voice mail or answer it? Nervously, I held my Sidekick in my hand. I'd missed the call. I unlocked my mother's door. I walked through her house, checking to make sure everything was in place. I smiled. My mom was the best mom. I stood in the kitchen, absorbing her love.

Ding.

I had a message. A letter was on the dining room table, with my name on it. I sat my Sidekick on the table and picked up the letter. It was from Alphonso, and it had been opened. Removing two pages, I read the letter.

"Why, Mama! Why did you make me go all the way to L.A., knowing Alphonso had sent this fucking letter!" I cried.

I gripped the top of the letter. There was no need to read the second page. Whatever Alphonso had to say wasn't worth my getting upset. I tore the letter from the top toward the bottom, but I stopped when I saw a perforated edge. Peeling away the top page, I couldn't believe it! I had a cashier's check from Alphonso, with my name on it, for seventy-two thousand dollars!

I flipped open my cell phone and called the concierge desk at the hotel where I worked. "Yes, this is Velvet. Let me speak to the manager." I jumped up and down so hard, my titties ached with joy. Nothing could ruin my day!

The manager got on the phone. "Hello, Velvet. I'm glad you finally called in. You're suspended for three days for not reporting to work," she said.

"I know that's your documented disciplinary way of avoiding firing me so you don't have to pay unemployment compensation," I said. "But I'm going to save you a few dollars. I quit. How's that?" I laughed in her ear. I wasn't laughing at her. I was thrilled beyond measure.

I opened my mother's door. My smile vanished. Tolliver's wife stood inches from my face.

CHAPTER 35

Valentino

Fuck Summer. We hadn't been married two hours and already she had a bad attitude. I should be the one pissed the fuck off. What had I done to her? It was my money, not hers. And it wasn't enough. She was going to have to come up with more than that. I got up from the couch, made my way into the bedroom, changed into a pair of slacks Summer had bought me, put on my casual-dress, brown button-down shirt, and went into the kitchen.

"Stop feeding him all the time. He's gonna be overweight," I said.

"He hasn't had anything to eat this morning," Summer said, beating a bowl of eggs.

"Ba, I gotta make this run. I promise I'll be back in a few days, a week tops. Then I'm home for good."

"Anthony, I did not bail you out for you to bail on us. If you leave, don't come back. You got what you wanted."

"Nah, nah," I said, shaking my head. I hugged Summer. "Right here is where I want to be, ba. With you and our son. I'm not going to miss my court date. I wouldn't make you pay a million-dollar bond. I wouldn't. I need for you to believe in me."

"Where're you going?" she asked, turning over the bacon. "Anthony, go upstairs, close your door, and stay there until I come and get you."

Yeah, straight. I was with her on that. Anthony did not need to hear our conversation. "I'm going to Atlanta."

"Atlanta! Just beat me and get it over with! No matter what you say or do, I'm never gonna be yours, you dirty bastard!" Summer yelled. Then she softly said, "Anthony, you can't leave the state of Nevada."

What the fuck? Not this shit again. Who in the fuck was that? Could a nigga's mind conjure up a bitch, or was this Sylvia Browne ghost shit for real? I played it cool. "Summer? I'm driving, okay? I won't stay a day longer than I have to. I promise. All I need is another blank check to cover me until I get back."

Summer started shaking her head before I finished my sentence. "Nope. Ow! My head hurts! Why did you slap me!" Summer yelled. Then she softly said, "Anthony, I don't approve of you going to Atlanta, and I'm not giving you anything."

Approve? Who the fuck did she think I was? "Fine. Then I won't come back."

"Then you'd better take this with you," Summer said, handing me her wedding ring. "You'll need it more than me."

Was that supposed to make me stay? I took the ring, put it in my pocket, then grabbed the car keys. I started backing up toward the door. "Summer, baby girl," I found myself saying.

Summer yelled, "I'm not your baby girl!" She threw the eggbeater at me. "I'm sorry, Valentino. I never should've come here. I quit. Ahhhhhhhh! No, please don't. I'm sorry. I'll be good. Noooooo! I'm not Summer, motherfucker. How many times do I have to tell you that . . . I'm Sunny." Her eyes damn near popped out of the sockets. Running toward me, she yelled, "Give me my keys!"

Pushing her away, I slammed the front door, ran to the Bentley. Fuck! Looking in my hand, I saw I'd grabbed the keys to the SUV. I wasn't falling on my ass again, that was for sure. The screeching tires left Summer standing behind a cloud of smoke. Fuck that. That wasn't Summer. That bitch I'd married was Sunny. As I headed to the casino, my hands rattled around the steering wheel. Benito had better be waiting, or I was leaving him in Vegas.

Was that why she'd bailed me out? To fuckin' torture a nigga? All I'd needed her to do was go along with my plan. Fuck. I was scared to go back there. Did my son have to live with that shit every day? Fuck that. Fuck them.

I made my way to the penny machine, and there Benito was.

"Nigga, that machine ain't gon' hit two days in a motherfuckin' row. Let's roll."

Getting in the car, Benito asked, "So did you do it?"

"I wish I hadn't," I lied. I loved Summer. It was that bitch living inside of Summer that I wanted to kill again. When I got back, I was performing an exorcism with my dick, and I was going to straighten her horny ass the fuck out.

Door-to-door, it was 1,968 miles from Vegas to Atlanta, which translated into a total of twenty-eight hours and fifty-six minutes in a car with Benito. That was going to drive me fuckin' crazy. I wanted to drive damn near 120 miles per hour to cut the trip in half, but I'd have to start a high-speed chase to escape beating down any of these Arizona, New Mexico, Texas, Oklahoma, Arkansas, Mississippi, Alabama or Georgia motherfuckers if they tried to pull me over.

Damn. It was gonna take two days for us to get to Atlanta. At least we were driving through northern, and not southern, Texas during the day, and we could sleep in my SUV overnight once we got into Oklahoma. I'd road kill every armadillo speed bump in Texas before I laid my head to sleep in that crazy-ass state. The only law I liked in Texas was the right to bear arms: handgun, rifle, and shotgun ownership was unrestricted.

In Texas a nigga didn't need a license or a permit to protect himself, but Texas had more black men on death row than any other state in the country, and I was sure they'd love to add one more, especially when they realized I refused to show my driver's license or give any information that would prove I was out on bail. I didn't care if Benito did have a valid driver's license. I didn't trust him to drive me to the corner sto' in daylight.

Benito started punching the air. "So, V, you done got all swole and stuff. Tell me how many dudes you had to rough up or cut up or beat the hell out of when you were in prison. I know they tried to get at you. What'd you do? Huh?" he asked, jabbing the air. "Tell me."

I told him, "I'll show you what happened before we go to sleep tonight." Ig'nant ass. Every man who got locked up didn't get raped. I knew that was where he was going. But my response shut his ass up quick. "Don't think I don't know some of those teammates of yours were on the DL. What about you? You shit packin', nigga? Or gettin' your shit packed?"

Benito shook his head. "I don't go down like that. Not me."

"Yeah, right. Shut the hell up."

I turned on the radio. Driving on Interstate 40, we left Texas and crossed the Oklahoma state line. I was tired from driving all damn day. I speed dialed the home number to check on whomever I fuckin' married.

"The subscriber has temporarily suspended this number. Please try your call again at a later time."

"What the hell?" I yelled. My heart raced. Was this a sign?

"You okay, man? Seems like you got a lot on your mind," Benito said, staring at me.

"Stop staring at me, nigga. Answer this. You ever loved a woman?"

Benito sat up straight. "Man, I don' had the finest females. One of them for three years. What? You don' forgot I lived with Lace? You forgot I played pro ball? I'm an icon in every community in America."

"Nah, nigga, I ain't forgot shit. I just brought it up an hour back. Sho' you don' had lots of bitches. I have too. But you ain't answered the question, either. Have you?"

Benito was quiet for a long time. I drove to downtown Oklahoma City, to a fancy five-star hotel, and parked in the lot outside. It was eight o'clock at night. Still enough time for us to have a good meal, a few drinks, and let down the backseats for a few hours so I could rest before I drove this bitch-ass SUV to Georgia.

I turned off the engine, waiting for an answer. "Nigga, get out of the car. You can tell me over drinks."

We went into the hotel and headed to the restaurant. I walked up to the hostess. She was bland but cute. "Two for dinner," I said.

"The wait is an hour and fifteen minutes," she said.

"For what? The fuckin' chef to arrive up in this deserted bitch?" I asked. Damn. Why was the wait so fuckin' long? The place was practically empty. Was she hoping to detour us to some other place? Fuck her. "James for two. We'll be at the bar." Hell. Wasn't like we had shit else to do but cram our asses in the car and sleep after we finished fucking. I meant eating.

I didn't realize that I'd asked such a tough question, but it did shut Benito the fuck up. Sitting at the bar, I ordered two scotch on the rocks. Looking at Benito, I asked him the question again. "Who in your lifetime have you loved unconditionally? Not your mother. Not your father. I mean a woman."

"Just 'cause you got married you tryna change up?" Benito exhaled. "Does it matter? These bitches don't love us. All they want is a permanent paycheck, or sex, or a man they can brag to their girls that they fucked or that they're dating. Women nowadays don't want no commitment, V. They too busy chasing paper, just like us."

"Nigga, what about your baby mama? You love her? I'm asking your ass because when I get my money back, you gon' need a place to lay low for a minute after I break you off. And this time, with the money you're gonna have, you can't lay your head between a woman's legs if she ain't got no love for you. And the only way to make sure she's got you is if you've got her, too. That's why I got married. Who you ever don' right by? Maybe you can answer that."

"When you get all soft and shit?" Benito asked. "I don't love them hos."

The only woman I'd ever done right by was Summer, when we first hooked up. I'd get her to trust me when I got back from Atlanta. But if she was still acting crazy, I was gonna commit that bitch to a mental. Damn. That wasn't a bad idea.

"I haven't gotten soft, nigga," I lied. I was missing Summer's warm smile already. But not that crazy bitch trapped inside her. Summer was selling that haunted house. No way was I spending another night there. "I'm not going back to jail. And that means I have to do what I have to do to stay out."

"Mr. James, we can seat you now. I'll have the bartender transfer your tab," the hostess said.

We followed her to our table. Fine fucking dining was the way I wanted to eat every day. I was not about to live out of the Dumpsters, like those freegans scraping up free food and shit.

"You have Lace's number?" I asked Benito.

Grinning, he said, "Yeah. She wants me."

Whateva, nigga. "Sapphire's?"

Shaking his head, Benito said, "Nope. But my brother has her number."

Hell, I probably had her number in Summer's phone. I pulled out the cell phone and pressed the power button. Nothing happened. *What the fuck?* I thought, putting the phone on the table. "Good enough. We'll call Lace tomorrow, when we're standing outside her fucking door. We can't give her a heads-up that we're coming, so don't your dumb ass dial her number."

The food was good, but I was tired. I wanted to get to Atlanta before sunset tomorrow. "You done?" I asked Benito.

"Uh-huh. I'm sleepy, man. That niggaritis don' kicked in."

I dropped a hundred on the table, and we headed to the door.

"Excuse me, sir," the waitress said, chasing behind us. "Your bill is three hundred dollars."

"What the hell!" I snarled. "All we had was—"

"Here's your bill. I need two hundred more, plus a tip," said the waitress.

I tossed two one-hundred-dollar bills at the bitch, then walked away. There was no way I was tipping her ass. She'd better see her boss about a fuckin' raise. I could put her on a quick stroll after she got off if she wanted to make us some money, but tipping wasn't happening.

Benito and I got in the car. I drove to the far end of the parking lot, parked under a tree in the corner, then turned off the engine and the lights. I climbed in the backseat.

"We ain't checking in?" Benito asked.

"Nigga, get your ass back here," I said.

Benito squeezed in beside me.

"Nigga, as long as we this fuckin' close, and you don' drunk and ate up three hundred dollars, roll the fuck over."

"A hundred and fifty. And I promise to pay you back with interest, but not that kind of interest." Benito shook his head. "I ain't like that, V."

"I know, nigga. Me neither. Shut the fuck up, and pull down your pants."

CHAPTER 36

Honey

During the time I spent in L.A. and Vegas, what I learned was we treat people the way we are . . . not the way they are. I didn't admit that what Velvet had said on the plane made sense and that she'd made me feel better about my feelings for Grant. But feelings couldn't change facts.

Velvet's mother didn't want what was best for Velvet; she wanted what was best for herself. The same held true for Grant, Sapphire, Velvet, and me. The only person that genuinely wanted what was best for others was Ronnie. He was special. When he grew up, I could tell he was going to protect his mother and grandmother. Children went along with adults, trusting that adults had their best interest in mind. Adults, myself included, claimed we loved others, until others didn't live their lives to make or keep us happy.

I guessed Grant had retreated to his corner again. He didn't call or respond to my calls. A woman shouldn't pursue a man. I was the one who'd said we should give it a few days, and here *I* was the one who didn't want to wait. Grant had gone to his home in D.C. and to check on his parents and his business. Was he a mama's boy? Was that a bad thing if he was?

I'd settled in, slept well, got up this morning. Now I was in the kitchen, singing and dancing and cooking breakfast. Onyx was setting the table for us. The time had come for each of my girls to talk to me.

"Onyx, go upstairs and tell everyone to come down for breakfast," I said.

Once the table for fourteen was set, we gathered around it. The only person missing was Sunny, and no one was allowed to sit in her seat, which was opposite the head of the table and across from me.

"Girl Six, I want you to sit to my left," I said, because I was right-handed, and if I had to knock her ass on her ass, I'd have a straight aim. "Onyx, you sit to my right."

This was the first time we'd all sat at the table at the same time. It was more like the first time I'd joined them at the table.

"I'll bless the table," Onyx said. "Lord, thank you for waking each of us up this morning. We pray the food that nourishes our bodies will give us strength to do good for ourselves, one another, and the women who come to us for help today. Amen."

"Girl Six, I want to formally welcome you home," I said.

Girl Six smiled. "Thanks. It's good to be here."

"You talked with Sapphire since you been here?" I asked her.

Girl Six looked away; then she looked at Onyx and at me. "Yes. She sent me here to spy on you. I told her I couldn't do that. And I haven't spoken with her since. If you don't want me here, be direct. You don't have to beat me. 'Cause I'm done dealing with abuse from you. It's not necessary. I want to stay. I want to work in the office with the other girls. I want to help other women. That's why I'm here."

Surprised at Girl Six's candor, I said, "I can respect that."

I didn't have an appetite. My stomach started churning. Before excusing myself from the table, I told everyone, "Carpool in groups of four to the office. I'll be there by eleven." That gave me three hours to recover from the queasy feeling invading my stomach.

"You want me to stay and wait for you?" Onyx asked. "You don't look so good."

"No, I'm fine. You go ahead with the others," I insisted.

The girls lingered, talking while eating. I went into my bedroom and closed the door and took a nice hot shower. "Ooh, it feels so good to be home," I said. I stepped out of the shower and opened my bedroom door. The mansion was quiet. I walked around my empty house, proud of my accomplishments. Returning to my bedroom, I didn't bother closing the door. I slipped into my power red pantsuit, then slipped my gun in the holder under my left arm. You never knew what abusive fool would follow his woman into my business.

I didn't know what came over me. For the first time in my life, I knelt on the floor, leaned into my chaise, and pressed my hands together. I closed my eyes. "Lord, despite all that has happened to me, I have so much to be thankful for," I whispered. "I ask that You bless Red Velvet abundantly. And I pray she gets that acting role in *Something on the Side*. If not this movie, another one. Within a day or two if you could. That'd be nice." I'd heard you had to be as specific as possible when praying.

I was proud of that woman. She was more than a pretty face. Velvet was smart, and she didn't take no shit off anybody, including me. I chuckled at how she'd slapped me back. I could've killed her if that seat belt had broken. "Thank You for keeping her safe," I whispered. I had more respect for Velvet than I had for Girl Six, that is, until today, when Girl Six proved herself worthy of respect.

"Lord, please bless my mother." I knew it was selfish of me not to pray for my stepfather, but I didn't want to be hypocritical. I had no love for that sorry-ass leech my mother married. I had to call Sapphire to find out if she had had a change of heart about killing Alphonso. I prayed not.

"Bless my biological father," I whispered. Maybe one day my father would stop being so stubborn and would acknowledge me. If not, oh well. His loss. What was wrong with black men not accepting responsibility for their children?

As far as my parents were concerned, some things were better left in prayer. *Listen at me, acting like I've been praying all along.* Maybe I had and didn't realize it. I decided to go to church on Sunday with Velvet's mother and Ronnie. Couldn't hurt. I was happy for Sapphire since she would be reuniting with her mother, and I was happy I'd been instrumental in that happening. I hadn't heard from her, so maybe, finally, she wasn't concerned about the money she'd given me. Probably best, because seriously I wasn't giving it back, anyway.

I thought about Grant. I didn't care if he got run over by a truck, swept under a bus, and dragged to hell. "What the fuck?"

Scrambling, I reached behind my head, clawing my nails into the hands of a person I couldn't see. "Motherfucker, let me go! Let me go!" I screamed, struggling to loosen the plastic bag tightening around my neck. This motherfucker was trying to suffocate me. I couldn't see. Now I could barely hear. I was thrown facedown on the floor. I fought to keep this maniac from taping my hands tightly together.

Did Girl Six set me up? She'd better pray she wasn't involved.

Rip!

More tape secured my ankles. Fuckin' amateurs! This wasn't even duct tape. Two people lifted me from the floor, carried me, then shoved me in the trunk of an SUV. At least I had more space to maneuver out of this cheap-ass tape, if I didn't suffocate first.

Whoever these sorry motherfuckers were, they didn't realize who they'd kidnapped. By the time they stopped this SUV, the tape would be off, and the minute they opened this trunk, I was shooting both of them in the head for fucking up my day.

I'm Honey, motherfuckers! Honey!

CHAPTER 37

Sapphire

What I learned was we listen to the words people speak, but it was more important to hear what they were not saying. Knowing my mother had never stopped loving me allowed me to drop my guard. Yes, I'd been hurt. Yes, I'd been molested. Yes, I'd run away from my pain.

I'd buried those feelings inside so deep, no one had heard my cries. Never again. Tiffany Davis was ready to face her fears.

Arriving at my mother's house, I parked in front and stared at the FOR SALE sign. This was the house I'd lived in for sixteen years. The house where bad things had happened to me. But on the other side of that front door, the door I sat staring at, lived a woman. A woman who gave birth to me. A woman who had never stopped searching for me. A woman who had always loved me.

I powered off my cell phone and placed it in my glove compartment. Then I took a deep breath. I got out of my car. I stood tall. I squared my shoulders. I walked up to the front door. And I rang the doorbell.

When the door opened wide, there she was. We swapped tears of joy, and tears of sorrow for so many years lost. Tears of cleansing washed me, washed us.

"Mommy, I love you."

"Oh, baby, you just don't know. I prayed every night that you were safe. Cried every day as I passed out flyers. I love you, Tiffany. I'm so sorry for what happened to you."

Click!

My body tensed. My feet froze. My mother had closed and locked the door. That sound haunted me. I had to ask, "Where is he?"

"Come on in, baby. You don't have to worry about him ever again. Alphonso is gone, out of our lives, forever. If you want to press charges—"

I interrupted my mother. "Let's not talk about any of that right now. I'll deal with Alphonso later. I want to talk with you. Did he hurt you after Honey left?"

My mother chuckled. "Nah, I beat his ass so bad, he thought I was possessed. He couldn't get out of here fast enough."

"Good job, Mom. That sounds like what I would've done," I lied. If I had a daughter, I would kill any man who thought about molesting or raping her. Oh, another reason why I shouldn't have kids. "Did you ever suspect anything?" I asked, looking in my mother's eyes. "Can we please stay in the living room? I can't go back to my bedroom, ever."

Sitting on the sofa, beside me, my mother rocked me in her arms. I felt like her little girl again. She began to cry. "I didn't want to believe that he'd do that to you. I didn't want to believe you ran away because he'd raped you." My mother's voice grew more intense. "That was my husband, and I never wanted to believe the man I had let move into our house, the man I had walked down the aisle with, the man I had exchanged vows with would rape my daughter!" She exhaled. "I didn't want to believe that I was stupid enough to make that big of a mistake and, worst of all, that I'd failed as a mother. My God, you're my only child, Tiffany. You're my baby."

I cried the entire time we talked. I wanted to scream at my mother, "I hate you!" But I didn't hate her. I hated what she'd allowed to happen to me. I hated that she hadn't protected me. I hated that she hadn't loved herself more than she'd loved her husband. And that she hadn't loved me enough to confront him. But no matter how much I was hurting inside, I could never hate my mother.

"Mommy, I love you. I gotta go for a while. Clear my mind. I'll be back to see you, but I can't help you pack. Here's five grand. I want you to hire a mover to dispose of everything in this house except pictures and videos. I'll buy you all new stuff and a new house. I've got a few things to handle."

"You want me to go with you?" my mother asked, following me to the door.

"No, you're safer here. I promise. I'll be back."

Being in the house had resurrected my anger for pimps and rapists. I was headed to Alphonso's job, and he was either going to turn himself in or end up with a bullet in his dick.

"Valentino," I mumbled. Where was he? He'd been too quiet. Hadn't heard anything regarding his whereabouts since I'd picked up the check from Summer. "Maybe I should visit them. Yeah, I'd better track Valentino and Benito down and handle those two before they sneaked up on me," I said aloud.

I got in my car, revved up my engine, check my gun, and powered on my cell phone. Twenty-six missed messages from . . . Honey? "Aw shit! What happened?" I yelled.

I listened to my voice mail. In one message, Honey said, "Sapphire, I've been kidnapped from my Atlanta home. I'm in the back of an SUV," she whispered. "I have no idea where they're taking me. I need you to take care of my girls. I'm going to get out of this alive, but I need your help. Please don't call me back. Wait until I call you again."

Alphonso Allen, that lucky bastard. He'd get to have his freedom for another few days, but I'd be back to kill him personally. I drove to LAX, parked in the daily parking lot, and got on the first direct flight to Atlanta.

I guess being a cop was in my blood. Anybody who fucked with my family fucked with me. And Honey was now my family.

CHAPTER 38

Valentino

Driving back and forth on the 85, with Honey in the trunk, I looked over at Benito, who was digging in his shitty ass. That nigga tried to act like he had leverage 'cause his cell phone had service and my shit was now terminated. Same fuckin' difference. Service or no service, that nigga's battery was dead, and I wasn't buying him no charger. Summer was wrong for leaving me out here like this.

I stopped off at a Wal-Mart to get one of those prepaid phones. Benito hopped out of the car and walked bowlegged and shit. "That's what you get for talking 'bout what you don't do, nigga," I said.

"You wrong, V. I'm supposed to be your boy, not your bitch," Benito, said tugging at his pants.

We started laughing. I could never fuck Benito. Yeah, he was different. He was annoying at times. But that nigga would do anything for me. "Cut that shit out. Walk straight." Entering the store, I asked him, "Nigga, did you remember to poke a hole in the plastic bag so that bitch won't die in the trunk?"

"Yeah, man. I took care of my business. You gon' get me a phone, too. I need to call my mama."

I swear I wanted to slap his ass. I hurried up and paid for two phones with one hundred minutes. I might have to send that nigga home early if he fucked up.

Driving to an abandoned lot, I powered on my phone and dialed information. "Atlanta, Georgia. Sweeter Than Honey," I said and asked to be connected.

"What's sweeter than honey and more valuable than money?" said a female voice.

"Who is this?" I asked. Her voice sounded familiar.

"Who is this?" she asked, with attitude.

"Bitch, don't fuck with me. Who the fuck are you?"

"Oh, my, God. Valentino? How long have you been out? Does Honey know?"

"I been out long enough to have kidnapped Lace, Honey, whatever the fuck she calls herself. Listen up and listen righteous, because I'm only going to say this one time. I want my fifty million dollars delivered to me in cash by tomorrow night, or this bitch is dead, and all of your asses are next. You can't run. You can't hide from me. I'm going to kill you first, then the rest of my bitches, you hear me! Y'all are my bitches! But I'ma kill every last one of you, one at a time, until somebody gives me all of my fuckin' money!"

"I don't know what you're talking about," she said calmly. "I can get you as much as I can before the bank closes today, but Honey is the only one who has direct access to her account. Where is she? How do I know you're serious? For all I know, you could be calling on a three-way from prison."

"I got your prison, bitch! Hold the fuck on," I said.

Looking at Benito, I said, "Here. Take my gun. Get that bitch out of the trunk. If she tries anything funny, shoot her ass."

The minute I said that shit, I got out of the car, too. Benito's dumb ass was guaranteed to fuck something up. I walked around to the back of the SUV with Benito. He raised the hatch. Staring down the barrel of that bitch's gun, I dropped the phone. Why the fuck had I given Benito's stupid ass my piece?

Pow! Pow! Pow! Pow!

CHAPTER 39

Grant

Oneness in love was key. Oneness in love was the key. When I looked at Honey, I saw a perfect imperfect being. I saw her shadow in my reflection. Our journeys differed along the same path. We saw things through our minds' eyes. We felt with our hearts. We touched with our words. We sung with our eyes. We cried with our souls.

When all else failed, and the world around us crumbled, we drifted apart, but love sustained us. If I had no money, no place to live, no shoes on my feet, no food to eat, no place to go, no mother, father, or ignorant adopted brother, if none of the people I loved were around me, and if I had one last breath to take, it wouldn't matter as long as I had Honey. I'd exhale my last breath with everlasting love for her.

I sat in my car, in my parents' driveway, watching my father wave to me. "Son, you been out there too long. Come in," he called. "Your mother and I want to know where you've been the last few days."

I smiled, but not from my aching heart. "Give me a minute. I have to respond to a few e-mails," I lied.

I dialed Honey's phone for the tenth time. It went straight to voice mail. Maybe I'd delayed responding to her too long. Maybe she really was done with me. But I wasn't done with loving her.

I texted her again. *Baby.*

There was no reply.

Exhaling, I dialed her office number. I didn't want to disturb her at work, but her silence was driving me crazy.

She answered, "What's sweeter than honey and more valuable than money?"

"Baby," I whispered into the receiver.

"Yes?" she answered.

"Baby." I exhaled a sigh of relief.

"Yes?"

I didn't want to put it off another second. I was tired of playing games. Honey was right. We did have an emotional relationship. I was ready to acknowledge all my love for her. I asked her, "Will you marry me?"

"Who is this?"

"Well, I guess you have so many men proposing to you, you don't recognize my voice. Has it been that long?"

"Grant?"

"Yes," I responded. "Of course. Who else?"

"You sitting down?"

I was so caught up, I was listening more to myself. Suddenly, I realized I wasn't speaking to Honey at all. I said, "Yes. Why?"

"This isn't Honey. This is Onyx."

"Well, I figured as much by now. What's up? Honey isn't speaking to me. You're her messenger now?"

"Grant, Honey might be dead."

"What the hell! Is this some sorta sick-ass joke she's playing?"

"No, I'm serious. Someone kidnapped her from the house. They called, demanding fifty million dollars. When I asked to speak with her, all I heard was four gunshots." Onyx started crying really loud.

"Onyx, calm down. I'm on my way right now."

The phone slipped from my hand. Benito's voice replayed in my head. *You'd better pray Lace doesn't have my money or she's one dead bitch.* I hadn't taken him seriously. No one had.

"Fuck! I should've told her," I yelled.

This was one situation my dad could not talk me out off. I backed out of the driveway and headed straight to Reagan National Airport. I'd never killed a man before, but I swore that if Benito had killed my sweet Honey, brother or no brother, I'd have his blood on my hands.

CHAPTER 40

Red Velvet

"Mommy, stop it! Stop tickling me! Mommy, you're not playing fair!" Ronnie screamed with laughter.

Not having to worry about money for a while felt good. I'd set aside sixty thousand dollars to develop and implement my business plan. Never again would I work for a man. And I might not get another penny from Alphonso, but getting such a large lump sum made all of us happy.

"Okay. I'll stop," I said. I hugged my son tightly, then smothered his face with kisses.

"Ooh! That's enough sugar, Mommy," he said, wiping his cheeks. "Let's go visit Grandma. I want to give her her surprise." Ronnie pulled me to our front door.

Opening the door, I looked to my left. No one was there. I glanced to the right and saw Mrs. Taylor.

"Hey, Red. You can come on out," Mrs. Taylor said. "That sure was a nice thing you must've done for that woman that she brought you all them beautiful roses."

I had had no idea what Tolliver's wife was going to do. She could've tried to beat me over the head with the one hundred roses she'd personally delivered. That wouldn't have been a good thing for her, 'cause I would've beaten every single thorn into her ass.

"Yeah, it was," I agreed.

I couldn't imagine what spending one hour in jail felt like, but I was sure Tolliver's wife saw her marriage differently.

Ronnie was so excited, he was in my mother's house before I locked my front door. I walked into my mom's kitchen, and I gave her a hug.

"Calm down, baby. What's all the commotion about?" Mama said to Ronnie. "Velvet, what's gotten into him?"

"Mommy, can I tell Grandma pleeaaaassssee? Can I tell her?" said Ronnie.

"Tell me what, child? Spit it out before you bust," demanded Mama.

"Mommy's going to Hollywood! She got the part in the movie! And . . . she's taking us with her!"

My mother looked at me from the corners of her eyes. "Come here, Velvet."

Here we go. I knew she wouldn't be happy for me. I was still going to start my business. I just wanted my big break in Hollywood. But if my mother wasn't going, neither were we. I wasn't leaving her behind. I couldn't make it without her being there to support me.

"Aaahhhhh!" Mama screamed.

She scared the shit outta me. "Wait, Mama. You're pulling my hair."

"Baby, I'm so happy for you! This is what you've always wanted," said Mama. "It's your time to shine, baby."

Ronnie hugged me from the side.

"Mama, thanks for always believing in me. I love you," I said.

"I love you, too, Grandma," Ronnie said, with tears in his little eyes. I wasn't sure if he understood how I felt, but I knew his love was pure.

"Ma, I have to make a quick run. Can you watch Ronnie for an hour?"

"Of course, Velvet, but where're you going?"

"I want to tell Honey in person. I want to thank her for all she's done for me," I said.

Mama said, "For us. Tell Honey thanks from me, too."

"Me too!" Ronnie yelled. He didn't have to yell. I was still in the kitchen with them. But my baby was just as excited as I was.

"Invite Honey to go to church with us on Sunday," Mama said. "You're going, too. To give thanks. Never forget where your true love and blessings come from, baby. Now go on. Take your time getting back. Ronnie and I are fine."

"Thanks, Ma," I said, skipping out the door.

I was so excited; I couldn't believe what was happening. What if I froze up? What if I couldn't gain the twenty pounds they wanted me to for the part? What if Ronnie didn't like L.A.? With Disneyland, Magic Mountain, Universal Studios, he'd love L.A. I'd put him in the best schools. I'd take damn good care of my mother. Buy us a big, fancy house. Maybe she'd meet one of those Hollywood producers and fall in love again. That would be nice. To see my mother in love again.

Driving to Honey's business, I wondered if she'd gotten back together with Grant. I bet they had. Those two couldn't stay away from one another long. They made a good couple. I parked in front of her place, then ran inside.

"Onyx, where's Honey?" I said, with a big grin on my face.

Onyx's eyes looked so sad.

My heart pounded against my breast. I inhaled, then exhaled. "What happened?"

"When she didn't show up, when she didn't show up . . . I went back to the house to get her." Onyx started crying, and I started crying, too.

"Where is she!" I screamed, holding on to Onyx.

"We don't know. We're afraid that Honey might be dead."

I fell to my knees. "Nooooo!" I screamed. "If anybody hurts Honey, and I don't give a fuck who it is, I swear I'm nailing a stiletto in their clit or their motherfuckin' dick."

They ain't seen how hot Red Velvet can really get down.

CHAPTER 41

Honey

People refused to leave me the hell alone. The closer I got to doing the right thing, the more of a setback I experienced. How in the fuck did I end up in the back of a SUV? And who in the hell had kidnapped me? Was I going to die? Was this my payback for all the horrible things I'd done?

Using my acrylic nail to poke a hole in the tape, I removed the tape from my wrists, balled it up, and then left it behind me on the floor of the SUV. I ripped away the plastic bag covering my head and slowly eased the tape from over my lips. Whoever kidnapped me definitely weren't professionals. But who was bold enough to enter my home? How did they get in? In my mansion, of all the rooms in my house, how did they know exactly where to find me?

Was it Grant? If he knew how much money I had, he could have arranged to have someone kidnap me. This was not the time to allow love to overrule my senses. I never put anything past a man. A jealous man would turn on a woman without hesitation.

Was it Sapphire? Maybe. She had threatened me. And she was capable of manipulating anyone she wanted. Was one of my girls working for Sapphire?

Was it Red Velvet? She was one bad bitch, but I didn't believe she was bold or heartless enough to set me up. Was she?

Was it Girl Six? Justifiably she was at the top of my list. What was the real reason she decided to come live with me?

Was it Benito? Nah, he was too scary. But he was also a foolishly bitter man desperate for money. Hmm.

Was it Valentino? He was in jail. Or was he? Had he found a way to get out? Did Sapphire get him out? Oh, fuck. Summer. With so many things happening, I'd neglected to keep my promise to check on her. If Valentino got to her . . . fuck.

Was it Rita? My mother always hated me but did she dislike me enough to kidnap me? No, but her trifling-ass husband did. Maybe he wanted revenge for my stomping on his nuts with my stilettos.

Damn, stilettos. Was it Trevor? He was quite angry that Red Velvet had quit working for him. Maybe he held me responsible for influencing his top moneymaker.

Was it Jean? My father. Good or bad, he wouldn't invest time in me.

Exhaling, I curled into a fetal position, trying to remain still. The fast movement of the car made me nauseous. I wanted to cry. The seemingly endless list of people—some I could name, others I knew only by face—that would have a motive to kill me was ridiculously long.

I wasn't ready to die. I refused to die. I had too many women to help, my girls depending on me, and I hadn't given up on marrying Grant and having his babies.

The car stopped. The engine silenced. The opportunity I was waiting for came sooner than expected. I removed my gun from the holder and pointed it at the trunk, praying someone was stupid enough to open it expecting to find me in bondage with that fucking plastic bag over my head.

The moment the hatch on the trunk opened, I saw Benito holding a gun and Valentino with a cell phone at his ear. I had to make a quick decision. Either shoot Benito's dumb ass before he fired at me, or shoot Valentino before he grabbed at me or my gun.

As shots fired, I had only one thought. *I was not going to die like this.*

Book Club Questions

1. In the beginning of most relationships, there's infatuation, lust, and/or attraction. At what point did you fall in love? Before you answer that question, how do you define love? Have you experienced true love?

2. In Chapter 8, Red Velvet says she loves her son unconditionally, but it's because of her mother that she didn't commit suicide. Can a person who contemplates suicide love themselves? Do you believe a parent can love their children unconditionally and not love themselves? Explain. Do you believe your parents love you unconditionally? Why?

3. Has love or a lack of love from your parents played a part in your relationships? Do you feel your parents love one another unconditionally? Have they given you good relationship advice? Would you marry a person with the characteristics of your parents?

4. Have you ever been molested or raped, and did you fail to tell someone? If so, why didn't you tell? If you've ever been violated, how has that impacted your relationships?

5. What is your position on adoption? Do you believe adopted people should be treated the same as birth siblings? Would you adopt Benito's offspring?

6. Has a pimp ever approached you and asked you to work for him? If so, what happened? Do you think prostitution should be legalized? Are you attracted to the fast life (i.e., money, cars, the nightlife, etc.)? Explain.

7. If you have children, do you love them in the way your parents showed you love, or do you show them love in a completely different way? Why?

8. Do you have a Benito in your family? Have you dated a Benito? Would you date a man like Grant? Why or why not? Do you believe Grant truly loves Honey?

9. Love or the lack thereof is a constant theme in the novel. Which relationships do you believe are the most conducive to an overall healthy love life?

10. If you were given fifty million dollars to do something with, what would you do, and why?

11. Have you dated a man who was in jail for a while? If you did, did you make him get tested before having sex? Do you practice safe sex at all times?

12. Do you love yourself first?

13. Have you ever invested quiet time in looking into your eyes? If so, how does the experience make you feel? What did you see? Have you looked into the eyes of your partner for more than five minutes straight? Do you glance at, or look into, the eyes of strangers to read their emotions?

Lagniappe Section

The lagniappe section offers a little bit of this and a little bit of that. I'm sharing my thoughts and views about relationships, and I've invited a few friends along. Enjoy!

Who's Loving You
(poem)

Now I lay me down to sleep
I pray for someone to love me
For me

Throughout my day
I search for love
I look but cannot believe
Again today I did not see
Anyone with love in their eyes for me

I notice one set of deep beautiful eyes
And when they stared at mine
Quickly I turn away

Afraid to come face-to-face
With love

I lay awake at night
Holding my pillow
Longing for someone to appear
Longing for someone who cares

And when that person comes near
Fear
Takes over my body
My mind
My soul
Beholding the pure essence
Of what I desire

To Love
To be loved

I wonder
If they wonder
Before we speak
Who's loving me

I scream to the highest heights
Send me love
Clouds gather
Rain pours
I run for shelter
Afraid to get wet
Afraid to get hurt

I try to figure out
Without help from my mouth
Do you have
Or have you lost love
And like me

Do you long for a human touch
That speaks to you
Not with words
With love

Or a smile that brightens your day
An unsolicited hug embraces your waist

Or do you simply let your feelings
Fade
Into the sunset
Hide behind the sunrise

Day after day
I kneel
My hands press together
My heart whispers
Now I lay me down to sleep
I pray for someone
Anyone
Just one
To love me for me

My prayers are answered
You step into my light
I hear your touch
I feel your voice

Love at last

We laugh together
We cry together
Come rain or come shine
We do everything together

And one day
Along the way

We drift
Love don't love
We're back
Where we started

Now I lay me down to sleep
I pray
For someone . . . anyone
To love me for me

My eyes meet
Anew
We go our separate ways
No longer together
Forever
Day after day
I look around
If only I could've found
The words to say
Baby please stay
Hum
Déjà vu
I've been here before
In my heart
As I search for love
Once more
I wonder
Who's loving you
And I no longer pray
For someone to love

I wish

Where is the Black Love?

Sometimes I wish I'd been an adult in the sixties, instead of being born about ten weeks after the Civil Rights Act was enacted on July 2, 1964, to establish the Equal Employment Opportunity Commission, which was supposed to enforce civil rights for blacks, which had been granted under two prior acts. I wish I'd been a woman when the majority of black men had been real men. The sixties were a time when blacks loved blacks, the best they knew how, despite the fact that white people hated blacks. Nowadays we don't go out of our way to display affection.

In the sixties, black men tipped their hats to black ladies, our men dressed impeccably, and they had pride. No, not pride . . . dignity, poise, and they never walked past black women without acknowledging them. "Yes, ma'am. No, sir," black children would say to elders. The sixties were a time when women wore heels, gloves, and dresses, not jeans, T-shirts, flip-flops, or tennis shoes. A time when every black woman, irrespective of size, strutted down the street, swinging hips and flaunting attitude with confidence, stretching her head to the sky, knowing, not wondering, that she was a goddess. Black folk struggled together. Together. But they also partied and danced with so much fire and passion in their hearts, everyone could feel the energy in their kicks, high steps, fast swings in midair, and fancy splits down to the floor.

I wish I were Madame C. J. Walker and my husband were a man like Malcolm X, a thinking man who wasn't afraid to stand up and speak out for justice. Yeah, the sixties were a time when black folks fought, not begged, for equal opportunities. It was a time when the majority of black men upheld character, morals, and ethics, which were rooted in actions that exhibited and warranted respect for self, family, friends, and those not so friendly.

Life ain't never been fair for blacks, but almost fifty years ago, black women supported black men, not financially, but emotionally and spiritually. Back then the white man's dollar couldn't put a price on black love. Today it seems like the only way to get love among blacks is to barter, sometimes your soul.

Does the character of one man beget the character of another? Because I'm wondering exactly when and why black men started disrespecting black women. Hell, when did black men start disrespecting their wives, their mothers, and degrading one another? Pulling triggers without a conscience . . . over what? The Eurocentric standards of success? This whole damn world is a mess. People lying, dying; babies and women crying and being raped; parents beating the kids; men assaulting women. Hatred and road rage have replaced love and respect. Black men, the most powerful race of men on earth, dead or alive, one by one, are vanishing into the meaningless unknown. But why?

Once upon a time, people cared about the feelings lurking in the hearts and heads of loved ones who shared their bed, nestling between their legs, stimulating more than their erogenous zones. A house was a home, and no one who dwelled within was alone or lonely. Positive or negative, people were genuine, not fake. The greetings "How are you?" and "How was your day?" did not escape one's lips without one pausing long enough not to listen, but rather to hear the answers. Men used to open doors and actually hold them open long enough for the women walking behind them to walk through without getting slammed in the face. Black men used to escort women on their arms with an unspoken self-awareness that told the world, "I'm her protector. I'm her man." Today a black man seldom holds a black woman's hand in public, in private, or after making love. If that's what they still call it. Love.

Nowadays, a lump forms in my throat and I choke on the infectious reality that most men care only about what's between a woman's legs and how fast they can slide into home plate and avoid taking her on a first date. Men make no concrete investment of their time, let alone their money, because today women generously pick up the tab. Madame C. J. Walker never would've done that, and Malcolm X never would've expected her to.

Once upon a time, black men labored for their loved ones. Nowadays most men are so busy chasing a dollar, like a dog chasing its tail, that they consider slowing down long enough to love or commit to any black woman a chore or a setback. Every part of her mind, body, and soul becomes boring after he's dripped his last drop of cum inside her womb. Once he's done, in a random act of contrived kindness, he says "Baby, I'll call you later." He says this just in case he wants to stick his dick in her pussy, reload, then explode another load again and again.

Boom!

There was a time, five decades ago, seemingly not so long ago, when a man cared about his seed before ejaculating inside of a woman. And if he impregnated that woman, he asked her father for her hand in marriage, ensured food was on the table, the light bill was paid, and actually reared his children. "Boy, what did your mother say? Don't make me take off this belt. You'd better listen to your mother, or you gon' have to deal with me . . . with me, with me, with me."

Nowadays a black man will deny his seed, even if the child looks like he spit him out. Words roll off a black man's tongue even when he cannot convince himself of his lie. He says, "That's not my child," or "How do I know for sure it's mine?" That is, until Maury tells him, "You ARE the father!" Then he wants to shed tears until the credits finish rolling. Then once again . . . he's fading back to black.

For a moment the mother wonders if a ghost had screamed, "Whose pussy is this?" right before her man's back tightened and his toes curled. She wouldn't dare use the word *spine*. Nowadays most men don't have one. They want all the perks, like free pussy; a complimentary hot meal; a cozy, warm bed in which to lay their head; a submissive woman to dump their problems on or invest in their dreams; and a few dollars in their pocket, irrespective of where the money came from and as long as they didn't have to earn it.

What's their justification? "I can blow her back out like no other man can," they say. Or laying claim to what they could never own, they say, "That's my pussy. You hear me?" But if game doesn't recognize game, she'll only hear what he wants her to. She'll do whatever he wants her to whenever he whispers, "I love you, boo." Even if the words are a damn lie, she'll cry for joy because she craves to be loved. She desperately wants to be held, if only for one night of pleasure, and her man trades places with the baby he left her to raise alone for the next eighteen plus years.

Once upon a time, a man wanted to blow a woman's mind. Tease her. Test her. See if she could conduct an intelligent conversation while holding his hand as they strolled together. He cared whether or not she had a strong head on her shoulders, because he didn't want an unstable wife nurturing his children. Education was a priority, and dropping out of school wasn't an option for a black man's kids. Now, well, a black man cares more about whether a black woman can give good head than finding out if she's got any degrees or asking his baby mama what his child needs.

No shirt. No shoes. No diapers. No food. By nature a black man is a man, but he's not man enough to handle his responsibilities. Say what? Give the money to his baby mama and let her get her hair done or buy food for some other man to eat? Owing to the fact that his baby's mama looks better than she did when she was with him, he can't see that his son never misses any of the meals he has neglected to pay for. But let a black man's child become a millionaire from all the sleepless nights the child's mother has invested, and a black man will stick his chest and hand out so far, his palm could go in his ass and come out the same mouth that denied the child was ever his.

A man used to greet a woman with a smile; he'd introduce himself. He used to charm her for a while, but now that cell phones exist, he insists on getting her number before asking, "What's your name? Are you married?" as if he honestly cared whether or not she had a husband at home or whether his wife or his babies' mama was at home by herself, with their children.

Men used to automatically pick up the tab, walk a woman to her front door, ask for a second date. A man would never invite himself into a woman's home or stay too late without her explicit consent. Now men ask, "Where you live? I'll be over. Got any good movies? What you gon' cook? Got anything to drink?"

Once upon a time, black men helped black men build character. Nowadays a black man's mouth is synonymous with a slaughterhouse. He calls black women bitches and whores. Voluntarily, he puts his dignity on a chopping board. Fuck you, trick. Bam! Balling up his fists and hurling punches at his black woman is his way of proving his manhood. The subliminal, and sometimes overt, degradation of a black woman makes him stand tall. The smaller he can make her feel, the less of a curve he has in his spineless spine as he lies to her face repeatedly.

Maybe it's just me, y'all. But has any woman met a black man with character lately? My frame of reference is predominantly black men, so I can't honestly speak about other races. Even though I'm fed up with black men, I haven't given up on the black men that do have character. I may be talking about your daddy or a black man you've dated or even the one you're with. Does he show you that he loves you? If so, how?

I know a few wonderful men and I've listed some of them in my dedication and acknowledgments. From celebrities to ordinary guys, the real men must be on sabbatical or on vacation or missing with no action, or maybe they're all dead or simply afraid to do the right things. Seriously, I understand that there's a plethora of reasons why it is sometimes difficult for a black man to do right by a black woman, even if she is the one supporting him.

Given the abuses of sorry-ass, need-to-have-their-badges-taken-away police officers and racist, pathetic district attorneys, who have more dysfunctional issues than the average black man; racial profiling; and an injustice system that locks a black man up ten times longer and a hundred times faster than a white man for committing the same crimes or, in some cases, for committing no crime at all, equal rights need to be reinstated like black men need to renew their marital vows to their wives, immediately.

After making a quick dollar off of the white man's drugs; or dressing up in a designer suit, trying to quietly fit in; or dangling gold chains or flashing gold teeth or rolling in luxury cars just to get women or damn . . . the list in my head of how white society plots and plans the demise and genocide of the black man is endless. I know that every black man is constantly pressured in hopes that he'll snap. And when a good black man gives up on himself, the people who are hurt the most are the black women who are left alone to do it all by themselves, his kids, and the entire black community.

Society perpetuates the notion that it's easier for a black man to do what's wrong. I disagree, because by nature, even the black man on the corner, selling drugs, in his heart wants to do what is right. Black men don't want to leave their wives or their baby mamas at home with the kids while they roam the streets, searching for new pussy that's really only new to them. But a black man stares a woman in the eye without blinking. His rehearsed script rolls off of his tongue. "You know I want you, girl. But we can't be together right now. I told you I have a wife." He makes the word *wife* synonymous with the recent purchase of a new pair of shoes.

Well, whosoever wrote those lame-ass civil rights acts of 1957, 1960, and 1964 needs their ass kicked for lying to black men and women. Because thanks to society, when the curtains close, what we truly have is an audience filled with lonely, emotionally castrated black women and characterless black men, waiting to perform the next act just in case their shallowness, their inconsiderate ways, their lies, and their alibis weren't convincing enough the first several times around.

But what are black women thinking when they watch this cast of characters, these pretenders who say, without any forethought, "I want you to have my baby." When black men are not required to show up and be accounted for as real men with character, why do black women spread their legs, share their bed, give their money, and freely hand them their hearts?

Could it be that most black women are clueless? How can a black woman not know her self-worth? I bet that Harriet Tubman is firing gunshots in the air all around Heaven right now, wondering why in the hell black folks are turning their backs on one another.

Black, white, or other, most women have no idea how they deserve to be treated. Maybe they're living a life like their mothers or choosing men like the fathers who never loved their mothers. Or perhaps, just perhaps, most black women don't know the meaning of the word *character*. Even worse, some women don't care about a man's character as long as his dick can stroke deep enough to make them forget that he doesn't give a fuck about them.

Lights. Camera. Silence.

Action speaks louder than words. At the end of the journey, when the curtains close and the show is over, very few lovers can whisper in the other one's ear, "I love you," and mean it. How can one love a person they don't know? How can any man or woman love another person without first loving themselves?

How can true love exist when a man's character is absent?

LACONNIE TAYLOR-JONES

Who's Loving You

It was 1975 and my freshmen year in high school.

Beads of sweat settled like raindrops on my nose as I dashed around a new school on a humid day in August, trying to locate my first period physics class. When I finally showed up ten minutes late, my greatest fear as I strolled inside the huge, auditorium-style room filled with mostly juniors and seniors should've been whether the instructor would allow me entrance. Instead, my biggest concern was inconspicuously finding someplace to sit. Scanning the room, I spotted a solitary desk in the rear. Once I settled in, I glanced to my left and saw a brother with a shy smile, wire-rimmed glasses, and one of the toughest Afros I'd ever seen. He smiled at me. Fate intervened again, because he was also in my fourth period advanced math class. Over the school year, I learned a great deal about the person I initially considered a nerd.

By all accounts, he could have so easily been lumped in the category our society preserves for black males that are fatherless and raised by single mothers—most likely *not* to succeed. Yet, he defied all the odds.

Every day, I'm grateful to that middle-school teacher who had the unmitigated gall to tell this man-child to his face that black folks, and especially black men, didn't have the intelligence or the discipline to become engineers. Whether that statement inspired my man to achieve—he delivered the valedictorian address to his senior class in

1975 and subsequently received a full scholarship to one of the top engineering schools in the country, earning a chemical engineering degree with honors—I'll never know.

What I do know is this: He's the man I married twenty-four years ago and the father of my four children. He's the man who sometimes heads out the door sick and works all day to earn an honest day's pay in order to support his family. He's the man who loves me in spite of my shortcomings. He's the man who honors and respects me and demands the same from others on my behalf. He's the man who's cried with me and for me. He's the man who's celebrated my joys and shared my pain. He's my lover, my best friend, my soul mate.

Who's loving me?

Not just any man, but a *damn* good man.

LaConnie Taylor-Jones
When A Man Loves A Woman
Genesis Press
www.laconnietaylorjones.com

K. L.

Who's Loving Me

My wife is everything I need in a woman and more. I've said often, along with God, she makes me the man I am today. She's exactly what I prayed for. She is my gift from God, but that gift didn't come without some pain. So that you fully understand what she means to me, allow me to share with you our journey. This journey has entailed a happiness that has overcome me being married when we initially met, reconnecting with each other after a five-year absence, infidelity, a miscarriage, my four children from three other women, former acquaintances that attacked our relationship, a mother-in-law who gambled part of our financial future away, and even Hurricane Dean. There is no way I could have scripted the way my life has been filled with pure happiness from the love of a strong African American sister who somehow fell and stayed in love with me. The one thing I do know is that the Lord was at work here, and he decided it was time for us to be together.

In 1995 I returned to York College in Jamaica, Queens. I needed to get my life in order. I had made the choice to be a full-time student. I had originally started college in 1985 and had spent four years playing ball and chasing skirts at this very college. I was sleeping with every woman I could, and ten years later nothing had changed, except my marital and parental status. I was a married man of four years and was expecting my second child with my wife. I also had a daughter, with another woman, who was living in South Carolina with her grandparents since her mother and I were unable to take care of her. Inside, I was the same dog and predator. I started hanging out with the younger guys on the basketball team because they loved my wisdom on how to get the ladies, and this fed my ego. Prideful discussions about my conquests and sexual prowess were an instant ego fix. I became one of the coaches of the women's basketball team. That is where I met Tiffany. She was cute, sexy, and thick. Oh, I could go on for days about how good-looking she was. I have always loved the thicker sisters, and she was perfect. One thing I noticed was that her clothes left a little something to be desired. Hell, it looked like she was poor. I was calling her my Section 8 sweetheart. Actually, I told another brother that she was my diamond in the rough. I was so vain that I told her, "You know, if I clean you up, you'd look pretty good." Of course, I got ignored.

I was definitely smitten with Tiffany. She was friends with one of the young women on the team, so I used my coaching influence to get a date. Getting together for lunch one day, Tiffany explained her home life. She told me that at nineteen she owned her own home. Here I was, almost ten years older than her, and she was telling me she owned a home. Yeah okay. Of course, I didn't believe her, but whatever will get me into her pants. I could see she was digging me, but she didn't act like other women. My school status and smooth romancing talk didn't move her. She asked me if was I married. I had to say yes. I didn't think lying was going to work. She said she didn't date married men. I was tight. I couldn't see the makings of a fine, stable, and together sister. All I saw was a lost victim I wanted to bed down. Not too soon after that conversation, Tiff dropped out of school.

Fast-forward to 2000. I was still lying with whatever women would let me. The only thing now was I had separated from my wife, and I was living back home with my mother and grandmother. One night, when I was heading to the store, I saw these hips and this soft, sexy walk. I never neglected to check out the stride of a full-figured woman. I wanted to get Ms. Sexy's attention, so I said, "Why are you looking so mean?" She ignored me. Wow! It was Tiffany. Five years later and she still looked great. I yelled out, "Don't act like you don't remember me." After talking for about two hours, I took her home, and it turned out she lived about three minutes from my parents. Of course, she asked if I was still married. "Keith, you know I don't date married men, so why are you trying to kick it?" she said. "Listen, Tiff," I said. "I am not with my wife anymore, and I am working on getting divorced. I even live out here in Queens now. I moved out." I told her to just take time and think about getting together.

We were married on August 12, 2007. To understand this woman, you have to know that she is not money or attention hungry: she is just committed to being a good person. That is what I love about her. Going into this marriage, we knew so much had changed in our lives. We had given our lives to Christ and had become Christians. When I hear women talk about men and say, "Once a cheater, always a cheater," I'm delighted that our relationship puts that to rest. You see, as I stood waiting for my bride to come down the aisle at my parents' home, my thoughts were on why God chose me to bless like this. Here I had spent my whole life trying to destroy all he had given me. I had cheated on Tiffany multiple times and had even got one woman pregnant, but she lost the child. I did the "I am sorry. I'll never do it again. Don't leave me, baby" thing just to keep her in my life. The last time was the time that the ice around my heart cracked. I had begun to change my life after I started attending church and trying to get closer to the Lord. Tiffany was doing the same thing. She even got baptized since it was something she'd always wanted to do. Her connection to the Lord saved our lives and our future together. The last time I cheated, she was ready to kick me out and end this union we'd had for six years. Before she could get the words out, I was leaving, because I didn't want to see her hurting anymore. With the Bible on the bed, Tiff asked me to come and sit next to her. "Keith, listen," she said. "You know I love you, but I can't keep doing this. Tonight you're going to have to decide to change. If you love God and me, then you have to change all the way, or we will never make it." Here the woman I'd helped bring to Christ was ministering to me. Here a woman nine years my junior was reaching inside my chest and healing what had been an ailment most of my life. Say what you want, but that night God touched my wife, and she touched me. My tears had never been so big. After losing a child of our own, hearing about another woman being pregnant for me around the same time, this angel chose to do

what she thought God wanted and attempted to fix this relationship. That was the night I fell so in love with her that only death could stop me from loving her. Standing there on our wedding day, with our friends and family, I was proud to be getting ready to say "I do." This is the woman God wanted me to have, and it was through the love of Him that we saved each other. My wife is the love of my life, and I'll fight to the death to make sure she is never hurt by anything I do or anyone. She is my friend, partner, and equal. This is who is loving me!
—K. L.

www.KLthewriter.com

Love Is . . .

Love means many things to people. What does love mean to you? The dictionary defines *love* as a profoundly tender, passionate affection for another person; strong affection for another arising out of kinship or personal ties; an unselfish loyal and benevolent concern for the *good* of another.

Any act of kindness that is done with forethoughts of expectations of reciprocity is not love. When you truly love another, you should freely perform acts of kindness simply because you care for the other person. If you have regrets or remorse for having expressed love for someone, then you don't honestly love them. You bartered your tokens of affection in hopes of gaining their love.

Love is a gamble. There is no guarantee that the one you love will love you. My advice is take a chance and don't hold back. Love fuels the spirit. Love soothes pain. Love protects the heart. The one thing love does not do is love. People love. Love is a noun; it's an immeasurable, insurmountable, intangible thing. Things are idle until people utilize them.

In your heart, you have the power to love and uplift everyone around you. Unhappiness is a choice that requires you to relive moments of your past that generally prevent you from appreciating the present. Try smiling when you feel like frowning. Give someone a hug just because you care. Be very clear that the first person you must love is yourself. When you love yourself, you elevate yourself. You do not allow others to bring you down by abusing, mistreating, or disrespecting you.

Don't confuse having sex with making love.

Too many babies are conceived from straight fucking. To the greatest extent possible, love the person you're having sex with. Discuss the possibilities and responsibilities of pregnancy. It saddens me to see so many single mothers struggling alone. I know there are a few single male parents, too, but 70 percent of African American women are single moms. This percentage is ludicrous and must decrease drastically.

Ladies, you must take dominion over your hearts, your minds, your bodies, and your lives. I urge you not to forget that your pussy belongs to you and no one else. Not your mama, not your daddy, and definitely not any man. Never feel pressured to have sex. MAKE HIM put on a condom, or put it on for him. Men and women who are sexually active must keep condoms on hand at all times, because you can't use what you don't have.

My favorite condoms are Magnums (the regular lubricated ones without all the added stimulants or effects) and Lifestyle Tuxedos. If the Magnum is too big for him, the black Tuxedo should fit nicely. Have at least one Magnum XL, just in case you hit the jackpot. If he's fairly small, you can try Kimonos. I find the elastic band at the base is too tight for large and average dicks but just right for a man who is smaller. Kimonos may also work better for men who are diabetic, by helping them to prolong an erection. The size of the condom does matter. The size of the dick does not.

I hear all the brainwashed, sexually inexperienced readers disagreeing with me, but what I find is most men, while they may not be able to count the number of sexual encounters they've had, are inexperienced when it comes to pleasing a woman. A smaller-size man generally works harder to make a great impression in bed than a man with a big dick. Lambskin condoms only protect against pregnancy, not sexually transmitted diseases. If a man is allergic to latex, he should maximize foreplay and minimize the time he wears the latex condom. He might try adding a drop of water-based lube on the head of his dick before putting on the condom, but by no means should the couple forgo protecting themselves.

Ladies, allowing a man to ejaculate inside of you is personal (and possibly terminal) and should never be done without first getting tested. HIV does not have a look, a taste, or a smell, and it is a disease that does not discriminate. What I'm hearing from college-age students is the ladies are the ones who don't want the men to wear condoms. In this case, guys you must accept the responsibility of wrapping up your dick, because you're at risk, too. You could contract sexually transmitted diseases from women. Those who prefer same-sex relationships or are bisexual, you, too, must use condoms and dental dams.

Ladies, before having sex, ask him, "If I get pregnant, what are you going to do?" If he already has children he's not taking care of, please don't foolishly think you're the chosen one and he'll do right by you. He won't.

Having a baby should be a choice, not a mistake.

Discuss the ramifications and seriousness of contracting a sexually transmitted disease. Protect yourself. Take birth control pills or use another form of birth control in addition to condoms. Innocent children are abandoned emotionally and sometimes physically because two irresponsible people with raging hormones decided to have unprotected sex. What's left after the sperm fertilizes the egg? A pregnant female, often a teenager, who will spend the rest of her life caring for her child, alone. And somehow, miraculously, that child is expected to learn how to love parents that don't know how to love them.

Often the people that you have sex with don't love you at all. Sometimes they don't even know who you are or what your middle name is or what your favorite anything is—your favorite color, food, place, or movie. Emotional infidelity is potentially worse than having sexual affairs. A true love bond cannot be broken. A sexual relationship can end at any time. Married or single, if you decide to engage in sex, fuck responsibly.

I imagine the most misused word in every dictionary is *love*. People say, "I love you," with their mouth, not their heart. So you hear what you want to hear, but you don't feel the power of love. It's easier to hate. Oh, people are so easily appeased and displeased nowadays, largely because they don't know how to genuinely love themselves or anyone else. But they think they do.

No, I take that back. *They don't think*. They simply believe.

Who's Loving
Mary B. Morrison

The answer for me is simple, "I am."

My life is fantastic! I get out of bed when I'm ready. I write when and where I want. I have a beautiful son. When I'm at home, I'm blessed to awaken to a breathtaking view of the sun shimmering on the lake. I have no reason, not a single one, to be unhappy. I work hard, and I know how to enjoy myself. I travel extensively. I appreciate people. For me, the master key to my internal joy is that I don't feel guilty about anything I do.

I see whomever I want, whenever I choose. I don't lie. I don't have to cheat. And I'm not a pretender. I don't say I like you if I don't. The word *love* and the words *I love you,* I only speak them if I mean it.

When I travel, I have the wonderful opportunity to meet new men and reunite with former acquaintances. I decide to what extent I'm interested in sharing time with the men I meet. I try my best to live in the moment, because memories last a lifetime.

I don't need a man to provide for my son and me. Nor will I take care of a grown-ass man. There are times when I think I'd prefer to be in a relationship, that is, until a man is in my space for more than seventy-two hours. Then I realize I want him to leave. I've discovered that three days is my threshold.

Black men nowadays are chronic complainers, and they have way too many hang-ups. By the time black men finish complaining, I'm drained. I accept responsibility in my role, and I consciously strive to accentuate the positive in their lives, because I am truly happy and I want the people around me to be happy, too. Black men dump their problems and won't listen to a woman for more than five minutes; then they gotta go. Who needs that headache? Definitely not me.

My concept of being in a relationship is having the ability to communicate openly, to not personalize what the other person says, to explore fantasies together (not behind one another's back), and to uplift and support one another to the highest heights possible.

The lyrics "I can do bad by myself" are so true. The opposite is my reality. I'm doing great dating openly. Sex makes me happy, so while I'm guilty of taking the dick and running, I don't feel guilty for doing so. Once in a while, I will slow down just to see if a brotha is sincere in his desire for a meaningful relationship. Then he'll say something like, "I want to take my time." In what? Dog years? I ain't got that kind of time to wait around on you. Next! Too many women miss wonderful opportunities—career, sex, traveling, hanging with their girlfriends, etc.—because they wait in vain for a man to decide how they should live their life. I'm honest, y'all, sometimes to a fault, because I tell guys that I'm having sex with other men.

Some men have told me they actually enjoy misleading a woman, treating her nice but never making a commitment to her. And when she gets jealous of the other woman, her tears or outrage stokes the male ego. That's why I keep it real with how I feel.

I must admit, my attitude is healthy for me but very intimidating for most men.

I have a guy friend or two in most major cities that I travel to, like Atlanta, New York, D.C., Los Angeles, Louisville, I had one for a long time in New Orleans, my Chicago friend moved to Philly, and in my hometown, there are always a few good dicks hanging around.

I'm not saving myself for when a special man comes along. I don't have that kinda time. For me, love is simple, love is consistent, love is powerful, and love is uplifting. There are some guarantees in life. For me, one guarantee is I love myself more than anyone else, and that keeps Mary B. Morrison extremely happy.

Acknowledgments

I am grateful for the finest things in life . . . love, happiness, peace, family, friends, fans (without you there'd be no *New York Times* best-selling author Mary B. Morrison), and God's grace.

My ultimate joy is my one and only twenty-one-year-old, six-foot-nine, super-handsome, intelligent, and talented son, Jesse Bernard Byrd, Jr. Oh my goodness, he's like totally legal now. Wow! I remember the day he was born. A lot has happened since then. Time flies. I respect single parents, like myself, who have the majority, if not all, of the responsibility for their kids and are constantly sacrificing to rear them. Instill good values in your children. Let them see you work hard, let them see you smile, let them see you cry, and constantly tell them, "I love you." Jesse is a young man of great character. God gave me the right child. Jesse is at the University of California, Santa Barbara, pursuing his dream of playing in the NBA.

Elester Noel and Joseph Henry Morrison are my biological parents. Both of my parents have made their transition into eternity, my mother when I was nine years old, and my father when I was twenty-four years old. For those of you who are blessed to still have your parents, cherish them.

I'm blessed with the greatest siblings in the world—Wayne Morrison, Andrea Morrison, Derrick Morrison, Regina Morrison, Margie Rickerson, and Debra Noel. Man, I don't know what I'd do without them or my cousins, Edward Allen and Treece Johnson-Mallard.

This is the first time I have had to call upon my friends to read my work and give me feedback, and I'm glad my ego didn't overrule my senses. I want to thank Eve Lynne Robinson, Malissa Walton, Denise Kees, Debra Burton (of Turning Pages Book Club), and Lisa Johnson (of Sistahs on the Reading Edge) for all saying yes. I love you guys!

Turbo Tongue, what can I say about you without writing a tell-nothing, keep-that-shit-to-myself, off-the-hook kinda book? Straight up, with your orgasmic voice, you need your own damn radio talk show. "Tell me a deep secret." Thank you for making me laugh until I cry, smile until my cheeks hurt, and you know you make me wanna shout! Throw my hands up! Cum on now! Work it. Work it out . . . LOL. You're the best.

When I think of the success I've had since self-publishing in 2000, I think of Felicia Polk, a true friend who supported me from day one; Vyllorya A. Evans, my mentor and friend; my son, Jesse Byrd, Jr., who has never complained about the sacrifices he's made to support my literary career; Selena James, my editor who cares about my vision; Karen R. Thomas, my editor who believes in every book I write; Laurie Parkin, a phenomenal woman who's never too busy to respond to me; Linda Duggins, my publicist extraordinaire; Adeola Saul, my publicist and superwoman; Karen Auerbach, my publicist who makes dreams come to life; LaToya Smith, my shero; Steven Zacharius, a man who holds my best interests at hand; Walter Zacharius, a visionary who includes me in his plans; Claudia Menza, my agent and dear friend who tirelessly supports me; Andrew Stuart, my agent and biggest advocate; Eve Lynne Robinson, my fabulous photographer and friend; Kim Mason, my web designer and so much more; and Lou Richie, my family for life.

When I began writing, there was a longer list of African American independent bookstores owned by die-hard booksellers with a passion for black literature and authors. I truly miss our huge supporters. My success is their success because of Michele Lewis, Emma Rogers, Sherry McGee, Maleta, Brother Simba, Brother Yao, and Vera Warren-Williams.

Feel free to hit me up with a piece of your world at www.mary-morrison.com and let me know Who's Loving You. Peace and prosperity.

Enjoy the following excerpt from HoneyB's

Single Husbands

Coming in March 2009 from Grand Central Publishing

WARNING!

Adult Fiction

Sexually Exquisite

If you are not eighteen years or older, do not, seriously, do not read this book.

PROLOGUE

Is There a Loophole in Marriage Vows?

If you are or have ever been married, does this sound *somewhat* familiar?

In the presence of God, and our family and friends, I offer you my solemn vow to be your faithful partner in sickness and in health, in good times and in bad, and in joy as well as in sorrow. I promise to love you unconditionally, to support you in your goals, to honor and respect you, to laugh with you and cry with you, and to cherish you for as long as we both shall live.

I encourage you to reread the above paragraph word for word. But don't stop there: read all the marriage vows you can find, and e-mail me any preexisting marriage vows where it states married couples cannot have sex outside of their marriage. If you choose to quote the phrase "vow to be faithful," I ask that you first seek the definition of the word *faithful*; then pay close attention to how the word *faithful* is being used.

There are beliefs rooted in Christianity, like "Thou shall not commit adultery" and "Thou shall not covet his neighbor's wife," but to my knowledge, correct me if I'm wrong, none of the ten commandments are quoted in marriage vows. So I must ask you, the reader, because you are intelligent, is there a loophole in wedding vows regarding infidelity?

The three couples in this story made a commitment to one another, but somewhere along their journey, after saying, "I do," Herschel Henderson, Brian Flaw, and Lexington Lewis took detours. Now take a moment to think about how people change after they get married. These three men didn't honestly deviate from their premarital behavior. Most people don't. What happened was the women they married thought that signing a marriage license would miraculously make their unfaithful fiancés faithful husbands.

Have you ever thought about the definitions for *marriage* and *license?* Marriage is the state of being united to a person of the opposite sex as husband or wife in a consensual and contractual relationship recognized by law. There are no prerequisites to getting married. In reality it doesn't matter if the parties exchanging vows even respect or love one another. Who cares? The law rules above all hearts. The law doesn't care if one is miserably or happily married. One's IQ and bank account can be below zero, and one can still find someone to marry.

Moving along, a license is permission granted by a competent authority to engage in a business, an occupation, or an activity. It is a document, plate, or tag that indicates such permission was granted.

A license is a document. Every license—except a marriage license—must be renewed and can be revoked, suspended, or terminated. A marriage license can either be annulled (reduced to nothing) or dissolved (decomposed or made to disappear), which means the marriage ends in divorce.

A marriage license is a façade. It's a piece of paper granted not by the parties involved but by an authority (the law) to the parties, who have no enforceable control over their spouse. In many cases, people marry strangers. What's my point? People who decide to get married are disillusioned, because they believe they have entitlements when, in actuality, they have zero authority to hold the other person accountable to anything that that person does not desire to commit to. You don't marry a piece of paper. What you commit to is a union with an imperfect being, who you somehow expect will become perfect when you hear, "I now pronounce you husband and wife."

A marriage license to me is synonymous with the enforcement rights of a birth certificate. It simply identifies a person's a legal commitment, but the license does not, cannot, will not, shall not make anyone whole, complete, or happy. One can literally break all the laws of marriage and never be penalized. Which brings me to the question, what are the laws of marriage? Hit me up with your responses.

One can throw in the towel and cut one's losses, but one cannot bring forth charges against a cheating spouse unless one is perhaps married or living in the state of Florida. I ain't gon' mention no names, but I wonder if that's why that famous, multimillionaire couple's affairs suddenly became hush-hush when a baby was allegedly conceived out of wedlock. Hmm? I'd better shut my mouth. Anywho, what good is a marriage license? Now if you marry the right person, a license may make you wealthy, but how much will it cost you?

The law cannot make any person accountable; it merely grants an immeasurable tool with no accountability. Every license in America, except a marriage license, has built-in requirements for renewal, or else it does what? It expires. So when a couple decides to get married, they need to determine with their heads if the commitment is one they're willing to keep forever. Not many couples stay married forever, and of the ones that do, many die unfulfilled.

What the women in this novel get is what they have had all along. Instead of dating a single man, these women voluntarily consent to . . . *Single Husbands.*

Single Husbands... Three men who married for all the wrong reasons.

Herschel Henderson said, "I do," to have access to his wife's money, Lexington Lewis vowed for his better and her worse, and Brian Flaw meant until death do us part. Herschel has a mistress that he sexes more than his wife, Lexington is making love to as many women as he can at the sex clubs, and Brian is fucking women of every ethnicity because he's become bored with his sex life. The one thing these men share is despite being married, none of them will give up the sexual freedom they enjoyed as single men.

CHAPTER 1

Brian

—I, Brian Flaw, take you, Michelle, to be my lawfully wedded wife. . . .

First Sunday, three o'clock, after church, before Michelle's mother dropped off the kids at eight, it was yoni massage time. The one day of every month that Brian reaffirmed his love for his wife.

Brian absolutely adored his wife. She was the mother of his two children, his very best friend, and his confidant. Brian told Michelle everything that he considered significant, but there were a few things not worth mentioning.

Red satin sheets covered their king-sized bed. A goddess of heavenly beauty stretched from the headboard toward the foot of the bed. The softest cocoa skin he'd ever laid hands upon wrapped around her flesh, making him the happiest man alive.

Michelle's yoni was a precious space and sacred temple. She'd taught him to love and respect her pussy before the first time they made love, before their wedding, and before she gave birth to their children, saying to him, "Baby, it's solely my responsibility to teach you how to appreciate and pleasure my entire body."

The day Michelle let him watch her masturbate was etched in his mind forever, but it didn't have to be. The videotape was safely tucked away in their safe, along with the other XXX-rated home videos they'd done during their ten years of marriage. Brian knew Michelle was especially unique, because she was the only woman that had taught him how to make passionate love to her without fucking her.

Sitting on the bench at the foot of their bed, Brian buffed his fingernails as he admired his wife. She'd taught him that it was a man's responsibility to make certain his fingernails didn't cut or scratch a woman's delicate pussy, leaving her miserably sore and with painful scars that would hurt her so much she'd resent him and regret having allowed him to touch her sacredness. He'd learned so much from his wife. Michelle was even more beautiful than the day they'd met.

Brian's dick got hard. Moving about their spacious bedroom, he lit twelve white candles, dripped a few drops of cinnamon oil on the lamps beside the bed. Then he walked over to their patio and opened the glass door. The salty, warm summer breeze off the ocean engulfed their bedroom.

Returning to her, he softly kissed her forehead. "Are you relaxed, baby?" he asked Michelle.

"Yes, baby. I'm relaxed and patiently awaiting my wonderful husband."

"I'm here to please you, not just today, but every day. Whatever I have to give, I freely give it unto you."

Carefully, Brian placed two red satin pillows under his wife's head so she could comfortably watch him whenever she desired. Then he put a pillow under both of her knees and one under her curvaceous hips. Once he started massaging his wife, she always got extremely wet, so as a wedding gift, he'd had a tailor make a washable pillow covering, which he put on top of the pillow before placing the pillow inside the satin case.

Seated at the foot of the bed, Brian whispered, "Spread your legs and bend your knees so I can look at my pretty pussy."

Together, they inhaled deep into their bellies, then exhaled as much air as they could, like they did in yoga classes on second Sundays.

"Inhale again," he said as they began to breathe deeply two more times.

Careful not to touch her yoni, Brian's strong yet smooth hands journeyed up Michelle's thighs, passionately massaging her legs, abdomen, thighs, breasts, nipples, and other parts of her body to arouse her. Picking up the bottle of Wet , he squeezed a few drops of lubrication in the crevice of his wife's thighs and on her outer vaginal lips.

Slowly, he caressed her pussy, starting from the outside, massaging her outer lips between his thumb and index finger. He gently twirled her outer vaginal lips all the way up then all the way down. He took his time before he began massaging her inner lips. The time had not yet come to penetrate his wife.

Noticing Michelle's shallow breaths, Brian softly said, "Breathe a little deeper, baby."

Their yoni massage ritual was a treat Brian never grew tired of doing for his wife. He wanted to make sure Michelle was always sexually pleased beyond satisfaction, as he was on the third Sunday of each month, when Michelle gave him a lingam massage. Brian's dick went from limp to hard as he imagined his wife's hands all over his body.

Brian kept his thoughts inside his head; he knew it was best not to talk too much. Excessive talking by either of them would detract from maximizing his wife's pleasure. Michelle's eyes rolled to the top of her head, exposing the whiteness of her eyeballs through the tiny slits in her lids. She'd told him that was the moment when she could feel his energy moving from her feet to the crown of her head.

That was the perfect time for Brian to massage her precious pearl. Brian had once admitted he was slightly jealous that a woman's clitoris was four times more sensitive than a male's glands, and that a woman could easily have five times more orgasms per session than a man. He remembered what Michelle had told him. "Look at me, Brian. I want to make myself clear," she said. "A woman's precious pearl has only one purpose, and don't you ever forget it . . . and that's to give her pleasure, pleasure, and more pleasure. So don't ever overlook touching, stroking, and kissing my clit."

Adding a little more lubrication, he stroked his wife's clitoris in tiny clockwise and counterclockwise circles, then gently squeezed her clit between his thumb and index finger, using various rhythms.

"Breathe, baby," he reminded her again.

Inserting his right middle finger into his wife's yoni, Brian lightly explored and massaged the inside of her vagina. Slowly stroking up, down, around, and sideways, varying the depth, speed, and pressure, he honed in on her G-spot, then moved his middle finger, silently telling his pussy, *Come here, my pretty pussy.* Sliding in his ring finger, he stroked Michelle's G-spot to her satisfaction. Putting his thumb to work, he massaged her clit in an up-and-down motion. Brian didn't stop there. Using the same hand, he slipped his pinkie inside her anus.

Lifting her head, Michelle gazed into his eyes.

Brian softly said, "Thanks for letting me hold God's greatest gift to mankind in the palm of my hand. I cherish your mind, body, and spirit." Then he caressed his wife's breasts with his left hand, pausing for a moment to feel her heartbeat.

Michelle's hips jerked. Silently, tears streamed down her cheeks, as though it were their first time bonding. Brian closed his eyes and said, "Thank you, God, for trusting me with the most beautiful woman in the world. Baby, I love you."

Concluding the massage, slowly, gently, respectfully, and passionately, he eased his fingers out one at a time from inside his wife, holding his left hand against her heart until all of his fingers were removed. Then he lifted his left hand away from her body. Joining Michelle in the afterglow of her yoni massage, Brian cuddled her in a spoon position, telling her, "Baby, I appreciate and respect you."

Michelle had greatly enriched Brian's life, and there was no way he could repay her. Therefore, no matter what happened in their lives, Brian would never divorce his wife.

CHAPTER 2

Herschel

—*I, Herschel Henderson, take you, Nikki, to be my lawfully wedded wife. . . .*

"**S**top choking me!" Nikki yelled, struggling to pry Herschel's thumbs away from her aching throat.

"Shut the hell up, woman," Herschel countered, repositioning his huge masculine hands for a firmer grip. "Why do you make me hate you?"

Hate was such a strong word, but the sight of his wife disgusted him more than it pleased him. Once Nikki got a ten-page spread in a major magazine, which was showcasing her culinary skills, the bitch thought her shit didn't stink. She flew all over the country, out of the country, joyfully leaving him at home alone. She should've called first and told him she was coming home a week early.

The argument Nikki had started six days ago was old but far from over this morning or tomorrow morning or the next day after that day. Herschel was the man of his house, and the shit wasn't resolved until he said so. Why in the fuck had he had to sleep on the sofa six nights in a row to appease Nikki? Why did he have to call her ass from the home phone every damn night just to prove he was at home? Wasn't like he stayed home or slept at home after hanging up the phone.

"You know I love you, so why do you keep threatening to leave me?" he said.

"I can't breathe," Nikki whimpered. Forcefully, her knee rammed into his balls.

"Ahhh! Bitch! Are you crazy?" Folding into a number seven, Herschel grabbed his nuts, then fell to the floor. Orange, tiger-stripe imprints of his hands remained on his wife's flesh, from under her earlobes to above her collarbone. Herschel witnessed the bruises turn to a deep red. Fuck! Nikki's debut television show was taping tomorrow, it was the middle of summer, and she'd have to wear another scarf around her neck to cover up what she'd made him do.

"Baby, baby," Herschel repeated. "I'm so sorry. I don't know what got into me. Nikki, I need you." Stumbling toward her, he pressed his lips softly against hers. His mouth circled hers, trying to pry her thick, luscious lips apart with his tongue.

"Umph, umph," Nikki groaned, placing her hand in the center of the chiseled chest she used to drizzle hot chocolate on, then lick until all of it was off. "No, not this time, Herschel." *Smack!* Nikki's palm landed against his face. "You need to go be with that bitch you had up in my bed when I got home!" Reaching behind her, Nikki kept her eyes on him.

Fuck. It was a good thing he had good reflexes. Herschel ducked just in time to dodge the porcelain lamp that came zooming toward his head. *Crash!* The freestanding bedroom mirror behind him shattered before falling to the hardwood floor. Glass flew up to the ceiling and then down to the floor. "You are so fucking crazy, Nikki! Stop this shit, baby," he said, snatching her biceps.

Swiftly turning her body sideways, Nikki couldn't break free. Herschel didn't believe in hitting women, but Nikki was pushing him to do the unthinkable . . . kill her.

"Herschel, please," she cried. "I just want you to take your things and get out of my house. Let me be. Why can't you just let me be?"

Oh, now that she'd made it, she didn't need him anymore. If she really wanted him out, Nikki would have to buy him out. "Baby," Herschel said, wrapping his burly arms around Nikki's tall, slender body, "Listen to me." He ran his hand over her short black hair, which was neatly tapered around her mocha face. "That bitch that was here don't mean shit to me. I was lonely. I miss you. I miss my wife. Damn, Nikki. You're gone all the time."

The woman who had been in their bed six nights ago honestly didn't mean anything to Herschel, but April Henderson meant everything to him. Truth was, April wasn't legally his wife, but he'd given her the title of wife and, unofficially, his last name. And if April had had half the money and assets his wife Nikki had, he never would've married Nikki, because he had never loved Nikki. Nikki had gotten what she'd paid for: companionship, a fine-ass man to escort her to public events, and a damn good lover.

The day Herschel proposed to Nikki, he promised April he'd never leave her, no matter what. The day Herschel stood at the altar with Nikki, he'd recited his vows for April. Sex with April was better than with his wife. Herschel laughed with April, cried with April. They dreamt aloud together. Unlike Nikki, April believed in him. Every man needed a woman who believed in him. But there was one thing he'd regret the rest of his life, and that was missing the delivery of his child with April while he stood at that fucking altar with Nikki's ass!

Why couldn't he respond when the pastor said, "If anyone has cause for why this man and this woman should not be joined in holy matrimony, speak now or forever hold your peace."

Herschel should've looked Nikki in the eye and said, "Baby, I don't love you." But that would've meant no all-expense paid vacations for April. No single-family, three-bedroom home for April and their son, Ryan. And April would've had to stop home schooling Ryan and get a job. The best part was April was his best friend. April was one helluva woman. Sunday mornings, when Nikki accompanied him to church, April stood next to Nikki in the women's choir, honoring their secret vows of for better or for worse. April would ask Nikki for recipes to cook for him, and Nikki would happily give step-by-step instructions to April.

"You are a fucking liar!" Nikki screamed. "You fucked some bitch in my house, in my bed! What's her name, Herschel? Who is she?"

Correction. Now that they'd been married almost ten years, it was *their* house and *their* bed. And the woman had been some bitch. She'd been a one-night stand, and Herschel couldn't remember her name. But April was his mistress. April was a real woman and the true love of his life.

"I don't have time for this bullshit," Herschel said, letting go of

Nikki. "You need to call somebody to clean up this shit, because I'm not doing it this time, and I'm not leaving."

Calmly, Nikki said, "You know what, Herschel? If you don't leave, I'm calling the police."

Let Nikki call the fuckin' cops, Herschel thought. Thanks to Nikki, April had more than enough of Nikki's money to post his bail and a house that was free and clear of a mortgage to use as collateral. Herschel had the best life. Nikki was seldom home, and April was always available.

Just in case Nikki was serious, Herschel softened his voice. "Baby, I said I'm sorry, and I mean it," he lied again. "Please forgive me." He raised his right hand. "I swear on my mother's grave, you are the finest, the sexiest, the most beautiful black woman in the world, and I am so fucking proud of you."

Herschel was proud of Nikki, but he also hated the fact that she didn't need him. He knew that shit. Nikki could have any man she wanted. Why she'd married him, Herschel knew. He'd spoken all the words Nikki and every other successful, single, sexy black woman wanted to hear. There were a lot of lonely black women in the world. They were so lonely that they'd marry down just to have a man in their bed, in their life, on their arms, and to have bragging rights over their single girlfriends. When a black woman married, her husband lost his identity, as she'd repeatedly refer to him as her husband, saying, "My husband this and my husband that." A black woman like his wife would stay in an abusive relationship to avoid being alone.

"Herschel, hush. Your mother is not dead," Nikki said, trying to conceal her desire to laugh.

"See, you wrong for that shit," he said, nodding. "You wish my mama was dead."

"Sure as hell do. She's responsible for you being so dependent on me."

"Baby, I'm not dependent. I'm supportive. There's a difference," he said, kissing his wife's lips once more. This time Nikki didn't pull away.

Taking his wife into the kitchen, Herschel hoisted Nikki up on the island, then spread her legs. Opening the refrigerator, he removed a fresh mango, peeled away the skin with his teeth, tossed his long locks behind his back, then ran the mango between his wife's breasts and around her areolas. Then he sucked her sweet juicy nipples until they were erect.

"Mmm," Nikki moaned, leaning her head back and running her fingers through her hair.

Moving the mango between her pussy lips, Herschel pulled his wife back so that she was lying supine on the cool island tiles, then buried his face between her thighs. "Damn. You taste so fucking incredibly delicious. Who's pussy is this?" he asked, firmly pressing his tongue against her clit the way she liked. "Don't move." He made his way back to the refrigerator. He retrieved an ice cube, melted it down a little in his mouth, pressed his cool lips against his wife's clit, slipped the ice cube inside her ass, right along with his middle finger, then began to finger fuck her in the ass. Herschel enjoyed eating pussy, and he buried his face deeper into Nikki's pussy until she came so hard, he had to catch her before she fell to the floor. Maybe he should've let her fall. It would've been a justifiable accident.

"Baby," Herschel pleaded, holding his wife in his arms, "Don't ever leave me. I really do need you."

"Be careful what you ask for," Nikki said. "I'm tired of you. So if you choose to stay, I promise to make you wish you had left."

CHAPTER 3

Lexington

—I, Lexington Lewis, take you, Donna, to be my lawfully wedded wife. . . .

"Meet me at the club. I'm going down . . . ," Lexington sang, driving up to the valet. Handing the parking attendant his keys, Lexington strolled into the sex club.

He was on the prowl for all the pussy he could suck and fuck before sunrise. Handing the front-desk monitor his annual membership card, Lexington held on tight to his supersized bottle of vodka. He wasn't big on consuming alcohol, but the club policy was bring your own drink. Walking through the swinging double doors, Lexington glanced at the posted sign he read each Saturday night: IF NUDITY OR LIVE SEXUAL ACTS OFFEND YOU, DO NOT ENTER.

Checking out the honeys in lingerie at the bar, their naked, bodacious booties squirming on fiberglass bar stools, Lexington slowly handed his bottle of vodka to the bartender, reciting his membership number.

"Man, you know I got you," the bartender said, jotting the number on a sticky. "The usual?"

"You bet," Lexington confirmed.

"Ladies, this round is on Lex," the bartender announced, pouring a round for all the women at the bar.

Generously sharing his alcohol with women generally gave Lexington premier pick of any, and sometimes all, the women at the bar that he wanted to suck his dick. Unbuttoning his shirt, he exposed the soft, curly hairs on his chest. Working out daily, while his wife, Donna, sat around the house, gaining weight, had paid off tremendously.

"Hey, Lex, Daddy," said a familiar voice behind him.

Lexington smiled, then turned around. "What the fuck are you doing here?" he asked.

Nikki gave him a kiss on the lips.

What the fuck was his boy Herschel's wife doing up in the sex club? Donna didn't even know his spot.

"Nikki, what's up? You need to take your ass home. Herschel is going to flip the fuck out if he finds out you're here. And for the record, you're not with me, okay?"

"And what about Donna? You saying you have permission to be here every Saturday night?"

Lexington's jaw tightened as he walked over to the dance floor and joined a group of three fine-ass, naked women in high heels. One bowed before him, unzipped his pants, took out his dick, and started licking him up and down. Another one joined her while Lexington eased his finger inside the third woman's pussy.

Glancing over at Nikki, he saw that she was bent over a table, with some dude fucking her in the ass. Damn. Nikki could take it like that. Shaking his head to erase X-rated thoughts of fucking his boy's wife, Lexington walked away from the dance floor, bypassed the restrooms, and asked the locker room attendant to open up one of the lockers for him. Undressing, Lexington placed his clothes and shoes in the locker, wrapped his towel around his waist, and headed to the Freak-a-Zone.

Strolling through the club to see what was happening and what regulars were on the scene, Lexington nodded his head at a few of the guys he knew. All six of the Jacuzzis were packed with women and men, who were sitting on the edge, getting their clits licked or dicks sucked. A few were bent over the sides, fucking doggie style.

"Aw, damn," Lexington thought as he spotted the finest woman in the club. She was sitting alone, checking out everyone else.

She looked classy, sophisticated, and very much in control of her hormones. "That's the one I'm fucking tonight," he whispered.

Patiently, he traveled throughout the community rooms. Beds were lined up under a canopy in one room and positioned around a Jucuzzi in another room. Everybody was in the zone. Men were leaning back on sofas, with their hands clamped behind their heads, while naked females with nice bodies and booties were lined up on coffee tables, sucking dicks like lollipops. Condoms were everywhere, but Lexington used Magnum XL exclusively, so he'd brought his own.

Lexington envied his boy Brian and the way Brian adored Michelle. Why couldn't Lexington feel the same way about Donna? It wasn't that Brian didn't do shit on the side. Brian's preference was to fuck every woman he could but never fuck any of them more than once. But Brian was different from Lexington and Herschel in that he genuinely loved his wife and kept her first. Brian had a plan for all the women he fucked: he rented hotel rooms, had the women put the room charges on their credit cards, then reimbursed them with cash. That way he never left a paper trail. And Michelle loved Brian so much, she'd never leave him, either. Brian boasted about how his wife would never take another woman's word over his, so basically Brian didn't give a fuck when chicks threatened to tell his wife about their affair.

Lexington wished like hell he could love his wife, but Donna was a straight bitch. She verbally humiliated him in front of her friends, his friends, their kids, and their family, so why should he give a damn about what Donna felt?

Making his way back to the woman who was sitting alone, Lexington extended his hand and asked, "You wanna join me in a private room?"

"Sit with me for a moment, and we'll see," she said, licking her lips.

Lexington sat next to her on an oversized cushion. "What's up?"

"I'm not from around here. This is my first time at a sex club, so instead of joining in, I decided to watch."

"What's your name?" Lexington asked, watching her nipples pop beneath the gold lace teddy covering her breasts. Yeah, she was new. Most of the women strolling through the club were either naked or had on basic bikinis.

"Irresistible is my name."

"Don't give me no fake-ass name," Lexington said. "What's your real name?"

"That's what my mama named me. What's yours?"

Lowering the lace covering Irresistible's breasts, he caressed a nipple before easing it into his mouth. "Lexington. Hey, let's go," he finally said, firmly gripping her hand.

Irresistible stood. Damn! Her sweet ass was working that gold thong. Lexington eagerly led her into one of the private rooms. While he eased the spaghetti straps over her shoulders, she unwrapped his towel. Sitting on the bed, she began sucking his dick.

Tearing off the edge of a condom wrapper, Lexington stepped back, but Irresistible wouldn't let go of his dick. Her mouth was tight and juicy and felt so fucking good, he wanted to cum but refused. "Whew, baby. You gon' have to ease up off of him so I can put on a condom."

"You like the way I suck this big-ass dick, Daddy?" she said, getting a bit aggressive and sucking a lot harder.

Aw, fuck. What the hell? It's her mouth, he thought. "If you don't back up, I'm about to explode a load," he replied. Lexington was enjoying that shit, that is, until the door opened.

"Mind if I join you?" Nikki asked, entering their room without permission.

"Get out!" Lexington said, holding back on squirting cum all over Irresistible's face.

Quietly, Nikki stood before Lexington, dropped the towel wrapped around her body, pushed him onto the mattress, straddled his dick, and began fucking him.

"Nikki, cut this shit out," Lexington protested.

Irresistible started sucking Nikki's breasts and rubbing Nikki's clit. "Ride him like a horse, baby," Irresistible said, cheering Nikki on.

"No, don't encourage her. You don't understand," Lexington said.

"Aw, now who's acting new?" Irresistible moaned.

Nikki started squeezing his dick. Irresistible sat on his face, facing Nikki. Lexington ran his tongue over Irresistible's shaft, then sucked her clit. *What the hell,* he thought. Inserting his finger inside Irresistible's pussy, Lexington began frantically finger fucking the shit out of her G-spot.

"Oh, my, God! Yes! Yes!" Irresistible screamed, "That's my spot, baby! Go harder!"

Lexington felt Nikki riding him faster. Grinding her pelvis into his dick, Nikki screamed, "Fuck you! Cum for me, Lex!"

Suddenly, it dawned on Lexington that he was ejaculating inside of his boy's girl without a condom, and as big and long as Lexington's dick was, his sperm didn't have to swim. He shot those motherfuckers straight to the eggs, like a fucking cannon ball. That was how Donna had ended up pregnant five years in a row.

"No, Nikki, don't do this to me. Stop. Please, get up."

"Ahhhh!" Irresistible yelled, squirting fluid all over his stomach and Nikki's pussy.

Nikki's pussy clamped down so hard, there was nothing Lexington could do except yell as he shot a full load, cumming harder than ever. Nikki's pussy was fucking great.

Lexington knew Herschel was a dog, but Nikki was a straight bitch for this shit. No matter how doggish men were, the one unspoken rule between friends was friends didn't fuck their friends' wives. Nikki had to keep this shit between them.

"Irresistible, you need to get up. You, too, Nikki."

"You two know each other?" Irresistible asked.

Shaking his head, Lexington walked out of the room, went to the lockers, got dressed, retrieved his car from the valet, and headed home to his wife. What should've been a great night had ended up all bad.

Stepping into his living room, Lexington found Donna sitting on the sofa, as usual.

"It's six o'clock in the morning, Lex! Where the hell have you been?"

Lexington did his usual. He grabbed Donna by the hand, led her to the bedroom, ate her pussy, and fucked the shit out of her. As long as Donna got hers, he could shut her up for a little while.

"Lex."

"Yes, baby?" he answered, dozing off.

"I think we should go to marriage counseling," Donna said.

"Okay, Nikki. Whatever you want, baby. Just promise me you won't tell Herschel."